Foss Man

Keith Fossey

First Edition

PAGE PUBLISHING, INC.
New York, NY

First originally published by Page Publishing, Inc. 2017

"Foss Man" is a work of fiction. Names, characters, places, and incidents are a product of the author's imagination or are used fictitiously. Any resemblances to actual persons, living or dead, events, or locales is entirely coincidental.

ISBN 978-1-64027-683-3 (Paperback)
ISBN 978-1-64027-684-0 (Digital)

Printed in the United States of America

Dedications

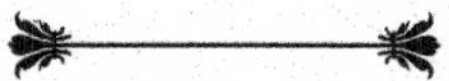

The "Foss Man" series is dedicated to the memory of Rich Fossey, my special younger brother and great friend who lost his courageous battle with cancer April 24th, 2017. Also to my mother, Shirley Fossey, who was simply the most remarkable human being I have ever known. Against great odds, it was her relentless strength and fortitude that served as the driving force behind the success and life-long happiness enjoyed by my 7 siblings and myself. Her shining example provided the real-life inspiration for the mother of the eight Foster children in "Foss Man".

ACKNOWLEDGMENTS

First and foremost, much appreciation to my wife Avis, who has faithfully served as my tireless and fearless sounding board. The "Foss Man" series would not have happened without her unwavering support. Thanks to Victoria Wright, popular Prior Lake High School literature teacher, who took time from her hectic schedule to critique my writing and provided the much needed encouragement to charge forward. Thanks to Dave Jennings, renowned Minnesota state congressman and career educator, who diligently critiqued the book. And to Mike Fossey, for providing the endless technical support. Thanks to sister Kathy Gainey, who offered persistent moral support and in the beginning wisely advised me, "don't try to be cute, just tell the damn story!" And brother Dennis Fossey, who was in my corner throughout the entire process and has volunteered to spearhead marketing of the book, a critical necessity for an unknown author. And finally, thanks to my junior in high school grandson, Tyler Breck, whose loyal support and beyond his years wisdom provided valuable input from a teen-ager's prospective.

JUNE 7, 1957

Jefferson, Iowa (Population: 900)

Chapter One

Like most of the small farming communities in Iowa, baseball was a big deal in Jefferson. Due to the high-paying jobs offered by the Morgan Road Construction Company, the largest employer in Wright County, along with the general prosperity enjoyed by the many grain and livestock farmers in the surrounding area, Jefferson had the luxury of constructing one of the most spectacular baseball complexes in northern Iowa. The cement-enclosed dugouts, manicured grass infield, and the two wire batting cages were rare features, but what made it exceptional were the large banks of lights attached to the giant towers that at night could be seen for miles. The night games were like playing in broad daylight.

Playing at night not only provided the benefit of escaping the stifling afternoon sun and stubborn humidity, but also, with the town team roster predominately filled with adults, the players could now work during the day and be free to participate on week nights. Foss Man's dad seized the opportunity for generating extra revenue by setting up and running the refreshment stand for all the home games. With the older kids happily pitching in, the operation became a source of pride for the entire Foster family.

The exceptional facilities generated great interest in baseball, and with promotion and special focus on the expansive little league program, the Jefferson High School varsity baseball team became a dominating force and enjoyed taking home many championship trophies.

Foss Man (Luke Foster) came from a large closely knit family which, for a combination of reasons, struggled to merely pay the bills. Meanwhile, Rocket's dad was sole owner of the prosperous

Morgan Road Construction Company. What Foss Man particularly loved about baseball, when he drilled a line drive into the gap, no one thought about the size of his house, whether or not it had running water, or the age or make of the family car. Foss Man and Rocket had just completed their sophomore year, and after playing key roles in bringing home another conference championship that spring, they were invited to play on the town team again that summer. Providing a level playing field and serving as the much-needed equalizer for the sensitive teenager, baseball proved to be a big deal for Foss Man!

Foss Man was 6'1" and weighed 160 pounds. He was a switch-hitting catcher and was blessed with a rifle arm. No one dared steal on him. Rocket was a 6'2", 185-pound, almost freakishly good athlete with a ninety-mile-per-hour fastball that had already drawn the attention of most of the college recruiters in the surrounding states. Rocket's huge potential for baseball stardom created a legitimate shot of putting Jefferson on the map someday. As battery mates since their little league days, in spite of living on opposite ends of town, the two became the best of friends.

It was a perfect sunny Saturday, and Foss Man had three lawns to mow before his parents would allow him to attend the first town team practice that was scheduled for 5:00 that afternoon. He was a little nervous about the important try out but was excited and could hardly wait to get the summer baseball season underway. On this typical Saturday, his buddy Rocket was scheduled to work in his dad's big rock quarry until noon that day. He had been trained to operate the giant bulldozer, and after the truckers dumped their eight-ton loads of gravel, it was his job to level the mounds around the giant stockpile.

Foss Man had agreed to go to work for Walter Olson again this summer and would be working ten-hour days in the giant cabbage fields alongside the Mexican migrant workers. With high hopes that the sixteen-year-old beauty Rosita Rodriguez would be returning from Texas with her parents this summer, he was looking forward to reporting for work bright and early Monday morning. The demanding and good-paying job would not prevent him from mowing lawns on Saturdays throughout the summer months. Lee Jorgensen, the about-to-retire high school custodian who had become a good friend, had promised to sell him his amazing '50 Ford the very day he turned sixteen next fall. They had already agreed on the $200 price tag, and Foss Man was determined to have the money saved well in advance. The previous fall, Rocket had driven his shiny new '57 Ford convertible off the showroom floor in nearby Boulder.

Most of Foss Man's buddies had their driver's licenses and owned their own cars by now. Skunk, Skeeter, and Horse had bought cars the day they turned sixteen. They were all in the same grade in school, but Foss Man was almost a full year younger. While Big Jake was old enough and could easily afford a car, having higher priorities, he and Foss Man were the only two members of the gang still relying on their bikes as their primary mode of transportation.

Foss Man mowed the first two lawns that morning and biked back home. His mom didn't work on Saturdays and, like always, fixed lunch for him and his five younger siblings. Older brother Allen was busy pumping gas at Rosie's Standard, and sister Catherine was working at the local vet's office. Triggered by a number of emotional setbacks in his early childhood, Foss Man had developed a special bond with his mother.

At 1:00 sharp, Foss Man enthusiastically jumped on his bike and pedaled out to his Grandpa Wentworth's place a mile west of town to complete his final job for the day. It was a huge sprawling lawn and paid the almost unbelievable sum of $3. His grandpa's beautiful estate set on the shores of the mighty Troy River. The big two-story house was just a short distance north of his prosperous feed mill operation that relied heavily on the powerful adjacent river. On the way out there, Foss Man rode by his summer boss Walter's big cabbage field, and with the heavy rains that spring, he could see the weeds were almost taking over. He figured it was a good thing the migrant workers were scheduled to hit town later that week. He couldn't help himself; it made him think about the amazing Rosita again.

A well-established Saturday afternoon ritual by now, the minute he finished mowing the last lawn, he'd pedal by Sallie's Drive-In and treat himself to one of his favorite hot fudge sundaes covered with nuts. More important than his fondness for hot fudge, he wanted to get his weekly fix of observing the Becker twins in action as they strutted around waiting on customers.

He wasn't surprised to see Rocket and Skeeter sitting there with the top down in Rocket's still shiny convertible. Foss Man parked his bike and climbed in the back seat to kill a little time with his buddies before he headed home to change and get ready for the all-important baseball tryouts later that afternoon.

Rocket was quick to point out, "Good news, Foss Man—they're both on duty today."

He was well aware of the fact the twins usually worked on Saturday afternoons, but it was comforting to have it officially confirmed. The boys in the locker room all agreed that Mary Jane and Myrna Becker had every right to be proud of what were clearly the four most amazing tits in Jefferson High. An astute businesswoman, Sally deliberately provided uniforms that accentuated all the car hops' striking attributes, but as evidenced by the fact business always picked up when the Becker twins were on duty, with little or no effort on their part, they easily stole the show.

Mary Jane had already taken Rocket and Skeeter's order, but when she noticed Foss Man sitting in the back seat, although she knew what he was likely going to order and now fully aware of the fact all their eyes were glued on her, she pranced over in her sassy manner and cheerfully greeted him, "Well, look who we have here—another one of the big sophomore hotshots. I suppose you want your regular, huh, Foss Man?"

They all knew what was coming; they had witnessed the same routine at least a dozen times by then. "Yes, Mary Jane, I want my regular, a hot fudge sundae with nuts. But a minor correction—I believe that would be *junior*, if you don't mind."

Her first quick answer, "Okay, okay, by all means, *junior*, but either way,"—then her well-rehearsed response, and she couldn't wait to say it—"would you like me to crush your nuts?"

After the requisite laughter, strictly for the benefit of his buddies, Foss Man would recite his assigned line: "Yes, Mary Jane, I would like you to crush my nuts!"

Rocket and Skeeter would burst out laughing again, and Mary Jane would close the deal with her famous cocky smirk. "I'd be glad to, Foss Man." And she boldly strutted her way back to the order window.

Foss Man proudly proclaimed, "There's no doubt about it, boys. Mary Jane simply can't help herself, she's madly in love with the Foss Man!"

Skeeter wasn't exactly buying it. "Yeah, right. Keep dreaming, good buddy, keep dreaming."

It never got old. The Becker twins were clearly the most provocative, playful, and free spirits in the high school, but the harsh reality was, they crushed the hopes and dreams of an entire determined male population with their strict "Look but don't touch" policy. While that was true, they were great kids and would be sorely missed next fall after they both accepted academic scholarships to, of all places, a prestigious private girl's school out east someplace. An all-girl's school—what a waste!

Like Foss Man and Rocket, Skeeter was an excellent ball player on the high school team and was more like a brother than a friend to Foss Man by now. They were all genuinely disappointed he hadn't been formally invited to try out for the town team. That being the case, before he took off for home, Foss Man insisted, "Hey, Skeeter, why don't you just come along with us to practice today?" He suggested, "Just volunteer to chase down fly balls, and we'll sneak you in for a little batting practice." Foss Man promised, "When the manager sees the way you hit line drives, there's no doubt in my mind he'll end up thanking us for bringing you along and will have to think twice about adding you to the town team roster." Skeeter loved baseball, and Foss Man was glad when he reluctantly agreed to show up for practice later that day!

Arriving home at about 3:30 that afternoon, feeling great about completing a prosperous day, and thinking only about how he was going to crush the ball during batting practice in less than an hour, Foss Man routinely pulled up to the shed to put his bike away. As he was approaching the front door, he was alarmed when he heard what sounded like a girl's voice desperately crying out for help. He quickly rushed inside, and the unthinkable scene so rudely thrown at him would turn his joyous life upside down.

Incomprehensibly, on the big old couch along the north wall of the wooden storage shed tucked remotely in woods behind their family's single-car garage, Catherine, his petite eighteen-year-old sister, was pinned underneath the notorious 230-pound town bully. Foss Man immediately recognized the crazy lunatic who was widely known for his outrageous and evil behavior. The unimaginable reality was, Ron Ferguson was in the process of violently raping his innocent and now helpless sister! Catherine was fighting him off with every ounce of strength she could muster but was clearly not succeeding. Her loud and desperate screams prevented Ferguson from hearing Foss Man enter the shed.

The first thing Foss Man heard as he entered the shed was the frightening and chilling threat, "Shut your fucking mouth, you little bitch, or I'll break your fucking neck right now!"

With immediate rage running through his veins and with an instant involuntary flashback to the horror related to his failure to save his baby sister from drowning twelve years ago, Foss Man impulsively grabbed the baseball bat leaning against the wall near the entrance to the shed and, with a bolt of inhuman strength, took a powerful swing, crushing the side of Ferguson's head. The sickening and haunting sound echoed throughout the small building.

Not knowing what hit him, the giant crumbled and flopped on top of Foss Man's horrified sister. Pinned under Ferguson's now limp body, Catherine was struggling desperately to get out from underneath the monster. As Foss Man got an accidental glimpse of the blood on his sister's lower extremity, with a sudden reinforced surge of wild fury, an instinctive decision that would ultimately prove to be the biggest mistake of his life, he delivered a second powerful blow that connected directly on the back of Ferguson's head, producing another resounding *thud*. His ravaged sister struggled to get to her feet while indignantly pulling her dress down and holding her torn underpants in her right hand. Not wanting to believe his eyes, Foss Man couldn't help but notice the blood streaming down the inside of her legs.

MARCH 1945

Shores of Troy River

Jefferson, Iowa

Chapter Two

The Foster home would be surrounded by the raging river, and during an average year, at least two feet of water came roaring through the kitchen, living room, and the three small bedrooms. A mild year might result in merely flooding the basement and not disturbing the main living quarters. Luke's family knew well in advance when the flood was coming and always took the precautionary measures at least a few days prior to its inevitable arrival. They had to be creative and elevate the furniture and would diligently remove all the vulnerable smaller belongings and furnishings. The only good thing about the disruptive annual event was it meant the family would be moving in with Grandpa and Grandma Wentworth and their beautiful huge home located safely on the hillside about a half mile north of their house for a few days. It was an undesirable routine every spring, but Grandpa Wentworth owned the smaller house and was happy to let the Foster family live there for a modest rent. With the income picture as bleak as it was, Luke's struggling family appreciated simply having a roof over their head.

It was a day late in March 1945, about nine months after the Allied Troops stormed the beaches of Normandy, and a few months before Hitler's surrender and the much-celebrated conclusion to World War II. Luke (Foss Man) hated the frequent pitch-black "lights out" sessions when he, his brother, and his two sisters would huddle together in the living room with their reassuring mom and dad. Not really understanding what it was all about but knowing it had something to do with the threat of German and Japanese bombers, it was always a chilling experience for the kids.

Luke Foster, age four, was sleeping in the same bed next to his five-year-old brother Allen. His sister Catherine, age six, and their little two-year-old sister Carol were sleeping together in the tiny adjacent bedroom. His eight-month-pregnant mother and his by-now-growing-concerned father were attempting to sleep in the nearby third small bedroom. With the persistent clapping thunder and the accompanying bolts of lightning illuminating the entire house, everyone was struggling to get much sleep that night. There had been torrential thunderstorms in the area for the past few days, but the annual spring flood was clearly not expected for another few weeks.

Suddenly, all hell broke loose. In a matter of mere seconds, the house was flooded with at least a foot of the rushing turbulent water from the now violent and raging river. The almost continuous drenching rains during recent days had unexpectedly caused the ice above the large nearby dam to break. With numbing ice-cold water now swirling around their waists and in total shock, Luke and his three siblings were screaming and crying as they frantically huddled together in the middle of the living room with their stunned parents. With no apparent solution for the sudden glaring danger facing them, Luke's mother and father were desperately attempting to calm everyone down when out of nowhere, like the angel of grace, Grandpa Wentworth's loud and thundering voice came echoing through the front door. The door had been forced open by the powerful surging river water. In a desperate attempt to get everyone's attention, their grandpa was screaming, "Hey, everyone, get the hell out here! Hurry, we don't have much time!"

One half mile upstream on the shore along the mighty Troy River, Grandpa's new, rather grand home had been wisely built on an elevated section of his expansive property not vulnerable to the spring floods. For decades, he had instinctively evaluated the kind of threatening storm that was brewing out there and was already a little concerned when he retired that night. As the storm intensified, Grandpa recognized the sudden looming danger it posed to his family in the house down on the always vulnerable lower end of his property. With the magnitude of the storm now a reality, he got dressed, hastily pulled his boat trailer, fishing boat, and motor out of the machine shed and backed it into the river already overflowing its banks. He motored down the turbulent fast-rising water and was now strategically positioned at the front door steps of the small and perilous home of his cherished loved ones.

Grandpa remained in the small aluminum round bottomed boat while Luke's dad, as calmly as possible, one by one, was handing him the four screaming kids. Scared to death but more concerned and worried about their mother's safety than anything, the kids were begging her to join them in the boat. Delirious with fear, their mother insisted they "just go ahead," clearly her only concern being the safety of her beloved children. Eight months pregnant, and with the boat rocking violently in the wild raging water, the task of simply getting their mother on board safely would, in itself, prove to be a difficult challenge. With no time to waste and severe eminent danger lurking, at her loving husband's insistence, their mother reluctantly agreed to join the kids in what would now clearly be an extremely overloaded boat. Their father was more than willing to remain behind and wait for Grandpa's hopeful and timely return.

With the boat finally in motion, the biting cold wind howling, and steady rain pounding down on them, they were in total darkness. The only remote vision was created by the continuous flashes of brilliant lightning accompanied with the inevitable persistent deafening claps of thunder. The four confused and frightened kids and their mother were clinging together in the center of the bouncing and rocking boat. Their grandpa, positioned in the back by the roaring motor, was trying desperately to maneuver the boat against the powerful surging waves.

Then the unthinkable happened. With giant chunks of broken ice hammering against the lightweight vessel, a sudden violent collision separated the family, who, with all their strength, had been desperately holding on to each other. Carol, the youngest and weakest, slipped from the grip of her older brother Luke's nearly frozen fingers and was thrown overboard. Nearly capsizing the boat, the hysterical mother made an instinctive desperate lunge helplessly reaching out to save her baby. But she was too late! Carol had disappeared into the pitch-black swirling water. Out of sight and blending in with the ferocious storm and roaring river, Carol's faint desperate screams, "Mommy! Mommy! Mommy!" would forever haunt the surviving family members.

Suddenly there was nothing! Grandpa Wentworth, stunned with the incredible turn of events and with growing concern about the now very real possibility of the boat sinking and drowning all of them, was making every human effort to calm everyone down when the boat abruptly slammed to a halt. They were all thrown forward into a heap.

What was very likely a life-saving development, they had run into dry land. Now safe but in a total state of confusion and shock, the kids continued their frantic crying and screaming. Their grief-stricken Grandpa hurriedly unloaded everyone. Knowing very well there was no realistic chance in saving her, in his desperate attempt to calm the still-crazed and hysterical mother, he promised his daughter he would go back to search for her baby. When in reality, he was merely going back with the fading hope of saving her husband from the now deadly river.

With the unforgiving, angry river still rising by the minute, now desperate, their dad was perched on top of the kitchen table. He was relieved when he heard the storm muffled roar of the approaching boat motor. Wading through the freezing water swirling above his waist and managing to reach the boat, Grandpa Wentworth had to give him the horrific news about his little girl. In complete shock over the gut-wrenching report, the stunned father went berserk.

Prior to this moment, William had never shown anything but the greatest respect and appreciation for all the generous and wonderful things his father-in-law had done for him and his family over the years. While his behavior was understandable, totally out of character, he unleashed a torrent of anger like never before.

Literally out of his mind, the insane father unloaded, "Jesus Christ, you miserable reckless bastard, how in the holy hell could you let something like that happen?"

Understanding his grief and trying desperately to remain calm and level-headed, Grandpa Wentworth responded firmly, "Get in the boat, God damn it, or I'll leave you here to drown!"

As misplaced and as undeserving as it was, now totally irrational and filled with wild rage, Luke's dad fired back, "Exactly where in the hell did she fall out of your stupid, goddamn boat. What on earth made you think this worthless tin can would actually get them out of here safely? For God's sake, let's get our asses moving and find Carol right now, God damn it!"

With the relentless storm not letting up, never one to lose control but growing more upset by the second, Grandpa barked, "If you don't shut up and sit down, we're not going anywhere and we're both going to drown. Now sit down and shut your goddamned mouth!"

The outraged, heartbroken, and defeated father begrudgingly sat down as they motored through the still-violent storm to safety. The river had risen at least another two feet since the first treacherous lifesaving trip, and as it turned out, wasn't close to cresting. The infamous Flood of '45 would prove to be the worst flood in decades.

The persistent storm made it next to impossible but alarmed by the unspeakable fast-spreading news, every fireman and law enforcement officer in Wright county, along with dozens of volunteers, started an intensive wide-ranging search for little Carol Foster. While determined and refusing to surrender, the exhausted and unwavering search party finally had to accept the inevitable: the unforgiving flood had washed the innocent soul very likely miles downstream to God only knows where. Carol's little body would never be found!

A memorial service was held a few days later in the First Lutheran Church in Jefferson, the small friendly farming community located a half mile east of the Troy River and less than a mile north of the soon-to-be-infamous small house. Many generations of Fosters and Wentworths, including Luke's mother and father and each of their three siblings, had graduated from Jefferson High School. The citizens in town would come to know and genuinely care for everyone else. With the church packed and overflowing, many of the nine hundred residents of the closely knit village were gathered on the street in front of the church and stretched down and around the next block.

Chapter Three

Moving in and living with Grandpa and Grandma Wentworth for an unknown length of time was a welcome distraction and helped blunt the intense heartache and the raw pain the Foster family was dealing with. Sick with their own unbearable personal grief, Luke's parents were deeply worried about what the ultimate impact of that horrible image in the boat that night would have on the three kids. With everyone grieving and suffering in their own way, Catherine and Allen displaying rather amazing strength, Luke's glaring condition became a grave concern. Always the most energetic, happy-go-lucky, and a nonstop talker, he would now only sit quietly with a haunting empty look in his eyes. Appearing totally lost in the strange, mysterious spell, he was either unable or simply unwilling to utter so much as a single word.

Throughout the previous summer, always demanding the center of attention and clearly the most mischievous one of the bunch, Luke was more than his mother wanted to deal with at times. That being the case, she looked forward to the much-needed relief when Luke would frequently join his fishing buddy Mr. Slim down by the river for hours on end. Luke's favorite times were the nights Mr. Slim would build a roaring fire. He loved sitting there under the millions of stars and bright moonlight, staring at the fire, listening to the crickets and croaking frogs, but more than anything, he enjoyed the sound of the rushing river current and the rumbling and roaring of the nearby dam in the background. Mr. Slim had a magical way with Luke, and spending all that time together, they had become the very best of buddies. Luke's mother knew getting them back together would be a good thing for Luke.

The other pressing issue was their longtime dream of finding a safer place to live and one with the much-longed-for luxury of running water. Grandpa Wentworth was well aware of the families growing need for financial relief and, with that in mind, offered to suspend the modest rent they had been paying him. He discreetly characterized the benefit as a reward for Luke's father's loyal and dedicated effort at the feed mill during the past seven years. As much as they wanted to get away from the threat of the now deadly spring flood, the irresistible offer combined with the fact there were no viable alternatives of paying no rent, moving was simply not in the cards.

That difficult decision behind them, Grandpa Wentworth immediately hired his good friend Art Hollatz, the owner of a large local construction company, to take care of the badly needed house repairs. That being the case, the Fosters moved back home exactly two weeks after the flood. A number of the Jefferson civic organizations coordinated a remarkable plan to fill the newly repaired house with used furniture, probably nicer than the furnishings that were ruined in the flood. The greatest surprise was one caring citizen had delivered what would be their first electric refrigerator. The extraordinary generosity of the small prosperous community included a systematic steady flow of casseroles and hot dishes as well as endless boxes of groceries dropped off in a timely manner.

The record-breaking flood had quietly dealt Grandpa Wentworth another gut-wrenching setback. Trapped in a shed that had always been considered safely located on higher ground, preoccupied with saving his loved ones, a half dozen of his prized pregnant sows had gruesomely drowned. Using a front-end loader, Grandpa Wentworth and Luke's dad had the miserable job of scooping up the carcasses, piling them on a feed truck, and hauling them away to be buried.

Less than two weeks after moving back home, providing welcome joy and a much-needed lift to their spirits, the family was truly blessed when their new baby sister Glenda came into the world. Along with caring for a son suffering through persistent nightmares, Luke's mother happily took on the burdens of an infant baby and the required middle of the night feedings. Spending endless hours in the comfort of his mother's arms, Luke often heard her quietly sobbing as she fought off her own desperate need for sleep.

Already struggling to provide even the basic essentials for the family, the deck was now severely stacked against the Foster family. But against great odds, with her unmatched inner strength and relentless determination, Luke's mother was the driving force to provide the much-needed joy and happiness around the home front. With her persistent warm manner and upbeat attitude, the kids absolutely worshipped and adored their mother.

Luke's father was putting in grueling long days in the nearby feed mill and willingly helped tuck the kids in bed every night. Following the bedtime routine, William richly earned the right to relax for a couple hours when he frequently grabbed a cane pole and retreated down to the river for some intense fishing. Usually pitch dark by now, you could see him searching for a new "hot spot" by watching for the small moving red glow on the end of the ever-present Camel hanging from his lips. As tight as the budget was, Luke's dad was somehow managing to scrape up enough money to quietly purchase a six-pack of his favorite Pabst Blue Ribbon on an almost daily basis. Many nights, he would succeed in pulling in a batch of crappies, or catfish, that he promptly cleaned and were likely served as the main course on the following night's supper table. The next morning, you could find the smelly fish guts wrapped in newspaper along with the inevitable six empty beer bottles strewn behind their sturdy and dependable one-hole outhouse.

While compassionately recognizing her loving husband was dealing with a life filled with painful personal heartaches, losing his mother at the tender age of five, being the victim of a ruthless hard driving father, and now the recent loss of his baby girl and Luke's troubling reaction while generously giving him his due credit for being a dedicated and hard worker, Elizabeth had growing concern over his drinking habits that she was afraid would threaten the fragile foundation of their already-struggling household. Witnessing this pattern for over seven years by now, her unwavering support and patience was being severely tested.

One morning, Luke's mother was busy washing a batch of diapers when she heard a knock on the front door. She was pleased when she recognized Luke's great fishing buddy Mr. Slim standing there on the porch. With his always cheerful tone he greeted her, "Hi, Elizabeth, I hope it's okay I dropped by uninvited like this. I wanted to see how you and my little fishing buddy are getting along."

Slim Carson, age 74, retired for over ten years after a long career working on the railroad, was generally considered the best and most dedicated fisherman in Wright County. Mr. Slim, as Luke respectfully labeled him, was a confirmed bachelor, at most 5'8" tall, weighed in at 250 pounds, with a bushy red beard covering a severely weathered face. He was a pleasant and delightful old gentleman with a great sense of humor and an endless supply of wild tales he loved sharing with anyone willing to listen. Long ago, Mr. Slim had staked out his own personal section of shoreline next to his favorite highly productive fishing hole in the Troy River.

Always happy to see Luke's great friend, Elizabeth cordially invited him in. With genuine warmth and sincerity, she said, "No, this is wonderful, Mr. Slim, it's great to see you. This is a perfect time. I just put our new little one down for her nap. It's kind of you to check up on us. I'm doing fine, Mr. Slim, but I have to warn you, Luke really isn't doing very well."

With that much appreciated heads-up, Mr. Slim accompanied Elizabeth as they entered the living room, where they found Luke sitting and staring out the window. Sadly, he had been virtually frozen in this position for hours every day since they moved back home. While Catherine and Allen had been carrying on in a fairly normal fashion, Luke was lethargic and had no interest in doing anything but sitting there in a trance glaring out that window. It was pretty obvious Luke had developed a powerful fear for another flood and wanted to do nothing but keep an eye on the threatening river he could only monitor when looking out that one particular window.

Understanding all this, Mr. Slim walked over by Luke and sat down beside him. Very gently, he asked, "Hey, buddy, you about ready to go pull in a couple of those big catfish? They've been biting like crazy this week!"

Luke slowly turned his head and looked directly at Mr. Slim. He had a frightening distant look in "unseeing" eyes and, without saying a word, acted like he had never seen Mr. Slim before in his life. It was gut-wrenching for Mr. Slim to see his buddy like this. Desperately fighting back tears, observing the strange, cold interaction between the two longtime fishing partners was absolutely heartbreaking for Luke's mother.

Mr. Slim tried everything he knew how to get some kind of response from his little friend, but it was soon apparent Luke simply wasn't going to acknowledge his presence. After a few minutes, Mr. Slim and his mother quietly retreated to the kitchen. Luke remained sitting there quietly, slowly turning his head back and once again began glaring out the window.

Chapter Four

Like most of the small communities across the country, the Jefferson civic leaders went to great lengths to organize a major celebration for the victorious conclusion to World War II. A rare event for an always productive and profitable Saturday, in respect to the special occasion, except for the popular Crazy Horse and Alibi Inn taverns on main street, all the local business owners willingly hung "Closed" signs on their front doors. It was a spectacular warm, sunny day.

Immediately following the parade down the crowded main street featuring the newly uniformed high school marching band, a vast majority of the jubilant nine hundred local citizens gathered down in the carefully groomed grassy grounds of the town park. Everyone proud and filled with pride, Mayor Fleming would soon be introducing and honoring the highly respected surviving war heroes.

The celebration just happened to fall on William and Elizabeth's eighth wedding anniversary. Still reeling from the recent family tragedy, the Foster family was excited and looking forward to going to town to celebrate both special occasions.

Exactly eight years ago, William Foster, after graduating from high school and working two long years for his unreasonable hard driving father, the handsome 6'2" muscular and determined young man had proposed to the love of his life, the beautiful Elizabeth Wentworth, the very night she walked across the stage and received her high school diploma. Knowing she was an excellent student and strong candidate for higher education, William wasn't about to let Elizabeth go off to college like her older sister Sylvia had done a few years earlier.

When Elizabeth promptly said yes, it was clearly the happiest day of his life. Highly motivated to get out from under the strict control of his demanding father and eager to seal the deal, William and Elizabeth were married two short months later. Elmer Foster, William's dad, was very religious and a highly respected and prosperous farmer. However, perhaps provoked by the heartbreaking loss of his beautiful young wife to a mysterious illness, there was an ongoing glaring sadness behind the scenes of what on the surface appeared to be a happy household. When William and his three older sisters were in their teens, they had renewed hope the atmosphere would improve around the house when their lonely father quietly married Ruth, the warm and delightful neighbor lady who lost her husband when he was struck by lightning a few years earlier. Sympathizing with the kids, Ruth made every effort to improve things around the home front, but unfortunately, she had very little influence in changing Elmer's by then well-engrained stubborn and bull-headed makeup. That being the case, also wanting to escape the unhappy home front, William's three sisters married soon after graduating from high school and hastily moved out of the area.

With the jubilant celebration well underway, subdued and remaining in his strange trance, Luke appeared totally confused and lost as he held his dad's hand and standing next to his mother who was holding Glenda, his new baby sister. As the only unaffected member of the family, with her permanent smile and bouncy disposition, Glenda was unknowingly doing her part to lift everyone's spirits. Mimicking the impressive soldiers in their striking uniforms, Allen was standing rigid and erect between his mother and sister Catherine while saluting and reciting the pledge of allegiance to the now more than ever revered flag. He knew right then and there he would become a soldier someday. The excited crowd was laughing, cheering, and singing along with the high school band now seated in the newly painted pavilion and enthusiastically playing all the popular inspirational military hymns. Patriotism was at an all-time high!

Grandpa Wentworth was standing close by, and while wrongly blaming himself for the loss of his beloved granddaughter, was getting some much-needed relief with the immense pride he and Grandma

Wentworth felt when they introduced Stan, their only son. The educated eye could quickly recognize several of the rare medals awarded for valor amongst the many other ribbons for distinguished and meritorious service all pinned to his barrel chest.

Luke's mother and her sister Francis were beaming with pride during the thunderous applause as their younger brother Stan was introduced and took center stage. Aunt Francis, also married right after high school to a truck driver who made a good living hauling Grandpa Wentworth's ground feed to the barges over on the Mississippi River, in sharp contrast to Elizabeth's warm, pleasant, and feminine makeup, was the gruff and hard-nosed chain-smoking local school bus driver. Aunt Sylvia, oldest of the three sisters and still single, after graduating with honors from the University of Wisconsin, was working for the Department of Agriculture in Washington, DC, and regretted not being able to return for the special occasion. With Sylvia's distinguished and aristocratic flare, the three girls couldn't have been more different.

Wrapping up the formal ceremonies, Reverend Thompson, the popular long-standing preacher for the First Lutheran Church, was at the microphone leading the suddenly hushed crowd in prayer. Reverend Thompson, of course, had presided at the recent memorial services for little Carol and, over the years, would become a prominent and powerful influence on the William and Elizabeth Foster family.

As the bustling crowd was dispersing, Uncle Stan, all decked out in his striking marine uniform, made a special effort and walked over and swept Luke up in his arms and gave him a big hug. It was the first time in months that Luke had so much as cracked a smile. He was clearly in awe of the powerful and handsome soldier. With that touching and uplifting conclusion, it was clearly a wonderful celebration providing some brief but badly needed relief for a family that had been going through a sad and difficult time in their life.

As they were piling in their car and ready to head back home, Rick Peterson, William's very best high school friend, who was one of the celebrated returning war heroes and looking mighty impressive in his brilliant, heavily decorated marine uniform, came running over and insisted William join him for a cold beer at the Crazy Horse, where a bunch of the old gang had agreed to continue the reunion. Ignoring the fact it was their wedding anniversary and the fact they had carefully planned a special dinner to celebrate the occasion, knowing William hadn't spent time with Rick since he went off to fight in the war years ago and knowing how much he would enjoy the spontaneous gathering, his generous and thoughtful wife sincerely encouraged him to go ahead and join his buddies.

William's hasty decision to spend his wedding anniversary with his best man instead of his bride was probably not one of his wiser moves. As it turned out, hours later, William staggered into the house while Elizabeth happened to be busy providing Glenda with her first middle-of-the-night feeding.

Chapter Five

In spite of their father's increased drinking, as they worked their way through the hot and humid summer months and time passed distancing them from the tragedy, laughing and good times had returned to the Foster household once again. Demonstrating their resiliency and great spirit for life, after the always challenging and busy weekdays, everyone enthusiastically looked forward to the Sunday routine when they could spend time together. All beaming in their Sunday bests, they'd pile in the old, rusty '38 Chevrolet and head for the First Lutheran Church. As they entered the church, they observed the two permanent fixtures in the back pew, Luke's fishing buddy Mr. Slim, and sitting next to him, his buddy Nute who owned the popular bait shop in town. Next to them, Grandpa Foster and step grandmother Ruth had already been settled in for a good half hour and were carefully monitoring exactly who was in attendance. After listening attentively to Reverend Thompson's short but always inspirational message, they'd head home and make the final preparations for the weekly picnic out in Jasper's Park.

Jasper's Park was a small public park adjacent to the Troy River a mile directly south of Jefferson. The kids loved the picnic that usually featured their mother's incredible fried chicken and all the trimmings. But their favorite part was when their mom and dad joined them in the silly self-made creative games that followed filling their bellies. Simple things like leap frog, ring around the rosy, wood tag, and the normal frolicking slowed down when the whole gang ended up competing in the weekly fishing contest, oftentimes lasting until late into the afternoon.

Birthdays and holidays were celebrated with uncles, aunts, grandpas, and grandmas who were quietly contributing and helping out whenever possible. Grandpa Wentworth was always finding an excuse for dropping off a box of groceries or new toys or games designed to bring more happiness into the lives of his cherished loved ones. He was never going to be quite the same after the horrible accident in his fishing boat, and while almost working at being a grumpy old bastard, he couldn't cover up the fact he actually had a big and caring heart. All in all, it appeared there was once again real hope for getting back on track with the vibrant and positive outlook the Foster family had always been known for.

On a personal level, Luke had been making only minimal progress. While he still refused to talk and remained uncharacteristically subdued, he was no longer stuck in front of that window and appeared to be doing his best to cooperate and go along with the daily routine around the house. The doctor told everyone to be patient, that hopefully it would be only a matter of time and he would be back to his mischievous and lively self again. The family was learning to accept his new low profile, and everyone went out of their way to cheer him up. Having no idea how long this behavior was going to continue, it was now an accepted reality—life simply had to go on!

With all that understood, it was encouraging when Luke appeared to at least partially snap out of his funk and once again looked forward to spending time with his buddy Mr. Slim down by the river. It appeared he had finally overcome his great fear for the threatening river, and Mr. Slim was encouraged when he observed a little of Luke's old spirit each time he pulled in another one of those big catfish. Knowing Luke still had a long way to go, he was more determined than ever to help pull him out of this strange and mysterious spell. Mr. Slim couldn't get a verbal response out of him, but digging deep into his bag of tricks, he was encouraged when Luke was at least responding with an occasional spontaneous smile. Not about to give up, Mr. Slim remained optimistic that Luke was going to bounce back one of these days!

Providing another source of support and a welcome break for his mother during those long, hot summer days, Luke was spending time with Grandma Wentworth over in the nearby feed mill office. His grandma spent hours in the office answering the phone and performing other secretarial duties while monitoring the always present cane pole that was extended through the open window conveniently positioned right next to the big old wooden desk. She kept the all-important container of night crawlers at arm's length in the bottom drawer of the old beaten-up gray metal file cabinet.

His grandma was a heavy-set, cheerful, warm, and wonderful lady. Perhaps explaining the academic excellence all the kids would enjoy throughout their school days, Grandma Wentworth was a brilliant student, skipping several grades in elementary school and graduating with honors when she was sixteen years old. Like Mr. Slim, with her great wisdom and pleasant demeanor, she tried every conceivable angle while patiently attempting to change Luke's disturbing behavior. She didn't succeed in getting Luke to say a single word either but was also encouraged when he'd get so excited whenever she pulled another big catfish through the window. Having personally witnessed the unique proceedings at one time or another, their many valued customers learned to accept waiting on the phone line honoring the fact the renowned "fishing secretary" had a higher priority, the chance of landing another "big one" through that open window.

Providing additional relief at the home front, brother Allen would be joining big sister Catherine and going off to school that fall. It became a welcome daily ritual when Luke would walk to the end of the driveway and watch his brother and sister climb the steps and board the big yellow bus. They may have been coached a little to do so, but they both willingly gave Luke the by now well-practiced "hug" goodbye. Of course their Aunt Francis was the school bus driver, and Luke looked forward to her friendly greeting every day when she swung the bus door open for Allen and Catherine. He got used to the strange sight of the cigarette hanging from Aunt Francis's mouth with the smoke steadily curling in her face. Luke would stand there quietly and watch the door close and the soon-to-follow cloud of dust that blocked the view of the big bus speeding down the gravel road. He hated to see his brother and sister leave for the day. He would return to the same spot at the same time every afternoon and got excited when he saw the bus roaring back down the road.

This routine continued late into the fall until one morning a disturbing event took place. After Allen and Catherine had given Luke the by-now-automatic hug and were climbing up the bus steps, a wise guy lowered a widow and hollered, "Hey, are you the dumb-ass brother who can't even talk?"

Hearing the outrageous comment, Aunt Francis just about exploded! Furious, she pulled the handbrake into place, flicked her lit camel out the still open door, stormed back, and grabbed the smart-ass kid, unceremoniously dragged him down the aisle of the bus, took him outside, and proceeded to beat his ass unmercifully! Luke took off running as soon as he heard the mean comments but couldn't help but hear the kid screaming and very likely now praying for his very survival!

Aunt Francis was famous for maintaining law and order on her bus and the superintendent of schools totally supported her approach. When he heard the story about what had taken place that morning, the next time he ran into her, he politely complimented her, "You're doing a great job, Francis, keep up the good work!"

In his still fragile condition, this unfortunate incident was the last thing Luke needed. The cherished trips to the end of the driveway came to a screeching halt. "Are you the dumb-ass brother that can't even talk?" kept ringing in his head. He wondered how many of the kids on the bus were mean like that. A small consolation, he was comforted by the fact he could stay home with his mother for at least one more school year.

Not having the slightest knowledge of it at the time, the experience with the wise guy in the school bus turned out to be only a brief introduction to the ruthless bully who would end up tormenting Luke throughout his school days. It was merely the first of many encounters for Luke at the hands of the mean and infamous Ron Ferguson. As it turned out, Ron and his older brother Frank would go on to become the most notorious troublemakers in Jefferson history.

Chapter Six

The winter months proceeded in quiet and uneventful fashion. Filling the void of no longer having his older brother or sister around, Luke looked forward to the time he spent ice fishing with his old buddy Mr. Slim throughout the winter months. Enjoying his mother's carefully packed lunches, they'd sit for hours by the gas heater in his fishing partner's small wooden shack. But it didn't matter what little tricks or strategies Mr. Slim attempted; nothing worked in getting Luke to respond verbally. He continued with that strange, distant look in his eyes and refused to say so much as one word.

On days when he wasn't ice fishing, he spent time with his grandma in the feed mill office, and between phone calls, they kept entertained playing checkers and card games. With the river frozen over, fishing out the window was no longer an option. Like Mr. Slim, his grandma tried every clever trick in the book to coax him into saying something, but nothing worked. In addition to their own endless personal efforts, Elizabeth and William appreciated the many hours Mr. Slim and Grandma Wentworth worked with Luke and could only hope that someday, he would be his free-spirited and fun-loving self again.

As the long winter months passed, once again, it was the time to start thinking about the spring flood. For obvious reasons, they were carefully prepared to move in with Grandpa and Grandma Wentworth and their grand home long before any serious threat presented itself.

A much needed and appreciated break, the flood that spring was the mildest one in many years. As expected, the Troy River over flowed its banks but as it turned out, only a small amount of water poured into their basement. With the river receding quickly, and after spending two nights with the grandparents, the Fosters reluctantly moved back home.

With that good news, the school year ended relatively drama-free. Always looking for any encouraging sign, Luke showed uncharacteristic excitement about the school year winding down and the whole family being back together every day for the summer months. Of course, that meant more hectic times and a bigger workload for their mother. To further complicate the picture, not startling news by now but at the same time always a significant development, it was announced that Luke's mother was once again pregnant.

Three small bedrooms. Mom and Dad and now soon-to-be five kids. Still no running water. The general outlook created a sense of urgency, and a larger house simply had to be given serious consideration. A move meant the additional financial pressure of once again paying rent. There was only one logical solution: Luke's dad had to find a better-paying job.

Probably not the greatest idea, William had been meeting his old high school buddy Rick Peterson with regularity in the Crazy Horse for a few beers after work throughout the winter months. However, either a blessing in disguise or merely a richly deserved stroke of good luck, his special friendship with Rick led indirectly to a major life-changing development for the Foster family.

Rick's dad, Paul Peterson, happened to be the second-generation owner of the prosperous Peterson Plumbing and Heating Shop, coincidentally located on Main Street, just two doors down from the Crazy Horse. Lyle Knudson, one of Peterson's dependable longtime employees, was retiring at the end of the year.

While his good friend may have had some influence on his dad's decision to ultimately hire him, in all fairness, William had a well-earned reputation as a dependable and hard worker throughout those long years at the feed mill. With Grandpa Wentworth's genuine blessing and much-deserved recommendation, Mr. Peterson offered Luke's dad the job. William would officially become an apprentice plumber the following January 1, 1947.

Hard to believe, but it was slowly sinking in, William had been offered an opportunity to learn a skilled trade. The remaining six months in what had become the "dreaded" feed mill seemed like an eternity, but this dream come true was well worth the wait. While Elizabeth was excited about the prospect of William making more money and knowing it would dramatically improve their chances of moving into a bigger house, she was genuinely happy her husband would soon be removed from the unhealthy working environment in the dirty and dusty feed mill.

Hoping to find a bigger house before the new arrival and within the limitations of their still tight budget, they had six months to shop around. Eager to begin the house search, did they dare dream of having a place with running water?

And there was more great news! It was the Fourth of July weekend, and Luke was quietly sitting there watching for the end of one of the two special propped-up fishing poles to start jerking. Like always, Mr. Slim was sitting right next to him, sharing one of his endless supply of wild stories. It had been over sixteen months since Luke had uttered so much as one word. Luke casually glanced down at the ground in front of him, when he thought he saw what looked like a penny. He reached down and picked it up and proceeded to brush it off.

Mr. Slim was sitting nearby taking it all in, and when he noticed Luke's sudden new focus, he asked him, "Hey, buddy, what'd you find there?" With a proud look on his face, Luke held up the penny. Taking a closer look at it, Mr. Slim discovered it was a penny all right, he could hardly believe what he was looking at. It was an 1856 Indian Head penny, and the more he examined it, he realized it was in almost perfect condition. He had never seen a coin that old in such flawless mint condition. Quickly thinking and always seizing the opportunity to get a response out of Luke, he calmly came up with, "Wow, you know what? I think you found something really special there, little buddy. Believe me, Luke, that penny is very valuable. Maybe you should thank God for your good luck in finding that amazing coin!"

Without hesitation and out of nowhere, looking up to the sky, Luke said loud and clear, "Thank you, God, for letting me find the special penny."

What had just happened here? Mr. Slim's heart about exploded. Struggling to control his emotions and trying desperately to keep his composure, he finally came back with, "Wait a minute here—exactly what did you just say, Luke?"

A little louder this time, and once again perfectly articulate, "Thank you, God, for letting me find the special penny."

He couldn't help it; the grizzly old man's eyes filled with tears. He didn't know exactly how to react. Mr. Slim had been waiting for this moment for months and hadn't given any serious thought to how he would handle it when it indeed finally happened. He wanted to be careful and make sure to say the right thing to keep the conversation going.

"Luke, it's really great to have you talking again. And you know, thanking God when you get a special surprise that makes you happy is always a good idea. I'm very proud of you, Luke!"

Looking him directly in the eyes, Luke said calmly, "Mr. Slim, you don't have to worry about me anymore. I'm going to be okay now. I'm sorry I made you worry. If it's okay with you, I want to talk to my mother now!"

Mr. Slim could hardly believe all this was finally happening! Thrilled and without hesitating, he said, "Now you know what, that's a great idea, Luke. Let's just leave our lines in the water, and maybe we'll hook into something while we're gone. Be sure to hang onto that penny now! Okay, I think we're all set here. Let's go, little partner!"

It was close to the noon hour, and Mr. Slim knew Luke's dad usually went home for lunch. He thought to himself, *You know what? This just might work out very nicely!*

Not taking a chance to let this startling development reverse course, Mr. Slim and Luke talked up a storm on the short walk back to the Foster's house. When he knocked on the front door, Luke's mother couldn't help but notice the huge smile on Mr. Slim's face.

Mr. Slim came right out with it: "Elizabeth, Luke has something he wants to say to you!"

Looking up at the person he adored more than anyone in the world, Luke rushed toward her, jumped up into her arms, and putting an almost strangle hold around her neck, said quietly the words she'd been desperately waiting to hear for over a year now: "I'm going to be okay now, Mommy, please don't cry anymore!"

Luke's mother couldn't contain herself. She broke down sobbing uncontrollably, and as she was hugging and swinging her precious son in circles, Luke's dad suddenly came through the front door. He knew immediately what he was looking at and, with no discussion, joined the joyous group hug.

As the three of them clung tightly together, Mr. Slim felt blessed to personally witness this special moment filled with such pure, unadulterated happiness. Catherine and Allen had been playing in the backyard, and when they came charging into the house and learned what was going on, they both jumped up and down and joined what turned into an unforgettable family celebration.

When things settled down, Mr. Slim told them the whole story about the Indianhead penny and how Luke quickly agreed it was a good idea to thank God for it. Proud and greatly relieved, William and Elizabeth gave Mr. Slim a hug and thanked him emphatically for the unquestionable role he played in Luke's remarkable recovery. Before Mr. Slim left, his last thought was, *Make sure Luke takes good care of that penny. It's not only worth a lot of money—I have a gut feeling it's going to bring him good fortune throughout his lifetime!*

The Fosters always had the greatest fondness for Mr. Slim, but they would now have an extra special place in their hearts for the amazing old gentleman fisherman! Slim Carson's newfound respect went far beyond the Foster family. It was notable how his basic standing in the community grew as time passed, and he became notorious for his critical role in the small miracle out on the shores of the mighty Troy River!

It didn't take long for Luke to regain his old form that summer. Seemingly making up for lost time, he was once again jabbering virtually nonstop. While his mother much preferred this constant chatter over the disturbing silence during the past year, his newfound energy level and mischievous tendencies were back to normal and, putting it mildly, kept her on her toes. While thoroughly pleased to see all this new spirit and enthusiasm, Luke's mother couldn't deny it—she looked forward to the days when he spent time with Mr. Slim down by the river as well as the more-than-welcome visits with his grandma over in the feed mill office.

Fishing through the office window was always the first option during the summer months. But a much-needed effort designed to burn up some of his boundless newfound energy, Grandma Wentworth gave Luke his very first cash-paying job. Sweeping the warehouse floor became an important part of the routine during each of his regular visits. The warehouse was partially filled with the hundred-pound sacks of ground feed. The huge room was conveniently located right outside the office door so his grandma could keep a close eye on the suddenly lively and unpredictable rascal.

Luke loved his new assignment and would sweep the floor with wild and furious abandon stirring up clouds of feed dust and, most likely, improving the situation very little. When his grandma generously determined it was a job well done, he proudly accepted the dime he knew he so richly deserved.

Years earlier, Grandma Wentworth recognized that the bright and colorful cotton feed sacks were made of suitable material for making shirts and dresses for the grandkids. A highly skilled seamstress, while sitting in the office waiting for the phone to ring and when the fish weren't biting, she spent hours converting the feed sacks into the much-needed school clothes for Catherine and the boys. Whenever new bales of the sacks were delivered, she'd carefully go through them and pick out the most striking and attractive ones.

It was just two weeks until the fall term started. A decision had to be made about enrolling Luke in school. They knew he would very likely be the youngest member of the first-grade class. Everyone was well aware of his sensitive nature and his well-documented emotional insecurities. There was no question he was ready academically.

His mother readily acknowledged that with his aggressive, unpredictable, and energetic tendencies, combined with Glenda and the new arrival, she made no secret about her desire to put Luke in school. They sat Luke down and carefully felt him out. He wasn't sure. He remembered that day when that jerk hollered at him out the bus window. He wondered, "Were there a lot of guys like that in school?" But he wanted to get on the bus with Allen and Catherine and learn how to read like they could.

It was a difficult decision, but they registered Luke for school that fall!

Chapter Seven

Luke bravely boarded the intimidating yellow school bus for the first time. With the ever-present smoking camel hanging from her lips, knowing he was nervous and scared, Aunt Francis gave him a big smile and warm greeting, "Well, look who's joining us on the bus this year. Welcome, big guy!"

Barely managing to get it out, Luke quietly responded, "Th-thanks, Aunt Francis."

Allen and Catherine were walking briskly and confidently down the aisle in front of him and promptly sat down with one of their old acquaintances. Carefully making his way one nervous step at a time, a little guy about his same size said firmly, "Hey, Luke, why don't you sit down here beside me!" A little startled and not knowing who the kid was, Luke cautiously sat down by the exceptionally friendly boy.

The outgoing and jovial boy went on, "I know who you are. My brother Stub's in third grade with your sister Catherine, and he knows your brother Allen too. Stub's that guy sitting over there with Allen." Luke couldn't help but notice Stub only had one hand. Very adultlike, his new friend was extending his right hand. "They call me Skunk, I'm Skunk Jensen." Luke extended his right hand.

That simple handshake was the beginning of what would prove to be an unbreakable lifelong bond!

Very proudly, Skunk proceeded to point out where his big sister Ellie was sitting. The cute Becker twins were sitting in the seat right behind Ellie. Ellie was in fourth grade, a year older than Luke's sister Catherine. At that very second, she happened to turn and look back at them. She gave Luke an amazing smile. Good grief, Luke thought she was about the prettiest thing he had ever laid eyes on. Already feeling a heck of lot better about things but knowing he was blushing with his typical "fire-red" face and bashfully looking down, he managed to return a weak smile.

Skunk continued, "Don't look back right now, but the biggest jerk in school is sitting two rows behind us. His name is Ron Ferguson. I know all about this guy, and I want to warn you. Stub told me about the incident last year when he hollered out the window at you. I guess Ferguson was embarrassed when everyone on the bus saw your Aunt beat his rear end. He picks on everyone, but he's probably going to single you out some time today. Trust me, Luke, if it happens, there's only one way to handle it. You have to ignore him and just walk away!"

It was true—the famous bully Ron Ferguson was sitting back there. And it was also true, Ron clearly remembered the incident last year, and the only reason he hadn't already mouthed off to Luke was because he knew Francis was watching him like a hawk in the big mirror. He knew if he said so much as one negative word, she would stop the bus, drag him outside, and beat his ass again. She caught him in the act a couple times last year, and Ferguson didn't want anything to do with her. As it turned out, sadly, Aunt Francis was the only one around the school setting who held him accountable for his persistent bullying.

Not wanting to think about the Ferguson kid, with his normal curiosity, Luke asked Skunk, "Is Skunk your real name?"

Skunk said, "No, it's my nickname. My real name's Larry. Last year, after I walked through the barnyard one morning before I went to Sunday school, I didn't wipe my shoes off very well, and Miss Wells, my Sunday school teacher, asked me to take them off, and she put them out on the lawn behind the church. I didn't really notice it, but I guess they stunk pretty bad. I had to walk out there in my stocking feet after Sunday school to get my shoes. Everybody in the class thought it was pretty funny. I suppose it was pretty funny, but who cares? My friends called me Skunk after that. Nicknames are cool. To tell you the truth, I kinda like the name!"

Luke's parents would have enrolled him in Sunday school last year too if he hadn't been dealing with the mysterious lingering spell.

Unfortunately, it didn't take long for Skunk's prediction to come true. As soon as they entered the school and were walking down the hallway searching for the first grade room, Ron Ferguson came up behind Luke and Skunk and blurted out, "Nice shirt, Luke, we have a bunch of feed sacks in the pig barn that look just like it!"

Before Luke could react, Skunk barked back, "Shut your big mouth, you big jerk!"

Although Skunk had come to his rescue, and as hard as he tried to ignore his comments, Luke was upset about what Ferguson said. Replaying the process of getting ready for school that morning, step one was accepting the fact he had inherited Allen's shoes from last year. They were pretty beaten up but only had a couple small holes in the soles. He was also wearing Allen's pants from last year, and they were only a little bit short for him. He knew his shoes and pants weren't the greatest. That didn't really bother him, but the fact was, he was confident his new shirt was darn cool. And his mother had given him a fresh new haircut Sunday night and that had given him a boost. All things considered, he felt pretty good about things until the big jerk mouthed off! Ferguson was about twice as big as he and Skunk put together. He was impressed that Skunk didn't seem one bit concerned. Luke was glad about one thing: Ferguson was a year older and in the second-grade room next door with Allen.

Successfully managing to put the bully out of his mind, Luke enjoyed school that morning. He liked it when Miss Chancellor read those interesting stories to them. She played the piano, and they all sang along. That was great. When it was time for lunch period, with the time remaining after they got done eating, they were encouraged to go outside on the playground. It was only minutes, and Ferguson was heading his direction again. Boy, Skunk sure knew what he was talking about. What the heck did he do to deserve this? It was pretty obvious the jerk must be retaliating because his Aunt Francis beat his ass last year. Luke was nervous and braced himself!

Ferguson began the proceedings. "Hey, Luke, why don't you wear one of your sister's feed sack dresses to school tomorrow!" A few of the kids in the area laughed a little bit. Skunk was running around some place having fun and wasn't there to rescue him this time. Luke was pretty shaken up but again just walked away from the big jerk. Skunk's pretty sister Ellie happened to be in the vicinity and heard what Ferguson said. Trying not to embarrass him but wanting to comfort him a little bit, Ellie politely said, "Luke, just ignore him!" Following her suggestion, he tried his best to put it out of his mind. How nice was she anyway? And there was no denying it—he was totally mesmerized by Ellie's friendly smile and those amazing dimples in both cheeks.

Before they found their way back inside for the afternoon, determined to take one more pot shot, Ferguson came up behind Luke, and making sure all the kids in the area could hear him, "Hey, Luke, where'd you get that goofy haircut? You look like a stupid porcupine!" Fed up with the bully, nobody laughed this time.

Luke ran into the school and was relieved to be back in his assigned desk and the comforts of the first-grade room. It was nap time. What the heck was this all about anyway? How were you going to learn how to read if you were sleeping? Lying there on his small assigned rug, Luke watched as the other kids were already sleeping soundly. He hated the idea of going to sleep afraid that the same ugly nightmare would occur like it did every night. His mother wasn't there to help him get through it. Noticing how he was tossing and turning, Miss Chancellor asked him if he wanted to color in a coloring book or draw pictures. Although he enjoyed the coloring, all he could think about was the fact he'd be facing Ferguson again on the bus ride home that afternoon. Then he remembered, Aunt Francis would probably take care of that problem. Boy, he couldn't wait to get back home that night!

Luke was hoping he could sit with Skunk on the way home on the bus that afternoon. It was comforting when Skunk sat down beside him. Skunk didn't know about the other two incidents on the playground with Ferguson during the noon hour, but he could tell something was bothering Luke. Luke knew Skunk wouldn't be around to solve all his issues at school, but it sure was nice to have a friend like him. What a great guy! Skunk may have been small in stature, but he carried himself with the kind of strength and confidence that Luke could only dream about having some day!

As it turned out, Luke had a pretty rough time that first week in school. Claiming he was sick, he told his mother he wanted to stay home from school the second day. Getting it firsthand from Allen and Catherine, his parents knew his main concern revolved around the Ferguson kid. They seriously considered talking to the school principal about the bully but were smart enough to know taking that action could easily backfire and only make things worse. They were confident that if Luke could somehow get through that first week, he'd be okay. After all, Allen and Catherine had gone through similar incidents in the beginning of their school days and they handled it without major problems.

Not wanting to surrender to the bully and knowing how much Luke enjoyed everything else about school, after lengthy discussion, they eventually talked him into going back that second day. They weren't aware of it at the time, but what really tipped the scale for Luke was knowing if he waited another year before attending school, he'd be sacrificing the opportunity to see Skunk's sister Ellie every day! While he dreaded the thought of dealing with the bully, he wasn't about to give that up!

While far from the fun-loving and free-spirited guy he was previously known for, it wasn't too long before Luke managed to feel more comfortable in the school setting. Knowing Allen and Catherine had been through the same initiation with their homemade clothes and haircuts, he envied the way they so confidently went about their business. Allen was glad Luke had allies like Skunk and Ellie, and it may have appeared selfish at a glance, but he took a bold position that Luke would be better off in the long run if he had to fight his own battles. Catherine, who inherited her mother's striking beauty while wearing those homemade feed sack dresses every day, walked proudly like she knew well in advance that someday she would be the envy of every girl in school.

The first week of school introduced three important new characters into Luke's life. There was Skunk, the thoughtful and caring kid, perhaps small in physical stature but with the heart and spirit of a lion. He was a lifesaver and would become a major player throughout Luke's schooldays. Then there was Skunk's sister, Ellie, in fourth grade. Ellie had a special genuine fondness for Luke and would go out of her way to be his friend. Then, of course, there was Ron Ferguson. The unfortunate truth was, Ron and his older brother Frank were in the process of establishing legendary status for their persistent bullying in school and around town. It was evident to everyone, Ron was merely in the early stages of going down the same dubious path as Frank, who after serving suspension after suspension for disruptive behavior, was on the brink of permanent expulsion from high school. Their 6'6", 300-pound father and strange and indifferent mother were fully aware of their bullying and persistently bad behavior, but either they didn't care or were simply not equipped to straighten them out. The unfortunate end result—Ron Ferguson would prove to be a thorn in Luke's side for many years to come!

Chapter Eight

Progressing through the fall months and looking forward to wrapping up his remaining days in the feed mill, with the possibility created by landing the exciting new job offer, Luke's dad was determined to find that much desired new house in town. Always trying to help out whenever he could, Grandpa Wentworth quietly assisted in getting the house search moving in the right direction.

Baseball had always been a big deal in Jefferson. Following a prolific high school career, the first Jefferson player to sign a professional contract, and after modest success bouncing around in the Chicago Cub minor league system for a few years, Grandpa Wentworth returned home, resigned to playing with the town team until he was in his late forties. An exceptional all-around athlete, Luke's Grandpa turned to playing golf and joined the nearby Boulder Country Club.

Boulder, twelve miles down Highway 318 with a population of about three thousand, was proud of its impressive nine-hole golf course. The Troy River split the course down the middle, creating a number of scenic holes along its shores. Tolerating the painful clean-up after the disruptive spring flood, it was a beautiful golf setting. Grandpa Wentworth was a regular for the Wednesday afternoon men's day outings, providing him with a chance to relax for a few hours, drink a beer or two, and bond with many of the other successful businessmen in Wright County.

As the leaves were busy turning colors on the sunny fall afternoon, Luke's grandpa was conveniently assigned to a foursome that included Paul Anderson, owner of the plumbing shop; Dr. Ellington, their longtime family doctor; and a gentleman by the name of Walter Olson. Walter was a prosperous businessman in Jefferson and, over the years, had invested in a number of properties in the area. He owned a large acreage west of Jefferson, where he raised a variety of vegetables destined to be sold in his popular farmer's market throughout the summer months. Grandpa casually mentioned to Walter that his daughter's family was looking for a place to rent after the first of the year when William was scheduled to start his new job as an apprentice plumber with their current golfing partner, Paul Anderson.

Walter said it just so happened he had a renter moving out of town over the Christmas holidays and the house would be available in January. The house was located a block south of his home. It was an older house with four bedrooms on a nice, big lot, but he was well aware of its one glaring shortcoming: it didn't have running water. He mentioned his other rental property next to his warehouse might become available sometime in the near future. He wasn't sure how soon that would be. The house by the warehouse was much nicer and had indoor plumbing but, of course, would require higher rent.

The next day, Grandpa Wentworth informed William about his conversation with Walter. He was thrilled with the news and wasted no time in going to see him immediately after work that night. He found Walter working in the warehouse, and he politely invited William back to his office. Following a short friendly conversation, in a matter of only a few minutes, they had worked out what William felt was a fair and reasonable rental agreement.

After ten long years in the house on the shores of the treacherous Troy River, the Fosters would soon be moving into the big house in Jefferson a block south of Walter Olson's beautiful estate. An important part of the deal, Walter promised William that when his other house with running water became available, the Foster's would have "first rights" to rent the place. While William knew his family would be disappointed about not fulfilling their dream of indoor plumbing, he also knew they'd be thrilled about moving into a bigger house in town and, more than anything, no longer having to worry about the threat of the annual spring floods. All things considered, this was a wonderful development and happy day for the Foster family!

With all this exciting news, their dad's new job, and now the new house, the fall months seemed to drag on forever! But before they knew it, in sub-zero temperatures and in heavy blowing snow, promptly on the first of January, thanks to a number of generous and enthusiastic friends and volunteers and the use of one of Grandpa Wentworth's feed trucks, the furniture and their sparse belongings were moved into the amazing new house in Jefferson.

William reported to his new job the following Monday morning, and the kids would no longer be boarding the big yellow bus. Catherine, Allen, and Luke would now be bundling up during the remaining winter months and making the daily six-block walk to school. Their mother would remain home with one-year-old Glenda thoroughly enjoying getting settled in their new home and preparing for the new arrival in May.

The fact was, the house was old, pretty rundown, and not the greatest-looking place. But more important than all that, it was well built and well insulated, so when they cranked up the coal furnace, it would always be cozy and warm inside. The two-story house, in great need for a fresh coat of paint, had three sizable bedrooms upstairs for the kids and another bedroom downstairs for their mom and dad. Luke would no longer be spending time with his nose pressed to the window in the middle of the night, worried that the river might catch them off guard. The first floor included a nice-sized living room, dining room, and big kitchen. The very truth was, running water or not, the entire Foster family loved the new place and felt truly blessed!

Not seeing any great advantage, the new property did feature a two-hole version of the all-important outhouse. Severely compounding the challenge of no indoor plumbing, the well on the property had gone dry sometime during the previous year. Walter had pointed this fact out before the rental agreement was reached, and it was understood his new tenants would be permitted to use his pump to provide all the water they needed. That of course meant hauling the water the long block from Walter's house to their place. Carrying the drinking water for the white porcelain bucket sitting on the kitchen counter was no big deal, but the many gallons of water needed for the washing machine and the big gray tub for the Saturday night baths would prove to be a formidable challenge. Hauling water would be only the first of many chores that fell directly in the hands of the two older boys, Allen and Luke.

Luke knew moving to town meant missing out on those special sessions down by the river with his buddy Mr. Slim and his grandmother, but the truth was, the spectacular outdoor features of the new place held great promise for many new adventures. There was the impressive big red barn setting directly between their house and Walter's place. Then the large apple orchard and sprawling pasture on the north side of the property that separated their house from the busy 109 roadway.

But clearly the most practical advantage of the expansive new property, there was a perfect spot for the vegetable garden Luke's parents had always dreamed of having. They could picture being rewarded with the endless bounty of sweet corn, tomatoes, peas, carrots, and cucumbers every summer. With the growing number of mouths to feed, there was abundant space where Luke's dad could easily enlarge the garden.

Chapter Nine

It was a glaring reality, Jefferson enjoyed exceptional prosperity. The proud citizens took great pride in keeping the public buildings updated and freshly painted, the black topped side streets pothole-free, and an always perfectly groomed city park. The lofty property tax levies provided generous revenue to build the very best schools, and with that came high expectations and demand for academic excellence. The outer perimeter of the city limits was distinguished with straight rows of dark spruce and evergreen trees. The perpendicular streets were bordered with mature oak, maple, and elm trees and were lined with handsome, well-kept homes and immaculately manicured lawns. One exclusive section of town featured older Victorian estates with ostentatious gated entrances to large front yards surrounded with classic black wrought-iron fences. The residents in the impressive neighborhood represented what was called the old money and were politically influential in setting the tone in maintaining a high standard for the entire community.

The no-stoplight main street was decorated with attractive hanging flower plants attached to tall, illuminating light poles. The modernized storefronts in the diversified business district reeked of profitability. Along with the normal business offerings, the Roxie Theater and popular Crazy Horse and Alibi Inn taverns attracted patrons from a large geographical radius. The handsome red brick post office, city hall, library, and fire station were a source of great pride. The large traditional schoolhouse was conveniently positioned in the center of town. The football field and spectacular baseball field were located along the southern border of town.

The lone community deficiency may have been in the police department, which employed one law enforcement officer. Al Hughes spent the vast majority of his time sitting idly in his shiny new marked car parked in front of the fire station diligently policing Main Street. It was more than a rumor that Officer Al tucked a flask of his favorite "hooch" under the front seat that led to the much-deserved title Alcohol Al. As questionable and ineffective as his performance may have been, the typical small-town political forces embraced the situation as it was, and the generally peaceful environment in the pristine community kept Al Hughes proudly wearing the badge.

The two worst known crimes committed in Jefferson during the past six months both involved the infamous Ron Ferguson's high school brother, Frank. Alcohol Al had to deal with Frank when he got caught shoplifting candy bars from the Dreyer Drug store, and he was also the prime suspect for painting profanity on the front door of the schoolhouse. It was discovered the day after Frank had once again been suspended from school, and unfortunately, the custodian didn't get it removed until all the students had walked through the door that morning. The incident caused a minor fury in town when dozens of parents of elementary-school kids were pulling their hair out, trying to explain what it meant to "get fucked"!

But on the surface, Jefferson had the characteristics of a desirable and pleasant small town and appeared to be an ideal place to raise a family.

The Foster household was an isolated exception to the general affluence of the vast majority of families in Jefferson. Although William's new starting wages were an improvement over his modest pay at the feed mill, the new monthly rent payments would devour the highly anticipated additional income. With the still growing family, Luke's mother was needed at home, preventing her from any serious consideration of supplementing the income picture. Replacing the old '38 Chevrolet wasn't going to happen any time soon. While the outlook was good and there was newfound optimism for the future, the challenging financial picture would simply be a continuing way of life for the Fosters.

But that wasn't a big deal. They'd proven over and over they could overcome challenges. They weren't about to let the shortage of luxuries prevent them from having a life generally filled with happiness and good times. Wearing clothes made out of feed sacks, perhaps a few small holes in their pants and shoes, the homemade haircuts, but led by their always inspired and vibrant mother, the Fosters focused on counting their blessings, keeping a positive attitude, and were determined to simply get on with their lives. In spite of their limited means, the citizens of the community would only marvel how this special closely knit family could walk so proudly and with their heads held high.

Luke was the exception. Still reeling from the lingering guilt of letting Carol slip from his fingers that unforgettable night and now dealing with the persistent bully almost every day in school, highly sensitive and insecure, Luke struggled mightily to carry himself with the kind of confidence Catherine and Allen appeared to simply manage in stride.

While enjoying the many improvements in their lives, there were a few new built-in dynamics that presented new concerns for Luke. The required walk back and forth to school meant walking in the direct path of their new landlord Walter Olson's mean dog, Rusty. There was no alternate route, walking on the busy 109 highway along the north side of their property was strictly forbidden. Rusty was of no special recognizable breed; he was just a big, ornery mutt. If you entered his marked territory and failed to stop and pet him to his full satisfaction, he would start his intimidating growling routine, and if you prematurely moved on, it was inevitable. He would succeed in biting you, sometimes more severely than others.

The miserable twice-a-day ritual was bad enough, but Luke and Allen had to go back into the unreasonable dog's danger zone to pump at least one pail of water every night. It was the same deal: you played his little game or simply paid the price. Like everything else, it didn't seem to bother Allen too much, but that was not the case for Luke. Almost as bad as dealing with the Ferguson jerk at school every day, the persistent threat presented by the mean dog became a major aggravation in his life. Luke absolutely hated dealing with that miserable dog!

The ongoing battle with Rusty did produce a rather intriguing revelation about Luke's big sister. Catherine demonstrated an uncanny knack for getting along with the mean dog. For whatever reason, and truthfully it annoyed Luke, Catherine mysteriously developed a harmonious rapport with Rusty and could freely breeze up and down the road with no threat to her safety.

Catherine not only had a special way with dogs, but she was also often found nursing a tiny bird that may have fallen from a nest. One time, using a delicate eye dropper, she patiently fed and cared for an abandoned baby rabbit. The fact was, fondness of animals developed into a powerful lifelong passion for Catherine.

But the benefits related to the move to town clearly outweighed the occasional setback. What turned out to be a major positive development in his life, Luke forged another special and invaluable friendship that fall. Like his buddy Skunk, Neal Fulmer was a shorter kid, and again like Skunk, he was an extremely friendly and likeable guy. Neal had a witty sense of humor, and Luke soon discovered there was never going to be a dull minute when he was around!

Luke learned early in their relationship that Neal never knew his mother and had lived alone with his father since he was real young. Luke couldn't fathom living without his mother. Neal's dad owned the Roxie Theater there in Jefferson and was an ambitious and successful businessman who could easily provide impressive new clothes and all the luxuries a boy could dream of having. Neal could care less about all that and envied Skunk and Luke for having what he thought were amazing families. He knew they were the lucky ones. Forging a special friendship, by the end of first grade, Skunk, Neal, and Luke were an inseparable threesome.

One of Luke and Neal's favorite things to do was getting invited out to Skunk's farm. It was usually on a Saturday, and the routine started with Skunk's mother serving them one of her incredible meals featuring her amazing "homemade" bread. Jockeying for position, Luke was in ecstasy after making no secret about his desire to sit next to Ellie at the dinner table. There was no way to hide it; Luke simply adored Ellie.

During one of their early visits to the farm, Skunk invited his two buddies outside to meet his true pride and joy, Thunder, their giant black workhorse. Along with the pure joy of feeding and taking care of the impressive beast, Skunk enjoyed riding Thunder to Sunday school every Sunday morning during the warm months of the year.

Skunk's two-year-older brother Stub was finishing up his daily chores, and the four of them hiked out to their secret hideaway in the dense woods on the north side of the big farmhouse. The previous summer, the Jensen brothers had cleared out a small remote area which, by careful design, included five sawed-off tree stumps that circled a big fire pit. With the endless supply of brush and fallen branches in the area, they built a roaring fire effectively killing the chill in the fresh spring air. A Saturday afternoon just couldn't get much better than this for a couple of city slickers like Luke and Neal.

Sitting on the tree stumps and enjoying the warmth of the fire, they were having one of their first of what would become regular bull sessions. Luke had always been curious about Stub's missing hand and hardly even noticed it any more. Luke politely asked, "Hey, Stub, I've always wondered, what the heck happened to your hand anyway?"

Having no problem talking about it, Stub quickly responded, "Let me tell you exactly what happened. I was about three years old, and I had been given strict orders to stay in the house. Ignoring all that, I snuck outside looking for my dad. Dad was shoveling shelled corn into a steel auger designed to lift the corn into that big storage bin next to the cattle barn over there. I guess he stepped away for a minute and had gone into the barn to do something. Determined to find my dad and curious about all the noise back there, I wandered back into the area by that auger. It was pretty stupid, just curious I guess, but I reached into the small opening where the powerful steel drill was rotating. My hand and shirt sleeve got caught in there. It happened so fast I can't remember exactly what was going on, but I guess I was lucky it didn't rip my arm off. They told me I could have easily bled to death."

Skunk was familiar with the story and just sat there watching Luke and Neal's eyes almost bulging out of their heads. A little sick to his stomach, Luke barely managed to say, "Boy, Stub, that must have really hurt!"

Stub continued the disturbing story, "Yeah, I suppose it did, but at the time, it mostly just scared me. My dad heard me screaming and came running over there. He grabbed me and had a heck of a time pulling me out of the machine. I'm telling you guys, it's a good thing Dad is really strong or I probably would have died that day. I don't remember much about it, but I guess I was bleeding like crazy all the way to the hospital. The doctors had to do a lot of surgery. They ended up cutting my hand and part of my arm off right up to here." He rolled his sleeve up so they could see the ugly scar and what was left of his left arm.

White as a sheet and visually shook up by then, Neal said, "it's really sad you only have one hand now, but I guess you were pretty lucky you didn't die!"

Stub said, "Yeah, but I'm okay with it by now. After all, I was the idiot who went out there and put my hand in the stupid machine!" And then he volunteered, "My real name's Kent, but after what happened to my hand, everybody started calling me Stub. But that's okay, I'm like Skunk, I kind of like my nickname."

Impressed with the whole ordeal, Luke said, "Wow, that's really a scary story." Expressing his genuine and sincere feelings, he said, "Boy, I'm sure glad you didn't die, Stub. And you know what, Stub is kind of a cool name. I can see why you like it! Nicknames are cool! Maybe someday I'll get one like you and Skunk, but I sure don't want my hand torn off to get one!"

Trying to be funny, Neal said, "Yeah, maybe someday you'll get your peter torn off and we can call you Peterless or No More Peter or something like that!"

Skunk had to add his two cents worth. "Yeah, or how about Peter All Gone?"

They were all laughing, and Stub added, "Don't worry, Luke, someday you'll get a nickname. But you know you won't get one until there's a pretty good reason. That's just the way it is."

Their discussions always included some reference to Ron Ferguson. Skunk and Neal knew how much he was bugging Luke around school and reminded him, "He's just a big windbag, and you just have to keep walking away from him."

Stub told them, "I hear Ron's older brother Frank is even a bigger jerk and might be getting kicked out of high school."

All Luke could say was, "Allen says I'm a big wimp. Sometimes I don't know if my brother really likes me very much, but I guess I kinda am a wimp. But—I don't understand it—why don't Ferguson's parents make them behave? School would sure be more fun if it wasn't for those jerks!"

Neal told Luke, "When Ferguson bugs you, just think about the Becker twins."

Luke came back with, "Not a bad idea, but I'd rather think about Ellie!"

When they wrapped up what was a comforting time spent with his buddies, Luke made up some kind of an excuse to go back inside the house so he could hopefully run into Ellie again before they headed for home. Luckily, she was sitting at the kitchen table doing her homework. Like always, she gave Luke a big smile accentuating those amazing dimples and said, "You guys be sure and come back and see us again, okay!"

That made his day. Luke would be looking forward to that—he knew that for darn sure!

In place of dealing with the flood, brother Gerald was brought into the world that spring. While adding to the endless workload for their mother, the good news was, their new house accommodated the new addition with relative ease. Three boys, two girls, and counting.

Chapter Ten

Luke's friendship with Skunk and Neal served him well throughout those early years in school when almost every day they bravely helped shield him from Ron Ferguson. That in itself made them invaluable, but their friendship also paid huge dividends on Sundays, always Luke's favorite day of the week.

Skunk once again came to his rescue when he provided one day of relief every week from Luke's personal running battle with Rusty. As soon as the weather turned nice in the spring and continuing throughout the summer months, Skunk rode his big workhorse Thunder to town to attend Sunday school. Luke could hardly believe his luck when Skunk asked him if he'd like to ride along with him. More important than the novelty of riding a horse for the first time, Luke loved the rare free pass through Rusty's danger zone every Sunday morning.

Luke climbed to the top of the wooden fence connected to the big red barn and, from there, jumped on the giant horse. Riding bareback with his arms clinging around Skunk's waist, they bounced and laughed every step of the three-block journey to the church. But the best part was when they approached Rusty's personal territory. As they expected and now hoped for, the mean dog would come charging toward them, barking and going crazy. Maybe a little annoyed but showing no real concern, Thunder would proudly strut by while indignantly ignoring the obviously frustrated pest. Luke thoroughly enjoyed watching the ornery hound cower away in the rare but much deserved defeat.

Once in a while, Skunk would invite brother Allen to join them. Now the three of them would be clinging to each other and bouncing crazily down the road. Not wanting a ride, many times Catherine stood there watching and laughing as her brothers awkwardly and clumsily mounted Thunder. More importantly, she was in total awe of the huge fascinating animal.

There was one minor problem when they victoriously arrived at the church. There was no healthy manner for Luke to dismount from the giant animal. Having no other option, Luke happily accepted the steep fall on the grassy lawn at the back of the church. Following Luke's painful fall, in one well practiced fluid motion, Skunk would swing his small body while gracefully landing on his feet. Skunk would tie Thunder to a tree behind the church and they'd head in for Sunday school class. An hour later, they'd head back home, again laughing out loud as they once again trotted unharmed directly in the path of the angry barking dog. Arriving home, Luke willingly accepted the second violent fall to the ground, and Skunk and Thunder proceeded to joyfully trot down the road for the mile trip back to the farm.

There was another thing Luke loved about Sundays. Attending church and singing with the church choir provided a much deserved and enjoyable break for his mother. Luke's mother had an amazing voice. It was difficult with the arrival of the new baby and her already hectic schedule, but when it was feasible, she looked forward to the rare privilege of attending choir practice for the one short hour on Wednesday nights. Elizabeth loved singing in the choir on Sundays and was oftentimes the featured lead soloist. The entire congregation loved listening to her beautiful voice. Luke and all the kids would sit together and beam with pride as their mother was up front belting out another popular hymn. Her popularity in church led to many requests over the years to perform at weddings and sometimes even for funerals.

Then it was his other buddy Neal who contributed to making Sundays special. During the early years throughout the winter months, Neal would sneak Luke and Skunk in the side door of his dad's theater for the Sunday afternoon matinees. Years later, after Neal had almost moved in and had become virtually a member of the Foster household, and with the full approval from his dad, the entire Foster family became welcome guests and could freely walk through the front door without being expected to purchase tickets. As their friendship grew, Neal would sneak candy bars out the back door of the snack counter and quietly slip them to Luke and Skunk in the pitch-black theater.

About once a month after the Sunday matinee, Neal would invite Skunk and Luke up the inside stairway to their apartment above the theater. The good-sized living quarters were filled with the nicest furniture Luke had ever seen. Better than that, there was always pop and ice cream in the refrigerator. Like around the fire pit in the woods behind Skunk's house, Neal's apartment became another one of their favorite hideaways.

One Sunday after taking in the first half of the matinee double feature, they decided to go upstairs and kick back, eat snacks, and relax. With Neal's great fortune of having every toy or game imaginable, the three could kill hours up there. During one of their many gatherings, by now famous for his wild and crazy stories, Neal was telling them about an overnight camping trip he and his dad were on recently.

Neal started out, "You guys probably won't believe this story, but it's the truth. I had to take a leak that night, and you know like you always do in the woods. You pick a tree, go behind it, and you pee."

Not very impressed, Skunk couldn't resist mocking him and responded, "Wow, that's really special, peeing behind a tree, don't you think, Luke?" Luke resisted saying anything, just chuckled, nodded his head in agreement, and politely sat there waiting for Neal to continue his story.

Neal continued, "Hold on, you jerks, now pay attention, there's more to the story. When I was peeing, a mosquito came buzzing around, and I couldn't believe what happened. As it buzzed toward me, it made a perfect safe landing on my peter, and before I could chase it away, it bit the heck out of it. It hurt like crazy, but worse than that, my peter itched for about a week!"

Skunk and Luke burst out laughing. Skunk said, "So let's get this straight—what you're claiming is this: you had a skeeter actually walking on your peter!"

Neal said, "That's exactly right. You said it. I had a skeeter walking on my peter, and it bit me," and they all burst out laughing again.

With Skunk unofficially in charge of nicknames, it was pretty obvious for him Neal would officially be called Skeeter from that day forward.

So that's how Neal became Skeeter.

As time passed, and Luke and Skeeter became inseparable, well aware of the lonely circumstances in his and his dad's apartment, Luke's mother made a deliberate effort to make Skeeter feel welcome in their home. She and Luke's dad agreed, "Skeeter was a funny, likeable, and caring kid and what was one more mouth to feed."

Skeeter would grow to absolutely worship Luke's mother. He had never been around anyone quite like her. He thought Luke was the luckiest guy in the world. Skeeter loved the chaos in the Foster home and, before long, felt comfortable jumping in one of the double beds upstairs almost every night. For all intents and purposes, Skeeter had moved in with the Fosters.

Recognizing how his son had never been happier in his life and fully aware of how preoccupied he was with his many business ventures, Skeeter's dad willingly accepted the new living arrangement. To show his support and familiar with his son's enormous appetite, he started dropping off large boxes of groceries on a regular basis. Periodically he would buy 100-pound sacks of potatoes and bushels of apples and oranges from Walter Olson's warehouse and discreetly deliver them to the Foster house. It was clearly a win-win situation for everyone.

Thanks to baseball, Sundays were even better during the summer months. The town team had a big game every Sunday afternoon. Home games always drew a big crowd. The summer after the Fosters moved to town, the baseball manager asked Luke's dad if he'd be interested in opening a refreshment stand. Seizing the chance to make a little extra money, William jumped at the opportunity.

Like Grandpa Wentworth, Uncle Stan was a terrific baseball player. Stan couldn't wait to join the team when he returned home from the war. Luke and his buddies loved watching him chase down those fly balls in center field and couldn't believe some of the long home runs he crushed over the fence.

It was a sad commentary, but Luke's dad never had the chance to play sports. Shortsighted, Grandpa Foster thought working around the farm was more important. A bad tradeoff, free from the strict training rules required of the high school athletes, Luke's dad spent hours behind the corn crib drinking quarts of home brew with his neighbor buddy. His neighbor's dad had a generous supply of beer produced in his elaborate brewery set up in their basement and never caught on.

The whole family pitched in and helped run the refreshment stand for many years. Luke's dad was in charge and made a habit of quietly burying a six-pack of his favorite Pabst Blue Ribbons below the ice in the pop cooler.

Luke, Skeeter, Skunk, Stub, and Allen attended every home game. They dreamed of the day they could wear one those amazing uniforms with "Panthers" across the front of the shirts and those shoes that clicked when you walked on the sidewalk. There was a mad scramble for the foul balls, and the lucky one would return it to Luke's dad in the refreshment stand for a nickel.

Sundays were the best!

Chapter Eleven

When Uncle Stan discovered they had access to the big barn, he asked Allen and Luke if they would be interested in raising a few pigs. They were excited about the idea, and within weeks of moving to town, the boys were officially in the pig business. Stan dropped off four of what he referred to as runts, along with a few 100-pound sacks of ground feed. The pigs were sickly looking things, but Stan promised if they gave them enough water and fed them every day, they would grow up and be perfectly healthy someday. Stan reminded them, "Do a good job, and before you know it, you'll be eating pork chops!"

After agreeing to a modest rental agreement, Ed Miller, the local postmaster, began storing Champion, his big Tennessee Walker palomino in their barn. There was a large open door that lead to a fenced-in area where the horse could freely roam around.

Ed was a good guy and would strap his fancy saddle on the beautiful horse, pull either Luke or Allen up there with him, and give them rides around town. Catherine spent every spare minute simply admiring Champion and was constantly demonstrating her genuine fondness for the amazing creature. With her special warm touch, she would affectionately scratch him behind the ears and feed him ripe apples from their big orchard. In response, Champion would nuzzle her and she loved it when he made that low, loving woofing sound from deep in his throat.

Mr. Slim still made a special effort to swing by the house and pick Luke up at least once a month for a trip back to their old fishing hole. Mr. Slim and Luke maintained their friendship after the move to town. He introduced Luke to his longtime buddy, Nute, the owner of the popular bait shop in town. The two of them would stop in for some minnows or nightcrawlers, and before they retreated to the river, they'd hang around Nute's shop for a while putting away a healthy share of glazed donuts. The three of them laughed and had a great time. Much like Mr. Slim, Luke thought Nute was a great guy. He loved spending time with the two old codgers.

Better than all that, their dad was learning a skilled trade and had a great chance for making more money in the future. Luke would continue to struggle with the recurring nightmares about that horrible night in the boat, but considering all the wonderful developments, the general outlook was never better for the Foster Family!

But there was an ugly trend that was growing and threatening to undermine all the positive developments and the fundamental stability of the household. It all started out innocently when Luke's dad and his old high school drinking buddy Rick Anderson, who were now working together for Rick's father, were making a habit of stopping in the Crazy Horse tavern, just a few doors down from the plumbing shop, for a few cold ones after work. The fun-loving twosome had a well-established reputation for their endless pranks and crazy antics during the good old high school days. As the weeks and months passed and they were growing more comfortable in each other's company, it led to the inevitable consumption of more and more beer. Rick was married and had one eight-year-old son.

What had become a pattern, usually on Saturday afternoons, Allen and Luke would go along with their dad, who perhaps had good intentions of running a legitimate errand when they left the house but would end up stranded for hours in the old Chevy parked in front of the Crazy Horse or Alibi Inn. Their dad was merely going to stop in for a quick one, but unfortunately, it was now regularly turning into one of those never-ending beer-drinking sessions.

Luke and Allen were pretty well-behaved for the first hour while cooped up in the car, but when the inevitable bickering set in, the car turned into a small war zone. When they were alone one-on-one, Luke and Allen had developed what was probably a normal contentious brotherly relationship. When the customary battle ran its course, they debated about which one was brave enough to go in the tavern and plead with their dad, "Come on, Dad, can we please go home now?" They knew the unfortunate volunteer would get barked at and it would likely end with the inevitable smack on the top of the head. These smacks only happened when their dad had been drinking.

One Saturday afternoon, things got totally out of hand. Allen and Luke were waiting patiently in the car and their dad ran into his regular drinking buddy, Rick from work. The boys knew this combination was bad news, usually leading to another unbearable long drinking session. Severely under the influence, the two creative minds found a convenient excuse that led to one of their crazier escapades.

Several months ago, Rick's dad had completed a major plumbing job for a pig farmer by the name of Tank Williams. Rick was tired of listening to his dad complain about the fact Tank hadn't made a payment on his bill for months. Clearly fueled by the heavy amount of alcohol in their system, the two cronies decided to take it upon themselves to help balance the books. With that in mind, they felt justified in carrying out their dubious little plan, which was to capture and kill a couple of the farmer's "ready for market" feeder pigs. Tank owned a remote pig shed with an adjoining outdoor lot where the pigs could roam freely. The shed was located in an isolated area about a half mile down the road from his house. They knew there was a protective grove of trees that separated the pig lot from Tank's house.

Shaking hands and sealing the deal after a quick stop at the plumbing shop to pick up two steel sledgehammers, Rick was flying down the gravel road in his shiny new pickup truck. Luke and Allen were sitting at full attention in the back seat with their dad dutifully following close behind in their old Chevy. In broad daylight but well-hidden and tucked in behind the dense grove of evergreen trees, the two determined and excited partners-in-crime pulled up and parked their vehicles.

Armed with the long-handled hammers, Rick and their dad boldly climbed over the fence and entered the heavily populated pig lot. Totally captivated, wide-eyed, and with their noses pressed against the side window of the car, Luke and Allen were about to witness a spectacular show.

Strategically positioned in the middle of the crazed herd of over 200-pound pigs, with adrenaline pumping through their veins and no concern for the risk of being trampled, the two powerful but distinctly impaired grown men were now swinging the deadly sledgehammers with wild abandon. After repeated aimless swings, having clearly misjudged the difficulty of their grand plan, they were failing to make a direct hit on the targeted foreheads of the much quicker and more agile animals. With continued futility, they kept flailing away. Not about to surrender, the vicious but unsuccessful blows were repeatedly glancing off the confused pig's heads, producing persistent loud excruciating squeals and severe headaches that had to linger for days.

The scene was growing wilder and crazier by the minute, with the entire herd now stampeding frantically from one end of the fenced in pig lot to the other. Mixed with drunken laughter and nonstop profanity, both exhausted and sweating profusely, Rick finally succeeded in connecting with a deadly blow to the forehead of the most unfortunate victim. Unleashing one final bone-chilling squeal, the innocent pig dropped helplessly to the ground. They both readily and wisely agreed to wrap things up at that point; one pig would have to do.

Wasting no time, they dragged the hopefully dead animal out of the lot, and applying all their diminished remaining strength, they threw it in the back of Rick's pickup, and abruptly got the hell out of there!

Having never seen anything quite like it, while there was no doubt the two boys in the nearby car were highly entertained and totally fascinated by the whole episode, and good or bad, it left a deep and lasting impression on them. Their dad's role in the whole event was unsettling to them. Luke was sure glad Catherine wasn't there to witness the vicious display of brutality to the poor helpless animals. He knew she wouldn't hesitate to let him know exactly how she felt about it.

It was painfully obvious their brilliant plan hadn't been thought out very carefully as they found themselves now parked behind the Foster's barn. Laughing nervously but proudly congratulating each other on the marginally successful mission, as they were slowly sobering up, they hastily decided to stick the dead pig in the barn. Exhausted and in no condition to attempt the complex butchering process but smart enough to know it had to be done soon, they decided to regroup early Sunday morning. Rick was an experienced deer hunter and had observed and assisted his dad butcher big bucks on many occasions. Butchering the pig would be no problem. It was past suppertime, and Rick abruptly headed for home!

Chapter Twelve

Slowly coming to his senses and more than a little nervous and concerned by now, their father gave the boys strict orders not to mention anything about the dead pig to their mother. As bad as they wanted to share the wild and crazy story, having no real choice in the matter, they agreed to keep it a secret amongst the "boys." Setting the crazy pig story aside, like many times before, they knew their mother was not going to be happy about the fact they had been riding in the car with their dad after he had been drinking.

It was a long and quiet Saturday night around the house, and it was a struggle, but the boys somehow managed to get through the night without leaking the wild and crazy events of the day. Although he was experiencing a severe menacing headache the next morning, after giving it much worrisome thought throughout the long night, Luke's dad reluctantly explained to his wife about the fact there was a dead pig in the barn and that it had to be butchered as soon as possible. He told her it was a complicated story and pleaded with her, "Please hold off on your questions for right now, I'll explain everything later."

Trying to buy a little time for what he knew was going to be an unpleasant discussion, they agreed to sit down later that afternoon and, in a calm and civilized manner, talk the rather bizarre development over. Having known William all through his crazy high school days and beyond, Elizabeth was well prepared and conditioned for almost anything. For the time being, she would remain open-minded and wait for the verdict on what she knew would more than likely be quite disgusting.

Rick showed up early the next morning, and along with Luke's dad, well hidden inside the big red barn, the two of them hung the pig by its hoofs and proceeded to butcher it. Through shared pounding headaches, they clumsily and rather sheepishly discussed yesterday's misguided sequence of events.

Rick cautiously started the conversation with, "Whose stupid ass idea was it to steal this goddamn pig anyway?"

Luke's dad quickly pointed out, "You know damn well whose idea it was, you crazy bastard!"

After a brief debate, they accepted mutual responsibility and agreed, "Our intentions were good, but it was probably not the smartest approach to balancing the books."

In the end, Rick took one large fresh pork loin home with him, and the rest of the meat was carefully packaged and frozen for consumption by the Foster family. The sudden generous supply of pork was a timely bonus since it had been several months since they butchered one of the full grown runts the boys had more honorably been raising since they moved to town. Pork had become a favorite staple for the large family's demanding dinner table.

Skunk, Luke, and Allen all piled on Thunder and headed for Sunday school that morning. With no fear and petting her friend Rusty, Catherine also safely made her way to Sunday school. With everything going on in the barn and the tension in the air, the rest of the family skipped church. Luke's mom had been looking forward to singing in the choir that morning, but while disappointed, she had too much on her mind and reluctantly stayed home. Upset but attempting to keep things as normal as possible for the kids, as always, she fixed a big Sunday dinner. She and William had agreed to sit down and talk that afternoon while the kids, including Skeeter, would be attending the double feature matinee at the Roxie. Less-than-one-year-old Gerald would be taking his regular long afternoon nap. A rarity—the house would be empty and quiet.

Luke's mom and dad had many serious discussions about his dad's drinking over the years. While that was true, Elizabeth had demonstrated a rather remarkable patient attitude about trying to understand why William not only enjoyed drinking a few beers with his buddies but even going so far as to generously understand that perhaps alcohol helped ease the pain created by some of the traumatic events throughout his life.

While all this was true, she was well aware of the fact William's drinking was getting more extreme and affecting his judgment in ways that reflected decisions that no longer represented who he actually was as a responsible human being. Yesterday's incident was just one example. In his right mind, she knew he would never outright steal. His behavior was becoming unacceptable, and unfortunately, these kinds of escapades were becoming more and more frequent. She was truly worried that alcohol was becoming a serious problem for him personally and, on occasion, might even be taking over his life.

Elizabeth was a bright lady and well aware of the unforgiving nature and destructive force of alcohol abuse. While she may have been an exceptionally reasonable and supportive wife, she was also a strong woman with the wisdom and fortitude to do whatever it took to protect and do what was best for the kids. Far from naïve or any remote form of shrinking violet, she was not afraid to confront a problem when it was necessary. The family had survived many setbacks due to her sensible approach in dealing with serious challenges over the years.

Luke's mother started the intense conversation by simply asking her husband, "William, I want you to tell me exactly what took place yesterday. I know you spent a lot of time in the tavern with the boys sitting out there in the car, which you know makes me unhappy, but I want to know how that stupid pig ended up in the barn!"

William knew he was guilty of many selfish and irrational decisions, but there was one consistent virtue he had never violated in their many years of marriage. He always accepted responsibility for his actions and had never lied to the person he loved more than he could put in words. Fully aware of how totally wrong and ugly the story was, he proceeded to tell her in complete detail exactly what had taken place the day before.

Elizabeth could do nothing but sit there and fume as she listened to the outrageous story. As repulsive as the whole thing was, she knew his version of what took place was the perfect truth. As embarrassed as he was about it, she always appreciated William's willingness to be honest at critical times like this. That being said, she was no longer going to sit back and let everything that had been going on continue without expressing her growing concern with what she knew was at the core of the problem. It was a delicate subject, but confronting it head-on was long overdue!

Calmly she started out, "William, I want you to listen carefully to what I'm about to say. We've talked about this many times before but unfortunately, nothing has changed. First, I want to make something perfectly clear: I accept my share of the responsibility in getting to this critical juncture in our marriage. I am guilty of giving you the wrong message in the early years when I said nothing about your drinking habits. You know how hard I tried to be reasonable and accept the idea that your drinking was innocent, not that unusual, and simply your way of having a little fun. And as your consumption increased—and again, I know now how wrong I was—I went a step further and rationalized that perhaps your drinking was motivated by your effort to ease the pain of some of your childhood experiences, losing your mother when you were a small boy, your dad's demanding and unreasonable approach to raising you and your sisters, then of course losing our precious little Carol. But I'm sorry—I've been as patient as I can be, and it's time for both of us to deal with the reality your drinking is getting worse every year. What happened yesterday is a perfect example of how dangerous your drinking has become."

She had a lot more to say on the subject but deliberately waited to see what his response would be to what she knew was an extremely sensitive and personal issue for him.

Taking his typical approach, always in complete denial, William attempted to lighten the subject and deflect the real issue. "Elizabeth, I know how serious you are about all this, but you know Rick and I just got a little carried away yesterday. It all started innocently when Rick mentioned Tank owes his dad a lot of money and we were just trying to balance the books a little bit. Yes, I suppose it was a little stupid, but remember, I work for his dad, and let's face it, as it turned out, there was no real harm done!"

Making one final effort to downplay the whole subject, William made a feeble argument, "you know how Rick and I like to have a good time, and yes, maybe we occasionally just push the envelope a little bit too far!"

She quickly recognized nothing had changed. This was his normal reaction to the subject of his excessive drinking. Not about to back down and no longer apologetic for her indirect role in letting his drinking get to this point, sticking to her guns, Elizabeth continued, "No real harm done? What you mean is you didn't get caught, that's all! William, you were stealing pigs, for God's sake. Good grief, you're not in high school any more. You're over thirty years old, and you have five children. Luke and Allen were sitting in the car watching you two idiots. What kind of a message is that sending them? That it's okay to steal, just don't get caught? Is that really what you want?"

William may have been guilty of overindulging in alcohol at times, but he was far from a stupid man. He knew he had no good answers at this point, and he could tell this was not going to be simply swept under the rug this time. He had never seen her this determined, and his instincts told him it was probably prudent to sit patiently and merely listen.

"And there's one more critical issue that we have to talk about. When you drink too much beer, you lose your temper and hit the boys. I know your dad hit you when you were a kid, but that is no excuse. That was wrong! You're going to have to manage your drinking as you see fit, and I don't like to give you ultimatums, but if you want to live under the same roof, I will no longer tolerate the hitting! It's wrong to hit any of the kids, but you don't know about the middle-of-the-night struggles Luke deals with almost every night. The hitting must stop!"

Recognizing the urgency in her voice, he knew these issues had reached a new level of concern for her, and he felt absolutely sick about it. He totally agreed on the subject of hitting the kids. That was never going to happen again, and the fact was, it didn't! Knowing it was time for actions and not just the same shallow words he resorted to in the past but knowing how much he had hurt and disappointed his amazing wife, William sincerely apologized like never before.

Having been concerned about how to thoughtfully deal with William's drinking for some time now, Elizabeth had quietly and discreetly consulted with trusted professionals. She knew it had to ultimately be William's decision to do anything about his drinking. With that in mind and accepting his promise to never hit the kids again, she accepted William's heartfelt apology, and they agreed to move forward. She could sense a more serious tone and commitment in William's apology.

Chapter Thirteen

It was closing in on three years since they had moved to town, and for Luke, except for Ron Ferguson's never-ending effort to make his life miserable at school and the fact Rusty was still determined to bite his rear end every time he walked by or was pumping a pail of water, life in general was good. As far as the school bully was concerned, while he much preferred fighting his own battles, Luke couldn't thank his buddies Skunk and Skeeter enough for their reliable moral support in dealing with the big jerk. Then as much as he hated to admit it, there was his sister Catherine and Skunk's older sister Ellie's role in trying to keep the bully under control. If Catherine got wind of some stupid thing Ferguson said to her brother, she would go right up to him and let him have it. It was the same for Ellie. She had a big caring heart and had developed a special friendship with Luke over the years. Ellie never hesitated to confront Ferguson and tell him exactly how she felt. Big brother Allen's position was consistent on the issue. He thought Luke should fight his own battles. Luke wanted to be as tough as Allen.

Not that it made it any easier for Luke, but it was comforting to know he wasn't Ferguson's only victim. The fact was, the bully was still out of control and picked on virtually everybody he came in contact with throughout the school day. It was becoming abundantly clear Ron's older brother Frank's continuous pathetic behavior was having a powerful influence on him. As hard as many people in authority tried to steer the budding delinquent in a new direction, it was obvious Ron was destined to follow in Frank's despicable footsteps.

And as far as Rusty was concerned, while still a persistent pain in the butt, as time passed, Luke was slowly learning little tricks in dealing with him. Like his slowly improving attitude toward the Ferguson kid, he was determined to quit losing sleep worrying about the stupid dog.

All in all, Luke's sensitive and insecure nature was improving. An important part of this positive frame of mind was the fact he couldn't help but notice how much his dad had changed. Luke didn't know anything about what had gone on behind the scene at the time, but in the aftermath of the pig killing episode, he loved the fact his dad was now coming directly home after work every night and was making a special effort to help out around the house. And his dad hadn't smacked him on the head for months. When Luke's mom recognized his genuine efforts, she constantly told him how much she appreciated his refreshing new attitude.

Although he was no longer spending long hours in the taverns with his buddy Rick, the harsh reality was, Luke's dad was still buying a six-pack on the way home from work almost every night. Still worried about this continuing trend, Luke's mother knew in the long run, as difficult as it was to sit back and merely observe, it had to be William's personal decision to change his drinking habits. She was smart enough to know pressuring him would only make things worse.

The Fosters were in a good place. No one could have predicted what was about to happen!

Easter was one of Luke's favorite holidays. Along with the built-in three-day vacation beginning on Good Friday, having the family together for fun and games on Saturday, and after scampering around to find the well-hidden Easter baskets at the crack of dawn Sunday morning and then all of them attending church and Sunday school, they always went to Grandpa and Grandma Wentworth's house for a fabulous Easter dinner. With all the wonderful improvements around the home front, Luke's mother was once again attending choir practice on Wednesday nights on a regular basis and was looking forward to singing another solo for the always-packed Easter morning church service. Everything was in place, and the stage was set for what Luke knew would be the happiest holiday weekend of all time.

The weekend suddenly took a shocking and tragic turn.

It started when Luke's dad wrapped up his work day at noon on Good Friday. He was supposed to have the day off, but his boss asked him to join his son Rick to finish up a special project that he promised to have completed prior to the holiday weekend. Offering him time and a half pay for working on Good Friday, Luke's dad was enthusiastic about the opportunity to make the extra money. Luke's mother fully supported the idea, knowing the additional money would provide a little welcome relief for their always-tight budget.

Luke's dad and Rick, his former drinking buddy and current working partner, finished the special project at noon earlier than they expected. Before handing William his weekly check, Rick's dad, pleased with his reliable and impressive work performance, surprised him when he included another 25-cent-per-hour raise in calculating his pay for the week. William was already feeling good about putting in a productive week and the extra money he made that morning, but the unexpected raise was a wonderful surprise. Looking forward to spending the long holiday weekend with his family, he made an impulsive decision to take Rick up on his offer to stop in the Crazy Horse for a couple of cold ones before he went home. After all, he hadn't been in the tavern for months now, and furthermore, Luke's mother wasn't expecting him home until much later that afternoon.

Like the good old days, Luke and Rick proceeded to start drinking beer fast and furious and were having what they readily agreed was a long overdue good time together. Not giving the idea of eating some food a second of thought, with their empty stomachs, the effects of the sudden heavy consumption of alcohol were significantly magnified. With any form of common sense now completely removed from his mind, Luke's dad lost all control of his senses, and there was simply no turning back. As inexplicable as it was, Luke's dad and his longtime favorite drinking partner proceeded to spend the entire afternoon in the tavern and were getting drunker than either of them had been in years, if ever. The drunken binge would end up stretching through the supper hour.

Although he had been consistent about coming directly home after work for months, it wasn't a great mystery for Luke's mother to figure out where her husband likely was when he failed to show up for supper. Surprised by the turn of events and wanting badly to salvage the special weekend they had so carefully planned for the family and fully aware of how much he hated it when she did it, Elizabeth felt she had no choice but to call the tavern. Quickly recognizing his drunken condition and severely disappointed for his and the family's good, she insisted he come home immediately. Literally out-of-his-mind drunk, William recklessly ignored her wishes and continued laughing, drinking, and having a good time. With growing concern and building anger, Elizabeth called again and again but got the same results. Needless to say, it was an extremely sad way to start the special Easter weekend.

Regrettably, before Catherine, Allen, and Luke's regular bedtime, their pathetic drunk father came stumbling through the front door. The unsuspecting kids were about to witness an unimaginable confrontation between their mother and father. On top of the fact he was drunker than she had ever seen him, their mother was furious about his driving the car home in his outrageous condition. In a hopeless attempt to defend himself, slurring his words, Luke's dad was shouting back at his mother, complaining incoherently something about her repeated calls to the tavern, claiming she had embarrassed him in front of all his buddies. It was a weak and feeble argument coming from an obviously desperate and defenseless drunk human being.

Fortunately, the two little ones, Glenda and Gerald, were tucked safely in bed for the night, and Skeeter was out of town with his dad for the holiday week end. But unfortunately, their father's sudden explosive behavior prevented their mother from having any chance to send the three older kids upstairs to their bedrooms. During the uncommon heated exchange that followed, their father's anger suddenly escalated like never before. It was obvious the ruthless and cruel effects of alcohol had relentlessly taken over, and the end result was an unfathomable scene.

Suddenly, out of nowhere, their powerful and muscular father took a wild swing with the back of his hand, smashing their mother squarely in the face. It created an unforgettable loud, cracking sound. Their much smaller mother flew across the room slamming into the kitchen table and, as she was falling, knocked over two chairs. She landed flat on her back in the middle of the kitchen floor. With blood gushing from her nose and her glasses broken and hanging awkwardly down the side of her face, it was a pathetic and sickening sight.

Gathered at the kitchen door and with eyes bulging, the kids were stunned with the unthinkable event they had just unfolded in front of them. Scared to death and crying uncontrollably, the three terrorized kids instinctively huddled around their fallen mother, trying desperately to protect and comfort her as she remained sprawled across the floor. Rattled, confused, and too drunk to even remotely comprehend the magnitude of the tragic scene before him, their frightened but totally irrational father barked at them, "You little shits get your asses upstairs to bed right now, goddamn it!"

Barely conscious but alarmed when she faintly deciphered the ruthless orders directed toward her shattered kids, still lying on the floor and through chest-heaving convulsive sobs, their mother bravely begged them, "Please, kids, go upstairs. Hurry, go on now, please go upstairs!"

Sadly incapable of providing the badly needed aid to his broken wife, William turned his back, stumbled into the living room, collapsed on the couch, and in a matter of seconds, passed out.

Chapter Fourteen

The three traumatized and sobbing kids ran frantically upstairs and huddled together in the boys' bedroom. The horrific scene they just witnessed scared them to death. Their mother was still lying on the floor with blood gushing from her nose. *What's wrong with Dad anyway?* Why did he do this terrible thing to their mother? They remained together, trying desperately to comfort each other. The always strong Catherine and Allen were crying. Luke couldn't cry. The frightening event cut him so deep that he was spiraling helplessly downward to that familiar dark place where he had landed once before, several years ago.

Dazed and with severe pounding in her head after disgustingly observing her drunken husband passed out on the couch, Elizabeth had one thing on her mind: she had to get upstairs to comfort her devastated children. While anxious to be with them, she knew she had to stop the blood running from her nose and make herself as presentable as possible. She had trouble getting the stubborn bleeding to stop, and with gauze stuck in both nostrils, she rushed upstairs.

Searching desperately for the right words to adequately explain what happened, the first sight of her intensified the kid's sobbing, but her mere presence was comforting to them. Knowing she wasn't very convincing, she repeated over and over, "Everything is going to be okay, kids. Everything is going to be okay." Compassionately hugging them, she pleaded, "I want you to be big kids and go to sleep now. We'll talk more about this tomorrow." And again she insisted, "Everything is going to be okay. I promise, kids, everything is going to be okay!"

Gently patting them both on the back, she remained close by until she could see Catherine and Allen were no longer sobbing and were finally sleeping. Luke was tossing and turning, and she knew he wouldn't be able to fall asleep. Not saying a word, he kept sitting up, and she recognized that familiar frightening look in his once-again-unseeing eyes. She put him in her arms and carried him downstairs and laid him on the bed next to her. Heartbroken, she compassionately patted him on the back until some unknown time, with human exhaustion mercifully setting in, they both physically surrendered and drifted into a strange, unsettling form of sleep.

With her motherly instincts kicking in, barely an hour had passed and it was time for Gerald's first middle-of-the-night feeding. Tired, confused, and worried to death about what the future held for her beloved family, she had no choice but to be strong and simply move forward.

William came to at about 5:00 the next morning. As he struggled to sit up and was bracing his pounding and pulsing head in the palm of his hands with his elbows resting on his knees, his first thoughts were, *My mind has to be playing drunken tricks on me*. What he thought may have happened last night had to be a bad dream! Was it even possible? The foggy recollections couldn't be real! *No way, please dear God, tell me they aren't true!*

With his mind gradually clearing, he was mortified as he suddenly realized, *Oh my god, what on earth have I done!* Totally petrified, it was slowly sinking in. *Good grief, it is all true, it all actually happened!* There was absolutely no doubt about it. *And there are no excuses—I'm totally responsible for what is now an unspeakable reality!*

As the sequence of events was slowly coming back to him and the brutal truth was settling in, the most dreadful and sickening part was the vivid picture of his beloved wife sprawled on the kitchen floor with blood gushing from her nose and his three frightened and sobbing kids huddled around her. It was undeniable: he was guilty of violently hitting his beautiful, precious wife in the face and unconscionable, he had done it in front of the kids. This was, by far, the lowest moment of his life! Totally helpless, William sank into a strange, dark place!

He wasn't sure how long he'd been sitting there, but he was slowly coming around. The solitude of the house was deafening. He'd never felt so lonely and desperate. His mind was whirling. And everything had been going so well! *How on earth could I let this happen? Where do I go from here?* Then the frightening question: *Am I an alcoholic, for God's sake?*

He only knew one thing for sure: *I would never hurt Elizabeth if I were in my right mind!* With that conclusion, he simply couldn't deny it any longer. *I need help! In one reckless insane moment, I've absolutely destroyed my marriage.* Never more serious in his life, he was committed. *From this second forward, I will search for answers and do everything humanly possible to make it up to her!* He could only pray she would someday find it in her heart to give him another chance!

Lost and tortured, he remembered when, several years ago, Reverend Thompson played such an important role in helping him recover from his severe depression after Carol drowned. He recalled the preacher telling him at the time to never hesitate to come and see him any time, any day, if another setback presented itself. He knew it would be easier for his family if he wasn't around when they got up. That was the answer. He would head over to Reverend Thompson's parsonage. There was no doubt the walk would do him good.

Before he left, he noticed his weekly paycheck sticking out of his shirt pocket. He had a flashback to the day before when his boss had handed him the biggest check of his life and informed him of the additional 25-cent raise he was getting for his dependable work record. *Dear God, why didn't I come home and celebrate the occasion with my family?* Under the circumstances, it was a small consolation and meaningless gesture, but he endorsed the check and left it sitting on the kitchen table.

As he stumbled his way over to the kitchen sink to throw some cold water on his face, he couldn't help but notice the two kitchen chairs tipped over on the floor. The sight was another punch in the gut. Was it possible to sink any deeper? With growing agony, he set the chairs upright. Then the final sickening blow! Almost stepping in it, he saw the puddle of blood in the middle of the kitchen floor. Hard to believe, it was the blood of the sweetest and most amazing human being he had ever known. The physical evidence and final undeniable proof of his insane behavior was more than he could handle. He rushed back to the sink and vomited violently! Trying desperately to regain his composure, the once proud grown man fell to his knees, doubled up, broke down, and cried like a baby!

Fully aware of how fond Reverend Thompson was of Elizabeth, William boldly proceeded to tell him the unabridged version of the entire bloody story. Taking full responsibility for his actions, he offered no excuses for his pathetic behavior! He made it perfectly clear. "Reverend Thompson, I know this is unforgivable." With jumbled thoughts, he aimlessly rambled on, "You've always been there for me. I'm asking for your help. I know I have to make critical changes in my life. It may be too late to save my role with my family, but I must do whatever it takes to assure I never hurt them again." He was desperate and confused. "Where on earth do I start, Reverend Thompson? For God's sake, where do I start?"

With his experienced and highly trained ear, Reverend Thompson listened intently, and as difficult as it was for him, he managed to remain calm and expressionless. While clearly a challenge to cover up his utter disgust with the violent nature of the ugly story, but at the same time demonstrating his involuntary compassion, he didn't hesitate to be candid and firm with him. "Of course I'll work together with you, William, but let's agree on one thing right now. It's time to get the help you need and take the steps necessary to move your personal habits in a totally new direction!"

The preacher explained, "I've worked with Dr. Ellington on other cases like this. Let's give him a call and see if he'll sit down with us today and maybe we can put a plan together!" William had no idea what the plan might involve, but in his desperate state of mind, he had total confidence in these two caring and giving men.

He repeated the ugly story for the doctor. Following the uncomfortable but necessary discussion, Dr. Ellington pointed out that Wright County had a wonderful program designed exclusively for adults with alcohol related issues. He explained, "A prospective candidate has to first admit he has a drinking problem, procure a formal referral from his family doctor, which of course I'll give you, and volunteer for the thirty-day in-house treatment. There are no charges or fees for local citizens who meet these criteria. Let me explain one important feature. While a court-ordered patient is required to stay for the entire thirty-day program, a willing volunteer like you, although it's discouraged in most cases, has the option of signing himself out after participating for a one-week minimum period."

What Dr. Ellington deliberately left out of the conversation with William was a significant discovery that had been made just the week before. His wife had been in the office for a minor health issue, and like many times before, they easily deducted the fact she was pregnant. Elizabeth had asked him to keep the somewhat surprising revelation a secret, that she wanted to wait until Easter when she would share the news with her husband and family.

As desperate and determined as he was to make changes in his life, this was not an easy decision for William. The obvious repercussions of enrolling in an in-house alcohol rehabilitation program were huge, and it was all suddenly becoming very real. It was only human nature to think about the embarrassment and inevitable attached stigma for him and even more so for his innocent family. Like all small communities, he knew the Jefferson gossip mongers would have a field day. Then there was his dad. His relationship with his dad had been severely strained since he had happily, abruptly, and enthusiastically moved out of the house many years ago. He couldn't imagine how he would react when he learned the gory details of what happened last night. They were disturbing emotional issues but the truth was, he could deal with all that.

From a practical standpoint, the greatest problem would be the impact of his not working and how difficult if not impossible it would be for Elizabeth to pay the bills. But what choice did he have? He had hit rock bottom! He wasn't quite ready to believe it, but if he was indeed an alcoholic, at all cost, he had to do something about it. It may already be too late, but he could not afford to make another mistake. There was no alternative! With no further hesitation on his part, never more serious about anything in his life, he told Dr. Ellington, "I want to sign up for the program and I want to get started as soon as possible!"

Fully supporting the decision, Dr. Ellington suggested, "Reverend Thompson, why don't you take William home, help explain things to Elizabeth, pack a suitcase, and while you're gone, I'll make a few phone calls and make sure they have an opening down there. Urgency is pretty common in this business and they're used to moving things forward on short notice." Turning and looking directly at William, "I'm confident if you can make travel arrangements, we can get you enrolled in the program today."

Easter Sunday being the following day, it was a busy time for Reverend Thompson, but he said he could make a few minor adjustments and would be happy to drive William down there. Humble and greatly appreciative, William thanked the two genuine and caring professionals.

Reverend Thompson and William went back to the parsonage knowing they had to call Elizabeth to inform her of her husband's potentially life-changing decision. With everything that had happened the night before, it wouldn't be fair to just drop in on her. William was an emotional wreck, but more important than that, he had to be man enough to face his wife, and while everything that happened was foggy and unclear, he knew he had hit her very hard and could only pray that she wasn't physically hurt too badly. Implementing his well-earned trust and credibility, the preacher called Elizabeth and tactfully orchestrated what undoubtedly would be the most difficult meeting of William's life.

Chapter Fifteen

Saturday morning, Elizabeth was curious but relieved when she noticed her husband was no longer passed out on the couch in the living room. She had no idea where he may have gone. This was a first. Confused about his absence, at least it gave her a chance to focus on the kids' well-being instead of having to sort out where her and William's severely damaged relationship stood. Although she got very little sleep, with her unmatched strength and perseverance, knowing very well she was facing perhaps the most difficult and challenging time in her life, the first order of business, she had to organize her thoughts and be prepared to sit the three older kids down and attempt to explain what happened last night. There were no good answers.

Before the kids woke up, the phone rang. Still confused and understandably upset, Elizabeth reluctantly agreed for them to come to the house but insisted she needed a little time. It was critical that the kids not be there when their dad arrived. Knowing they'd be suspicious, she had to come up with a logical explanation and find a comfortable place for the kids to go. With that in mind, she told them to come over in about an hour.

It was unbearable for William to suddenly have to directly observe the end results of his violent drunken behavior the night before. Luke's mother had taped her glasses together, and they were resting on a Band-aid that covered a nasty cut on the bridge of her nose. The areas just below both her eyes were in the early stages of discoloration, and it was inevitable, within a few days, they would be totally black and blue. It was a gut-wrenching and sickening sight. He never felt so helpless in his life knowing there was nothing he could say or do that could undo the irreparable emotional and physical pain he had inflicted on this special human being. As bad as he wanted to, he knew it would not be fair to make a feeble effort to merely apologize. It was a time for action and not a time for hollow words. Humiliated and heartbroken and not able to look her straight in the eyes, with his elbows resting on his knees, looking down, he buried his face in his cupped hands.

Reverend Thompson gently but convincingly laid out the surprising and drastic proposal. Elizabeth was visibly startled by the dramatic revelation but quickly demonstrated her clear understanding and full support for the whole concept. Not suggesting for a minute she was willing to forgive William for his egregious behavior but demonstrating her incomparable compassionate heart, she kept things simple and brief. "William, for your own personal well-being, I want you to know, I think you're doing the right thing." Emotionally charged and struggling to hold back on the much-deserved and tempting critical editorial comments, she boldly added, "Let me pack some clothes for you and you can be on your way!"

It was difficult to see, but she knew the plan was necessary and would be the best decision in the long run as she observed her dejected and defeated husband carrying their one and only suitcase in his hand as he climbed into Reverend Thompson's car. Reverend Thompson and William began the three-hour journey to the alcohol rehabilitation center in Independence, Iowa. For the first hour, they sat there without saying a word. Reverend Thompson wanted William to have some time to fully digest everything that had transpired during the last twenty-four hours.

In an obvious deep state of depression, William sat there doing just that. The jury was in; the verdict was now final. He had failed miserably in holding up his end of the deal as a husband and father. Would he ever be given another chance to return and make it up to them? He knew beyond a doubt Elizabeth would never allow him to hurt the kids like that again! It was now a very real possibility! He may never live under the same roof with this amazing woman again. His heart ached like never before!

He had to snap out of it! *Okay, get a grip here, enough whining! It's time to quit feeling sorry for myself! It's time to dig in and do something about this horrible mess I and I alone have created! It is time to shape up and act like a man!* Then it struck him, the obvious and stark revelation! *This will only happen if I quit drinking. I simply have to quit drinking! I'm ready, I will definitely quit drinking! This is the first step necessary in clinging to any hope for winning my family back!*

Reverend Thompson shared a few thoughts. "Let me suggest something while you're dealing with what happened last night. William, you can't let this episode define who you are as a human being. Instead, let the way you deal with it define who William Foster really is. Let this—what is very likely the darkest time in your life—become your brightest hour! Let this be a fresh new start for you. Take full advantage of this opportunity in front of you!"

His final comment: "When you're not under the influence of alcohol, you are as caring, giving, and thoughtful as anyone I know, William. Elizabeth knows this is true. That's why she married you in the first place. Don't forget, I was there that glorious day. Now I'm no expert on the subject, but if it's that darn alcohol that derailed you, keep all this frozen in your mind as you enter this difficult and challenging week. I have faith in you, William!"

They walked into the institution together. After completing the registration formalities, they embraced. William thanked him for everything, and he was unceremoniously escorted the long, lonely walk to his small assigned room. Reverend Thompson headed back to Jefferson.

Shortly after her husband and the preacher left that morning, Elizabeth was startled when she heard someone knocking on the door. She was glad the three older kids were still in bed. The only unaffected ones, little Glenda and Gerald, were innocently scampering around the house. When she saw Mr. Slim at the door, Elizabeth remembered that Luke had a date for their first fishing trip of the spring. This would be just the first of what she knew would be many awkward encounters in dealing with the undeniable physical evidence in the aftermath of what happened last night. It was inevitable; the whole unbecoming story was going to get out there. A longtime cherished friend of the family, Mr. Slim was the last person she feared would be judgmental of her or her family.

Mr. Slim couldn't help but notice the rare flaws in Elizabeth's normally unblemished face. Quick thinking and demonstrating his always thoughtful consideration, he focused strictly on his reason for being there. "Hi, Elizabeth, is my little fishing buddy ready for the big season opener?"

Recognizing and appreciating his deliberate polite profile, she skipped the small talk and answered him directly. "Hi, Mr. Slim. No, I'm afraid Luke's going to have to miss out on fishing this morning. He's a little under the weather and is still in bed. I know he's going to be upset, but he'll have to look forward to your next outing. I'll sure tell him you were here though."

As awkward as the interaction was, Mr. Slim kept things simple. "Okay, Elizabeth, tell Luke we'll just have to catch the big ones next weekend!"

Concerned about Elizabeth's unusual nervous demeanor, the loyal friend that he was, he couldn't help but wonder if he should offer some kind of help or support. Deciding it was best to mind his own business, he reluctantly left and headed for the old fishing hole.

That was only the beginning of what obviously would be a long and difficult weekend. When Reverend Thompson called about wanting to bring William over for what turned out to be a lifechanging meeting, as sad and heartbreaking as the nature of the meeting was, Luke's mother was relieved they at least had a plan to move forward. Having no idea of what the future held for her family, she was determined to take it one day at a time and simply focus on one thing, and that was doing whatever was best for her amazing children. As always, her kids' well-being would be the driving force behind every difficult decision she had to make from this day forward.

With that in mind, while there were more immediate pressing issues to deal with, she couldn't help but think about the child she was carrying and her original plans to share the news with William the next day, Easter Sunday. It was hoped to be another happy occasion.

How was she going to deal with Easter Sunday? She had attended choir practice Wednesday night and had been looking forward to her solo performance scheduled for the special services Sunday morning. The easy thing would have been to tell Reverend Thompson during their meeting that morning that for obvious reasons, she would not be able to attend church tomorrow. The truth was, preoccupied with the weight of the decision made that morning, it hadn't entered her mind. As it turned out, she was glad the subject didn't come up.

In formulating her personal approach in moving forward and dealing with their friends, neighbors, and relatives, she felt the best thing to do was what they had always done before. Hold their heads high, be proud, and simply get on with their lives. Knowing very well her presence would stir up provocative curiosity, she decided there was no better time than Easter Sunday to start the long, difficult task of recovering from this terrible ordeal. What better way to prove to the kids that things were going to be okay? That's exactly what they were going to do. They would all go to church and go over to Grandpa and Grandma Wentworth's house for Easter dinner as planned!

The first order of business that morning was explaining why their father wasn't going to be at home for an unknown period. She made vague reference to the fact he was sick and had to go away for a while to get well. After what took place the night before fresh in their minds, they seemed to be okay with that. Her plan was to take it one day at a time and only explain more if they inquired. The sad truth was, she didn't know herself what the future held or when their father would return, if ever!

With that difficult discussion behind her, it was an understandably strange and subdued atmosphere around the house throughout the rest of the day. Elizabeth tried to shift the focus on preparing for Easter. She was always impressed how resilient and strong the kids could be, and this was clearly going to be their biggest test. Her greatest concern continued to be Luke's severe depression and the protective shell he was forced to put around himself. She was relieved about the fact he was at least up and around and, to a limited degree, interacting with the other kids. While it was her first and greatest fear, it didn't appear to be like the frightening deep spell he had plunged into after Carol's tragic death, but she could tell he was extremely upset. She asked him to help hide the Easter baskets, a job normally reserved for his dad. Luke reluctantly and begrudgingly went through the motions while weakly attempting to help his mother.

As could be expected, the normal excitement while searching for the Easter baskets the next morning was missing, but it helped keep their minds off the conspicuous reality that their dad wasn't going be there that day. Sticking with her bold decision to attend Easter church services, she got the kids dressed up, and after applying rarely used makeup to camouflage the growing black and blue discoloration below her eyes, they all bravely headed for church.

Ignoring the spectacle their presence may have created, with Glenda bouncing on Catherine's lap, little Gerald resting his head on Allen's shoulder, and a subdued Luke sitting next to them, their mother was free to join the choir in front of the church. Extremely upset with his dad but aware of his strange absence, Luke was having trouble getting it out of his mind: *Exactly where is Dad anyway?*

A welcome distraction, Luke beamed with pride as his amazing mother, bruises and all, was now proudly standing amongst the choir in front of the overflowing congregation and was belting out one of his favorites, "Just a Closer Walk with Thee"! With their general awareness of the tragic event that took place Friday night, this was a stirring moment for everyone in attendance and set a positive tone for the overwhelming support the Foster family would receive throughout the challenging days and weeks ahead. As the story unfolded, with full appreciation for the difficult circumstances behind the scene that memorable Sunday morning, the level of respect and admiration for Luke's mother reached another new high!

Something else very telling took place that morning. As they were exiting the church and shaking the preacher's hand like they had done virtually every Sunday over the past forty years, Reverend Thompson's asked Luke's grandpa and step grandmother, Elmer and Ruth Foster, if they would join him in the vestibule for a few minutes. As the church emptied and they were inquisitively huddled together, Reverend Thompson got right to the subject.

As it turned out, Elmer and Ruth were in the vast minority when it came to the members of the congregation that hadn't heard about the unfortunate incident that took place in the Foster home Friday night. It so happened that the part-time bookkeeper for Dr. Ellington, who was sitting in the next-door office Saturday morning and had overheard the conversation between Luke's dad and Dr. Ellington, in typical small town fashion, had shared the solicitous content of the meeting and the story spread like a brush fire in high winds. It was inevitable that the story would get out there; it just happened in record-breaking speed in this particular case.

Reverend Thompson was familiar with the history of the strained relationship between William and his parents, and the very truth was, generally speaking, he had sided with William. But he also knew Elmer and Ruth were good, God-fearing folks with strong principles and the highest moral character. He proceeded with the unenviable task of telling them very candidly about what happened Friday night in the Foster home. But more importantly, he informed them about William's sincere regrets and how he had boldly swallowed his pride and volunteered for the alcohol treatment program. Considering the fact the strongest and only alcoholic beverage Elmer Foster had consumed in his entire life was the wine modestly served during communion services on Sunday mornings, he was sickened by the incomprehensible nature of the pathetic and repulsive episode. Elmer's first reaction was as Reverend Thomson expected: he was humiliated, ashamed, and understandably furious with his son William's inexcusable behavior. The veteran preacher let him vent for a few minutes, and when he settled down, he continued with his real objective and the urgency he felt in sharing the event with William's father.

"Elmer, there's a very lonely young man sitting down there in Independence, Iowa, who is doing a very brave thing and is in great need of moral support and a loyal friend right now. I can think of no one in the world who could be of greater benefit to him than you at this critical juncture." Recognizing he was perhaps striking a nerve, he continued, "As someone who has witnessed your flawless attendance record in that same seat every Sunday morning for over forty years and someone who knows the depth of your true character, I'm asking you to seriously consider going down to see your one and only son. I know I don't have to remind you what Easter is all about, the fact God sacrificed his only son for all our sins. Including yours and mine, I might add! I beg you, Elmer, go home and think about it. Keep in mind, yes, your son made a huge mistake, but you and I both know he is not a bad person. Try to understand, alcoholism is a disease."

The preacher knew he had put Elmer on the spot, but that was okay. By now a master of human nature, he knew this could prove to be richly rewarding for him as well as his son!

Chapter Sixteen

William was surprised when an attendant knocked on his door and informed him of a guest waiting for him down in the lounge. It had been a long lonely day, and it was 6:00 p.m. on Easter Sunday. He could hardly believe his eyes when he recognized who was sitting there. He tentatively walked toward the man and, filled with a wide range of emotions, was now standing in front of the last person he would have expected, his own father. The distinguished gentleman stood up, and without saying a word, he opened his arms and reached out to his tired and severely defeated-looking son. The long overdue embrace was only the beginning of what proved to be a pivotal turning point for a fractured relationship that was in serious need of repair.

It was awkward for both of them in the beginning, but when his dad recognized how desperate William was, his previously cautious and guarded fatherly instincts kicked in, and leading the way, it wasn't long before the conversation between them flowed with surprising ease. Deliberately avoiding meaningless apologies, after readily acknowledging his personal shame and how he had failed miserably as a husband and father, William informed his dad it was time for action and not idle promises. Step one, he would completely remove alcohol from his life and then do whatever it took to get his family back. That was his only remaining reason for living.

Totally convinced his son was committed to these dramatic changes in his life, he promised to be there for him every step of the way and to do whatever he could to help him get through this difficult time in his life. Following a lengthy heartfelt conversation between the two of them, feeling better about himself than he had in years, William's dad was back on the road for the three-hour drive back to the farm. He too had a new purpose in life!

After removing any trace of alcohol in your body, which in his case only took a day or two, the primary objective was the intense evaluation of the individual patient's personal condition. Whether you consume alcohol because you merely enjoy the euphoria, to simply have a good time, to perhaps ease the pain of past events in your life or any of the multitude of motivations, they got William's full attention when they pointed out the fact, "When drinking interferes with the basic happiness of your loved ones, you clearly have a drinking problem!"

He didn't have to hear any more! William didn't care if he qualified for any formal definition of alcoholism or not. He knew he was guilty of abusing alcohol, that his alcohol consumption was at the core of his problems, and he wasn't going to drink anymore. He knew he qualified for what they called "hitting rock bottom," and it was very simple: he was done drinking! He would participate in all the tedious group discussions, pay careful attention during the daily individual counseling sessions scheduled throughout the week, and he would sign out on Saturday as soon as he met the seven-day minimum attendance requirement! There was no alternative. He had to get back to work, and whether he lived under the same roof or not, as he had always done, he would do his very best to provide for his family!

That same Monday morning, shortly after the older kids left for school, including Luke, who was not really himself but was reluctantly willing to attend school, there was another unexpected knock on the front door. Luke's mother was surprised when she recognized it was Paul Peterson, William's boss from the plumbing shop.

After apologizing for stopping by uninvited and awkwardly acknowledging his awareness of what took place over the weekend, Paul got directly to his reason for being there. "Elizabeth, I want you to know we're going to sorely miss your husband for this unknown period, but I also want you to know we fully support him and are glad he's getting the help he feels he needs. There are two things you should know. First, I promise you, your husband's job will be there for him when he successfully completes the program. And second, William hasn't missed a day of work in three years, and while we don't have a formal sick leave policy, he will be receiving his check this Friday and every Friday until he feels comfortable about returning to work. Elizabeth, your husband's a good man and a highly valued employee. Please understand this is not a handout. William has richly earned these benefits!"

As pleased as she was about William getting the help he so badly needed, Elizabeth had been tormented all weekend over the glaring reality that his sudden bold decision would cut off their only source of income. While putting on a brave front, the truth was, she had been worried sick. She had no idea how they could move forward under these circumstances. Always a pillar of strength and not one to show her emotions, this incredible news was more than she could handle. Seeing the tears forming in her badly swollen and black and blue eyes, Paul opened his arms, and sobbing quietly, Elizabeth rested her head on his broad shoulder. She thought to herself, *Small towns may be famous for their unbecoming gossipy ways, but it should never be overlooked that they are also filled with wonderful, caring, and loving people!*

That Wednesday, with his mind made up about signing out on Saturday and with his father already agreeing to pick him up and bring him back to Jefferson, William owed it to Elizabeth to keep her up to date on his plans for the immediate future. He'd never written a letter in his life but decided it would be the best way to express his current feelings about everything:

> Dear Elizabeth,
>
> I will never ask for your forgiveness. What I have done is unforgivable.
>
> You and I both know I would never physically hurt you if I was sober. But there are no excuses. The fact is, I made a thoughtless and foolish decision to drink on Friday, and now I have to live with the consequences. I accept full responsibility for my actions on Friday night as

well as my persistently selfish behavior all those days and nights over the years. You deserve to hear it directly from me. It is now a proven and conclusive fact: I cannot handle alcohol!

No apology from me will change the damage that has been done, and I don't expect you to ever accept it, but for my own survival, I have to at least put my feelings on the record. Elizabeth, from the bottom of my heart, I'm truly sorry for the unbearable pain I have caused you—not only Friday night but also all those hours I spent in the taverns and my failure to be there for you and the kids when you all so badly needed me.

There's nothing I want more than to return home and spend the rest of my life making it up to you and the kids, but I know very well that it may be too late for that. I saw the unbearable hurt in Luke's eyes, and with my full understanding of his history and vulnerable makeup, combined with your unmatched care and love for all the kids, I know you cannot take the risk of letting something like this happen again. Those things have to be your first consideration, and I will always admire and respect you for that.

My dad came down here Saturday night, and while he—and rightfully so—is absolutely repulsed by my behavior Friday night, prompted by Reverend Thompson, he genuinely wants to support and stand by me throughout this difficult time in my life. With that rather amazing development, he has agreed to pick me up Saturday and, fully understanding my questionable status with you and the kids, has generously invited me to move back home. He made it clear I am welcome to stay there as long as it may be necessary.

In his classic style, he promised to provide ample opportunity for me to "earn my keep."

Assuming you and the kids aren't ready for me to return home—and again, don't misunderstand me, there's nothing in the world I want more—I will move back on the farm and return to work next Monday. I pledge to get my full paycheck directly in your hands every Friday from this day forward. When I placed the difficult phone call to Paul Peterson to tell him about missing work this week, he informed me about his intentions of paying me and promising to deliver the check directly to you this Friday.

My dad and I will come by Saturday afternoon at about 5:00 p.m., and if you will kindly pack my clothes in some boxes and have them sitting on the porch, we'll pick them up, no explanation needed. While I'm dying to see you and the kids, I fully understand that my presence would not be sensible at this time.

I will spend the rest of my life regretting what I have done, and you know I will love you forever! I know how big your heart is, but please believe me, this letter is not intended to seek your sympathy or your forgiveness. I know you'll put what's best for the kids before our personal relationship. And that's the way it should be!

Talk is cheap, and it should be given no consideration as you move forward. But for whatever it's worth, I swear to you I will never drink another drop of alcohol as long as I live!

Your loving husband,
William

As planned, William's father appeared promptly at 2:00 p.m. on Saturday, and they were now speeding down the highway on their way back to Jefferson. What historically would have been a highly unlikely and awkward scenario, stuck three hours as fellow captives, they openly and boldly addressed many of their misunderstandings of the past. The honest and candid conversation proved to be the perfect tonic for their long-strained relationship. If there was a silver lining in the dark cloud hovering over William, it was the fact it proved to be the catalyst for a remarkable fresh new beginning for him and his father. Hard to even imagine a week ago, his dad was now squarely in his corner and would be his greatest ally from that day forward.

As they approached the Jefferson city limits, William had privately let himself dream of the remote chance there wouldn't be any boxes sitting on the porch when they arrived at the house. He had informed his dad in advance about the likely presence of the boxes and of his intentions to quietly pick them up and promptly head out to the farm.

Then reality set in. There were indeed three large boxes stacked on the front porch as proposed with a rather conspicuous envelope Scotch-taped to the top box. While fully aware of this likely outcome, the now very real physical evidence of the ultimate end result of his pathetic behavior that infamous night hit him like a 2 × 4 in the forehead. With tears running down his face, he threw the boxes in the back seat, and with the envelope in his shaking hand, William and his dad headed out to the farm.

Never imagining he would ever be sleeping in his high school bedroom again, it had been years since he had been in the long-uninhabited room. Confused and filled with raw emotion, he looked at the picture on the wall above his old dresser. It was of him and Rumble, the prize-winning steer he showed in the Wright County Fair when he was in eighth grade. The purple ribbon was still pinned to the wooden frame.

He flopped on the bed and nervously opened the envelope:

> Dear William,
>
> After being married to you for over ten years, I know how painful this is for you. It's not my

intention to make it more hurtful for you, but in order to move forward with any hope for the best possible outcome, it's a time for pure honesty. Let's be clear—your actions Friday night were exactly like you said in your letter, totally unforgivable. What you did to me personally was bad enough, but the fact you did it in front of the kids is simply unimaginable.

While that's true, I agree, we both know you would never do anything like that when you were sober. Your actions were clearly fueled by the alcohol in your system. That being the case, it would serve no purpose to demonstrate how disappointed or how angry I am with you. We can remain civil and respectful as we sort out the best way to move forward. But it would be a mistake for you to interpret my reasonable tone as any remote form of acceptance of your behavior.

We both want the same thing, and that is whatever is best for the kids! The future of our personal relationship can only be determined with the passing of time. The emotional and physical wounds are so deep and fresh I honestly don't know if or when I will be comfortable living under the same roof with you again. Living with your parents will provide the time I need to make a reasonable and healthy decision about any future we may or may not have together.

You deserve to know exactly what we're up against. More than the other kids, Luke keeps asking about where you are. Do you know why? Like years ago, when he for so many weeks stared out that window fearing that the dangerous Troy River would ruthlessly take another one of his brothers or sisters, he now lives with the constant threat that you will come home and hurt me again. Luke's nightmares have become more intense than ever. We simply cannot afford to let something like this happen again. His recovery from this whole thing will be instrumental in determining how we handle our personal future.

One more thing. You have every right to know, I'm pregnant.

This isn't about whether or not I love you, William. It's about what's best for the kids.

Elizabeth

Chapter Seventeen

As the weeks passed, William had increasingly been allowed to spend carefully selected time with the kids. Knowing how much he missed the kids and how much he was suffering with the current setup, Elizabeth compassionately organized Sunday afternoons so their dad could spend some time with them. Recognizing the struggle Luke had with being in his dad's presence, as heartbreaking as it was, William willingly and patiently didn't force himself on him. They casually crossed paths in church on Sunday mornings, but Luke conveniently spent the time at the matinees at the Roxie theater with Skunk and Skeeter during the time his dad was at the house on Sunday afternoons. Less than two weeks after the incident, when things settled down a little bit, Skeeter was back staying with them on a regular basis. Luke's mother recognized that Skeeter's presence was comforting to Luke and helped keep his mind off things.

Mr. Slim had been stopping by every Saturday morning to pick up Luke for their regularly scheduled fishing trip. Continuing in his still lingering funk, knowing Mr. Slim understood what was going on, his mother politely told him each week that Luke wasn't in the frame of mind to go fishing. Having been through this kind of thing with him once before, while he was deeply concerned, Mr. Slim only wished he could find a way to help his little buddy. Finally, one Saturday, after six weeks of continuous failure, for no apparent reason, out of the blue, Luke was up and raring to go when Mr. Slim came to the door. With no questions asked, the two longtime fishing partners headed for their old fishing hole.

After getting the poles rigged up and sitting there quietly for about an hour, Luke was the first to strike up a conversation. He started out with, "Mr. Slim, can I ask you an important question?"

"Sure, good buddy."

"You know what my dad did to my mother, don't you?"

Not knowing for sure how much to admit he knew, Mr. Slim responded cautiously, "Not exactly, Luke, but I know it was a pretty bad thing and that it happened after your dad had been drinking beer with his friend that day."

"Why do people drink that stupid beer anyway?"

"People drink beer for a lot of reasons, Luke. It's something that's hard to understand until you get older. But I know one thing for sure. Even good people can do pretty dumb stuff after they've been drinking."

Thinking about that a little bit and understanding his dad had quit drinking beer, Luke said, "he hurt my mom really bad, Mr. Slim. I'm really worried. Do you think he would ever do anything like that again?"

Knowing how influential his answer might be but wanting to be honest at the same time, treading carefully, Mr. Slim said, "Your dad's a good man, Luke. I know how hard it is for you to understand, but he would never think of hurting your mother if he wasn't under the influence of exactly what you called it, that 'stupid beer.' I've known your dad for a long time, and I know one thing for sure. He loves your mother and you kids more than anything in the world, and if he said he intends to quit drinking, I believe him. You know I would never lie to you, Luke. I honestly don't believe your dad will ever hurt your mother again!"

"Boy, am I glad I asked you about this. I know you'd never lie to me. I believe you, Mr. Slim."

The next day, Sunday afternoon, after the first half of the matinee double feature at the Roxie, Luke and Skunk joined Skeeter upstairs in his dad's apartment like they did whenever the second movie was something other than a cowboy movie. Skunk and Skeeter were well aware of the fact Luke's dad wasn't living at home, and they knew he never wanted to talk about it. Skeeter, who had almost been living with Luke since his dad moved out, overheard the other kids talk about how much they missed their dad.

As they were busy scooping up giant bowls of their favorite chocolate ice cream, Skeeter thought it would be okay to ask him about it. He came right out with it. "Don't you ever miss your dad, Luke?"

A little surprised by the question, Luke told them the truth. "I'm mad at my dad for hurting my mom. You guys didn't see what happened. It was really bad. I couldn't stand it if he did something like that to her again. Mr. Slim told me yesterday that I don't have to worry about it anymore. He said people do dumb things after they drink beer. I think my dad quit drinking beer. I feel a little bit better about things now."

Listening carefully to Luke, Skunk added, "My dad gets loud and ornery after he drinks beer too. He doesn't hit us, but he gets mean and hollers at everybody all the time. I don't like it either. I just go upstairs to my room or out to the woods when he gets that way. It's really stupid when our dads drink beer."

Luke added, "Mr. Slim said when we get older, we'll probably understand it better. But I agree with you, Skunk—I think it's really stupid!"

Skeeter added, "I understand how you feel, Luke, but your dad always seems like such a great guy. When I'm at your house, he's always nice to me. He's a funny guy, always making jokes and plays catch with us all the time. My dad doesn't have time to do that. I agree with Mr. Slim. I think your dad is sorry for what he did, and I bet he never does anything like that again. It's none of my business, but I'm going to tell you the truth. And you know I think your mom's amazing. It upset me too when I heard what he did to her, but I really miss your dad!"

Luke was glad Skeeter brought the subject up. He was still upset about what his dad did, but after talking with Mr. Slim yesterday and now his two best friends, maybe he didn't have to worry so much anymore.

Elizabeth could see signs that Luke appeared to be recovering and warming up to the idea of his father moving back home, what she had been hoping for all along. When she recognized the consistent and determined effort William was putting toward doing all the right things, it helped immensely with her emotional recovery from the traumatic event. The bouquet of flowers he dropped off at the house almost every night didn't hurt anything either. The flowers served two meaningful purposes. It not only made Elizabeth feel better about him personally, but she made a special point to explain to the kids that he was doing it to show them how sorry he was for what happened that night.

Having every reason to make things work between her and William, Elizabeth was trying desperately to put the horrible episode behind her. When she carefully separated William's behavior when he was drinking from when he was sober, she once again recognized the caring, fun-loving, and thoughtful man she had fallen in love with so many years ago. Was it finally time to sit down with William and have a serious talk? Knowing there were no guarantees, the fact he had not touched a drop of alcohol for over two months now was an encouraging sign and a legitimate reason to believe they could be happy again. She had never seen him so serious or determined about anything in her life.

After an intense and satisfying heart-to-heart talk with her humble and apologetic husband, before any decision was made, she knew she had to sit down and talk to Luke. She wasn't going to move forward until she was sure Luke felt totally comfortable with his dad moving back home. Luke's final guarded but sincere comment was, "Mom, I'm still really mad at Dad for hurting you, but I think it would be good for the family if he moved back home. I like it when he makes jokes and makes everybody laugh. I miss not seeing everybody laughing. And I like playing catch with him. Skeeter says he misses Dad too."

Observing their dad carrying his boxes of clothes back into the house bright and early that Sunday morning was a strange and emotional experience for the kids. William joined his once-again-united family as they attended church together that morning for the first time in over two months. They proudly walked in as a loving family, and as always, with their heads held high.

After enjoying one of their mom's amazing Sunday dinners, they sat down in the living room to celebrate being together again and for what their parents informed them in advance was an important family meeting.

After much careful thought, their mother made an honest effort to hold their dad accountable for what happened that night without undermining the still important and much-needed respect the kids should have for their father. She had the compassion but, more importantly, the wisdom to maintain this balance. For his part, keeping things as brief and simple as possible, in his own genuine but proud manner, their dad convinced them how sorry he was for hurting their mother and promised they were going to get back to having picnics, playing more ball, and having fun again. Catherine and Allen appeared ready to move forward. Luke was listening intently, but it was obvious by his body language that while he was glad his dad was back home and he would try his very best, it was unlikely he would be able to truly forgive his dad any time soon.

While Luke had been making great progress in getting back to his old self after the difficult years following his sister's drowning, unfortunately, in the aftermath of this traumatic episode, generally speaking, he had clearly taken a serious step backward. As he struggled to get to sleep every night, in addition to the long-standing picture of his sister slipping from his hands and going overboard, he now had to deal with the horrific image of his dad hitting his mother and her bleeding and lying on the floor. He dealt with it all fairly well during the day when he kept busy, but sadly, bedtime had become more torturous than ever.

Chapter Eighteen

It didn't take long for the kids to recognize how much their dad had changed and how he was doing everything humanly possible to be a better husband and father. Still putting in long hours at work, when he came home from work, he was fully energized to help his pregnant wife and was contributing around the house like never before. His determined fresh attitude pumped new life into the home front, and before long, genuine happiness had been restored for the Foster family.

With things getting back to normal, it appeared Luke was getting along pretty well when he entered fourth grade that fall. By now a foregone conclusion, the Ferguson jerk kept at it and was never going to back off or refrain from pestering him. But with continued moral support from Skunk and Skeeter, he was getting more comfortable and stronger every day and learning to simply turn his back and ignore the jerk.

One chilly Saturday afternoon later that fall, Skunk, Skeeter, and Luke were sitting on the tree stumps around a roaring fire in their favorite hangout in the woods out on Skunk's farm. There were a few snowflakes in the air signaling winter was just around the corner, but with the heat from the fire, they didn't mind one bit. Before they hiked out to the fire pit, Luke managed to find an excuse to go in the house with hopes of bumping into Ellie. She was always friendly toward him, and when she greeted him with that amazing smile and those big dimples, it made his day. If it was even possible, Luke thought Ellie was getting prettier every day!

The talk around school that week focused on what was going on with Ron Ferguson's older brother. Frank had turned eighteen and, to the great relief of the school administration, had been expelled and was no longer attending high school. After being in and out of the juvenile court system following a string of misdemeanor charges over the years, Frank was finally being tried in adult court for a week-long crime spree that included armed robbery and sexual assault, both felonies. With indisputable evidence stacked against him, he was found guilty and sentenced to ten years in the state penitentiary. It was the biggest news to hit Jefferson in years and a rare blemish on the flawless and peaceful reputation of the always proud community.

Stoking the already roaring fire with a long stick, Skeeter started the conversation. "My dad was sure glad to hear Frank Ferguson was finally sent to prison. He could never catch him in the act, but he knew he was the idiot who was cutting big slashes in his new cushion seats in the theater. Boy, my dad hated that guy!"

Skunk added, "Yeah, now if we could just get rid of his jerk brother Ron. Man, have you noticed how big he's getting? It looks like he's going to get just as big as his dad!" His dad was 6'6" tall and weighed over 300 pounds.

The three buddies were making small talk when Skunk's older brother Stub came by and decided to join them. In his always friendly mood, he asked them cheerfully, "It looks like you guys are pretty serious about something. What's going on?"

Luke thought the world of Stub and, always glad to see him, enthusiastically answered, "Hey, Stub, how you doing anyway? We're talking about the stupid Ferguson brothers. What do you think of those guys?"

Stub offered, "Well, I hear we don't have to worry about Frank any more, but let me warn you, I'd sure stay away from that younger one—what's his name, Ron? He's already bad news, that's all I can say."

Luke fired back, "Boy, you don't have to tell me, the big jerk's always on my case giving me crap!"

Skunk, the "nickname" guy, for a long time had been trying to come up with a fitting name for Ferguson. It just so happened they were learning about the eclipse of the moon and the sun in science class that week. It finally struck him. *Eclipse—yeah, that's perfect.*

Ferguson is so big when he walks by, he blocks out the sun. This had to be his best nickname ever. With that, he quickly shared his idea. "I've got it, you guys. We're going to call the big jerk Eclipse." And he went on to explain how he came up with it.

Skeeter loved it. "I don't know how you do it, Skunk. Boy, that's a beauty. Yeah, that's perfect. Let's call the jerk Eclipse from now on!"

Lightheartedly, Luke joked, "Sure, even stupid Ferguson has a nickname now. Thanks a heck of a lot!"

Skunk promised him, "Don't worry, you'll get your nickname. Be patient, it will just happen someday, but it has to be one that fits!"

Changing the subject, knowing Luke was still hurting from what he had been through at home recently, Stub wanted to make a sincere effort to make him feel better. Wording it carefully, he said, "I know you went through a tough stretch at home, Luke, but I want to remind you of something. The word's out and everybody really respects your dad for the way he's handling everything now. Believe me, there's a lot more guys in town that would be a lot better off if they quit drinking so much. From what I hear from some of my friends, drinking is screwing up a lot of families in Jefferson!"

Skunk boldly added, "You can say that again. Our own dad's a good example. Stub, you've seen how he gets so mad after he's been drinking. He's always screaming and barking at everybody when he drinks too much beer. It sure wouldn't hurt if he quit drinking too!"

Appreciating their support, Luke quickly agreed, "Yeah, things are a lot better around our house. But what my dad did was really bad. I'm still having trouble getting it out of my mind!"

Still wanting to encourage him, Stub said, "It may take some time, Luke, but if I know you, you'll forgive your dad someday!"

The fire was burning down, and before long, it was time to head for home.

During the first week in December, Luke's brother Gerald was forced to move to one of the upstairs bedrooms to make room for another brother, Frederick, the new arrival that winter. Middle-of-the-night feedings continued to be a way of life for Luke's mother, and while it appeared she would never enjoy a full night's sleep, his dad was now taking his turn once in a while and was making a genuine effort to make things easier for her. As always, the new bouncing and smiling baby helped take their minds off the recent family struggles and contributed to the joy and happiness in their lives as they were nearing the Christmas holiday season.

Sunday afternoon, the weekend before Christmas, once again skipping the second half of the double feature at the Roxie, Skunk, Luke, and Skeeter were hanging out upstairs in Skeeter's place. There had been a huge snowstorm that weekend, and there was a really good chance they'd be closing the schools Monday.

Big snowstorms always put them in a festive mood, and on this particular occasion, with his wheels always turning, Skeeter came up with one of his better schemes. The wet snow was perfect for building snow forts, and there were dozens of fresh new snowmen of every size and shape spread across town. A typical front yard snow scene included a wholesome family featuring a mom, dad, and one or two smaller snow kids.

Prompted by the liberty of watching the endless wide range of movies featured in his dad's theater over the years, Skeeter was in the early stages of developing what would almost have to be considered, at the very minimum, a lightweight pornographic mind. His current dubious idea consisted of inserting a "pecker" on each and every snowman in town.

Luke and Skunk thought the idea was pretty dumb at first, but Skeeter was very convincing, and before long, the fun-loving threesome were all on board. The spent almost an hour breaking up the branches from the big pile stacked behind the barn. With darkness conveniently setting in, they got a good start on their little scheme prior to reporting home for supper that night.

The snow was still coming down hard, and the wind was howling. With the temperature a balmy twenty-five degrees, the minor blizzard was just about perfect for their covert operation. Scampering from one yard to the next, neighborhood to neighborhood, they were laughing hysterically as they inserted their homemade "peckers" into the lower extremities of every snowman they could find. Their favorite trick was to insert the largest branches into the lower front side of the smaller childlike snowmen. Proud of their efforts, they couldn't resist pausing on occasion to admire their good work.

It was suppertime, and they had only covered about half of town. Satisfied with their progress, Skunk headed back to the farm while Luke and Skeeter returned to Luke's house. The snow continued coming down, and with the wind still blowing, it was announced early that night that the schools would indeed be closed on Monday. With that exciting news, determined to finish the job, Luke and Skeeter came up with some excuse to go back outside after supper. They were having a blast, and Luke congratulated Skeeter for what had to be his best idea ever.

When daylight hit the next day, the widespread presence of the distinguishable "male gender" snowmen generated much laughter and lively conversation amongst the adult population around town. As bad as they wanted to be recognized for their clever contribution, the fact the schools were closed Monday prevented the normal buzz in the halls and helped in keeping it their own little secret. As proud as they were, the responsible parties would remain a mystery.

Skeeter proved once again to be invaluable in lifting Luke's spirits!

Chapter Nineteen

The winter months were rolling along nicely, but Luke's return to the fun-loving days came to screeching halt when out of nowhere, a startling event threw him and the entire Foster household into another unexpected tailspin!

Around the middle of January, the first symptom surfaced when Luke came down with a terrific headache one morning while sitting in reading class. Luke hated to miss school, and although he was suffering tremendously, determined, he somehow managed to make it to the end of the school day. He staggered his way home immediately after the last bell rang that day. The last thing he remembered before he was rushed to the hospital that night, proving he still had some of his senses, was petting Rusty on the way home so he wouldn't have to deal with getting his rear end bitten along with the pounding headache.

Extremely worried after Dr. Ellington's initial prognosis, with the old '38 Chevrolet on its last legs and barely capable of chugging its way around town, they recruited Uncle Stan, and they quickly put Luke in the back seat of his spanking new Chevrolet. With his nervous father riding along in the front seat, they rushed Luke the thirty-five-mile trip to the larger, more reputable hospital over in Buffalo Center. Scared to death and badly wanting to go along, it only made sense for Luke's mother to stay back and care for her newborn son and the other four confused siblings.

After surviving the excruciatingly painful spinal tap, it was determined conclusively, Luke had the deadly and crippling disease called polio! There had been a few recent polio victims in Wright

County, and the results had always been bad. Luke's parents were worried sick!

Knowing every minute was critical, Luke was quickly loaded in an ambulance and rushed the three-hour trip to the University of Iowa hospital in Iowa City, Iowa. The next forty-eight hours were considered the most crucial period for surviving the oftentimes deadly disease. Meanwhile, with the aggressive and contagious nature of the mysterious illness, the Iowa State Health Board's mandated quarantine was immediately put in place. Another stunning development with far-reaching implications, Luke's parents and his five brothers and sisters would no longer be allowed to leave their house for an undetermined period. As it turned out, the strict isolation required under these extreme threatening circumstances would disrupt the family's immediate future in profound and unimaginable ways.

By now fully unconscious and oblivious of what was going on, nine-year-old Luke was admitted to the intensive care unit and given the very highest priority in the University of Iowa Hospital. Stubborn high temperatures were threatening Luke's life. With the highest alert and now in the direct care of several of the best medical specialists available, with Luke now virtually packed in ice, as the hours passed and the high temperatures persisted, it was a frightening and scary time.

While it was characterized as an extremely close call, when the deadly high temperatures finally broke, Luke had survived the first critical stage. Following forty-eight hours of close observation and persistent care, with great relief, he was transferred from the intensive care unit to the general polio treatment ward designed to combat the next very real threat, the dreaded paralysis.

While ecstatic about the first good news, Luke's family was keenly aware of the story about John Fleming, the most recent polio victim from Wright county, who had returned home a paraplegic and faced the reality of being wheelchair-bound for the rest of his life.

The fact remained, with the limited existing medical knowledge, there were few options available in terms of treating polio. Exercising the one known hopeful remedy, Luke was given persistent scalding hot pack treatments over his entire body around the clock for the next two weeks. He was totally isolated from other patients, his only contact being with the nurses and doctors who, it seemed, never came near him without a needle in their hands. The persistent tension and nervous concern on all their faces were undeniable.

Throughout the two long nerve-wracking weeks, there was an amazing outpouring of love and support demonstrated by the many cards, letters, and gifts from friends, relatives, and the general citizens from the always caring Jefferson community. His personal favorite was, of course, the amazing card he got from Ellie, who had signed it "With love, Ellie." He made up his mind right then and there, *I'm going to marry Ellie Jensen someday!*

After two weeks of regular intense hot pack treatments, it was the critical time to test Luke's legs for the extent of the threatening paralysis the doctors had grown to expect with polio. It was an encouraging sign when they discovered Luke had feeling in both legs and feet. However, they were disappointed when they discovered he was unable to support his own weight when attempting the simple task of standing on his own two feet. His desperate attempts to walk were simply not successful. Knowing this was a common outcome, the doctors were deeply concerned about what now appeared to be a reality. Clinging to the hope his legs were perhaps just weakened from spending two weeks in bed, every day it was the same thing: after repeated determined attempts, there was no improvement in his ability to walk.

With limited options facing them, the decision was finally made to extend the hot pack treatments for another week. First, the gut-wrenching concern about Luke's ability to ever walk again was scary and terribly sad for the home front. But secondly, the fact the almost unbearable quarantine had to be extended for yet another week was deeply upsetting for the beleaguered and totally emotionally drained family.

After the extended third week of treatments, while it was officially determined he was not paralyzed, Luke's legs simply refused to function properly. It was a sad development, but it was decided they had no choice but to send him home in a wheelchair with the hope that intensive therapy would improve the strength in his legs to enable him to walk again someday. With the endless hours of determined and dedicated effort made by all the many attending nurses and doctors, a powerful bond had developed between each of them and Luke. They had all become genuinely attached to this particularly gentle soul. It was an emotional time when the hospital staff expressed their heartfelt farewells to Luke as they greeted his Uncle Stan and both of his parents as they nervously entered the private room. It was finally the time to take the stricken polio victim back home to face what would be a much different world than the one he had left less than a month ago.

After many hugs and tears, Luke instinctively refused his dad's offer, and Uncle Stan awkwardly stepped in and proceeded to carry him out to the car. Luke was already familiar with the strong arms that picked him up and hugged him at the World War II victory celebration.

You could recognize the deep hurt in his father's face, but his dad knew exactly what provoked Luke's involuntary painful reaction. While already suffering immense guilt over the regrettable incident, he knew, now more than ever, that there was a serious and urgent need for healing between him and his still hurt and troubled son.

Thanks to the amazing March of Dimes organization, who had contributed immensely to comfort the Foster Family throughout the long quarantine, the dreaded but badly needed wheelchair had been delivered to the house prior to their return to Jefferson that day.

In the beginning, it was disturbing for the other kids to see their brother stuck in that strange wheelchair. But as always, they were resilient and excited to get back to school and anxious to get on with their own personal lives. Luke tried his best to not let it bother him, but the fact was, he was deeply embarrassed about all the attention he was getting from now having to get around in the awkward wheelchair. With his already built-in sensitive nature and the unfortunate deep-rooted insecurities he dealt with throughout his life, this setback wasn't going to help matters.

But driven by a genuine burning desire to no longer be a burden to his concerned parents, Luke had a glaring newfound spirit and determined will to lick this new challenge. Knowing it loomed as a very real threat, he simply refused to accept the horrifying idea of being stuck in the miserable wheelchair for the rest of his life like the Fleming boy. He knew he was going to get back on his feet and play ball like his buddies.

Refusing to waste time feeling sorry for himself, Luke found a powerful new inner strength and could only think about one thing: he wanted to get started immediately with the therapy sessions the doctors talked about! He knew beyond a doubt that he would not be riding around in the wheelchair for very long.

Knowing how meaningful it would be, Luke's mother invited Skunk and Skeeter over to the house the first day he returned home. They were glad to have Luke home, and Luke was ecstatic to be back together with his two best buddies. Like only these two special friends could do, Skunk and Skeeter made it obvious nothing had changed, and they quickly moved on to the other more important subjects than the insignificant wheelchair. The happy reunion gave Luke a much-needed boost.

Luke hated it when a teacher met him by their car and volunteered to carry him into the school as he was watching Allen and Catherine struggling to carry his wheelchair up the front steps. He knew everything would be a little weird finding his way around school in the conspicuous wheelchair, but before he wheeled his way into his classroom, out of nowhere, a special kid by the name of Jake Simmons came up to him and welcomed him back. Knowing he might need a little boost, the thoughtful kid went out of his way to be particularly friendly toward Luke. Jake was a tall, gangly, nerdy-looking guy with round wire-rimmed glasses, whom Luke was fully aware was in his class but up to now hardly knew him. With his obvious caring heart and outgoing personality, Jake was a perfect candidate to become another great friend for Luke. Jake clearly lifted Luke's spirits, and it was only days before he became a fixture along with Skunk and Skeeter.

Jake's exceptional height was a glaring contrast to the much shorter stature of Skunk and Skeeter. All but inevitable, Skunk, the nickname man, immediately labeled him simply "Big Jake." What proved to be another huge bonus was, Big Jake just happened to be the smartest kid in their class. Although they were all serious students, Big Jake proved to be a highly valued complement to the gang and, before long, would be sharing incredible wisdom well beyond his years.

Skunk, Skeeter, and now Big Jake, and of course, his special friend Ellie played a huge role in getting Luke back on track, particularly when Eclipse, though hard to believe, would go out of his way to make fun of him as he struggled to make his way around school in the cumbersome wheelchair. The first time Eclipse saw Luke struggling to squeeze his way through the classroom door, he blurted out, "Why don't you learn how to steer that stupid thing, or better yet, why don't you quit trying to get everyone to feel sorry for you and just stand up and walk like the rest of us, ya big baby?"

None of the other kids were impressed with his unconscionable comments, but naturally, it upset Luke. It was impossible to understand how anyone could be so cold and heartless, but it was simply the way Eclipse freely operated throughout the school day. With a persistent and ruthless jerk like Eclipse around, having loyal and supportive friends during this difficult time in his life was more important than ever to Luke!

It took three months of biweekly therapy sessions combined with diligent hard work at home between appointments, but miraculously, with the steady support from his buddies and Mr. Slim, Luke was able to stand on his feet again. Faithfully, either Skunk, Skeeter, or Big Jake would be by his side and encourage him during each of the grueling exercise sessions that consisted of endless knee bends and weighted leg extensions. With their loyal support, he pushed himself and worked harder than he had in his entire life. Mr. Slim made a point to stop by the house at least one night every week. For a few weeks, Luke was limited to only a few careful steps at a time, but as time went on, with his boundless determination, there was a quiet growing optimism that it would only be a matter of time before he might actually be walking normally again.

Six months into the process, and as he was slowly regaining his confidence and becoming fairly stable on his feet, the physical therapists recommended the bold idea of jumping rope. Luke became obsessed with the exciting new challenge. Knowing it was strengthening his legs, he was soon jumping rope by the hour. Everyone was worried that he may actually have been overdoing it.

While the steady loyal support from his three best buddies was invaluable and appreciated immensely by his parents, they could see an exceptional renewed commitment in Luke after each of Mr. Slim's regular weekly visits. One night, Mr. Slim asked him, "You still have that old Indianhead penny, don't you, Luke?"

Luke quickly responded, "Sure I do. I keep it in an envelope hidden under my underwear in the top drawer of my dresser upstairs. What about it?"

Mr. Slim suggested, "I've been thinking about it. I know God's in your corner, Luke, and that's more important, but this might be a good time to start carrying that special penny around with you. I have a feeling it could bring you some good luck when you could really use some."

Luke didn't hesitate. "You know, that's a good idea, Mr. Slim. I'll put it in my pocket tomorrow and just keep it there, and we'll see what happens."

It may have been a pure coincidence, or maybe he just felt inspired with a new surge of motivation and confidence, but rather amazingly, a few days later, out of nowhere, Luke abruptly and dramatically was not only walking at a much-improved steady pace but was pushing himself harder than ever and, for the first time, was actually able to jog a short distance. Fully aware of its presence in his pocket, Luke couldn't help but wonder if that special Indianhead penny had something to do with his sudden dramatic improvement. Mr. Slim was right—maybe there was something magical about that penny.

After that sudden drastic improvement, it was soon a foregone conclusion. Luke would not only be walking away from the despicable wheelchair, but within a few weeks, he was also actually running and, hard to believe, would someday become the fastest runner in his class.

In less than a year since returning home from the hospital, he was back to his old physical self, and for all practical purposes, the polio nightmare was over. The only visible aftereffect was the fact his legs were now significantly bowed. But that was no big deal. His buddies made a joke out of it, claiming it was more than likely a result of all the hours he spent riding Skunk's workhorse Thunder.

The fact was, every polio victim was unique. The doctors had no good explanation for what had taken place. From a medical standpoint, they knew Luke's particular case was obviously one from the little-understood nonparalytic polio strain. But in the end, they considered the remarkable outcome nothing short of a miracle. They were optimistic that the severity of Luke's bowed legs would improve over time, and fortunately, that turned out to be the case.

Although once again severely tested, the Foster family was stronger than ever in the aftermath of the long and difficult polio ordeal. While they would continue to struggle with the same old financial issues, once again feeling truly blessed, they were more determined than ever to get back to living with their once-famous positive spirit and that familiar bounce in their step.

CHAPTER TWENTY

During the remaining four years in the house along Highway 109 prior to entering high school, Luke's life was like a roller coaster. While building great friendships and having good times on one hand, in spite of his dad's hard work and vastly improved new attitude around the home front, Luke was troubled with the constant self-conscious reminders of everything from their ugly, old rusted-out car, the oftentimes unbecoming clothes he still wore to school, things like his friends all having flushing toilets while he was embarrassed when directing them to their outhouse or a porcelain pot, and other sensitive social issues that he knew shouldn't bother him but they just did. And the steady supply of bullying incidents generated by Eclipse undermined any real or long-term comfort level in school. Luke did his very best to be strong like Allen and Catherine, but due to his personal makeup, life in general would prove to be an ongoing struggle for him.

One dramatic change took place during this pivotal time in the Foster household. With Catherine taking on the burden of babysitting and managing the home front, sandwiched around the significant addition of two more arrivals in the family, Luke's mother started working outside the home for the first time. Luke and Allen were also discovering a wide range of opportunities for making money. The two older boys and their mother working took a little of the pressure off the always challenging financial picture. However, with the endless demands of the growing and dynamic family, it would always be a struggle to pay the bills.

Their parents always made having fun a priority, particularly after their father's childhood experience with his unreasonable and hard-driving father. Luke loved working and the concept of bringing in money knowing very well he'd always have his share of fun along the way. There was a great balance between work and play, and life was more than fair as far as Luke and Allen were concerned.

The apple orchard and massive green pasture offered endless hours of fun and games. Baseball was huge. Organized games usually got started around ten o'clock every morning, and guys from all over town would come and go throughout the day. The perpetual game would continue until it was either too dark to see the ball or the pesky mosquitoes chased everyone home. Luke could hit the ball a mile and was always one of the first guys picked when they chose up sides. His natural baseball ability served him well in providing the much-needed boost to his self-esteem.

Then there was one disturbing piece of news. Eclipse's family bought a house in Jefferson and moved out of the farmhouse they'd been renting for many years. This meant the kids in town had the great misfortune of dealing with the bully around the clock and on weekends instead of just during the regular school hours throughout the weekdays.

With his move to town, it was inevitable Eclipse would show up for the coveted baseball games. Having no real choice, Luke and his buddies were forced to eventually pick him when they were choosing up sides. As expected, on defense he would deliberately throw the ball across busy Highway 109 that ran along the north side of the pasture. After batting, he'd throw the bat as far as he could into the tall weeds. Eclipse succeeded in ruining the game.

Sick of his behavior, refusing to give up the cherished ball games, and well aware of the fact they were risking their health, Eclipse was no longer picked to play. Rebelling in his classic style, he would go after one or two randomly chosen victims and ruthlessly throw them to the ground. After swearing and threatening to kick everyone's ass, Eclipse would eventually get on his bike and peddle his way home. It's just the way it was.

Their apple orchard became famous for the declaration of the many great green apple wars. They'd choose up sides, and the battle was on. There were no rules, they'd just open fire, pummeling the enemy from every direction. There were frequent painful direct hits below the belt that may have left them walking a little funny for a day or two, but that was okay.

Along with the wars, they'd load up with a bucket of those same hard green apples and hide in the tall grass along Highway 109. When a car came by, they'd open fire. There were many direct loud hits on the side of an innocent passing vehicle. Every hit was followed with the automatic laughter and mild celebration. The unsuspecting drivers were confused about what happened and usually just shook their head and proceeded down the road. Sometimes their reaction included a verbal outburst that sounded something like, "You little fucking assholes!"

Skunk, Skeeter, and Luke clearly understood the concept of what an asshole was, but the "fucking" part was a new one on them, even for Big Jake. They assumed it was something not very nice but would have to make a point of asking Skunk's older brother Stub about it at their next meeting in the woods. If one of the angry drivers was mad enough and decided to turn around and come back, they responded the way every logical and responsible kid would, they ran like hell and hid in the much-appreciated big red barn.

Luke must have climbed every tree in that orchard a hundred times. There was one lone giant oak tree standing conspicuously in the middle of the much shorter apple trees. Luke found a special spot at the top of the tall oak tree where the branches formed an almost perfect natural seat where he could sit comfortably. This became Luke's private safe haven for those times when he wanted to escape his oftentimes troubled world allowing him to think and sort things out. He loved swaying back and forth in the seemingly ever-present fresh breeze while enjoying the impressive panoramic view including the northern border of the evergreen tree-lined community. If Luke was reported missing in action, everyone soon learned where they could find him, in his personal hideaway on top of that special oak tree.

The Foster Sports Complex offered wide ranging activities, but the always-violent tackle football games were Luke's favorite. He loved hitting home runs, but he got his greatest satisfaction viciously tackling guys—the bigger the better. A badge of honor, he usually had a bloody nose by the end of the football games. Luke proved he was tougher than nails and, perhaps motivated by the wheelchair experience, was anxious to prove it to the other players.

One typically hot and humid July day, Luke and Skeeter made what turned out to be a rewarding discovery. They were more than familiar with the cement Beaver Creek bridge within walking distance west of town down Highway 109 but they had never paid any attention to the impressive stream running lazily about twelve feet below. They learned that except for the short period following the annual spring floods, Beaver Creek was a gentle, crystal-clear slow-moving stream that emptied into the mighty Troy River about a half mile south of the bridge.

Sweating profusely from the just-completed three-hour baseball game, with the convenient seclusion created by the bridge and the wall of tall weeds bordering the shorelines of the creek, wasting no time, Luke and Skeeter stripped down bare-ass naked and plunged into the irresistible refreshing cold water. After frolicking for about an hour, enjoying their newfound pleasure, they headed home and couldn't wait to share their wonderful discovery with the rest of the ball players. The next day the whole gang headed out to the impressive creek, and predictably, it became a valued ritual that followed virtually every sweaty baseball game the rest of that summer and for the many years to follow.

It may not have been fully appreciated by the guys with fancy bathtubs at home, but now, having a viable alternative to the dreaded Saturday night bath line in front of the big gray metal tub, as soon as the spring flood settled down and the water temperature was bearable, Luke and Allen grabbed a bar of soap and headed down to Beaver Creek several times a week throughout the hot summer months. Throughout the next four years, until the special day they moved into the house with a tub and running water on the east side of town, Luke and Allen thoroughly enjoyed the regular dips in the nearby creek following every ball game or lawn-mowing job.

The Foster brothers were the only kids in town to offer rides on the big horse Champion, all-day baseball games, apple wars, the bloody tackle battles, and now swimming, fishing, and bonfires under the Beaver Creek Bridge. These cost-free activities served as great equalizers for the glaring economic shortcomings that were still prevalent in their lives. However, Luke's frame of mind and general outlook continued to run hot and cold. Hitting home runs and dominating the tackle football games always gave him a shot in the arm throughout the daytime hours. But he still dreaded bedtime every night when he struggled with the same two demons, his sister slipping from his hands and going overboard and the image of his dad hitting his mother, knowing the same inevitable nightmares were soon to follow.

Chapter Twenty-One

Luke preferred walking to school even if it meant dealing with Walter's pesky hound, Rusty. He hated to have the other kids see him getting out of their old, ugly, rusted-out '38 Chevrolet with the front fenders crudely cut off. On those rare occasions when he got dropped off, he would duck down, stay well hidden in the back seat, and as soon as they arrived, he'd quickly jump out of the car and run as fast as he could into the school.

Much like their Grandma Wentworth, the Foster kids were blessed with exceptional academic abilities. Luke and Big Jake took turns winning the spelling bees. Luke won all the arithmetic speed contests held on the blackboard in front of the classroom. The decisive victories made the walk back to his desk dressed in the feed sack shirt, the familiar holes in the knees of his pants and in the soles of his beaten-up shoes a little easier to deal with. Catherine and Allen were good students as well, and Luke still marveled how they never let anything bother them.

Eclipse's behavior in school and around town grew more egregious every year. A ruthless character like Ferguson should never be allowed to have a gun, but the fact was, he owned a new Red Ryder BB gun as well as a Remington 410 shotgun. When he was in sixth grade, with legitimate intentions of hunting rabbits in the groves of trees surrounding the privately owned farm buildings, one of his favorite tricks was resorting to shooting cats instead. Engaging his abundance of charm, he'd start the ugly process by saying, "Here, kitty, kitty, here kitty, kitty," and when the cat slowly and curiously walked toward him, he would carefully aim his shotgun, pull the trigger, and blast the innocent cat to pieces. As the fur was flying in all directions, he would burst out with his mysterious and evil laughter. Then the chickens. It was well documented that on more than one occasion, he doused a chicken with gasoline, lit it on fire, and with the chicken screeching and running frantically, it would suddenly fall over dead. This accomplishment was followed with more eerie, bone-chilling laughter. He would capture pigeons in the hay lofts of the farmer's barns, take them outside, either tie a firecracker to one of its legs, or shove it up their butt, light it with a match, and let it fly away. The length of the fuse would determine how soon the pigeon exploded in mid-air! Again, as the feathers flew, he thought it was hilarious. No animal was safe in his presence—or human being for that matter.

Like everyone, Catherine had always been upset about Eclipse's constant bullying, but her greatest anger was over the way he picked on Luke when he returned from the hospital and was stuck in the wheelchair. And when she heard about his cruel behavior toward animals, she was furious! Although she understood she was probably limited in what she could do about it, she made a personal pledge to do everything in her power to stop this monster's evil behavior.

Only an eighth grader, after reporting her concern to some of her teachers as well as the principal on a number of occasions, who told her they couldn't do anything about it until they caught him in the act, she bravely confronted Eclipse and threatened him right to his face, "You better stop killing animals, or trust me, you're going to be sorry!"

Not slightly concerned, he just laughed and told her, "Shut your big mouth. You don't know what the hell you're talking about! What do you think you're going to do about it anyway?"

Refusing to back down, not slightly intimidated, Catherine screamed back at him, "You wait and see, you big bully, I'm not going to stop until you're held responsible for all the mean stuff you do!"

Brushing her off, Eclipse just laughed again, and as he strutted away, he said, "If you're smart, you'll back off and keep your big nose out of it. You're just a little bitch anyway!"

Catherine was livid and more determined than ever to get him arrested or whatever it was going to take. She said to herself in total frustration, “There has to be someone in this town willing to do something about this monster’s outrageous behavior!”

There had always been a mysterious curiosity about the Ferguson household. Eclipse’s dad, a 6’6” 300-pound giant of a man, and his younger brother, who was just as big, owned their own small construction company. They were extremely private people and kept a strange low profile. His mother was a meek and reclusive lady who was never seen in public. Putting in long hours, his dad worked hard, minded his own business, and other than his weekly Saturday night trips to Schuster’s Grocery and the Corner Liquor Store, was rarely seen around town.

Chapter Twenty-Two

When Luke was in sixth grade, his mother delivered baby sister Connie, and the following year, a boy they named Leonard. That would now make it eight siblings with the oldest being fourteen-year-old Catherine. Adding Skeeter, who was a valued and appreciated fixture in the family by now, the bigger house by Highway 109 would soon become seriously overcrowded and even with their dad's hard work and improved wages as a skilled plumber, it was a growing challenge to pay the bills and put food on the table.

Catherine would be entering high school that fall, and with confidence and maturity far beyond her years, she virtually took over the household throughout the summer months so their mother, for the first time, could get the much-needed job outside of the home.

Elizabeth's first paying job was serving as the local telephone operator, which proved to be the perfect complement for her second job, selling magazines door to door. Highly motivated and with her warm and infectious personality, Elizabeth proved to be a booming success in the magazine business. While not eliminating the financial challenges, her efforts were richly rewarded and improved their ability to balance the budget.

Catherine was not the shrinking violet her image may have suggested. Her friends at school had the impression she was this sweet, angelic, pretty little girl, when in reality, she was a 100-pound spitfire who ruled with an iron fist. With her fully designated authority in managing the home front, their parents didn't have to worry for one minute when they were both at work. Allen and Luke didn't always appreciate her unshakable stern approach, but it proved to be a highly effective discipline game plan over the years.

After completing their assigned chores around the house, Luke and Allen willingly found an endless variety of jobs around town. Except for sweeping the warehouse floor in the feed mill years ago, their first cash-paying job was mowing their great Aunt Naomi's lawn. Using a push mower and working up a sweat, Naomi gave them each fifty cents and a glass of lemonade followed by a much-deserved dip in Beaver Creek. But the bad news was, Eclipse's new house was only two blocks from Aunt Naomi's house, and they lived with the constant fear that the big jerk would come waltzing by before they got the lawn mowed.

There was a serious confrontation with Eclipse a week earlier that lead to an unfortunate incident on Naomi's front lawn. The usual gang—Skunk, Skeeter, Big Jake, Allen, Luke and a couple of other guys—were hanging out in the popular Jefferson town park. Their innocent fun and games were once again rudely interrupted when Eclipse came riding along on his bike proudly displaying his new Red Ryder BB gun. After the expected verbal exchange, they casually stood by and observed as Eclipse proceeded to start shooting his shiny new gun at any bird or squirrel that had the great misfortune of being in the park at that particular time.

Not having much luck with his gun, suddenly and out of nowhere, Eclipse announced, "You know what, I think I'm going to shoot one of you dick heads!"

Allen, who was the same age but of course much smaller, always the more confident and bolder one of the gang, said, "Yeah, sure you will. Go ahead, why don't you try shooting me?"

Completely caught off guard with the surprisingly brave challenge, without hesitating, Eclipse calmly asked, "Where exactly would you like me to shoot your stupid ass?"

With the other guys standing there dumbfounded, usually quite intelligent and always confident, Allen pulled up his pant leg and said, "Go ahead, shoot my leg, I dare you!"

Holding his new Red Ryder about five inches from Allen's leg, without hesitation, Eclipse pulled the trigger. Stunned, Allen let out an excruciating scream that had to be heard all over town. Allen was jumping around holding his leg and unleashed a previously unheard of streak of cuss words, "Shit, goddamn, you go to hell, bastard!"

As painful as they knew it must have been, they couldn't help it—the rest of the guys erupted in convulsive, bend-over-at-the-waist laughter. They felt bad about laughing, but it was absolutely hilarious. When everyone finally regained their composure, as much as they dared, owing it to Allen after their unsympathetic reaction, they cautiously condemned Eclipse for the mean stunt.

Expressing their disgust toward him didn't bother Eclipse in the slightest. The last thing he said before he got on his bike and proudly rode away was, "If any one of you little assholes tell anybody about this, you will pay for it! You got that?"

Having little choice, they all nervously agreed, "Yeah, sure, you bet, we got it."

On bath night the following Saturday, their mother couldn't help but notice the big ugly red welt on Allen's leg. The BB was buried in his leg and had become badly infected. She insisted Allen tell her what happened. After a serious attempt to cover up the truth, Allen had to come clean. His mother was furious when she heard the frightening story, and after Allen and Luke's lengthy pleading with her not to do it, while clearly understanding how it might put them in harm's way, she said, "I've got no choice, boys, I'm going to talk to Eclipse's parents. This nasty business has got to stop—that's all there is to it!"

It was about a week later on Aunt Naomi's lawn. Well aware of the fact their mother made the phone call and knowing it was now only a matter of time, their worst fears became a reality. Taking turns with each pass, Luke and Allen were mowing the front yard between the sidewalk and the curb along the street. Eclipse came slowly pedaling down the sidewalk. He calmly got off his bike, flopped it on the ground, and started the inevitable proceedings.

He aggressively started out, "I told you assholes not to tell anybody about what happened in the park last week, and I just got my ass chewed out by my mother. She said your mother called complaining about shooting you in the leg. Now I promised if you told anyone you were going to pay for it, didn't I?"

With no good answers, they both stood there trying desperately not to shit their pants. There was no denying the fact they had indeed shared the story with their mother and they would now simply have to face the consequences.

He started the formalities by systematically tipping the lawnmower over. Clearly having their attention, with no serious harm done, okay, they could live with that. Not even slightly concerned with the fact there were two of them, Eclipse very methodically chose to put Luke in a headlock and violently crushed him to the ground. With his brotherly instincts kicking in, Allen immediately jumped on the giant's back, but the harsh reality was, as gallant and brave as it was, his effort did very little to alter the direction things were heading. With Luke down on the ground and virtually helpless, Eclipse flicked Allen off his back, and he landed directly on top of his fallen brother. With both of them indignantly sprawled out on the ground, he ordered, "If you know what's good for you, you'll stay right where you are!"

With their distinct individual makeup, there was a stark contrast between what Allen initially thought would be the proper response at this critical moment and what Luke's first thoughts were on the subject. Luke's first consideration was, *I could probably attempt one of my vicious tackles, but then what?* He next thought was, *I'm only eleven years old and I have my whole life ahead of me. This crazy idiot kills animals without so much as batting an eye.* Allen's leg was still hurting from the recent shooting incident. He was still humiliated about the whole ordeal, and he wasn't about to just lie there and not get up and fight this big jerk. Not surprising, Allen's inclination was to go down swinging!

Not really having time for a reasonable debate on the subject and what was very likely a good thing, Luke's position won out. Both of them may have been very proud and with an abundance of pride, but they were also pretty bright boys. And there were the obvious practical factors. This guy was a mean giant. And furthermore, the good news was, at the present moment, they weren't in serious physical pain. Fighting back would dramatically improve their chance of serious injury. Common sense and logic won out, and as difficult as it was, they swallowed their pride and cut their losses by reluctantly remaining on the ground.

With his mission accomplished and proud once again of a job well done, Eclipse calmly got back on his bike, started to joyfully whistle, and triumphantly pedaled down the sidewalk.

Luke and Allen had taken their medicine, sheepishly got back up, turned the lawnmower back upright, and finished mowing the lawn. It was another hard earned fifty cents, a glass of Naomi's lemonade, and a badly needed dip in Beaver Creek.

The following summer, they added Grandpa Wentworth's lawn, which was an all-day job that paid an amazing $3 per mowing. Grandpa's place, out by the Troy River, was a healthy distance from Eclipse's house and where they could work safely and peacefully.

In less than two years, Luke and Allen grew their lawn mowing business to fifteen lawns, all with a push mower, resulting in a steady revenue stream often totally $25 a week. This was big money and would allow them to help out with paying the bills at home, which they were more than happy to do!

Chapter Twenty-Three

Not satisfied with the income generated from their lawnmowing business, which of course was only productive during the summer months, Luke and Allen seized the opportunity and soon became the most prosperous paper boys in town. Their first paper route was delivering the Des Moines Register every morning. They had 50 weekday and 120 Sunday morning customers.

The important collection days were Friday night and Saturday morning. After they paid the weekly bill from the company, they split the normal $10 profit. That kind of money made getting out of bed early every morning well worth it.

They inadvertently overlooked the fact the Des Moines Register Company was deliberately padding the bill an additional $2.50 every week designed as a built-in savings plan. It was a proud day when they saved enough and willingly contributed it all toward buying a new car for the family. The boys were happy to donate their hard-earned money if it meant getting rid of that ugly old Chevrolet. The much newer '48 Ford was a beauty, and it gave Luke a huge boost, particularly on the days he was dropped off in front of school.

The paper route business was so lucrative Luke picked up another job delivering the Boulder Globe Gazette after school every night. The Gazette had no Sunday paper, so it was just a six-day obligation for his forty valued customers.

Delivering papers proved exceptionally profitable, but there was a disturbing paper route–related incident that took place that fall. Robbie Duncan, whose dad happened to be the superintendent of schools, had the best outdoor basketball setup in town. Robbie had a backboard, hoop, and impressive black top surface. The paper boys would meet over there for games after school almost every night but the biggest games were held on Saturday mornings after they had diligently completed their collections for the week!

There were usually about eight bikes with paper bags and money bags draped on the handlebars lying around on the ground next to Robbie's elaborate basketball court. Luke had recently purchased his very first bike from an older kid named Sonny Schwab for the modest sum of $4. After the hundreds of trips around town delivering papers on foot, he was more than familiar with every pothole, broken chunk of sidewalk, tree root, and all the worn paths in the well-used grassy shortcuts. The landmarks never changed, but what did change was the newfound freedom and independence he enjoyed when he could finally fly around town on a bike like the other guys had been doing for so many years.

The new bike was a big deal on many levels! One major reward: the bike would permit him to lift his legs up from the pedals and he could now fly right past Rusty. His days of dealing with neighbor Walter's ornery dog were officially over. But as luck would have it, the exact same week he bought the bike, Rusty had been run over while chasing a car on the busy nearby Highway 109. Rusty was killed instantly.

A new bike and his longtime nemesis Rusty now totally out of the picture. It was against his basic nature to think this way, but he couldn't deny it, after all those torturous years dealing with that miserable dog, Luke quietly thought it was one of the best weeks since they moved to town!

There was a short break in the basketball game, and Robbie went in the house to take a leak or something. On his way by the bikes, with the game resuming play and no one paying any attention to him, Robbie stuck a randomly selected paper boy's money bag in Luke's paper bag. A few minutes later, he returned and innocently joined back in the big game.

When the game ended and as they were leaving, Big Jake noticed his money bag was missing. Luke was shocked when he discovered Big Jake's money bag in his paper bag. Rattled and confused, he immediately gave it to his friend, insisting he didn't know how it got there. There was no reasonable explanation, and Luke knew his good buddy had to be curious about this strange turn of events. It was getting late, and everyone jumped on their bike and headed for home. Robbie witnessed the whole thing, and fully aware of how upset Luke was, didn't volunteer a word to clear it up.

After tormenting and tossing and turning more than usual at bedtime that night, Luke finally figured out what happened. He remembered that Robbie had gone in the house for a few minutes that morning and concluded that's when he "planted" Big Jake's money bag in his paper bag. Luke was so upset he boldly confronted the much bigger jerk that following Monday morning at school. After a heated exchange and seeing how angry Luke was, Robbie reluctantly came clean.

Offering no apology and taking a stubborn position, Robbie's feeble response was, "I didn't even know whose paper bag I was putting the stupid money bag in. It was nothing personal, so just forget about it." Clearly embarrassed about his selfish stunt, he went on, "If you bring it up to Big Jake, I'm just going to deny it anyway. So if you're smart, you'll just drop it!"

The disturbing incident required a trip to his favorite thinking spot, the private sanctuary on top of the tall oak tree out in the apple orchard. After spending a little time enjoying the always comforting scenic view and in deep thought, he was struggling with exactly how to handle it. The stupid thing was still bugging him, so he decided to make a quick visit to the bait shop, hoping he'd find Nute and Mr. Slim playing cribbage. After explaining the whole story to his wise old buddies, Mr. Slim offered, "Luke, at some point in every Iowa boy's life, you have to learn about the nasty aroma created when you foolishly stir up what is a harmless 'cow pie.' Big Jake is a trusting and loyal friend of yours and I'm sure has already forgotten about the whole thing by now. You should do the same and simply move on!" It wasn't easy, but Luke decided to accept his trusted friend's advice.

Mr. Slim was right. The subject never came up, but that didn't mean it simply went away. It was the kind of incident that Luke's mind would cling to. Unfortunately, the experience would prove to be another setback for Luke's fragile makeup. It seemed just when he was gaining confidence and building up strength in dealing with setbacks, there would be something stupid like this that sabotaged any significant progress.

Chapter Twenty-Four

Knowing Catherine, Allen, and Luke were all more than willing to pitch in and work hard, their parents made sure things balanced by arranging so they could participate in the many organized activities offered in school and in the community. Along with the little league sports, they were involved with things like swimming lessons, choir, band, Boy Scouts, and Girl Scouts. The fact that their dad had never been permitted to participate in school activities, that was simply not the way it was going to be for the kids.

The thing Luke loved about Cub Scouts and Boy Scouts was that when he saved up enough money to buy a uniform, it was the one rare time he could be dressed exactly like everyone else. He knew it shouldn't be that way, but this was important to Luke.

A major highlight for Luke was getting decked out in that striking scout uniform and marching in the Memorial Day parade every spring. The proud scouts marched down Main Street positioned behind the local war veterans. He could hear his Uncle Stan shouting out the commands to his fellow veterans as they were performing impressive drill routines along the parade route.

Positioned in front of the war veterans were the many parade horses, which included Ed Miller's familiar high-stepping palomino, Champion. Some scout would invariably step in some fresh horse turds, making all his fellow scouts burst out laughing and throwing them out of step. Knowing how much Catherine loved his horse, one year, Ed asked her if she would like to ride the handsome animal in the parade. Proudly dressed in the new hat and cowgirl outfit she had bought after weeks of savings from her babysitting money, she was never more excited in her life.

The final destination was the local cemetery, where each scout respectfully placed a bouquet of lilacs beside the headstone of one fallen war veteran's grave. Uncle Stan continued his leading role during the graveside ceremonies as he shouted out the sharp commands to the six rifle honor guards. The dramatic blasts echoing from the simultaneous firing of the powerful guns created a jolting effect, made even more chilling with the timely coordination of taps blaring from a trumpet in the distant background. It was a stirring experience for all the scouts but even more so for Allen, whose great passion for an Air Force military career skyrocketed after the riveting ceremonies every Memorial Day.

The Boy Scout leaders sponsored a three-day-and-two-night camping trip on the shores of the Troy River every summer. Pitching and sleeping in tents, cooking on the open fire, and building roaring bonfires at night, it just couldn't get much better than that. It was Luke's first experience with singing around an open bonfire, and as the years went by, it would become one of his very favorite things to do.

Hard to believe, but the infamous jerk Eclipse actually made a significant contribution during the popular camping trip that summer. No, he didn't save a drowning scout from the nearby raging Troy River—what he did was much bigger than that.

Eclipse a Boy Scout, could this really be happening? The fact was, as they had attempted with his brother Frank over the years, desperate efforts were made to change the younger, by-now-renowned bully. A number of concerned adult community leaders were searching for ways of trying to influence and hopefully alter his outrageous behavior. The most unlikely development, Eclipse actually became a member of the honorable and respected Boy Scout Troop 52.

Sitting around the bonfire the first night, the scouts were laughing and taking turns exchanging silly juvenile stories. Demonstrating unusual restraint, Eclipse was sitting quietly listening to the other guys and their (what he considered) childish and stupid tales. Suddenly and out of nowhere, in the typical manner he always addressed his peers, he proceeded to introduce the shocking question, "Do you dip shits know your pecker has another benefit to offer besides pissing?" Having everyone's attention, he went on to explain, "There's a technique. When you manipulate your pecker just right, you'll get amazing results." As only Eclipse could describe, he promised, "Stick with it long enough and it will eventually feel like your pecker is exploding!"

The other scouts burst out laughing, but there was no doubt Eclipse had their full attention, and they were more than a little curious about this crazy idea. Anxious to share his expertise, after a brief and crude demonstration, Eclipse went on, "I recommend all you stupid idiots give it a serious try when you crawl in your tents and slip into your sleeping bags tonight!"

Hastily deciding to not throw more wood on the dying fire, motivated with a newly provoked objective, the curious and eager scouts returned to their assigned tents.

During the next hour, there were an assortment of distinctive vocal expressions coming from a number of tents that validated Eclipse indeed knew what he was talking about. Luke, Skunk, and even Skeeter were impressed and had to admit the results really were quite amazing. Thanks to Eclipse, it turned out to be an exciting night—perhaps life-changing—in the young lives of a vast majority of the members of Boy Scout Pack 52.

At that bold and carefree age, no one was self-conscious about the incredible new discovery. Like Eclipse correctly labeled it, the amazing "pecker explosion" was the dominating subject and provided much lively discussion throughout the next day. All the lifetime skills the scout leaders had so carefully scheduled and were diligently attempting to teach that day, things like starting a fire by rubbing sticks together, recognizing poison ivy, or identifying what wild plants may or may not be edible, had very little impact on the preoccupied scouts. Nothing could compete or compare with the new and exciting potential lifetime skill introduced around the bonfire the night before.

That night, it was more of the same. Deliberately cutting the always favorite bonfire experience short, many scouts retreated to their tents conspicuously early that night. It soon became obvious by the frequent uninhibited loud declarations that there was once again undisputed widespread success throughout the campsite!

It was inevitable—introduction to the "pecker explosion" triggered some intense conversations amongst Luke, Skunk, and Skeeter. Big Jake happened to miss out on the overnight campout the previous week end, and considering the fact he was clearly the smartest one of the gang, they wondered if he was familiar with the novel idea. The next day they cornered him, and Skeeter asked him, "Hey, Big Jake, have you heard about the amazing technique Eclipse told us about that makes your pecker almost explode?"

Big Jake couldn't help but laugh. As the only modest member of the gang and not wanting to pretend to know more on the subject than he did, he made a quick suggestion: "Yes, I think I know what you're talking about, but I have to confess, I honestly don't know enough about it to explain it very well. You guys should ask Skunk's older brother Stub about it sometime. You have to promise to bring me up-to-date when you learn more on the subject, okay?"

They could tell Big Jake didn't feel comfortable talking about it and agreed talking to Stub was a good idea. With that in mind, they headed out to Skunk's farm hoping Skunk was home.

Standard procedure when they visited the farm, they went in the house so Luke could run into Ellie. When they entered the kitchen, they noticed she was busy helping her mother with baking cookies. The first thing she said was, "Boy, Luke, I think you're an inch taller every time I see you. Skunk and Skeeter, you better get going if you're going to keep up with this big guy." *Good grief, what did she call me? Are you kidding me? "Big guy"?* She may have been three years older, but he was already taller than she was. He knew they'd make a perfect couple someday!

It wasn't long before Stub came in from doing his chores. Wasting no time, Skeeter asked him if he would join them out by the fire pit in the woods. Always willing to join his younger brother Skunk and his two best buddies, they headed out to the woods and proceeded to build the required roaring bonfire.

Luke, Skunk, and Skeeter really didn't know where to start; they had a million questions. Luke got it started. After first seeing the term painted on the front door of the school and hearing it on more than one occasion when the drivers got mad at them for hitting their cars with green apples, he came right out with it and boldly asked, "Stub, what the heck does *fucking* mean anyway?"

Stub couldn't help it; he burst out laughing. Then quickly recognizing how serious his younger buddies were, trying to put it in the simplest terms possible, he decided to give it a shot. "*Fucking* is just a slang term for sexual intercourse. It's not a very nice word, and you really shouldn't even say it, especially in front of girls!" Stub knew he was getting in way over his head, but he attempted to explain how sexual intercourse related to the human reproduction process.

He did his best tying sexual intercourse, the pecker explosion, and human reproduction together. But Stub could tell by the look on their faces, *Boy, this is getting crazier by the minute.* Deliberately gearing things down a little bit, Stub suggested, "When you guys get in biology class in a couple years, trust me, it'll all make more sense. I'll still do my best to answer some of your questions, but it's pretty complicated, and I really don't want to confuse you."

Accepting Stub's cautious position but wanting to keep the conversation going, Skeeter chipped in, "Okay, this whole sexual intercourse thing is pretty confusing, but let's get one thing cleared up. We all know girls don't have peckers, right? So obviously that means they'll never experience the amazing pecker explosion. I'm sure glad I'm a boy, I'll tell you that right now!"

They all laughed and totally agreed with that concept! Luke knew Skeeter was familiar with some of this stuff from watching all those movies at his dad's theater, and Skunk didn't talk about it much, but he had put some of it together living on the farm and observing the animals. Catherine and Glenda's naked presence on Saturday bath night educated Luke about the fact girls didn't have peckers, but he had to admit that's about all he knew for sure.

After bouncing a few theories around for a while, Luke felt a little better when he realized his best buddies had a lot of questions on the complicated subject too. They agreed to share what they learned with Big Jake and figured amongst them, they'd get this thing figured out someday.

When Luke got home later that day, proud of his new limited wisdom, he couldn't wait to ask his always wiser big brother, "Hey, Allen, do you know what *fucking* means?"

Completely caught off guard by what he considered to be a totally stupid question, Allen said something indignant like, "Of course I do, you dumb ass!"

In typical brotherly fashion, Luke fired back, "You're the dumb ass. I bet you don't really know!"

As always, following this kind of contentious interaction, the proud brothers wound up wrestling their way to the ground, and they'd go at it for a few minutes. These regular confrontations were never too serious and evenly matched, the outcome usually resulted in a healthy welt or two on both of their faces. When their dad caught them fighting like this, he made them put on the boxing gloves Santa had cleverly brought them the previous Christmas. After many bloody battles, the once cherished boxing gloves soon became the most dreaded gifts of all time. The obvious solution was for them to stop fighting, but that wasn't about to happen.

Stub warned him about using these words in front of girls, but he was looking forward to his next conversation with Grandma Wentworth; she wasn't really a girl. She always told him the pigs were just being friendly when he asked her what the heck was going on when he saw them climbing on each other's back. He couldn't wait to share his rather amazing newfound knowledge and tell her what the pigs were actually doing was having sexual intercourse, or perhaps even more boldly, that they were fucking. Either way, he knew she'd be impressed!

Chapter Twenty-Five

The following school year brought some challenging new dynamics into Luke's life. All the Foster kids were eligible to start working in the school cafeteria the day they enrolled in seventh grade. It was Catherine's third year and Allen's second, and now Luke would be joining them with his first lunchroom assignment. They were generously rewarded for their efforts when, after all the other students were served, the three of them would sit down together and eat for free. The school administration was well aware of the family's strained financial circumstances, and the Fosters were the only family in town discreetly offered this special deal. Perhaps a little self-conscious in the beginning, the truth was, the three Foster kids appreciated what they agreed was a wonderful opportunity. The work part of it didn't bother them in the least.

Luke's specific job description was to make sure the other kids scraped their plates and stacked them neatly. If they failed to do so, he was expected to get on them about it. Fortunately, most of the kids were really great and cooperated, but some of the high school guys would just laugh and tell him, "Scrape the stupid plates off yourself, idiot." The real mean ones—and fortunately there were only a few of them—would laugh and suggest, "Why don't you just help yourself to my leftovers? You don't pay for your stupid lunch anyway!"

Comments like that were hurtful, but the pain didn't last long when Luke was soon sitting down and filling his belly with the endless supply of the delicious hot food. On the average day, Luke probably ate more than the entire third-grade class!

The toughest part about working in the cafeteria was knowing all the other kids were out on the playground playing softball during the time remaining in the noon hour. Once in a while, Luke would get out there in time for one at bat before the bell rang. One day, he crushed one and it shattered a big window in the biology lab located just beyond left field. He was the first seventh grader to accomplish such a feat, and although he didn't like the fact, he was probably going to have to pay for the broken window. The truth was, it made him feel a lot better for the next few days.

Luke's special friendship with Skeeter had many benefits, and it led directly to another unique job offer that winter. No longer having to sneak them in the side door, everyone in the Foster family had unlimited free admission to all the movies featured at the Roxie Theater. As Skeeter got older and his dad was training him to do things like running the movie projector, selling tickets, or working behind the snack counter, he hired Luke to sweep out the theater every morning. Skeeter's dad paid Luke $1 a day for the tedious job of sweeping between the rows of all the seats, but more rewarding than that, it was a rare day that he didn't find at least a few coins on the floor, and he looked forward to finding the occasional partially filled box of Milk Duds. Although he had to get up a half hour earlier to squeeze the sweeping job in before his morning paper route, for that kind of money, Luke happily accepted the job offer.

Luke eagerly took advantage of every moneymaking opportunity, but his favorite job was helping his old friend Nute "seine" minnows throughout the summer months. A two-man job, Luke recruited his brother Allen. Nute and the boys would go down to the familiar Beaver Creek Bridge, and with Nute leading the way to his reliable hot spots, he taught them the "art" of seining minnows. After netting at least a week's supply of minnows, they'd go back to the bait shop; Nute would hand each of them a crisp dollar bill; and they'd sit around, drink lemonade, and eat glazed donuts. Like Mr. Slim, Nute never ran out of interesting wild stories.

Along with the other job opportunities throughout their seventh- and eighth-grade school years, most of their lawnmowing customers hired them to shovel their sidewalks throughout the winter months. They may have worked hard, but that was okay—they had plenty of time to play ball and have fun.

Following eighth-grade graduation, neighbor Walter Olson offered Luke a full-time summer job, and he would now be getting paid by the hour for the first time. Enjoying a dramatic growth spurt during the past two years, Luke was a little over 6 feet tall, and as a result of his many challenging work experiences, his physical maturity had improved dramatically.

With his increased strength, after a few weeks of the tedious job of pulling weeds in the giant vegetable fields, Walter found a variety of more challenging tasks around the farm. He had two big chicken coops, and shoveling manure became one of Luke's new assignments. Impressed with his willingness to tackle any job thrown at him, Luke was promoted to junior foreman and became Walter's right-hand man, now overseeing several other kids his age who were stuck hoeing weeds in the cabbage fields. The new job title made Luke feel good, but more important than that, his pay was increased from fifty to the hard-to-believe rate of seventy-five cents an hour.

Always excused for late-afternoon baseball games, Luke still managed to put in between forty to forty-five hours a week and was taking home over $30 a week. His parents were proud of his impressive work habits.

One Saturday night, as he was handing Luke his weekly check, Walter told him there was something he wanted to talk to him about. He knew later that night, Luke and Allen would be making their regular trip to his water pump to fill the big gray tub for the family Saturday night bath ritual. Walter had privately witnessed many of their wrestling matches over the years when they always blamed the other one for splashing the water out of the tub and had to begrudgingly return for a refill.

When the Fosters moved into their current home eight years ago, Walter promised their dad that when his other house became available, they would have first rights to rent it. The same family had lived in the house all these years, and while he thought they would be moving out long before this, his current renters were finally moving out of town. Before Luke could respond, Walter reminded him of the fact the house had indoor plumbing.

Luke could hardly believe what he was hearing. He couldn't wait to get home and tell his parents the wonderful news. Seeing the excitement in Luke's face, Walter told Luke, "Go ahead and mention the idea to your parents, and if they're interested, tell your dad to come over tomorrow morning and we'll talk about it."

It was an unforgettable night in the Foster house! Luke could hardly get it out fast enough. He could tell his mother and father were equally thrilled about the wonderful news. Could it be true? Was Walter Olson actually offering them a house with a toilet, tub, and kitchen sink? Knowing the increased rent could still be a stumbling block, while clearly overwhelmed about the exciting possibility, his parents tried to calm everyone down, not wanting the kids to get their hopes up too high, knowing how disappointed they'd be if, for some reason, it didn't work out. Trying his best to remain calm, Luke's dad promised he would talk to Walter about it the next day.

Early on Sunday morning, Luke's dad eagerly made the journey up to Walter's house. Meanwhile, after a long night of tossing and turning and dreaming about the now very real possibility of having a bathtub and flushing toilet in the near future, everyone but their father got ready for church and Sunday school. After sharing the news with Skunk, Luke and Allen climbed the fence and jumped on Thunder's back, and they trotted their way to the church. Thinking Reverend Thompson's inspirational sermon would never end, noon finally arrived. With the whole family and Skeeter gathered around the always special Sunday dinner table, following grace, with a huge smile on his face and no longer able to contain himself, with all eyes riveted on him, Luke's dad said, "Listen up, everybody, I've got some pretty amazing news."

Bubbling over with excitement, their dad finally made the announcement they had been dreaming of for all those years. "Walter and I've reached a final agreement, and it's now official—we'll be moving into our new home on the first of August, which is exactly six weeks from today."

The news sent the entire family into a jubilant frenzy! It was their happiest day in a long time! Everyone was screaming, and the hugs were so generous, Allen and Luke were jumping up and down and they found themselves actually hugging each other. As soon as they realized what they were impulsively doing, they stopped and simultaneously acted like, *Oops, sorry, let's pretend that didn't happen!*

Another small miracle had taken place during that pivotal meeting between Walter and Luke's dad. Walter offered the house with the indoor plumbing for the same rent the Fosters were paying for their current place. Enjoying prosperity from his many successful business interests, the fact was, Walter was an incredibly generous, caring, and giving person. After getting to know the Foster family on a personal level and many years of observing firsthand how hard they all worked just to make ends meet, he genuinely liked them and decided he was simply going to give them a break. When Luke heard the story about the reduced rent, he felt guilty about celebrating and being so happy when Walter's beloved dog Rusty had been run over by the big truck on Highway 109 the previous summer.

The summer of 1955 would prove to be an amazing time for the whole family but especially for Allen and Luke. First the new house with running water and then an offer to attend their first major league baseball game in Milwaukee that summer. Luke wondered, *Is there any way life could get any better than this?*

When Gary Sanders moved to town a few years earlier, the lives of virtually every young boy in town would be dramatically changed for the better. Coach Sanders not only served as the head coach for all the major high school varsity sports, football, basketball, and baseball, for little or no compensation, he volunteered to run the summer little league baseball programs as well. He had coached Allen and Luke in Pee Wee baseball and was currently coaching them in "Midget" ball. Coach Sanders always had a special place in his heart for the less fortunate and would spend a lifetime championing the underdog!

No one was a greater benefactor than the Foster family. Much like Walter Olson, Coach Sanders liked the boy's attitude and appreciated how hard they worked to improve their lives. After coaching Allen and Luke in little league for several years, and recognizing how much they loved baseball, he was enthused about taking them to their first big league game. Having room for three more kids in his big Chevrolet station wagon, and knowing they were good buddies, loved baseball, and would all get along, Coach Sanders invited Skunk, Skeeter, and Big Jake to join them for the trip. Luke said to himself over and over again, "Boy, the new house and now this. I've got to be the luckiest kid in the world. This has to be the greatest summer of all time!"

They departed from Jefferson at 5:00 a.m. on the Fourth of July. Hardly able to sleep all night, they had sprung out of bed and were now on what would be the trip of a lifetime. Allen and Luke had never been out of the state of Iowa.

First there was the stunning view of the mighty Mississippi River as they departed Prairie Du Chen and crossed over the gigantic bridge connecting Iowa with Wisconsin. A few hours later, their jaws dropped at the sight of the impressive Milwaukee skyline. They had arrived in the big city two hours before game time. They drove past the Brave's impressive stadium on their way to their scheduled visit to the shores of Lake Michigan. With their noses glued to the windows, they thought, *Was that giant place actually a baseball field?* The excitement was building, their hearts were pounding in their chests, and they could hardly wait to get back to the huge stadium!

The stunning view of Lake Michigan was mind boggling. Coach Sanders stood there and proudly observed as the boys had a ball running up and down the beach frolicking and throwing rocks into the giant pounding waves as dozens of seagulls were dipping and diving for the dead fish on the endless shoreline. Beaver Creek and not even the mighty Troy River could compete with this remarkable raging body of water.

With wide eyes and in a state of total wonderment, the five overly excited boys and their beloved Coach entered the voluminous Milwaukee County Stadium. Overwhelmed with the large crowd and surroundings, they climbed their way up to their seats, which were in the first row of the second deck. There Luke sat next to his best buddies, Skunk, Skeeter, Big Jake, and of course big brother Allen, and with his head spinning, he was totally mesmerized by the view of the perfectly manicured baseball field. He tried desperately to calm down, gather himself, and quietly take it all in! *Could all this be happening?*

Coach Sanders bought a program and was busy pointing out some of the famous players as they were running around and warming up before the game. The great Hank Aaron would be playing center fielder for the Braves. Eddie Mathews played third base. Lefty Warren Spahn was the scheduled starting pitcher that day. The New York Giants were the visiting team. The third batter up in the top of the first inning was the one and only Willie Mays. All this was combined with the generous supply of peanuts, hotdogs, and orange crush. Hank Aaron and Willie Mays both hit a homerun that unforgettable steaming-hot July afternoon.

They returned home late that night, and the five boys would never be the same. For the first time in years, Luke was sound asleep in only minutes and slept like a baby throughout the night!

Chapter Twenty-Six

Touring the new house for the first time that hot August day was an unforgettable moment in the lives of the entire Foster family. After delivering papers to the house hundreds of times, Luke knew it was a nice big place, but he had never been invited inside. A full porch wrapped around the front and down one side of the white two-story house. There were four bedrooms, the same number as the old house, but they were much larger, providing the badly needed space for additional beds. Of course, the most appreciated new feature was something they had dreamed about for years, the amazing indoor plumbing.

There was the kitchen sink with the faucet that so magically produced a beautiful stream of cold water by simply turning the handle. The second faucet, with its almost instant hot water, was an unexpected bonus. Then the mad race upstairs and discovering it was now truly a reality—there was the flushing toilet sitting right next to the porcelain bathtub with the four odd-looking short legs. They all took their turn flushing the toilet one time and smiled and marveled at the amazing results.

Beaming with pride, Luke's parents stood back and proudly watched their children revel as the reality of these life-changing developments was starting to sink in. Catherine was entering her junior year in high school, Allen would be a sophomore, Luke a freshman, and they had never experienced the luxuries their friends had been enjoying for all those years. The long wait had been toughest on the three oldest kids, but the five younger siblings were equally excited.

The day after the furniture was delivered, the whole family, along with Skeeter, were sitting around the supper table enjoying their first meal in the new dwelling. Luke's dad had been looking forward to announcing to everyone, "Okay, I want all of you to go sit down in the living room. I've got a little surprise for you." He instructed Allen, Luke, and Skeeter to come outside with him. A few minutes later, they came back carrying a big box. There was no clue on the outside of the box that gave away the contents. They put the box in the middle of the living room, and their dad proudly said, "Go ahead, open it up." Aggressively tearing it open, it was almost more than they could handle. There it was—a spanking brand-new black-and-white television set. All the kids erupted, screaming and jumping up and down in total disbelief.

The front yard was small. There was a gravel driveway running along the west side of the house to a single detached garage. The small garage would prove to be a tight fit for the new family car. The back yard extended a good distance behind the garage to a thick cluster of bushes and a small wooded area. It was a nice enough layout, but they would sorely miss the huge pasture, apple orchard, and the big barn.

There was an unbecoming storage shed tucked in the bushes behind the garage. The badly weathered old shack was barely visible from the house, and Luke's mother thought that was probably a good thing. The previous owners left a hard-on-the-eyes old green, yellow, and orange upholstered couch and a matching overstuffed chair in the building. The furniture sat along the north wall below a long horizontal window that provided the badly needed ventilation during the hot summer months. With all the furniture, there was just enough space to store their lawnmower, lawn chairs, bikes, garden tools, baseball bats, gloves, and balls. Luke's dad put an old radio on a wooden shelf above the stuffed chair, and it became his and the boy's favorite hideaway for listening to the Iowa Hawkeye football games on Saturday afternoons throughout the fall months. Alternating with the fire pit in the woods out on Skunk's farm and Skeeter's apartment above the theater, the remote shed soon became the favorite hangout for Luke and his buddies.

Luke was looking forward to having his friends over to show them all the cool things about the new place. His plan was to invite them to the house after the first football meeting scheduled for the next day. The upper classmen met early Monday morning, earning the privilege of picking out the newest shoulder pads, helmets, and the best-fitting black high-top shoes. At one o'clock that afternoon, Coach Sanders welcomed the fifteen nervous and excited freshmen candidates. Luke had been looking forward to playing football for a long time, and after the coach's inspirational pep talk, he was so pumped up he could hardly wait for the first practice Tuesday morning. One more day and he could put on those impressive shoulder pads.

Nothing really changed. Skunk swung by the new place. Standing on the front porch, Luke jumped on Thunder's back as they trotted their way to the important football meeting. Skunk tied the big old horse to the swing set in the playground area behind the school. Skeeter and Big Jake pedaled their bikes to the meeting.

Skunk and Skeeter, both 5'4" and at most 110 pounds, were clearly the smallest guys at the meeting. That was okay—they'd more than make up for their limited physical stature with their toughness and boundless spirit. Then there was gangly Big Jake, 6'3" and 150 pounds, and Luke, 6'1" and 125 pounds, who would have been just as tall as Big Jake if it wasn't for his bowed legs. They were both built like their last decent meal had been a distant memory.

The meeting lasted about an hour, and Skunk and Luke climbed back on Thunder, and as planned, the other two jumped on their bikes and headed for Luke's new place. Skunk tied the big horse to a tree behind the garage, and Skeeter and Big Jake parked their bikes on the gravel driveway in front of the garage.

The four high school freshmen toured the new house with Luke enthusiastically pointing out the incredible running water features and, of course, the brand-new television set in the living room. With his buddies having enjoyed all these luxuries for many years by now, they acted politely impressed with everything, knowing how much it meant to their proud friend. The tour only took a few minutes before Luke guided them back to the small remote building tucked in the woods behind the garage. It was a typical hot and humid day, so Luke quickly opened the window above the couch for the much-needed fresh air. Huddled together on the ugly couch and the matching chair, the gang settled in for the first intense meeting of the new school year.

Coach Sanders handed out his carefully assembled Panther Football pamphlet to each of the new prospects. Instructed to study the important information before attending practice the next morning, they all brought their newly stapled booklet along with them. The first page included the important training rules: no drinking alcoholic beverages, no smoking cigarettes, and the strict curfew regulations. On the bottom of the last page, in large bold letters, was a reminder that everyone should be sure to bring a jockstrap for the first practice session.

Sitting there deeply engrossed and busy reading through all the critical information, Luke blurted out, "What in the holy hell is a jockstrap?" The other three guys burst out laughing!

Like he was in the habit of doing by now, once again coming to Luke's rescue, Big Jake, with his round wire-rimmed glasses perched on his nose and the by-now-proven intellect of the bunch, knowing Luke was dead serious, took charge. "Settle down, you wise asses. Don't worry about it, Luke, these clowns probably haven't worn a jockstrap in their whole life either. Okay, let's see, how can I put this?" He struggled for the right words but finally came up with "What a jockstrap is, I'd say, is basically an abbreviated special kind of underwear designed to prevent injury to your pecker and your hanging balls."

Everyone laughed again, and Luke, still confused and determined to get a better answer, boldly stuck with it. "I think I understand the whole pecker concern, but do you guys' balls really hang down that far?" They couldn't help it—they burst out laughing again, and having enough by now, Luke barked, "You guys are really a bunch of assholes. You know that, don't you?"

They all finally agreed that how far your balls hung down was really not the key issue. If you had two of them, you had no choice—you'd better just go buy yourself a jockstrap. With that little matter cleared up, the next discussion revolved around the second item on the list: a towel. That of course was self-explanatory; it was needed for the required shower after practice. While never openly talking about it, the truth was, the towel reminder triggered something that Luke had been worrying about for a long time: the dreaded shower room scene! The fact was, at thirteen, he was by far the youngest student in the freshman class. His three buddies were all fourteen, almost a full year older than he was.

Although he was still a little upset about their reaction to what he thought was a legitimate jockstrap question, Luke decided he might as well get it out there. This was as good a time as any to address his real concern, the lack of hair above his pecker. Luke frequently got words mixed up, so his buddies weren't sure if he was just being funny, but either way, he got another big laugh when he assumed, "I suppose all you guys have gone through *publicity* already?"

Even Big Jake was laughing too this time, and he politely pointed out, "I think you probably mean *puberty*, don't you, Luke?"

Luke quickly corrected himself, "Yeah, *puberty*—that's right, *puberty*—that's what I meant to say. Mom introduced the word a while back when she was explaining to us younger kids why Catherine and Allen needed more privacy on bath night the past couple of years because they were going through *puberty*, *publicity*, whatever the heck you call it."

Skeeter, almost having lived with Luke the last few years and more like a brother than a friend, with the nagging subject coming up on more than one occasion during their many private late-night conversations, knew Luke had been worrying about this lack-of-hair issue for a long time.

Skeeter had been the unofficial designated expert in the all-important pecker department since he had bragged years ago how the bold mosquito had used his peter as a landing strip. Proud of his well-established locker room sense of humor, Skeeter had taken full ownership of his famous "peter meter" guidelines. It was far from a perfect science, but with the basic understanding there was approximately a two inch gap between two mosquitoes theoretically standing on your pecker, a guy may be credited with a "two," a "three," and in very rare cases, a "four-skeeter" peter.

Knowing Luke was serious about this whole deal, not laughing any more, Skeeter thoughtfully explained to the gang, "Let me explain something to you guys. Luke's got himself a healthy enough pecker—I'd say very likely a solid three-skeeter job—it's just the lack of hair that has him so worried."

They were still laughing, but having enough fun and deciding it was probably time to show a little support for Luke, always his most caring and sincere friend, Skunk suggested, "Hey, don't worry about it Luke. When you start tackling those smart-ass upper classmen, trust me, hair or no hair, they won't be making fun of you for very long!"

Rallying behind Skunk's generous reminder, keeping things lighthearted, Big Jake offered another idea: "I'm going to make a sign for you tonight, Luke. You can tie it around your waist when you go into the shower room tomorrow: 'Hey, you big assholes, I'm only thirteen, give me a damn break!'" They were all laughing again this time, including Luke.

Proving he was feeling better about everything, making a deliberate effort to convince them he was okay, Luke said, "Good idea, Big Jake, you make the sign, and I promise, I'll wear the damn thing!"

Skunk, knowing deep down Luke was more concerned than he was letting on, like only he could do, making another genuine effort to help his best buddy out, thoughtfully offered, "Luke, we all had to learn the hard way during all those vicious tackle football games in your backyard. When you tackle somebody, it's like getting hit by a damn truck. No question about it, when it comes to tackling, you're the man." Then out of nowhere, he said, "You're the man, Foss Man!"

Foss Man—where did Skunk come up with that? Coach Sanders did have the habit of calling him Foss during baseball season, but the name really never caught on. They all liked the sound of it! They quickly and simultaneously agreed, "Yeah, you're the man, Foss Man. You're the Foss Man."

So that's how it happened. The name would stick from that day forward. Finally, Luke had the cherished nickname Foss Man! He had finally arrived! Everything was going to be all right now—hair or no stupid hair above his pecker!

With that significant development behind them, as always, the subject switched to girls. Skeeter said, "I hear there's a bunch of healthy farm girls transferring in from the country schools this year. It's not likely they can compete with the amazing Becker twins, but our class could sure use an upgrade." Proving his mind was back on track, Luke's immediate response was, "That's good news, Skeeter, but I've got to be honest—all I'm looking forward to is seeing Skunk's sister Ellie on a more regular basis now!" He had no reservations. "I know she's a senior, and I may not have one stupid-ass hair below my neck, but I want you all to know something: Ellie will be mine someday!" They all rolled their eyes and shrugged their shoulders, suggesting, "Yeah right, keep dreaming, Foss Man! I guess there's nothing wrong with dreaming!"

The first meeting in the new shed had proven to be very comforting and meaningful to Luke. His long time nagging concern suddenly wasn't going to be a big deal any more. He was looking forward to practice tomorrow and couldn't wait for the first live tackling drill. *Foss Man, that's right—Foss Man is going to be seriously knocking some guys on their ass!*

Those were the only two things occupying his mind as he struggled with getting to sleep that night: the first live tackling drill and his new nickname. Foss Man—yes, he was now Foss Man. He didn't care what anybody thought; a nickname was a big breakthrough for him. He absolutely loved it. He also realized how lucky he was to have the best friends in the whole world! Thanks to them, everything was going to be okay tomorrow. For the second time that month, he slept peacefully throughout the entire night.

Chapter Twenty-Seven

There were two full weeks of grueling practices before the school year got underway. With the intense humidity and under the stifling hot August sun, the two-hour practice sessions every morning and again in the afternoon about killed most of the exhausted but still enthusiastic prospects. Foss Man absolutely loved football and was disappointed there were no live tackling drills permitted during the first week of practice.

After all those months of fretting about it, as it turned out, the shower room scene was really never a big deal for Foss Man. While that was true, on the first day in the locker room, he did make a few rather startling observations. He couldn't help but notice about a half dozen upperclassmen who could compete with healthy Shetland ponies. What was it with these farm guys and their peckers anyway? Then there was the amazing Herbie Hansen, the muscular freshman farm kid who had transferred in from a neighboring country school. Herbie was an absolute physical specimen and could easily provide serious competition for Skunk's work horse Thunder. He had legs covered with thick black hair and looked like he was a week overdue for a shave. He would soon be recognized as the proud owner of the only certified four-skeeter peter in not just the freshman class but the entire varsity football team. Skunk immediately rewarded him with the much-deserved nickname—at first Herbie the Horse, then simply, just Horse. Except for Horse and a few of the older guys, as it turned out, Foss Man actually stacked up fairly well in qualifying for that all-important jockstrap. All that worrying about "man land" had been a complete waste of time.

Foss Man was the fastest player on the freshmen team, and there were only a few upper classmen on the varsity team faster than he was, but as predicted, it was when the hitting started the second week when he made the greatest impression on everyone. Finally, live tackling! The ball carriers were assigned to one line, and the tacklers were lined up about five yards right across from them. When Coach Sanders blew the whistle, the ball carrier would slowly run straight forward and the other guy was expected to tackle him at full speed. All those vicious games in the backyard had Foss Man well prepared for this day. He didn't disappoint! On the first whistle, he exploded forward. The poor ball carrier didn't have a chance! Foss Man almost killed him. Coach Sanders had carefully organized the lines so the players approximately the same size would be competing against each other. But to keep him from injuring his teammates, the coach had to keep moving Foss Man up to the next line to compete against the much bigger guys.

It was inevitable brother Allen, who was far from a slouch in the toughness department, was going to do battle with Foss Man. Again, they didn't disappoint! It was nothing short of a blood bath! Impressed, Coach Sanders made examples out of their vicious one-on-one battles, oftentimes making the entire squad stand by and watch them go at it. With all eyes on them, the loving brothers were relentless and proceeded to absolutely beat the living hell out of each other. Many times, clearly after the second whistle blew, the victorious brother would deliberately stomp on the other guy's hand or ankle as he staggered his way back to the end of the line. Coach Sanders knew he had two great prospects and was pleased how the Foster brothers' toughness influenced the rest of the players.

As they moved through the second week of practice, the primary job for the freshmen was serving on the famous "hamburger" squad. The rookies were carefully assigned positions, lined up, and would get totally annihilated playing defense against the varsity first-string offense. Due to his well-known tenacious tackling reputation, Foss Man was rewarded with the key middle linebacker position. Skunk's brother Stub, with the one hand disadvantage, was the best running back in the junior class, but the star running back and captain of the varsity team was a popular senior by the name of Randy Watkins.

During his many overnight stays out on Skunk's farm, Foss Man had witnessed this Watkins character picking up Skunk's sister Ellie for dates all the time. For that reason, Foss Man didn't like this guy one bit. He was about forty pounds lighter than Watkins, but he didn't care. He made a special effort to absolutely destroy Watkins every chance he got. Confused and not understanding the freshman punk's motivation, on more than one occasion, the star running back got angry and barked at him, "Hey, cool your jets, will you, dick-head?" Foss Man loved it and would hit him harder the next time. Football was the greatest!

Brother Allen, only a sophomore, was a starting receiver on the varsity offense, and during the live scrimmages, when he wasn't going out for a pass, whether it was his designated assignment or not, would deliberately and violently blindside block his younger brother every chance he got. It was brotherly love at its very best! That was okay—Foss Man loved everything about football and could hardly wait for the big game under the lights Friday night.

It was a major milestone when Foss Man's mother told him to spend his last summer paycheck on some new clothes. His mother knew the shortage of clothes had been a persistent source of insecurity for him. After finishing his paper route the next morning, Foss Man went directly to West's Clothing right there in Jefferson and, for the first time in his life, proceeded to buy several shirts, two pairs of pants, and a new pair of shoes. With the new clothes and a fresh new-bought haircut from Shirv's on Main Street, Foss Man couldn't wait for the first day of school. He was going to be looking mighty fine and knew Ellie would be more than a little impressed when he hopefully ran into her between classes Monday morning.

The cheerleaders had a tradition of sponsoring a welcome back-to-school "sock hop" after the season opener on Friday night. Combining the dance and big game, it was going to be a special night, particularly for the freshmen.

First, there was the rousing pep rally with the blaring band, and now, sporting the bright red varsity game jerseys and white game pants, their hearts were pounding as they ran onto the field for the first time. With a vast majority of the Jefferson citizens in the stands cheering wildly, there was a special electricity and excitement in the air. During the pregame warm-up drills, Foss Man couldn't help but glance over and notice the cheerleaders doing their thing. Ellie and big sister Catherine were busy leading the cheers.

At this special happy time in their lives, little did these two sweet innocent girls know—or did it seem even remotely possible?—that horrific violence would enter their personal lives, the likes of which the always tranquil community of Jefferson had never seen in its long and peaceful history.

During the national anthem, one of the parents took a picture of the proud reserves standing along the sidelines. Taken from behind, the "big four" were proudly standing together facing the freshly mowed and white lined field. On the left was the miniature Skunk with his jersey tucked deep into his game pants, making it difficult to read his number. His pant legs overlapped with the top of his black high-top shoes, preventing any exposure to his legs. Next to him was Big Jake, standing tall with his game pants barely reaching his knees and exposing long legs about the size of a number 2 pencil. Skeeter stood to his right and could have passed for Skunk's twin brother. Then it was Foss Man, whose bowed legs would allow a full-grown feeder pig to easily jump through them. If this picture represented the nucleus of the Panther's future football fortunes, truthfully, it did not look real promising!

The four buddies stood there well prepared for action, knowing it was highly unlikely they'd get in the game, except for Foss Man, who would be the first reserve in the game if the senior middle linebacker needed a breather or got injured. The Jefferson Panthers didn't have a great winning tradition in football, and fittingly, tonight's game was not going well. As they were falling behind in the third quarter, the "big four" got restless, and with their by-now-well-documented free spirit, they launched a rather unbecoming ritual that would continue throughout the season.

A determined, fun-loving character, Skeeter usually got it started. During the heat of the game, he would quietly sneak behind the other three guys, randomly pick one of them, and viciously tackle him, knocking him to the ground. Caught totally off guard, the victim would swear out loud something like, "Damn you, little pecker head," and the other two guys would burst out laughing. Before the game ended, making sure to even the score, they all took their turn in carrying out a number of the violent blindside attacks. Coach Sanders would get mildly upset when he caught them in the act. With their white pants now severely grass-stained, a badge of honor, whether they got in the game or not, they were pretty beaten up and battle-weary by the end of the game. Football had always been a rough sport!

The Panthers got beaten, 28–7. The star running back, Randy Watkins, Ellie's current boyfriend, scored the only touchdown, and Foss Man played the last few minutes on defense. He was the only freshman who managed to get in the game.

Throughout the next week, Skeeter proudly informed everyone around school he had the distinction of being named the first-string "ass back" for the mighty Panthers. As the unofficial leader of the spontaneous sideline frolicking, the coach was constantly yelling at him, "Skeeter, get your ass back on the sideline, will you!"

Skeeter and Skunk may have been small in stature, but their great spirit and fun-loving attitudes provided a much-needed boost for a losing team's morale during the long practices as the season progressed. Their contributions were greatly appreciated by Coach Sanders as well as all their teammates, including the upper classmen. The "big four" became well known for their ability to balance having fun while being serious about football at the same time.

When the blaring horn signaled the end of the game, it was time to hit the shower room, share Big Jake's deodorant, and head to the big sock hop. Foss Man and his buddies were now standing around the outside wall in the gymnasium, wide-eyed and nervously watching the upperclassmen dancing up a storm. Skunk and Skeeter couldn't keep their eyes off the Becker twins. Clearly the most shapely girls in school and always dressed provocatively, they were easy to single out on the crowded dance floor. They knew they were probably dreaming, but they were dying to slow-dance with either one of the raving beauties. Foss Man was wearing his shiny new shoes, shirt, and pants and feeling pretty good about himself when out of nowhere, Ellie came directly toward him and said, "Come on, cutie, you're dancing this one with me."

His eyes had been glued on Watkins and Ellie dancing together, and he had been quietly praying for a miracle like this. But now what was he going to do? He had never danced before in his life! Grabbing his hand, Ellie was tugging and slowly pulling him out on the dance floor. Similar to the day Eclipse tipped over Aunt Naomi's lawnmower, he honestly thought he was going to shit his pants. Knowing it was his first dance, trying to comfort him, the popular senior girl said sweetly, "Just relax, Foss Man, don't worry, I'll lead the way. Come on, this will be fun!"

It was a dream come true for the tenacious reserve middle linebacker, but the fact was, he was totally petrified! Could this really be happening? Was he actually with the girl he had absolutely worshipped and adored for so very long, the incredible, one and only Ellie Jensen? It was a slow dance, and Ellie aggressively pulled him in close to her. Tightly clinging to her, slowly rocking back and forth from one foot to the other, Foss Man noticed they really weren't going anywhere. Her amazing breasts were pressing against his chest. Man Land was suddenly responding to all this contact and was now totally out of control. The threat of shitting his pants was no longer his greatest concern. He was seriously worried. *Good grief, can she tell what's going on down there?* He was suspicious he may have gotten the answer to that dubious question when the song ended and he noticed what looked like the "Mission accomplished" smirk on her beautiful dimpled face as she thanked him and politely walked away.

Randy Watkins, the star running back who scored the only touchdown that night, was waiting on the other side of the gym and had been taking the whole thing in. A happy and proud Foss Man said to himself, *Too bad, big guy, your days with Ellie are numbered. It's only a matter of time!*

Life was good! Foss Man had nothing but pleasant dreams after the truly amazing night!

Chapter Twenty-Eight

A spitting image of her mother, Catherine had become an absolute knockout. With her exceptional maturity and the high level of responsibility developed in the process of running the household in her mother's absence, Catherine was an extremely proud junior in high school and carried herself with an abundance of confidence. She was an honor roll student, and again, like her mother, she was blessed with an amazing singing voice, played French horn in the band, was a varsity cheerleader, and was the only real competition for Skunk's sister Ellie and, of course, the sexy Becker twins when it came to popularity amongst the high school male population. Although he was often the victim of her firm hand and her persistent attempts to keep him in line over the years, Foss Man simply adored his big sister.

Allen was an honor roll student, a terrific all-around athlete, and much unlike his younger brother, he was always serious and had no time for clowning around. Foss Man marveled at the great ease Allen had dealt with most of the same issues that persistently bothered him. Other than varsity sports, Allen focused exclusively on working, saving money, and preparing for his career in the United States Air Force. Allen knew what he wanted, had a plan, and nothing was going to get in the way. The brotherly battles were going to continue, but if the situation demanded it, Foss Man knew his big brother would have his back.

Foss Man was serious about his school work, but the fact was, being accepted by his peers was a higher priority, and always a fun-loving free spirit, he put a greater premium on having a good time. As far as career goals were concerned, other than the possibility of taking over his buddy Nute's bait shop someday or, even better, simply joining Mr. Slim in his favorite fishing spot on the shore of the mighty Troy River, he really didn't spend much time worrying about his future. There was the one lofty goal: his quiet unspoken dream of replacing Hank Aaron in the batting order for the Milwaukee Braves someday.

Foss Man's parents continued working the long hours necessary to provide the growing needs for their demanding large family. His dad had steadily improved his standing during the eight years of employment with Peterson Plumbing and Heating. His mother was carpooling with several other ladies to nearby Boulder where she had been candling eggs forty hours a week for over a year. With both parents working full-time, babysitters were needed at home during the school day for the two youngest kids, three-year-old Connie and two-year-old Leonard.

With the full approval of Mr. Gladding, the high school principal, Catherine, Allen, and Foss Man were set up on a rotating schedule, excusing each of them to spend one-third of their school day at home watching little Connie and Leonard. All honor roll students, their schedules were carefully crafted to include all the important academic subjects. Only missing out on the electives like shop class, home economics, and physical education, everyone was confident the unusual schedule wouldn't undermine their education. Always considered a top priority, special effort was made so the time spent at home didn't interfere with the boys' participation in sports after school or Catherine's many extracurricular activities. Keeping busy was a way of life for the Foster kids, the only life they had ever known. Living in the amazing new house and everything else, they felt blessed and were genuinely a bubbly bunch of happy kids.

Foss Man reported to the Roxie at 6:30 a.m. on Monday morning. Sweeping the theater only took a half hour. Then he biked over and picked up the fifty Des Moines Register papers and had them delivered by 8:00 a.m. when he headed back home for his babysitting shift. He covered the first shift with brother Allen reporting home at ten o'clock for his two-hour shift. Catherine was expected home by twelve o'clock for the final afternoon stretch. Glenda, who was in sixth grade, was expected to hurry home after school so Catherine could go back to school for cheerleading practice. Cafeteria duty was suspended for the Foster kids until the following year when Glenda would be enrolling in seventh grade. Foss Man had to give up his after-school paper route so he could attend football practice.

Skeeter was right—there were a bunch of great-looking female additions to the freshmen class, the popular transfers from the surrounding country schools. Hounded by the upperclassmen, the new girls pretty much ignored the lowly freshmen boys. After all, how could freshmen be expected to compete with these older guys and their deep voices and thick hair under their armpits? And most of them owned cars with impressive loud mufflers! Wasting no time, by the end of the first week of classes, big brother Allen picked out the most striking one of the bunch, a shapely girl named Rhonda; they became virtually inseparable throughout the rest of their high school days.

The deck may have been stacked against the freshmen guys, but Foss Man honestly didn't worry about it; his focus was exclusively on Ellie. He could hardly wait for the bell to ring, and he'd be searching for her in the hallway between classes. It didn't take long, and he'd learned Ellie's entire class schedule and managed to run into her several times a day. Making the effort more than worthwhile, Ellie would give him a big smile and say, "Hi there, cutie," almost every time. Foss Man absolutely loved the high school scene!

There were a few sophomores mixed in with the freshman typing class, and as luck would have it, Eclipse had to be one of them. Foss Man really didn't waste much time fretting about the big jerk anymore, but his presence was always a pain in the butt. Eclipse stood 6'2" and weighed in at about 220 pounds by now.

Poor old Ms. Wuertzel, in her seventies, had served as the sweet and lovable typing teacher at Jefferson High for several decades. After the regular practice drills and assigning the typing lesson for the day, sitting quietly and innocently doing work at her desk in front of the room, Eclipse threw one of those little balls that exploded like a firecracker when it hit the wall directly above her head. The dear old lady literally flew up off her chair and must have nearly had a heart attack. The class erupted in loud and ill-advised laughter. It's a sad commentary, but while most of the students may have quietly sympathized with their beloved teacher, as Eclipse had grown to expect, no one was brave enough to rat on the big jerk.

The school year was moving along pretty smoothly. Then as expected, later that fall, Eclipse once again left his mark. Mr. Phillips, the soft-spoken gentleman biology teacher, the nice guy who had to replace the big window in the science lab two years ago when Foss Man proudly blasted a ball through it during the noon-hour softball game, was badly shaken up when he observed the popular pet squirrel lying motionless on the bottom of the cage sitting on the table in the back of the room. After closer examination, Mr. Phillips discovered a sharpened pencil had been driven through its throat and the poor squirrel was deader than a doornail.

There was no conclusive evidence who was responsible for the ugly deed, but more than a coincidence, Eclipse just happened to be in attendance during the final biology class that day. It was just one more example of his persistent cruel behavior. The ruthless character was obviously out of control by now, and his reign of terror would continue seemingly unchallenged.

Except for Catherine. With her undeniable powerful love for animals, when she heard about the despicable squirrel incident, knowing very well who was responsible, having no fear, she tracked Eclipse down after school and boldly confronted him. This would be just another one of many contentious face-to-face dialogues that would take place between the two of them in the months and years to follow.

In typical fashion, Eclipse's reaction was simply, "You don't know what you're talking about, and if you're smart, you'll shut your big fat mouth." Having no fear about being held accountable, Eclipse laughed it off and had no intentions of changing his ways! Catherine was furious and felt totally helpless!

The ongoing mystery for Catherine and many other concerned citizens in the community was, when was the school administration or local law enforcement going to do something about this obviously troubled kid? Mr. Duncan, the superintendent of schools, and Mr. Gladding, the high school principal, wanting to avoid taking the easy route, and simply expelling him from school set up frequent meetings with the parents, but they would rarely show up. Limited in what they could realistically do with the delinquent, they could only assume his parents wanted to prevent him from going down the same bloody path as his older brother Frank, who was currently serving time in the state penitentiary for his recent crime spree. But the indifferent and detached attitude displayed by the parents was confusing and obviously not working. Not surprisingly, the patience and inaction displayed by everyone in a position of authority only provoked and magnified his already despicable behavior.

As the football season progressed, Foss Man was getting more playing time every week. He was now sharing equal time with the senior middle linebacker and making as many tackles as anyone on the team. Coach Sanders loved his aggressive attitude. Brother Allen was a good receiver and scored several touchdowns that season. The Foster boys were establishing a reputation as exceptionally tough football players as they continued to pound on each other during the live one-on-one blocking and tackling drills in practice. Allen was his equal in the toughness department, but having no honorable choice in the matter, Foss Man wasn't about to back down!

As the season wound down, the big homecoming dance was approaching. Foss Man was proud and happy for Ellie when she not surprisingly received the coveted honor of being selected as the Homecoming Queen. However, he was not thrilled when Randy Watkins was crowned as the Homecoming King. He knew this development was a setback for his master plan in winning Ellie over.

Standing along the gym wall with Skunk and Skeeter, Foss Man felt helpless when he could do nothing but stand there taking it all in. As expected, the king and queen were the featured center of attention for several of what seemed like endless dances. Depressed and with things looking hopeless, like another small miracle, he saw Queen Ellie suddenly walking directly toward him. He had been looking forward to the dance all week, and homecoming or not, he could only hope and pray Ellie would ask him to dance again like she had during the sock hop two months ago.

He had given some thought to what took place below his waist the last time they danced, and he didn't know exactly how he was going to prevent it from happening again, but he was determined to handle it in a more mature manner this time. The slow dance proceeded exactly like last time. They were clinging together, and while cherishing every second of it, sure enough, old One Eye—a term straight out of Skeeter's infamous "Peter Manual"—was once again behaving in normal fashion. What made him think it would be any different this time?

Here he was now, the totally mesmerized freshman dancing with the beautiful senior homecoming queen with the sparkling crown sitting elegantly and gracefully on her meticulously groomed head, and his stupid pecker was rudely poking her in the direct vicinity of her belly button. This was not right! There had to be an answer! It had become a legitimate question, and he wouldn't hesitate to bring it up at the next meeting with the boys in the shed.

Skunk and Skeeter, perhaps shorter but charming and good-looking guys, were popular and always seemed to be in demand for the next dance with the many eager upper class girls. Foss Man's two best buddies loved every minute of it as they took the dance floor and deliberately rested their faces directly between the healthy breasts of the much taller farm girls. They came off the dance floor with satisfied smirks on their faces and oftentimes with proud bulges in their pants that didn't appear to concern them even slightly.

Big Jake had no interest in the school dances. He preferred spending his time on things like wrapping up the few remaining merit badges required for the revered Eagle Scout Award. He didn't attend the dances but was always a good sport and looked forward to hearing about the other guys' more recent dance reports.

The Panther varsity managed to win two games that year. Along with Foss Man, there were two other freshmen who distinguished themselves by the end of the season. There was Horse, the physically mature over-six-foot-tall farm kid who had become a terrific wide receiver, and a guy named David Morgan, another big muscular kid and a promising quarterback candidate with an exceptionally strong arm for a freshman. Everyone knew he could throw a baseball with amazing velocity, but he really got their attention when he was effortlessly throwing the football well over fifty yards. Skunk immediately labeled him the Rocket Man. For the first time in years, Coach Sanders was optimistic that with the freshmen players like Rocket Man and Horse, and the tougher-than-nails Foster brothers leading the way, there was finally legitimate optimism for improvement in the win column.

Before basketball season began, the gang scheduled another of their regular meetings in the shed behind the Fosters' house. After replaying the highlights of the football season and satisfactorily addressing Foss Man's concern with his persistent untimely erections, they shifted to the more pressing subject on the agenda. With Halloween just around the corner, it was time to put the plan together for the annual goat release. An ornery old codger named Herb Thorson was always barking at them if they so much as stepped one foot on his carefully manicured lawn. They felt a little payback was only reasonable.

Herb lived on the west edge of town just south of Foss Man's old neighbor and boss Walter Olson. He had a fenced-in area connected to a small barn where his twenty prized goats were free to roam. Successful execution of the plan would result with Herb chasing down his goats for a few days following Halloween every year.

After the painstaking job of corralling his precious goats last year, he made it perfectly clear how he felt about it when he publicly announced, "Don't even think about doing it again next year, you little bastards! I promise you, I'll be on the lookout with my loaded shotgun and I'll shoot any asshole that comes near my property!"

Knowing the crazy old fart was more than capable of doing just that—actually shooting them—it might have been prudent to simply abandon the whole idea this year. However, after lengthy and serious discussion, the gang all readily agreed they had no choice but to move forward with what they considered their yearly obligation.

It was Skunk who came up with the brilliant strategy of "dodging the bullets" by simply carrying out the plan a day later, the night after Halloween. Proving Big Jake wasn't the only one in the group with brains, Skunk's plan worked like a charm! They opened the gates, relieved when there were no subsequent shotgun blasts, and the twenty goats, like every year, took off running wild and free as the breeze.

Once again, the unsuspecting citizens witnessed the goats frolicking around the streets of Jefferson, joyfully eating the ample supply of green grass from the well-groomed lawns and enjoying their annual short stretch of freedom. Relieved and pleased when he thought he had finally made it through Halloween unscathed, Herb was so angry he about blew a gasket! Furious and swearing like a wild man, he spent the next few days running around town corralling his beloved goats determined to strangle the little pecker heads who were responsible.

Not looking forward to it but having no choice, Foss Man cautiously knocked on Herb's door to collect for the morning newspaper the following Saturday morning. Herb indignantly asked him, "You heard any rumors about who may have released my goats?" Normally not really good under these pressure-packed circumstances, Foss Man responded calmly and politely, "No, I sure haven't, Herb, but I promise I'll keep my ear to the ground!" A nervous wreck, Foss Man thought Herb bought it. Mission accomplished! Another proud moment for the big four!

Chapter Twenty-Nine

Foss Man absolutely loved the high school scene. For months now, he had been living the good life with the luxury of the flushing toilet, the regular hot baths in the porcelain tub, and no more lugging water in the big gray tub that long block from Walter's pump on Saturday nights. He had successfully conquered the locker room scene and completed a satisfying football season. There was great progress with his personal friendship with Ellie. And of course, he now had a bunch of new clothes and a much-improved comfort level with the general social scene in school. Another grading period where he once again landed on the honor roll. And of course the cherished nickname! With all the good news, he was finding it a little easier to get to sleep at night, and the persistent nightmares were becoming more manageable.

To celebrate all the good things going on in his life, Foss Man decided it was time for a visit to their former apple orchard for a climb up to his favorite safe haven in the tall oak tree. With their old house still unoccupied, he confidently jumped over the fence and effortlessly climbed up the tree. He sat up there, enjoying the solitude while taking in the inspirational scenic view from the lofty perch. He loved the always-present cool breeze but, on this occasion, missed the gentle rustling of the now fallen leaves. Facing the cold winter months, he would be temporarily suspending his visits to his dependable sanctuary. With the tree stripped of its leaves, he could see Ed Miller's horse Champion prancing around in the fenced-in area behind the big red barn. He could barely see the Beaver Creek Bridge but was reminded of the many hours spent frolicking in the cool stream far below. He had deliberately stuck the special

Indianhead penny in his pocket that morning, knowing the special effect of merely holding it in his hand when perched up there for some mysterious reason was almost magical. All combined, a visit to the tree top always lifted his spirits and outlook on life!

Football was Foss Man's most important activity that fall, but for a combination of reasons, he had included the mixed choir in his busy schedule. His mother, of course, had an amazing singing voice, and it was obvious Catherine had inherited her talent. In conjunction with that puberty thing, Foss Man couldn't wait for his voice to drop an octave or two, but the fact was he still had a pretty good high tenor voice. When he, Skunk, Skeeter, and Big Jake observed the addition of the shapely new young choir teacher that fall, they all flocked in for their individual vocal tryouts. It may have been a mere coincidence, but when Ms. Swartz persistently wore those amazing low-cut blouses during tryouts, male participation in the choir reached a new all-time high.

Basketball season was well underway, and the annual high school Christmas concert was coming up. The program, featuring the mixed choir, had always been a popular event in town, and the auditorium would be jammed. Foss Man and his buddies had all qualified for the choir and were enthusiastic about performing in what would be their first big performance. Ms. Swartz, the by-now popular and provocative choir director, had been working diligently for many weeks determined to make the program a success. All the choir members had grown to genuinely like Ms. Swartz and, knowing this was her first big test, went out of their way to cooperate and worked extra hard in preparing for the big night. Choir proved to be a nice diversion from the intense basketball season and Foss Man's demanding workload.

With the packed house in an already-overheated auditorium, as the choir was belting out "Joy to the World," tall, gangly Big Jake, probably the best male singer in the entire high school, with no warning, fainted and dropped like he had been shot in the head. He had been proudly standing in the back row of the risers and, fortunately, fell forward—a backward fall could have been disastrous. While falling forward was advantageous, it created a wild, chaotic scene. His long, gangly body knocked over the entire soprano section and half of the altos. Everybody was scrambling, and there was the lovable Big Jake lying peacefully passed out and spread across the top three rows of the risers. Ms. Swartz, in the early stages of her first major production, was startled and totally confused about how to handle the crazy, unexpected development. The concerned audience made a gasping sound and leaned forward on the edge of their seats.

The confused accompanying pianist was clearly distracted but somehow managed to keep on playing. A few of the shaken choir members continued singing a weakened version of "Joy to the World" while Foss Man, Skunk, Skeeter, and the rest of the brave tenor section quickly swung into action. His good buddies, sincerely caring about him but knowing very well Big Jake would fully recover and be just fine, were quietly thinking this whole thing was a pretty cool deal. Trying desperately to keep from laughing out loud in the process, each grabbed an arm or a leg and, while struggling to lift Big Jake's long, limp body, unceremoniously managed to half-drag and half-carry their unconscious long string bean friend off the stage.

As things on the stage were slowly settling down, and with Ms. Swartz bravely regaining her composure, she nervously announced to the crowd there would be a short intermission. The curtains were pulled, and the crowd was buzzing and could only wait and hope everything would turn out okay.

After throwing cold water in Big Jake's face, like his buddies knew all along, he came around in a matter of just a few minutes. With his quick wit, he comforted everyone when he confidently announced, "Perhaps I was a little overzealous in my effort to bring 'Joy to the World,' but you have to trust me, I had everything under control. My only real concern now is whether the audience may be shaken up over my little episode. What do you think—did they appear to be handling it okay?"

They were all laughing now. Foss Man assured him, "Yes, Big Jake, the people will get through it just fine!" Ms. Swartz told Big Jake to take the rest of the night off. The choir regrouped, including the heroic tenors. The curtains were once again abruptly pulled open, the dedicated rookie director bravely explained to the crowd that everyone was fine, and the Christmas program proceeded.

Big sister Catherine stole the show with her solo, a stirring rendition of "O Holy Night," and the audience rewarded her with a standing ovation. The longtime residents of the community commented about the irony as they recalled her mother receiving the same kind of applause when she had sung the same popular carol some twenty years ago. After the choir's successful version of the always popular "Silent Night," Big Jake, completely on his own, made an unscheduled appearance to center stage, took a deep bow, and got a rousing applause, nearly as big as Catherine's a few minutes earlier.

Christmas was a great time to be a paperboy, and Foss Man regretted the fact it would be his last year delivering the morning newspapers. The much-appreciated tradition of receiving a box of chocolate-covered cherries or an extra dollar bill as Christmas presents from his many customers was going strong. He picked out the nicest box of chocolates from the tall stack in his bedroom, had Catherine help him wrap it, and the day before Christmas, when he was visiting Skunk on the farm, he proudly walked up and handed it to Ellie. In her typical caring manner, she said, "Well now, how sweet is that, Foss Man?" and without hesitation, she proceeded to plant a big kiss on his cheek. This was almost more than he could handle. He knew she was still dating the Watkins guy, but he knew he had to be gaining ground on him. He would remain patient and cool and just let things take their natural course.

Along with running into Ellie between classes several times every day at school, Valentine's Day presented another built-in opportunity for Foss Man to express how he felt about her. There were plenty of leftover Christmas chocolates to carry him well through the winter months. During another one of his visits to Skunk's farm in the middle of February, he gave Ellie another carefully wrapped box of candy, and he promptly received another big fat kiss on the cheek. His confidence was growing by the day, and he knew it was just a matter of time before she would willingly forget all about the stupid Watkins character!

Big Jake, Foss Man, and Horse, the big new guy in town, led the freshman basketball team to an undefeated 14–0 record that winter. According to Coach Sanders, Foss Man, perhaps as a result of all that rope jumping years ago, could almost jump out of the gymnasium. Along with Big Jake's height and shooting touch and the impressive all-around athletic Horse, the three of them were strong candidates to crack the starting lineup on the varsity team next year.

The Panthers had a winning tradition in basketball, and as expected, the varsity had another good year. Although they did not qualify for the state tourney, it was a practice for all the players, including the freshmen, to be excused from school for a day to attend the state tournament down in Des Moines. It was a fun day that everyone looked forward to, and the team was in good hands with the always dependable bus driver Aunt Francis behind the wheel for the two-hour trip. Coach Sanders politely asked Francis to open the window next to the driver's seat to ventilate the steady cloud of smoke floating from the Camels permanently hanging from her lips.

Rambunctious and always looking for ways to keep things interesting, between two of the afternoon games, Foss Man gave Big Jake his billfold and had him turn it in to the tournament manager's table, claiming he found it. Before long, it came blaring over the public address system: "Would Luke Foster please report to the scorer's table?" After repeating his name a few times, Foss Man boldly went down and claimed his lost billfold. When the varsity guys gave them the inevitable crap about the juvenile stunt on the way home on the bus that night, Big Jake fired back, "Hey, give us a break, we're just lowly freshmen dealing with all these raging hormone issues as we struggle our way through puberty!" Big Jake always knew how to handle any hassle from the upper classmen and could readily put the wise guys in their place!

It came as quite a surprise to even the Foster family when in March it was announced Foss Man's mother was going to bring another little one into the world. The baby was due in November. Little did they know at the time how this, what had always been a routine risk-free delivery process, the Foster family would be facing an unthinkable tragic outcome.

Foss Man had a promising future in football and basketball, but baseball was clearly his best sport. He could hit the ball a mile and had a powerful shotgun arm. Coach Sanders immediately put him in the varsity line up as the starting catcher, and he maintained a .300 batting average throughout the season that spring. There was another relevant freshman player on the team, Dave "Rocket" Morgan, the lanky 6' kid who had gotten everyone's attention last fall when he had impressed everyone the way he threw the football. Rocket was a great all-around athlete and a phenomenal pitcher. A fastball in the mid '80s was unheard of for a freshman in high school. Rocket and Foss Man combined for a formidable battery, which was a rarity for two rookie freshmen as they proceeded to play key roles in winning another conference championship. Brother Allen was the slick fielding shortstop and was known for his timely hitting.

After their outstanding performance that spring, Foss Man and Rocket were invited to try out for the amateur town team that summer. The town team roster included adult players of all ages, and they played their games on Sunday afternoons. Hard to believe, Foss Man would now actually be playing in the games instead of working in the Foster refreshment stand and chasing down all those foul balls.

Rocket's dad, owner of the Morgan Road Construction Company, was the largest employer in town and with that came much power and influence. Big Jake's dad, an exceptional baseball player in his day, was the manager of the second largest workforce in town, the Rural Electric Company. He too was a highly respected and active political leader in Jefferson. Big Jake, a good player in his own right, had an older brother named Will, who as a catcher, was one of the best baseball players to ever came out of Jefferson. Foss Man could remember some of Will's towering home runs. He had idolized Will and was the primary motivation to become a catcher in the first place. Will was a walk-on for the University of Iowa Hawkeyes and, currently a senior, was getting significant playing time. With this proud family history, Big Jake's dad had become a huge baseball fan, and joined by Rocket's dad, the two of them formulated an ambitious plan to get lights for the baseball field. A field with lights was an extremely rare feature for a small community like Jefferson.

Big Jake's dad's lofty status with the electric company put him in the perfect position to recruit volunteers with the kind of expertise needed to get the lights hooked up properly. Rocket's dad encouraged his many employees to volunteer their skills as well. With their influence, personal dedication, and hard work, combined with generous contributions from most of the active ball players, Jefferson ended up with the first amateur baseball field with lights in northern Iowa.

What all this meant was those blazing hot Sunday afternoon games could now be moved to night games. The night games proved to be so popular, in less than a year, a new Wednesday Night League was formed. The lights permitted all the players to work during the day, play games on both Wednesday and Sunday nights, and a residual benefactor, the Foster refreshment stand would now have the opportunity to double their revenue. Baseball had always been a big deal in Jefferson, but with the impressive new lights, it soon became one of the most successful programs in the entire state of Iowa.

CHAPTER THIRTY

It was the last week of school, the successful high school baseball season was just completed, and confirmation ceremonies for Allen and Foss Man were scheduled for the following Sunday. When you were formally confirmed, you were expected to teach Sunday school for at least a year or two, and the Foster brothers were both actually looking forward to that. With the school year moving along smoothly and winding down, things suddenly took a horrible turn!

Teammates throughout the football, basketball, and baseball seasons, Horse and Rocket had become close friends of Skunk, Skeeter, Big Jake, and Foss Man. Great additions, Horse and Rocket were invited to join them for the first time, and the six cronies were now jammed in the Foster shed for the important year-end bull session. Before they replayed the highlights of their freshmen year, everyone noticed that Skunk had been particularly quiet lately, and Foss Man asked him, "Hey, Skunk, what's going on with you anyway? You haven't been yourself lately." It was pretty obvious something was bothering him, but Skunk didn't want to talk about it. After friendly prodding, Skunk finally came out with a stunning bombshell!

Almost crying, Skunk put it very short and simple: "My sister Ellie is pregnant!"

Everyone got quiet as they desperately tried to digest the shocking news. Foss Man turned white as a sheet and thought he was going to be sick. His first confused thoughts were, *Oh my god, this can't be possible!* Putting it mildly, he was absolutely shattered!

The news was so unbelievable the six freshmen boys could do nothing but sit there in stunned silence. Staring down at the floor, it suddenly dawned on Foss Man that he was focusing completely on Ellie and feeling sorry for himself and not thinking even for one second about Skunk. Skunk had always been there for him when he most needed it. He looked over at Skunk. It about killed him to see his very best buddy sitting there so brokenhearted and torn apart. Skunk had always been the pillar of strength. He knew how much Skunk loved and idolized his big sister. They all just sat there for a few minutes with their heads hanging down, not knowing what to say.

Finally, the much wiser and always thoughtful Big Jake calmly came up with, "Boy, that's really tough news, Skunk. But you know, it's not the end of the world. There are certainly ways of dealing with this kind of thing. Ellie's a strong person, and with you and Stub and everyone's love and support, you know she'll get through this." Then a perfectly logical question, Big Jake asked, "Do you know if Ellie and Randy are going to consider getting married?" Randy was Big Jake's first cousin.

As sensible as it may have been, Big Jake's question was like another violent punch in the gut for Foss Man.

Skunk said quietly, "I don't know, the old man is so pissed about the whole thing I don't know what's going to happen! You talk about love and support—the old man was so mad last night he wouldn't stop screaming at Ellie. I was afraid for a minute he was going to hit her! Ellie kept saying over and over, 'I'm sorry, Daddy. I'm so sorry, Daddy.' Hearing her plead for mercy like that just about killed me! Ellie's been crying for hours every night for over a week now, and I don't think she knows what she's going to do. It's been an absolute nightmare around the house. I hate the way my dad is handling this whole mess, and watching him drink all that stupid beer is only making things worse!"

Hearing Skunk's explanation crushed Foss Man. He could hardly breathe. He was an absolute emotional wreck. He couldn't get the incredible sadness Ellie must be going through out of his mind. Knowing there was virtually nothing he could do to help her, he felt totally helpless. With no more that could be said or done at the time to help their badly shaken friend, all the guys gave Skunk an uncharacteristic but genuinely caring hug. Abruptly cutting the meeting short, they all headed for their given homes, including Skeeter, who had been spending more time at home with his dad throughout their freshman school year.

Virtually blind with confusion and emotion, Foss Man inconspicuously found his way upstairs and lay on his bed and began to cry, deep, wracking sobs that went on and on!

Later that day, his mother finally came up stairs and asked him, "Hey, what's wrong, buddy? It's almost suppertime!" It was a struggle to get it out, but he somehow managed to tell his greatest friend and ally in the whole world what he was so upset about. His mother knew he had a serious crush on Ellie but had no way of knowing how strong his feelings were for her. After doing her best to demonstrate her love and support but at the same time knowing he had no choice but to be strong and move on, she bravely told him to wash his face off with some cold water and come down for supper in a few minutes.

Sadly, Ellie's pregnancy was only the beginning. There was more shocking news that came out the next day that would rock the entire community! When Big Jake and Skeeter heard the unspeakable story, while their first thoughts were with Skunk and his family, they knew how unbearable this stunning revelation would be for their buddy Foss Man. They decided to get together and go up to his house to share the incredible news in case the Foster family hadn't heard about it. When they got to his house, with it being Saturday, Foss Man's mother was home and came to the door. Always jovial, fun-loving characters, she could tell right away they had something serious on their minds. She told them that Foss Man was mowing his Grandpa's lawn at the time but they should come on in. They sat down in the living room, and as difficult as it was for them, the boys proceeded to tell her the horrible news.

Like every citizen in Jefferson reacted upon hearing the report, Foss Man's mother was stunned and in total shock. She could see Foss Man's two buddies were extremely shaken up about the whole thing, but it was heartwarming to see how genuinely concerned they were about Foss Man. Together they discussed a plan on how best to break the unfathomable news to him. As they were mulling things over, usually only working until noon on Saturday, Foss Man's dad came through the front door. He had heard the news at work that morning and was planning to share the story with the family when he got home. He agreed to go pick up Foss Man while Big Jake and Skeeter decided to go home, knowing it would probably be best if they weren't around when Foss Man heard what happened. Foss Man's deeply appreciative mother hugged the boys and thanked them for coming over, and they headed for home.

Foss Man had just finished mowing his grandpa's huge lawn when his dad pulled up. His dad told him to throw his bike in the trunk and made up some excuse why they had to get right home. Foss Man, who had two more lawns to mow that day, was a little confused but did what he was told, and they made their way home.

While he was gone, Foss Man's mother told the younger ones to go outside and find something to do. Catherine was babysitting for some neighbors, and Allen was working at his new job at the gas station.

When Foss Man and his dad got home, his mother told him to sit down and said that they had some very bad news to share with him. Nervous and confused, he sat on the living room couch, and his mother proceeded to tell him what had taken place sometime during the late hours the previous night.

Already worried about how fragile her son's current frame of mind was, struggling to find the right words, she put it as gently as she could: "Your friend Skunk's sister Ellie was found dead this morning from an apparent gunshot wound." Knowing how extremely difficult this would be for him, his parents braced for every conceivable reaction.

Foss Man sat there in quiet disbelief. He didn't say a word, just sat there. His parents tried to comfort him with supportive words, but he was in such an intense state of shock he could do nothing but sit there staring at the floor. The pain was so deep and so raw he was literally numb. After a few minutes, he got up involuntarily and slowly stumbled up the stairs to the bedroom he shared with his younger brother Gerald. They decided just letting him be alone for a while was probably all they could do at the time. Fearing he might fall into the dark place that had swallowed him over ten years ago following his sister's tragic death, they were deeply worried and agreed it was important to stand by and diligently monitor the situation.

Although there was great controversy swirling around Jefferson with the disturbing circumstances surrounding Ellie's shocking death and all the appropriate Wright County law enforcement officials were busy doing their due diligence behind the scenes, the immediate focus was exclusively on giving her family the badly needed support as they were going through the unimaginable grieving process.

With the unexpected incident and pending funeral, Reverend Thompson hastily postponed Allen and Foss Man's confirmation ceremony scheduled for that Sunday morning.

Three unbearable, miserable long days later, Foss Man was sitting in the second pew of the First Lutheran Church with his parents and sandwiched between Catherine and Allen, who of course were also deeply saddened and heartbroken over Ellie's death. Sister Glenda remained home with the four younger kids. Skunk was sitting within arm's length directly in front of them with his brother Stub and their grief-stricken parents. With his head looking down, a very somber Randy Watkins, his two younger sisters, and their parents were sitting in the front pew across the aisle. The church was jammed, and the overflow crowd ran out the front door, spilling onto the street in front of the church.

With the open casket positioned only a few feet from where he was sitting, Foss Man's eyes were glued on Ellie's beautiful flawless face. For the first time ever, there was no smile, and the dimples were gone. With tears running down his cheeks, he quietly begged her, "Please open your eyes, Ellie, and bring an end to this horrible nightmare. Dear God, how could you let this happen?"

There wasn't a dry eye in the church as Foss Man's sister Catherine and his mother, who with their amazing voices were in demand for occasions like this in Jefferson, together, sang a stirring rendition of "Amazing Grace."

Foss Man was physically and emotionally unable to go to the cemetery for the burial services.

CHAPTER THIRTY-ONE

There were many critical questions that needed to be answered! First and foremost, any criminal element related to Ellie's death was quickly dismissed when the county coroner officially ruled the death was caused by either an accidental or self-inflicted gunshot wound. Included in the medical examiner's completed analysis, the final determination was that the shot was indeed self-inflicted. Impossible for Foss Man to accept or believe, Ellie's tragic death was officially ruled a suicide! The overwhelming conclusive evidence proved she had deliberately positioned the shotgun so she could reach the trigger with the barrel of the gun pointed directly toward her stomach!

That was the official story, but quietly behind the scene, there was widespread unbecoming conjecture swirling around the community for the months to follow. No one wanted to put blame directly on Ellie's heartbroken and grieving father, but the few people aware of his great anger and the way he treated her after hearing the news of her pregnancy, while not holding him accountable for literally pulling the trigger, felt he was at least indirectly responsible for placing the gun in her hands! Foss Man knew better than anyone that there would be an endless struggle to reestablish the love and happiness that had always been so prevalent in Skunk's home. He knew Skunk would never forget Ellie's desperate pleas with her dad: "I'm sorry, Daddy! I'm so sorry, Daddy!"

While Foss Man was obviously deeply affected by the loss of his special friend, he was fully aware how much his parents were worried and concerned about him. Like the short time he had spent in the wheelchair, he was more determined than ever to prove to them that this horrible tragedy was not going to break him. But rather, like

Reverend Thompson and Mr. Slim had reminded him so many times in the past, dealing with this tragedy was going to make him a stronger person. There was no denying the struggle to get to sleep at night was going to be greater than ever, but that was something he alone would have to deal with. If he didn't want his parents to fret about him, he had to be strong, and now more than ever, somehow, he had to find a way to move forward and get on with his life.

On top of his own personal grief, his thoughts were dominated with deep and genuine sympathy for his great friend Skunk and his brother Stub. The sickening thought of losing his older sister Catherine helped put things in perspective! That would simply be unbearable! With that in mind, no longer feeling sorry for himself, he couldn't fathom what his great friend Skunk must be going through and was determined to be there for him!

With the hole in his heart, Foss Man would make a calculated effort to focus exclusively on three things throughout the long and difficult summer months ahead: his important new job with Walter, his love for baseball, and supporting his special friend Skunk.

Always the ambitious and innovative businessman, Skeeter's dad was in the process of converting the Roxie Theater into a six-lane bowling alley. With the elimination of the theater in town, his dad was in the early stages of constructing the first drive-in theater about a mile west of Jefferson. This development eliminated Foss Man's job of sweeping out the theater every morning. With the more demanding summer job offer from Walter Olson, it was also time to turn his longtime productive Des Moines Register morning paper route over to younger brother Gerald. Foss Man knew Gerald would do a good job and was impressed the way he sprung out of bed at 5:00 a.m. on Sunday mornings while he enjoyed the rare teenage pleasure of rolling over for another hour of much-appreciated sleep.

Highly industrious, Walter Olson had bought two hundred additional acres of rich farm land the previous year that made him one of the largest cabbage farmers in northern Iowa. His vast property now stretched westward to the shores of Beaver Creek. The new land, combined with his already sizable vegetable operation, demanded significantly increasing his workforce. Knowing there weren't enough workers amongst the local population willing to do the tedious hard work in the punishing humidity and stifling hot sun throughout the summer months, it was necessary to bring in migrant workers from faraway Texas.

Already impressed with his level of responsibility and conscientious work habits the previous summer, Walter offered Foss Man the important job whose primary responsibility would be to work closely with the new migrant workers. His job title, which he loved, was to officially serve as the junior foreman at the unprecedented wage of ninety cents per hour. The healthy promotion took the financial pain out of losing the sweeping job in the theater and giving up the morning paper route.

A built-in part of the decision to hire the temporary workforce, Walter knew he had to provide comfortable sleeping quarters for his valued new employees. As part of his long-range plan and the need for hiring the migrant workers for many years down the road, the astute and organized business man had carefully planned ahead and invested a significant amount of money in the construction of five sizable shacks strategically positioned along the shores of Beaver Creek. Knowing there was competition with the other large cabbage farmers in the area to rehire a reliable workforce year after year, along with his natural compassion, Walter deliberately went the extra mile in providing comfortable living conditions for the migrant workers.

It was a memorable scene when the five Mexican families came rolling into town that first time. Each family owned an old beat-up car jammed with little ones or a pickup truck with their personal belongings stacked high and tied together with a complex network of ropes. Totally exhausted from the long two-day journey from southern Texas, they were excited when they first observed their new living quarters. An unexpected luxury, the impressive shacks would provide each family with their own private place to live. With every family member pitching in, they made quick work of getting their belongings unpacked. Foss Man was busy helping them get settled in and could sense right away he was going to like these bubbly, happy, and spirited people. After the long hot ride cooped up in the stuffy cars, the younger kids were running around, frolicking, and laughing and wasted no time stripping down and bare-ass naked, jumping into the irresistible rippling cold water provided by the convenient nearby Beaver Creek.

During all the hustle and bustle, Foss Man's first order of business was to make a formal nose count of the members in Walter's dynamic new workforce. Early in the process, there was a startling observation that stopped Foss Man cold in his tracks. His eyes were suddenly locked on an attractive girl who was busy assisting her parents with the strenuous job of getting their belongings moved into their assigned new home.

Good grief, who was this amazing creature anyway?

Wasting no time the next day, Foss Man quietly learned more about the shapely beauty. Her name was Rosita Rodriguez. Along with her mom and dad, Rosita had three younger siblings, fourteen year old brother Pedro and four and five year old sisters. Her family represented six of the thirty members in Walter's new workforce. Rosita was fifteen, one year older than Foss Man, but obviously physically mature beyond her years. She had long coal-black hair, huge brown eyes, flawless olive skin, and full lips that complimented a perfect white smile. There was no denying it, her natural raw beauty was simply breathtaking. Nothing could remove the raw pain of losing his special friend Ellie, but her mere presence provided Foss Man with at least a small distraction from the heavy burden on his severely broken heart.

With the expenses related to their long journey from Texas, anticipating the likely need for cash upon their arrival in town, Walter thoughtfully advanced them a week's projected wages.

Following a quick trip to the grocery store, with impressive efficiency, the women prepared an elaborate spread of food. Walter had six newly built picnic tables delivered to the campsite the previous week, and with mealtime never neglected in their demanding lifestyle, they would be put to great use over the next three months.

Making an instant hit with his new friends, Foss Man readily accepted their invitation to join them for the first of what would become regular "feasts" throughout the upcoming weeks. The food was different from anything he had ever eaten, but he found it delicious and, as always, proceeded to absolutely gorge himself.

After everyone had filled their bellies, having been through the routine many times before, they proceeded to pitch additional tents, erect several makeshift canvas shelters designed for additional storage space, and tie clotheslines from tree to tree and shack to shack. Highly organized, the clotheslines were promptly filled with diapers and clean clothes that had been already washed in the crystal-clear creek water.

While all this was going on, a credit to his typical quick thinking, Foss Man found a thick rope in one of Walter's storage sheds and recruited Rosita's brother Pedro to help him tie it to the big oak tree conveniently standing next to what would soon become their favorite swimming hole. Although most of the little ones had already taken advantage of the refreshing water of Beaver Creek, with the exception of Rosita and another striking young lady who was extremely pregnant and clearly ready to deliver in the very near future, in varying degrees of dress, virtually everyone, adults included, took their turn swinging out on the rope, and while laughing and screaming with uninhibited delight, they thoroughly enjoyed plunging and splashing into the irresistible cold water far below.

Before darkness set in their first night in town, two of the older boys volunteered to dig a fire pit, gathered a pile of kindling and logs from the ample supply in the nearby wooded area, and in no time, they built a roaring fire. With the vast majority of the work done by now and everyone refreshed by the quick dip in the creek, accompanied by the two fathers who were accomplished on both the guitar and ukulele, everyone gathered around the fire and was belting out their favorite well practiced Spanish songs. Foss Man soon discovered the younger kids could speak both English and Spanish fluidly and were accustomed to serving as interpreters for most of the adults who spoke exclusively Spanish.

Already deeply impressed with these friendly people, Foss Man happily accepted their warm invitation and stuck around that night until the fire burned itself out. As he was sitting and enjoying the intriguing festivities, as inconspicuously as possible, he couldn't keep his eyes off the striking girl sitting directly across from him on the opposite side of the bon fire. It may have been his imagination or wishful thinking, but he swore he caught her glancing his way on more than one occasion.

With the lingering memory of Ellie's death, Foss Man's struggle to sleep at night would continue, but he had a good feeling about how this amazing group of human beings, a most unlikely source, who had been in town less than one day, could be invaluable in providing the much-needed relief for his still fresh and painful heartache. With the glaring absence of any materialistic items of great value, he was immediately impressed and could only marvel how these confident, proud, and happy people carried themselves.

Chapter Thirty-Two

Bright and early Monday morning, after a quick breakfast, the vast majority of the workforce reported directly to the fields. The job consisted of the back-breaking work of hoeing the fast-growing weeds from the endless rows of cabbage in the giant sprawling field. No training or instruction was necessary; by now they were well-practiced in the all-too-familiar tedious work. Paid by the acre rather than by the hour, except for the little ones under five years old, the entire family, including several seven-, eight-, and nine-year-olds, huddled close together and were all moving up and down the fields working feverishly to maximize their production. Rosita and her first cousin Juanita, the seventeen-year-old unmarried pregnant girl who could easily have passed as her twin sister, remained at the campsite on alternating days assigned to take care of the three youngest ones. Overshadowing her distorted physical condition, Juanita had the kind of radiant beauty enhanced by her pregnant condition.

A normal work day for the migrant workers started promptly when the sun came up, which was at approximately 5:00 a.m. Foss Man usually reported to work at 7:00 a.m., and following Walter's strict orders, immediately delivered two buckets of fresh cold drinking water from the same pump he and his brother had used so many years. Providing fresh water throughout the day was one of his primary duties. Uninterrupted, the group worked diligently until noon, 12:00 sharp, when they took a well-earned full one-hour break and gathered at the picnic tables under the shade trees along the creek for their quickly prepared first major meal of the day. Understanding and appreciating the critical need for nourishment to maintain the necessary energy and strength for the challenging long work days, they made a point to eat heartily and made a big deal out of every meal. Then it was back to work until 6:00 in the evening, when they would break again for one hour and another special Mexican feast. Then, remarkably, it was back to work until the pesky swarming mosquitoes became unbearable or total darkness set in.

After a quick dip in the refreshing creek water, it was either a short gathering around the fire and a few songs for most of the older folks or straight to bed for the badly needed sleep. Motivated to maximize the much-appreciated opportunity to make money during the short time they were in faraway Iowa, they proved to be relentless hard workers, taking only Sundays off to attend church in the morning and then a few hours of greatly deserved rest in the afternoon. Sunday nights were their favorite designated times for the largest group celebrations, big bonfires, and song fests that often stretched late into the night. Monday morning they were up once again with the sun and, pleased to have the great opportunity, willingly and enthusiastically went directly back to work!

On the subject of church, Reverend Thompson had thoughtfully made an unscheduled visit to a fireside sing-along one night during their first week in town. Between songs, he stood before them and cordially welcomed the group to Jefferson and invited them to join him for church services and Sunday school during their stay in town. Not knowing what their response would be, he was pleased when they enthusiastically accepted his warm invitation, and most of them became regulars at the First Lutheran Church starting that very next Sunday. The five loving and devoted families were warmly embraced by the long-standing members of the congregation.

Foss Man's relationship with the migrant workers grew to the point where he not only got to know each of the families but he also grew deeply and genuinely fond of every single family member, young and old. Although he spent part of his work day with Walter's other workforce in the nearby tomato, strawberry, and squash fields, within a month, he knew everyone by name and was familiar with the structure of each and every family. It soon became obvious the feelings were mutual when throughout the workday, all the younger ones would holler at him when he came anywhere near them. "Hey,

Boss Man, what cha doing? Come on over and see us, Boss Man!" The closely knit families hung together always working in close proximity to each other throughout the long, tedious work days. Before long, they were insisting that Foss Man join them for the noon meals, and taking full advantage, he soon learned to love the carefully prepared hot and spicy Mexican food, but more importantly, he enjoyed every minute he spent with the infectious and spirited group.

Well aware of each other's presence, less than two weeks of the summer had passed when Foss Man and Rosita managed to break away from the group for the first of what would become regular walks along the shores of Beaver Creek. There was an instant attraction between the two of them, and they quickly became great friends. Rosita was a likeable, very sweet, and genuine girl, but it didn't take long, and Foss Man recognized she was far more experienced and comfortable in dealing with the opposite sex. With her aggressively leading the way, Rosita would be the first girl Foss Man would actually kiss on the lips. As the summer weeks moved along, things between them were advancing in directions and territory previously unknown to him. The shapely beauty made Foss Man a little nervous and was proving to perhaps be more than the inexperienced fourteen-year-old was prepared to handle.

One night, when they broke away from one of the many sing-alongs around the roaring fire, Rosita asked him, "Why Foss Man so sad? Foss Man's eyes always sad, yes?" It was true—while thoroughly enjoying her company and the presence of the entire group, it had been a long time since he had been through a stretch of time like this when he was so uncharacteristically subdued and dispirited. During their many conversations, there never seemed to be a good time or reason to mention anything about Ellie's death. In response to Rosita's sincere inquiry, he decided it probably wouldn't hurt to tell her a little bit about what happened earlier that summer. Proceeding cautiously and knowing he would give her only an abbreviated version of what actually took place, he started out with, "I lost a very good friend last spring."

Tenderly, Rosita inquired, "Rosita sorry, was it girlfriend?"

He emphasized his relationship with Ellie was more like a serious crush than any kind of true romance. Seeing no logical reason for digging into the whole pregnancy and suicide part of the story, he simply told her his best buddy Skunk's older sister Ellie had been killed in a gun accident. Without going into great detail, he wrapped it up by saying, "Ellie was a beautiful person, a great friend, and her death was very painful for her family and everyone that knew her. I'm extremely sad about losing such a special person, but I feel really bad for my best friend who is dealing with losing his one and only sister!"

Listening intently, very sweet and heartfelt, Rosita came back with, "Rosita not like when Foss Man sad. Rosita can make you happy. You like Rosita make you very happy, Foss Man?"

A little confused and nervous about her intentions and desperately trying to steer things in a new direction, Foss Man came back with, "Oh, don't worry, Rosita makes me happy. I don't want you to feel sorry for Foss Man. Rosita already makes me happy, very happy!"

Questioning his own stupidity—and it was difficult and a little awkward, but with his instinctive and sincere reaction to whatever it was she may have been suggesting, they abruptly found their way back to the safety and comfort of the weekly celebration around the big bonfire.

Foss Man loved his job and the special relationship he had developed with the migrant workers throughout the difficult months following Ellie's death, but baseball would always be a top priority. It was highly unusual for a fourteen-year-old to take over the starting catching duties on the Jefferson adult baseball team. Foss Man and Rocket, the young fire-balling pitcher, made a major contribution to another successful season. Every line drive helped keep his mind off Ellie. The whole team was happy when Skunk showed up and decided to try out for the team. He didn't crack the starting lineup, but he was a good player, and of course, Foss Man loved having him around. It would be a long time before Skunk could possibly recover from his terrible loss, but once again, he impressed everyone with his amazing strength and resiliency. Skunk's positive attitude helped Foss Man get back on track. Everyone went out of their way to be supportive of Skunk, and the truth is, baseball served as a catalyst for all of them to put the horrible tragedy behind them and move on with their lives.

Far too early in the grieving process, Skunk was suddenly facing another gut-wrenching setback. The last Sunday night in June, right after the game, Skunk and Foss Man were on their way home when Skunk informed him, "Hey, Foss Man, I've got some bad news. Why don't you stop out tomorrow and say goodbye to Thunder?" Confused and giving Skunk an inquisitive look, Foss Man asked him, "What the heck are you talking about? What do you mean 'Say goodbye to Thunder'?" Obviously sad and emotional, Skunk went on, "Thunder must have stepped in a pothole or something in the pasture, but my dad and I noticed he was limping really badly this morning. We had Dr. Dockstader—you know, the old vet in town—come out and look at him this afternoon. After examining him, he said Thunder fractured a bone in his lower leg and that we have no choice but to shoot him or put him to sleep."

That night, as he was going through his normal struggle to get to sleep, Foss Man was replaying all the good times they had riding on the big work horse. He marveled at how strong Skunk appeared to be in handling this new heartbreaking development. Echoing through his mind was, *Shoot Thunder or put him to sleep? There has to be a better answer!* He knew how much Skunk loved that big old animal. Foss Man was inspired by Skunk's amazing attitude, and it made him more determined to be stronger then he had been in the past when dealing with what had become regular emotional setbacks. He knew it was going to be tough saying goodbye to Thunder tomorrow, but he made up his mind that night that he would be strong.

Foss Man reported to work at seven o'clock sharp the next morning. A couple hours later, he ran in to his boss Walter. After explaining what happened, having seen the boys bouncing by his house on the big old horse dozens of times, Walter sympathetically told Foss Man to take whatever time he needed to go out and visit Thunder. Appreciating his bosses' consideration, he jumped on his bike and headed out to Skunk's farm.

It was the first time Foss Man had been out to the farm since Ellie died. He had known it was only sensible to give Skunk and his family some private time to deal with the grieving process. Making things worse, he knew there was undeniable anger that Skunk, Stub, and their mother felt toward Skunk's dad. Seeing how much he too was suffering, they were trying their very best to forgive him and didn't want to believe his bad temper provoked Ellie's drastic decision to take her own life. But knowing her always happy disposition and positive outlook in life, it was inconceivable to think she would have done it otherwise. For that reason, the normal expected grief was overshadowed with almost unbearable tension around the Jensen home front. On top of that, Foss Man deliberately stayed away from the farm, knowing going into their kitchen and not seeing Ellie sitting there at the kitchen table doing her homework, that it was now a reality; he would never see those dimples and that amazing smile again.

Parking his bike, he was relieved when Skunk told him his dad was out in the field cultivating corn. Foss Man was personally struggling to forgive Skunk's dad after he learned about the way he treated Ellie when he found out she was pregnant. As much as he hated to think about it, he didn't know if or when he would ever feel comfortable in Skunk's house again.

Usually free to frolic and roam around the fenced-in barnyard, they could see Thunder was not very happy being penned up there in the barn. But no longer able to put weight on one leg, it was obvious to both of them he was in severe pain. Knowing the outcome was inevitable, Skunk and Foss Man only spent a couple minutes with the ailing animal, but they wanted to, one last time, thank Thunder personally for all those memorable trips they made around town together. Foss Man told him out loud that all those painful steep falls to the hard ground were well worth it, considering the many safe trips he provided while escaping the wrath of that pesky dog Rusty. Like he fully understood, Thunder responded by snorting and giving them that familiar woofing sound from deep in his chest. Thunder was euthanized that afternoon.

Again, Foss Man knew how much Skunk loved that big old cuss and was reminded once again how he had to be the most resilient human being Foss Man ever knew. His strength helped Foss Man deal with his own personal sadness over losing his good friend, Big Thunder!

There was some good news that week. His mother received a call from Coach Sanders, and Foss Man's new letter jacket had been delivered to the school. Rocket and Foss Man were the only members of the freshmen class to earn a varsity letter in baseball, or any sport for that matter, during the past school year. Ignoring the always prevailing financial pressures and lofty price tag, Foss Man's mother had insisted he go ahead and order himself a new lettermen's jacket. It was the middle of July, and in the now steady 95-degree heat and intense humidity, he had to be reminded more than once he probably didn't have to continue wearing that most cherished and beloved jacket every day. But he wore it anyway!

He was also the proud owner of one of the town team's all-wool uniforms with "Panthers" emblazoned across the chest and a brand-new pair of baseball shoes with cleats that clicked when he walked on the sidewalk. He always loved that sound. Along with a couple of impressive towering home runs that summer, he was hitting foul balls that now, like he had done so many times over the years, his little brother Gerald was having to duck under the Foster refreshment stand counter and chase them down in order to collect a nickel from his dad.

Their dad was still in charge of the foul balls, but the only difference was, now he was proudly throwing them back to the umpire or his son, the starting catcher on the town baseball team. His dad was quietly beaming with pride as Foss Man was fast becoming one of the budding star baseball players in town. Younger sister Glenda and brother Gerald had become their dad's right-hand helpers in the profitable now-twice-a-week refreshment stand operation.

Chapter Thirty-Three

As the summer moved forward, it became a common practice for many of the Jefferson citizens, while relaxing outside on their patios at night and when the wind was just right, to sit and enjoy listening to the cheerful singing drifting in from the happy people gathered around the roaring bonfire a short distance west of town. In the beginning, Rosita and her brother Pedro were the lone regulars attending the Sunday night baseball games. But as the summer passed, one section of bleachers was now filled regularly with bubbly, enthusiastic fans consisting of the fascinating new citizens in town. With her glaring beauty significantly enhanced by her always tasteful but provocative outfits, Rosita's presence at the game caused quite a stir, particularly amongst the general male population, including the ball players from both teams.

As the migrant workers began receiving regular paychecks, the local businessmen, particularly the two grocery store owners, were pleased to see them come to town for their always robust shopping sprees. An interesting observation—not one penny was spent on beer or liquor. With their regular visits to the ball park and grocery stores, combined with their regular attendance at church and Sunday school every week, the five Mexican families had become a welcome and positive force in the community.

Foss Man brought the bases, bats, and balls from home and helped organize Sunday afternoon softball games for his new friends in the familiar pasture that had been sitting idle since his family moved to the other end of town. He was impressed when he saw the way Pedro was throwing and hitting the softball. He asked him if he might be interested in serving as the batboy for the game that night.

Pedro was excited about the idea, and before long, he was not only serving as the batboy but taking batting practice along with the rest of the team. Impressed with the way Pedro was crushing the ball, the team manager told him to keep working on it over the winter months and next year it was very possible he'd be suiting up and playing with the Jefferson Panthers. Pedro promised to practice every day when he returned to Texas that winter and could only dream and hope to be back and actually become teammates with all these great guys. Rosita sat there every game and proudly watched her brother diligently fulfilling his bat boy duties and freely cheered out loud every time Foss Man came up to bat. Decked out in that brilliant sparkling uniform, Foss Man was trying hard not to get caught looking over at her.

The migrant workers thoroughly enjoyed the good times singing around the fire at night, the softball games on Sunday afternoons, the always bountiful meals, and the regular dips in the refreshing cold water in Beaver Creek, but the harsh reality was, the vast majority of their waking hours were spent in the intense humidity and under the scorching hot sun in the insect-infested cabbage fields. The fourteen-hour workdays consisting of the miserable, back-breaking work would have proven unbearable for the vast majority of people in the world. And of course they lived without indoor plumbing. It was far from a glamorous lifestyle, but the truth was, they always thought they had it good and appreciated the comfortable shacks Walter had provided for them. Foss Man continued to be impressed the way they carried on with that seemingly permanent smile on their faces!

A small example of their inherent culture and work ethics was illustrated when Juanita, the striking seventeen-year-old pregnant girl, worked right up to the day before she delivered the baby and promptly returned back to work in less than a week. Walter and Dr. Ellington were long time golf partners, and the week before the baby was due, Walter informed the doctor about the upcoming birth and told his friend that if he would assist in the delivery, he should send him the bill. The migrant workers, of course, had no formal work benefits, but it was the kind of gesture that Walter knew would encourage them to return the following summer. Dr. Ellington was more than happy to help with the delivery and apparently forgot to send Walter the bill.

With the questionable circumstances still swirling around Ellie's untimely death, it was a glaring contrast and heartwarming when Foss Man witnessed firsthand the way the new bouncing baby of the unwed mother brought such great joy to her family, particularly for Juanita's supportive and loving father. Foss Man couldn't help but admire the powerful loyalty and compassion they felt for one another.

As the days and weeks passed throughout the summer months, Foss Man and Rosita were spending more time together and had developed a relaxed and comfortable relationship. He knew he may have been behaving like a naïve fourteen-year-old, but with his respect and fondness for Rosita's parents and after what happened to Ellie, he continued to resist her more mature and aggressive attitude. She accepted that position, and their special friendship proved to be a much needed and appreciated dimension in Foss Man's life as he struggled with his personal loss.

Working long hours and keeping busy with baseball, the weeks were flying by for Foss Man. Before he knew it, the leaves were slowly changing colors and the school year was closing in on them. Once again successfully fulfilling their mission for the summer, by now an expected built-in part of their lives, the migrant workers were emotionally well equipped for their inevitable looming departure. With the same zest and enthusiasm they displayed on their arrival, they spent their final two days packing up their things, diligently preparing for the pending long journey back to Texas. Rosita and Foss Man hated the thought of her leaving town, but the sad day was upon them.

Looking back at the summer, the strong bond Foss Man developed with Rosita and these incredible people helped immensely in dealing with the difficult healing process. Their presence in town was truly a godsend for him personally. Those were his thoughts as he was observing the five overloaded pickup trucks, each with a packed trailer hitched behind, and the five aging cars now lined up and were about to be jammed full with his amazing new friends.

His emotions were escalating as he hugged and said goodbye to the now thirty-one people he no longer felt comfortable calling migrant workers; they were much more than that. After final heartfelt handshakes with Pedro and his father, an affectionate hug from their mother, and a final tender and tearful embrace with Rosita, the caravan was now pulling onto the road, and he could hear several of the kids screaming out, "See you, Boss Man. See you next summer, Boss Man." Even more gut-wrenching, he could see the tears sliding down Rosita's gorgeous cheeks as she looked out the back window and waved goodbye! It was far from a sure thing but a little comforting to him; they had talked in great length the night before about the possibility of her returning the following summer!

Walter's farm land was just a short distance from the apple orchard in Foss Man's former backyard. As his friends departed, he rushed over, and from his lofty perch in the tall oak tree, off in the distance, he could see the long caravan slowly moving down the black top highway south of town. Knowing Rosita was huddled in one of those old beaten-up cars that hopefully would be arriving safely in faraway Texas in a few days, he knew it was highly possible he would never see his special friend again. It was a different kind of heartache this time, but it was another sad day for Foss Man!

Walter had recognized the strong relationship Foss Man had developed with the Mexican families, and he attached great value to it, knowing it would influence their decision to return the following summer. It was a well-understood luxury to rehire a workforce that had proven to be reliable, responsible, and productive, all at the same time. As the years passed, maintaining a good workforce had become a very competitive issue with other vegetable farmers in northern Iowa. Walter was extremely pleased with Foss Man's contributions that summer and had every intention of giving him a healthy raise and the same responsibilities next year.

Chapter Thirty-Four

The football scene would be much different that fall. Skunk quit football when his dad offered to buy him a car if he agreed to stick around the farm to help with the fall harvest. Skeeter, who was living back home now, had become his dad's right-hand man in managing the theater and preferred making money to playing football. He bought his own car the very day he turned sixteen. Both weighing in at about 140 pounds and hovering around 5'5" tall, the fact was, baseball was a much better fit than football anyway. Big Jake, 6'5" tall by now, gave up football to focus on his promising basketball career and maintaining his number one academic class rank. That left only Horse, Rocket, and Foss Man from the gang who had played sports together throughout the previous year. The three of them reported promptly at nine o'clock on Monday morning and enjoyed picking out the better football gear, a privilege that went along with their new lofty sophomore status? All six of them still agreed to meet in Foster's shed at three o'clock that afternoon for the annual fall meeting.

Parking his new car on the street in front of Foster's house, Skunk was the first to show up. It was a beastly hot and humid August day, and Foss Man quickly opened the window above the old couch along the north wall of the shed. Before the other guys showed up, Foss Man and Skunk got into a serious personal conversation the two of them could comfortably and freely talk about exclusively with each other. The subject revolved around the major struggle they were both dealing with. They were still trying desperately to forgive their dads.

Foss Man started out, "Ya know, Skunk, my dad has really changed since he kept his promise to quit drinking. It's been several years now, and boy, I'm telling you, he's been a great dad since that night he hit my mother. But I have to admit, I can't get what happened out of my mind, and I'm still having trouble completely forgiving him."

Skunk responded, "My dad has been meeting with Reverend Thompson every Wednesday night all summer, and I understand they sit and talk about how he reacted to Ellie's pregnancy. Another good thing was, he didn't quit completely but he has cut way back on drinking beer. I know it was hard for him, but in his own way, he's tried to apologize to us and has asked Stub, Mom, and me to forgive him. But I agree with you, it's going to be really hard for me to forgive and forget."

Foss Man reminded Skunk, "My friend Mr. Slim has preached over and over about forgiving people who apologize and are willing to accept responsibility for their mistakes. It's probably going to take some time, but someday I hope we'll be able to forgive them."

Skunk agreed, "Yeah, I hope so too. I promise you, I'm sure going to try."

Big Jake parked his bike in the driveway. He and Foss Man were the only two members of the gang who still didn't own their own car. Ducking his head as he came through the door, Big Jake came in and plopped down on the couch beside them. A couple of minutes later, Rocket, Horse, and Skeeter came barging through the door.

Earlier that day, following the kick-off meeting with Coach Sanders, with the new playbooks tucked under their arms, Rocket and Horse jumped in Rocket's new Ford convertible, the dream car he had driven off the showroom floor over in Boulder just last week. They were going to make a stop at Sally's Drive-In for a malt and a quick fix of the shapely Becker twins. The popular hangout was jammed with football prospects who were undeniably competing for even brief attention from Mary Jane and Myrna Becker.

Mary Jane came over to the convertible and greeted the two good-looking over-six-foot-tall physical specimens in her sassy and flirting style, "Well, look who we have here—two of the big hotshot sophomore jocks. Wow, nice car, Rocket!" More than used to this kind of attention from girls by now, Rocket modestly thanked her, and they ordered their malts.

A confident and aggressive senior, Mary Jane brought out their orders a few minutes later and, with a flirting tone, suggested, "Hey, Rocket, I get off work at five o'clock. I would sure enjoy a ride home in that big fancy car of yours!"

Not exactly sure what his plans were, Rocket politely said, "I can't make any promises, Mary Jane. I've got a lot going on today."

With everyone jammed in the shed, jabbering and clowning around, finally getting down to business, Rocket asked, "Ya know, Foss Man, you've been my reliable catcher all summer and you've hardly said anything about that amazing Mexican girl who came to all those games this summer. What's her name—Rosita?"

Knowing Rocket was the big ladies' man and could be a wise guy, a little indignantly, Foss Man said, "Yeah, what about her?"

Rocket came back with, "Boy, those are some pretty amazing knockers. What can you tell us about those two beauties, you dirty old man?"

Foss Man came right back with, "Okay, Rocket, I know you're just having a little fun here, but let me make something perfectly clear." Trying to remain calm and keep things lighthearted, he firmly continued, "Rosita is back in Texas and, more than likely, won't ever make it back to Iowa again. She's a great kid, Rocket, and trust me, I don't know any more about those knockers than you do!"

Rocket's comments were totally fair game for shed conversation, but he quickly backed off. "Easy, my man, don't get all bent out of shape. All I'm trying to say is that she sure is a beauty!"

Skeeter knew Foss Man was a little touchy when it came to talking about Rosita and tactfully changed the subject. "Speaking of knockers, did you guys hear about Ms. Swartz marrying Tom Fulton this summer?" Tom was the wealthy banker's son, clearly the most eligible bachelor in town. The story was that with her no longer having to work and a desire to start a family, the sexy choir director had resigned from teaching after one short year on the job.

As one of the top performers in the choir, Big Jake had heard all about it and expressed his disappointment. "Yeah, I'm afraid that's all true. I understand they hired some guy, an old fart from a small school down in southern Iowa. Not good news as far as I'm concerned!"

Surprised to hear the report, Foss Man reacted, "Well, I guess that makes my decision a lot easier. I think I'll be saving my beautiful new baritone voice for singing around the bonfire. But I agree, I'm sure going to miss seeing Ms. Swartz bouncing around up there!"

Big Jake mildly objected, "Keep an open mind, Foss Man, who's going to drag my butt off the stage if I pass out again during the Christmas program this winter?"

They were surprised when there was a knock on the door. Foss Man's pregnant mother got home from work early that day and, seeing all the cars, knew there was a big meeting going on in the shed. She had great appreciation for Foss Man's loyal friends and decided to treat them to a plate full of her popular chocolate-chip cookies. In turn, the boys always thought she was the coolest mom in town, and Foss Man beamed with pride as she squeezed into the crowded premises.

Volunteering as the spokesman, Big Jake graciously took the heaping plate of cookies from her and said, "Wow, thanks, Mrs. Foster, you're the best. I'll make sure we split these up evenly. Looks like about three a piece, you bunch of animals." Noticing her glaring pregnant condition, Big Jake politely asked her, "When's Foss Man's new little brother or sister going to enter the big world?"

"The baby's due in about three months, sometime in November. Actually, it could be pretty close to Foss Man's birthday on the fourteenth. Well, enjoy the cookies, boys. I'd better let you get back to your business." With that, Foss Man's mother excused herself.

Horse, the newest and shyest member of the gang, made the observation: "Boy, your mom's amazing, Foss Man. She doesn't look a heck of a lot older than your sister Catherine!"

Skeeter, who of course never had a mother at home and until this year had almost lived with the Fosters, agreed, "You got that right, Horse. She's got to be the coolest mom in the whole world." Turning to Foss Man, he proudly proclaimed, "She's sort of my mom too, isn't she, Foss Man?"

More like a brother than a friend, Foss Man reluctantly agreed, "Even though you've been kind of a wise ass lately, yes, I suppose you can still consider her your mom!"

Switching gears to a totally unrelated question, Foss Man was serious when he asked, "You know, those stupid jockstraps are making more sense every day, but I have to ask you guys, how much trouble do you have with jock itch? Boy, I'm telling you, I've had a heck of a time with it this summer!"

They all had to laugh. They had to be thinking, *What is it with this guy and his ridiculous jockstrap questions?* Not really happy about their reaction, Foss Man insisted, "No, darn it, I'm serious. Don't any of you jerks have a problem with your crotch itching during the hot summer months?"

Skeeter, the self-appointed expert in the crotch department with his infamous "Peter Manual," with his quick wit and crude sense of humor, quickly pointed out, "Boy, you are a damn rookie, Foss Man! Of course we have jock itch just like you do, but it's not something you necessarily want to get rid of. Just scratch it and enjoy it, for God's sake. I promise you, give it a chance. In time, you'll learn to appreciate it!"

When Skeeter's questionable theory appeared to get full support from the rest of the guys, laughing too but sympathetically thinking he better come to Foss Man's rescue, Big Jake slipped in, "Incidentally, they do have powder for that stuff at Dreyer Drug Store—*numb nuts*!"

Surrendering, all Foss Man could come back with was, "My nuts aren't numb, they just itch. But thanks, Big Jake, and as far as the rest of you boneheads are concerned, I hope your nuts rot and fall off!"

Skeeter, particularly wound up and loaded with advice, started up again, "I got something else I want to warn you guys about. And Horse, with your considerable healthy instrument, this is more important for you. I bought my new pair of jeans for the school year last week, and I assume most of you will be doing the same sometime this week. I don't want you to make the mistake I did. I recklessly bought a pair with a stupid zipper instead of buttons, and

I already did some serious damage to old One Eye. I'm serious—if you're smart, you'll stick with the good old-fashioned buttons!"

A good sport but not overly impressed with the conversation to this point, Horse felt obliged to point out to Big Jake, "So this is where you've been getting all your smarts. Now that I'm officially part of the gang, maybe there's hope for me too!" Horse was a big, strong farm kid. Skeeter always insisted he had to have muscle in his shit. He knew why they all called him Horse and was okay with it as long as the teachers didn't call him that. He really didn't care much about the social scene around school and much preferred quietly going hunting for squirrels or perhaps shooting himself a big buck deer. Horse was a likeable guy and proved to be a great addition to the gang.

After the normal bull session about the highly anticipated crop of new freshmen girls, sharing their enthusiasm about being proud car owners and touching briefly on the forecast for next year's sport's scene, Rocket said, "You know what, after all that discussion about knockers, I really hate to eat the cookies and run, but I think I'll swing by and give Mary Jane a ride home. I don't get that kind of invitation from a senior girl very often! You know it's been a little crazy this last week, but that convertible seems to have a strange effect on girls!"

Skeeter had to respond, "Boy, that's a real shocker!" They all accepted it by now—Rocket simply lived a charmed life!

Wrapping things up, Horse offered, "Hey, if any of you guys want to go hunting tonight, let me know. There's still at least a couple hours of daylight after supper, and I promise you, we'll be able shoot a couple of squirrels."

Always up for new adventures, Skunk, who was still uncharacteristically quiet and subdued, and Foss Man agreed simultaneously, "You know what, that sounds interesting. What time do you want us out there?" With that, the meeting was adjourned.

It had been a pretty rough summer for Foss Man, but he had a good attitude and fresh outlook for a promising sophomore year in high school. Little did he know what the next year had to offer.

Chapter Thirty-Five

Coach Sanders had to pull Foss Man and his brother Allen apart at least once a week after he blew the whistle designed to conclude the live blocking or tackling drill. The coach credited their fierce battles and competitive attitude with setting the tone for what turned out to be the most successful football season in many years.

Horse and Foss Man served as the two inside middle linebackers for the varsity defense that fall. Thanks to Rocket's powerful throwing arm, the Panthers had a couple big unexpected wins, which resulted in a respectable 5 win, 4 loss record. Rocket connected with Allen for a bunch of touchdown passes, and impressive for only a junior, Foss Man's brother earned first team all-conference honors as a wide receiver. Horse also played tight end on offense and made headlines when he made a one-handed catch delivered perfectly by Rocket and streaked down the sideline eighty yards for the touchdown that ended Red Oak's record forty-five-game winning streak. A powerful inspiration to everyone, Skunk's brother Stub had an amazing season as the featured running back and a record that would stand forever, becoming the first all-conference player with "one" hand. Foss Man, who lead the team in tackles, Horse, and Rocket, all sophomores, were named to the all-conference second team.

A crazy thing happened during the football season that year. Similar to the Boy Scout experiment years ago, after getting arrested for shoplifting and repeatedly suspected for window peeking that summer, concerned community leaders and the school administration continued their desperate search for ways of involving Eclipse in school activities with dwindling hopes of changing his persistent disturbing behavior. Now a junior and strong as a bull, at 6'3" inches tall and weighing in at about 225 pounds, overlooking the fact that he had very little athletic ability and no genuine interest in football, playing football may have seemed like a logical consideration. Detached, indifferent, and strangely disinterested, having little choice in the matter if they wanted their son to remain in school, his parents reluctantly went along with the idea. Contrary to the better judgment of Coach Sanders, who was forced to surrender to administrative pressure, and against the wishes of the players, Ron Ferguson checked out gear and, hard to believe, was now a member of the Panther varsity football team. Foss Man was repulsed with the idea of having his longtime tormentor on the team but loved football and could only hope the whole thing failed quickly and he'd be dropped from the team.

In the beginning, it drove the coaches crazy when Eclipse absolutely refused to do anything he didn't feel like doing during practice. When they tried to teach him to bend over and get into the fundamental three-point stance, he insisted the idea was "gay," and furthermore, "Get used to the idea, I'll be standing up when I play football!" He persistently refused to do the wind sprints or any of the other grueling conditioning drills.

The players hated having Eclipse on the team, but they understood why he was out there; it kept him off the streets, making it safer and more peaceful for all the other citizens in the community. Coach Sanders pleaded with the players to be patient and, doing his best to go along with the hopeless experiment, was clinging to the remote chance he might at some point be able to contribute in some positive way during a game. After all, he was the biggest, strongest, and meanest kid in Wright County.

Falling well behind in the season opener, with the game out of reach, Coach boldly decided to take a chance and put Eclipse in the game in the middle of the third quarter. Not remotely capable or willing to learn the offensive plays, the only feasible option for Eclipse was to be assigned to play defensive nose tackle. Foss Man was the inside middle linebacker and, playing right next to him, had the pleasure of directly witnessing the whole wild episode firsthand.

Instead of getting down in the normal recommended three-point stance, Eclipse stood straight up, directly over the football. When the offensive center snapped the ball and came after him attempting to block him, Eclipse hollered at him, "Well, you son of a bitch," and with a wild swing, he violently punched him on the back of his helmet. The referee threw the flag, and the team was penalized fifteen yards for unnecessary roughness. Foss Man heard Eclipse mumble something like, "Hey you, big dick head, what's up with that bullshit?" The referee didn't hear him. On the very next play, this time, two offensive linemen came after him, and again he screamed, "Well, you dirty sons a bitches!" and he proceeded to pound on both of them with wild haymakers. About half of the opposing team pounced on him, attempting to rescue their teammates. No one came to Eclipse's defense, and as should have been expected, he reacted like a crazed wild man. Both head coaches came running out on the field, and before Coach Sanders could take him out of the game, after throwing another flag and assessing another fifteen-yard penalty, the referee promptly kicked Eclipse out of the game. When Eclipse approached the sidelines, he put his hands in the air and complained, "What the hell's going on out there anyway? Two of those assholes came right after me, for Christ's sake!" Eclipse just didn't get it! He honestly thought he had done what anybody would have under the circumstances.

The players on both teams were shaking their heads and couldn't help but laugh out loud about what had just taken place. They had never seen anything quite like it on the football field.

That was the end of Eclipse's football career: two plays, two penalty flags, and a negative thirty yards for the Panthers!

Everyone on the team was relieved when Coach Sanders had a meeting with the administration and they agreed he had no choice but to kick Eclipse off the team. Needless to say, the little experiment was not a great success. It went down as an honest effort to at least try to do something about the obviously severely troubled teenager.

The homecoming dance would prove to be much different this year. First and foremost, there would be no special Queen Ellie present for Foss Man to dance with. But there was a happy development when Catherine was selected by the student body to reign as the homecoming queen. While Foss Man didn't exactly appreciate his parents giving her all that boundless authority, and always fearing her never-yielding firm hand, he was extremely proud of his sister.

Skunk pulled up in front of Foss Man's house and honked the horn of his new car as they headed for the dance. Fortunately, Skunk's car had an automatic transmission. With his short stature, he had to tuck his left leg under his rear end so he could see over the steering wheel and dashboard. It was a comical sight, but Skunk had it down to a science.

On the way to the dance, they reminisced about their first encounter ten years ago when Skunk had graciously invited Foss Man to sit down by him on the school bus that first day of school. Then their many rides on Thunder flying by a disgruntled Rusty on their way to Sunday school. And now their first ride in Skunk's new car on their way to the homecoming dance. They'd been through a lot together, and their friendship had never wavered.

When it came to the high school dances, the dynamics for most of the gang had changed as well. Big Jake, the first kid in town to receive the coveted Eagle Scout Award the previous summer, still found dances to be a distraction for his preoccupation with academics and would have much preferred spending the night in the science lab if he could have arranged it. Horse skipped the dance. He was more concerned about a big raccoon that had been killing his chickens, and he was determined to shoot it that night.

That left Skunk, Skeeter, Rocket, and Foss Man with free reign at the big dance. Skunk and Skeeter no longer wasted time standing along the gym wall waiting for something to happen. With their new confidence and same old devilish spirit, they were now promoting their own cause and boldly going up to and asking the junior and senior girls to dance.

They agreed the Becker twins would be their first prospects. Skeeter sighted them first. He bravely said, "There they are, Skunk, let's go to work." Without hesitation, they walked directly across the dance floor, and within a minute, they were each clinging to one of the amazing Becker girls. It was really that simple, and they were now magically resting their faces squarely between the generous breasts of Mary Jane and Myrna Becker. One slow dance would end, and according to their carefully thought-out plan, they'd smoothly switch partners. At the happy conclusion, along with the inevitable perpetual erections, which didn't seem to bother their dance partners in the least, they couldn't get the smile off their faces. Foss Man thought it was great to see Skunk becoming his old fun-loving self again.

Enjoying his popularity with the girls, Rocket was always in demand for the next dance. Foss Man felt totally lost and was depressed when he thought about those amazing dances last year with Ellie. The high school dances would always be about dancing with Ellie, and being there brought back nothing but hurtful memories. On top of that, he had trouble getting Rosita off his mind, and as it turned out, it would be quite a while before Foss Man had any serious interest in other girls. He told Skunk he was heading home and left the dance after about an hour of standing along the wall of the gymnasium.

Coach Sanders took the football team on the bus to attend an Iowa State Cyclone football game the first Saturday after the season ended. Aunt Francis was driving the bus, but this time, the coach didn't have to remind her to open the window to provide the much-needed escape for the steady cloud of smoke from the always-present Camel hanging from her lips. It was a perfect sunny fall day. The trip was a new experience for most of the team, and after listening to all those Iowa Hawkeye games on the radio in the shed all those Saturday afternoons with his dad, Foss Man was excited about attending a college football game for the first time.

Sitting together but with plenty of time to kill before the game, Coach Sanders suggested the guys should feel free to roam around the huge stadium and take in the sights. For Rocket, Horse, and Foss Man, the sights meant heading straight down for a closer look at the cheerleaders.

It only took minutes to track down the home team cheerleaders. Horse wouldn't say much, but Rocket boldly hollered something suave like, "Hey, cheerleaders, come over here and talk to us!" He wondered, *Why didn't that work?* After a persistent effort, at the very most, the preoccupied cheerleaders may have managed a brief wave or two in their direction but evidently were too busy to join them for even a few minutes. For three second team all Corn Bowl Conference football stars like them, they were curious. *Exactly what was that all about?*

As they continued milling around, Foss Man noticed the choir group standing in the end zone, getting ready to go on the field to sing the National Anthem. Still licking their wounds after the rejection by the stuck-up cheerleaders, the three of them were standing close to the choir with only a five-foot-tall wire fence surrounding the field separating them. Foss Man noticed there was a small gate right next to where the choir had gathered. Without any discussion, as the choir was taking the field, Foss Man opened the gate and, catching Horse and Rocket by surprise, quickly joined them in stride as they were making their way out to the fifty-yard line.

There were about twenty-five singers in the choir, and Foss Man casually took his place in the back row. While a few of the choir members were giving him a funny look, it didn't appear the director even noticed him. Seconds after reaching the middle of the field, they proceeded to sing the Anthem. Foss Man sang quietly with his proud new baritone voice but was getting nervous thinking about how his cute little stunt was going to end.

Honoring America seemed to go on forever that day, but when they finally wrapped it up, the choir and Foss Man marched off the field together. As soon as they got back to the end zone, with the choir director now well aware of his presence and aggressively walking directly toward him, dispelling the notion that white guys can't jump, highly motivated, Foss Man cleared the five-foot fence with room to spare and took off running in search of his buddies.

When he finally tracked them down, they were shaking their heads in total disbelief. Knowing he was a little crazy at times, they honestly thought he had lost his mind. Foss Man admitted it was a little nerve-wracking in the beginning but maintained, "You know what, guys, the experience of looking up at that big crowd from the middle of the football field just might serve me well some day!"

Chapter Thirty-Six

Foss Man found a new job that fall working at Schuster's, the busy and prosperous grocery store on main street. The alarm went off at 6:30 a.m., and he reported for work before school every day at 7:00 a.m. sharp. His primary responsibilities were filling the dairy cooler with milk, orange juice, cottage cheese, and eggs and then switched gears keeping the fresh fruit and vegetable displays filled up and looking good for the day. After all those long hours in the hot, blazing sun all summer, he loved working indoors. With his outgoing personality and bubbly disposition, his boss, Vaughn Schuster, recognized what a perfect fit Foss Man was for not only efficiently getting the work done, but more importantly, interacting with his valued customers with such great ease. Vaughn had a great sense of humor and, much like Foss Man, was a total free spirit. The two hit it off immediately and developed a great friendship.

There was another significant development on the job front. Catherine finally landed her first job outside the house. Other than her weekend babysitting revenue, this was her first opportunity to generate her own personal income. And it wasn't just any job, but her perfect dream job. She would now be working six hours on Saturdays for Dr. Dockstader, the local veterinarian. Thinking she was the luckiest kid in town, Catherine would be directly involved on a regular basis with her first love and true passion, working and caring for pets of every size and shape. And she would be getting paid for it!

As the Saturdays rolled along, her new boss was so impressed with the genuine love and tender care Catherine displayed toward all the animals he asked her if she ever thought about becoming a veterinarian. The idea struck an immediate nerve with Catherine, and as they continued having discussions over the winter months, the concept became more and more serious.

Their working relationship was progressing nicely, and Dr. Dockstader came up with a pretty amazing plan. He wanted Catherine to enroll in veterinarian school at Iowa State University. He would take care of the tuition and all the other college expenses if she agreed to return and go to work for him after she graduated. He had expanded his business over the years and was spending more time dealing with new adventures, like his lucrative artificial insemination business. Looking into the future, he knew he would need help dealing with the "pet" end of the business.

As it turned out, Catherine applied to Iowa State University, and with her virtually straight-A transcript and impressive extracurricular resume, she had no problem getting accepted. When she officially got the good news, she had to be the happiest girl in town. Needless to say, the whole family was extremely proud of her. The fact was, by now, anything Catherine Foster accomplished would not surprise anyone!

Allen was working at Rosie's Standard Gas Station on Saturdays. He was a natural mechanic and loved working on cars. His future had already been determined; he was going to enlist in the United States Air Force the day he graduated from high school. A huge breakthrough, Allen bought a big old black Buick from his boss Rosie when he turned sixteen that fall. The car, of course, meant spending more time with Rhonda, his by-now longtime steady girlfriend.

The gang held another one of their seasonal meetings in the shed the weekend before the first basketball practice. They replayed some of the football season highlights, and after the expected scrutiny of the new crop of healthy freshmen girls and agreeing the boring choir director guy they hired to replace Ms. Schwarz was a serious setback, the conversation switched to basketball. Big Jake, now a towering 6'5" giant, was expected to be a star this year, and Horse, Rocket, and Foss Man would be battling it out to get some playing time on the varsity team. After the normal heavy dose of bantering, badgering, and laughter, agreeing their sophomore year was humming along pretty smoothly, they adjourned the meeting.

Foss Man didn't make the starting lineup for the varsity, but he was one of the first guys off the bench when one of the regulars needed a breather. About the third game into the season, coincidentally on his fifteenth birthday, November 14, they were having a real barn burner against their always big rival Riceville. With about five minutes left in the game, Big Jake, who was off to a great start, averaging over twenty points the first two games, fouled out of the game. Losing Big Jake was a major setback!

Coach Sanders hollered, "Foss Man, get in there!" Sitting next to his buddy Horse, Foss Man said something cocky like, "Pay close attention, my good buddy, it won't take long, I'll get this game back under control for the Panthers!" He tore off his warm-up jacket and hustled over to the scorer's table.

A few seconds after the Riceville guy missed the second free throw, the Panthers got the rebound, and after fast breaking to their end of the floor, there was a loose ball, a wild scramble, and a jump ball. The ball was tipped to Foss Man, and he took off like a streak to the other end and laid it up for an uncontested basket. He had only been in the game about ten seconds and had already scored two points in the tight, important conference game. The jampacked crowd went crazy, and confident he had lived up to his bold promise to Horse, Foss Man strutted proudly back to the other end of the court.

Suddenly, for some unknown reason, Coach Sanders was waving his arms wildly and calling for a time-out. When the team was approaching the bench to huddle up, Foss Man noticed a strange look on the coaches' face, and his teammates were not excited or patting him on the back like he felt he so richly deserved. He had made a basket, but unfortunately, it was on the Riceville end of the gym. It was the Riceville fans who were screaming and going nuts.

Upon learning this, Foss Man was rattled, to say the least, and Coach had no choice but to immediately take him out of the game. Brother Allen, who had played the entire game and was busting his rear end to secure the victory, demonstrating a little typical brotherly love as Foss Man headed back to the bench, mumbled something that Foss Man thought sounded like, "Nice job, dip shit!" He quickly took his place next to his buddy Horse, where he had been sitting no more than a minute earlier. Ten seconds in the game and he had made two points for Riceville. Horse, by now his good hunting buddy, didn't say anything. He just looked down at the floor and shook his head back and forth with a sympathetic look on his face, not believing what he had just witnessed. Foss Man knew he had to be thinking, "Nice job of getting the game quickly under control for the Panthers, you dumb ass!"

The Panthers lost the critical conference game to their big rival, 54 to 52. Even his loving Aunt Francis, who of course was driving the bus, was shaking her head, and he thought he could detect her rolling her eyes through the cloud of smoke from the burning Camel as he stumbled his way up the steps getting on the bus for the long ride back to Jefferson.

He wasn't feeling much love that night, and as it turned out, it wasn't the happiest of birthdays. Speaking of that, he was happy to finally turn fifteen, but it signaled it was still another long year before he could get his license to drive. He and Big Jake were still the only members of the gang who depended on their bikes as their primary mode of transportation. That was okay—Foss Man's $4 bike was holding up just fine.

After making two points for Riceville, Foss Man was depressed for a few days, but the perfect truth was, after some of the much bigger setbacks in his life and remembering the lectures from Mr. Slim and Nute about the advantages of being upbeat and positive, he was learning to keep things in perspective and managed to get over it with relative ease. His wise and supportive coach reminded him, "When the going gets tough, the tough get going!"

As the season progressed, Foss Man recovered from the setback, got more playing time, and managed to score his share of points for the home team. Along with earning a varsity letter, unwanted sources informed him that he also made the Riceville yearbook, where he was listed as the thirteenth leading scorer for the Riceville Wildcats that year. His response was, "Real funny!"

Chapter Thirty-Seven

Foss Man was sitting in world history class when someone knocked on the door. Mrs. Patterson went to the door and, with a startled look on her face, said, "Foss Man, it's for you."

It was Aunt Francis, his mother's tough, no-nonsense older sister standing in the hallway, and alarming to Foss Man, she was crying. She was obviously badly shaken about something and trying to keep her composure and wanting to wait for a better setting to give him the bad news, she told him to grab his books and come with her. Catherine and Allen were already on their way to their lockers, and the three confused kids exited the school and jumped in Aunt Francis's car.

On the way home, struggling to find the right words, Aunt Francis managed to inform them, "Your mother delivered your baby brother this afternoon, but I'm sorry, kids, there were some complications and the little guy didn't make it." Not letting on about her greater concern, their mother's critical condition, hesitating and still sobbing, she continued, "As of right now, your mother is doing okay."

Everyone gathered at home that night, all totally confused about what took place earlier that day. Their mother was in the hospital, and all Foss Man could think about was, what exactly did Aunt Francis mean by "As of now, your mother is doing okay"? He had never spent so much as one night without his mother at home. It was a lonely and strange feeling, and he hated it!

While losing their new baby brother was terribly sad news for the kids, their concern continued to grow when their mother remained in the hospital. Their shaken father tried to explain the best way he could about what happened to the baby. "This is hard to put in words, kids, but your little brother was what they call stillborn. I'm sorry, kids, it just happens sometimes."

Not having a legitimate answer when it came to their mother's condition, he deliberately left that out of the current discussion. The truth was, he was frightened out of his mind, and as incomprehensible as it was, her chances of surviving was in serious doubt.

Complications related to the umbilical cord strangulation of their infant child caused severe hemorrhaging, and they could not stop the bleeding. Their mother was receiving constant transfusions, and they were struggling mightily to keep her alive. Nothing was working, and a shortage of her blood type was a fast-growing concern. Her life was clearly hanging by a thread!

An emergency announcement was made over local radio and television stations appealing to the public for the desperate need of blood donations, identifying the specific blood type needed. When the word spread whose life it was that was in danger, the response was overwhelming. Virtually every adult citizen could remember the sweet and warm greeting they heard over and over, "Number please," when Foss Man's mother served as the local telephone operator years ago. Then the genuine admiration for her humble and determined effort in selling magazines to the vast majority of the citizens in Wright County. And almost everyone at one time or other had enjoyed her amazing singing voice going back to her solo performances in the high school musicals and, more recently, church services, weddings, or funerals. But more than anything, it was the respect they had for her strength and fortitude in overcoming the frequent challenges thrown at her and her large demanding family. She may not survive, but it would not be due to a shortage of her blood type!

As the days passed and their mother remained in the hospital, not knowing exactly what was going on but well aware of the fact it was something extremely serious, the kids were growing more and more concerned and were scared to death. Like all the kids, Foss Man was absolutely ravaged with fear. He had been learning to deal with setbacks throughout his lifetime and, as a result, was getting stronger every year, but this was threatening to be more than he could handle. He and the entire family were facing a loss with the potential of delivering a blow they might very well never recover from!

Some of the emotional setbacks in Foss Man's life were improved by spending time with his buddies Mr. Slim and Nute in the bait shop. Some were remedied by talking them over with his buddies in the shed. Some dictated a climb to his personal sanctuary in the tall oak tree. But this one clearly required help from Reverend Thompson and the Good Lord. Foss Man went to the church almost every day when his mother was in the hospital, and while kneeling in the first pew in front of the church, he begged and pleaded with God to please let his mother survive this terrible thing that was threatening to take her life. He promised God over and over to be a better person in the future if he would just grant him this one wish. Unknown to Foss Man, Reverend Thompson was touched as he quietly witnessed these heartfelt prayer sessions looking on from the vestibule in the back of the church. The preacher had witnessed Foss Man's dad doing the same thing on a daily basis.

Now desperate, after intense consultation and much deliberation, the team of doctors decided the only way they could stop the bleeding was by performing a hysterectomy! While it was an extremely risky operation under the circumstances, it was an easy decision for William if it was truly the only option to give her even the remote chance of living.

Following the surgery and around-the-clock vigilance by the best medical team in the area, combined with endless prayers from friends and family, sadly, things were not improving. They identified the ultimate problem as acute circulatory failure. Her heart and vascular system, for some unknown reason wasn't pushing blood through her body in normal fashion. Elizabeth's heart was simply no longer capable of carrying the load.

The famous Mayo Clinic in Rochester, Minnesota, perhaps the greatest medical facility in the world, was only an hour and a half drive from the Boulder Memorial Hospital. Although extremely concerned about her ability to survive the trip, transporting the deathly sick woman to Rochester was the only remaining option. With the ambulance's siren screaming and their desperate, heartbroken father at her side holding her hand, the emergency trip was now underway.

William was stunned by the now very real possibility that he was going to lose the human being he loved more than life itself. During his prayers and repeated trips to the church, he pleaded and begged the Good Lord to spare his beloved wife. How on earth were he and, more importantly, the kids going to survive without this incredible woman? Shocking him into an unprecedented level of awareness and responsibility, he now fully understood how critical it was for him to step up to the plate and, like never before, be strong for their eight surviving children.

After thorough evaluation of her condition by several of the best heart specialists at Mayo Clinic, they all agreed there was nothing more they could do to save her. She remained in a deep coma and was now literally hanging on by a thread. It was heavily debated if the kids should come and see her for what would be the last time.

Reverend Thompson was in the room and prepared to read her final rights. Also in the room were her loving husband and her three siblings, Aunt Francis, Uncle Stan, and Aunt Silvia, who had immediately flown in from Washington, DC, when she learned of her younger sister's critical condition. Waiting in the hallway was the rare gathering consisting of both sets of grandparents. It was extremely tense for all the adults present, but they were prepared to provide the much-needed moral support during the heart-wrenching process the mother and father were about to go through. It was a most difficult decision, but after much thought and discussion, visits by the kids were deemed necessary and appropriate so they could say their final goodbye.

Foss Man and the other kids had not attended school for a number of days. His buddies were worried sick about Foss Man's mother, and when they got the news about her grave condition, they held an emergency meeting around the fire pit out in Skunk's wooded lot. While they were all badly shaken and deeply concerned, well aware of his special relationship with Foss Man's mom, they fully understood why Skeeter was such an absolutely shattered mess. When they heard all the Foster kids were going to Rochester to say their final goodbyes to their mother, Big Jake wondered if there was any chance of Skeeter going along. He talked to Foss Man's dad about it, and without hesitation, the decision was made and Skeeter joined the people who had been like family to him for the past ten years.

Solemn and petrified, each of the deathly frightened kids were escorted into her room, one at a time. The sight of their mother hooked up to the complex network of tubes and multiple IVs, as well as the oxygen mask covering her mouth and nose, was a confusing and horrifying picture for their young minds to grasp.

As the gut-wrenching process inched forward, the last to enter the room, it was finally decided to let Skeeter accompany Foss Man. Skeeter stayed one step behind as the two nervously and cautiously approached the bed where Foss Man's mother lay motionless, totally unconscious. Like all his siblings, Foss Man was virtually numb and, what was probably a good thing, at least to some protective degree, in a state of shock. With tears flooding down his cheeks, with both hands, he held the limp hand of the only human being on earth who had been capable of getting him through those horrible nightmares that had been so persistent throughout his lifetime. Perhaps a small thing but following Mr. Slim's recommendation, he had privately put that special Indian head penny in the palm of his right hand. He had been keeping it in his old beaten-up billfold and only pulled it out at critical moments like this. It may seem trivial, but for whatever reason, it always comforted him and helped make things better. Would this be the first time it failed him? Still gripping her hand and while fighting through chest-heaving sobs, barely legible, Foss Man pleaded, "Mom, please, please don't die! We all need you, Mom! Please, please, Mom, don't die!"

He was alarmed when he thought he felt his mother weakly squeezing his hand in return. Was it his imagination, or was this really happening? He squeezed her hand again but more firmly this time. Suddenly, Foss Man knew it was real. His mother was definitely responding and squeezing his hand in return and with what seemed like a little more strength. There was no doubt in his mind; his instincts told him she was trying desperately to tell him something! What was it she was trying to say? Was it merely her way of saying goodbye to him? He wasn't about to let himself believe that!

He made up his mind right then and there that his mother was not going to die. As always, he knew she was the strongest human being in the world and was going to pull through this horrible ordeal. She had always been there for them, and she had to know there was no way they could survive without her. She was still going to be there for them; there was simply no alternative. Trying desperately to keep it together through all this, Skeeter came closer to her and briefly squeezed her hand, and with tears now streaming down their cheeks, the two grief-stricken boys slowly turned and stumbled their way out of the room.

After all the kids had been in to see their mother for the last time, ravaged and heartbroken, they were quietly and solemnly split into three groups. Uncle Stan, Aunt Francis, and their father were each designated to haul several of them back home. Needless to say, it was a long, sad trip. Foss Man was sobbing uncontrollably but kept repeating over and over to younger sister Glenda, younger brother Gerald, and Skeeter, who were assigned to his car, "Don't worry, Mom is going to get better and will come back home someday!" Glenda and Gerald didn't know what to think, but they were sure hoping and praying big brother Foss Man knew what he was talking about! Skeeter, normally brash and thick-skinned, still crying, was quietly staring out the window, and while he wanted to believe Foss Man, he was busy praying for the same miracle.

The day following the visit from the kids, the doctors were surprised when they noticed Elizabeth had a slightly stronger pulse. They were cautious to read too much into it, and while still filled with great doubt, it was at least a small favorable indicator. They remained vigilant and continued monitoring her with even greater intensity, now with a small a ray of hope.

The fact was, they were surprised she had made it through the night. Then she made it through the next day. Each day she remained alive, they were more confused. Her pulse was getting stronger, and she was slowly becoming more responsive every day. They now had renewed hope that for some unknown miraculous reason—could it be possible?—she might actually pull through this thing. They were reluctant to give the family too much optimism and false hope, but the truth was, they knew there was now a legitimate chance for her survival. They decided to tell her husband, her three siblings, and the grandparents about the new optimistic signs and the now real ray of hope. They were all ecstatic but agreed to be cautious and wait until everything was more stable before they raised the hopes of her eight still horrified and devastated children.

As each miserable long day passed, there was no doubt in Foss Man's mind. They didn't have to tell him; he knew exactly what was going on. His mother was getting better and would be coming home. He kept insisting and promising his brothers and sisters of that fact. They each had a different reaction. While his persistence and optimism actually made them feel a little better, the always stronger Catherine and Allen told him to stop talking about it; they didn't want the younger ones to be more hurt and confused if it didn't turn out that way. All Foss Man kept repeating was, "You wait and see. Mom is coming home. I promise you, Mom is coming home!"

And Foss Man turned out to be right! Their mother was getting stronger every day. There was no plausible medical explanation for her sudden turnaround. Not feeling comfortable in referring to it as a miracle, the doctors credited it to a classic case of a human being's powerful will to live! Elizabeth Foster simply knew she had to pull through to care for the eight amazing and demanding children she brought into the world. After two weeks of persistent care and steady improvement in Mayo Clinic in Rochester, she would be making the triumphant return home to her jubilant family.

During those long days and weeks, with their father spending the majority of his time in the hospital, and only rarely capable of squeezing in a day at work, Catherine had literally taken over running the household, and as everyone grew to expect, she was doing an incredible job. With everything the family was going through, there was a growing special closeness and level of cooperation amongst the kids, even between Foss Man and Allen. Catherine once again demonstrated maturity far beyond her years.

Their mother's homecoming was the happiest day of their young lives. While always confident about her recovery, Foss Man was overwhelmed with relief. His mother was going to live and would always be there for them. The frightened and horrified family knew they had been given a remarkable gift from God. They would never be the same after experiencing the very real threat of losing their mother.

There was another significant life-changing event that took place the day after his mom returned home from the hospital. Foss Man had gone back to the church to thank God for answering his prayers. When he first entered the church, he noticed a man kneeling in the first pew down in the front of the church. His head was down and appeared to be in the middle of intense prayer. As Foss Man walked to the front of the church, he suddenly recognized who the man was. It was his dad. He entered the same pew and went over and kneeled beside him. Without saying a word, his dad reached over and firmly held his hand. Kneeling together in silent prayer, they thanked God for answering their prayers. A few minutes passed, they stood up, and the first time in years, with no conversation, they turned and firmly hugged each other.

Unknown to them, Reverend Thompson had been sitting in the vestibule in the back of the church and witnessed the entire heart-wrenching exchange. He reached over and pulled out the top drawer of his old, badly worn wooden desk. He removed the long white envelope and, while staring at it, held it in his hands for a few minutes. He proceeded to promptly tear it in half. He had a sudden change of heart. The letter to the church deacons giving them his six months' notice of his retirement plans would have to be put on hold. Although he was approaching seventy years old and had been with the same church for over forty years, it was touching moments like this that kept him inspired and motivated in continuing to do his small part in promoting God's work. His recent and frequent thoughts and dreams of that steady diet of fishing up north on the lake in Minnesota was going to have to wait.

Chapter Thirty-Eight

The kids were incredibly relieved and thankful to have their mother home again, but they could easily recognize it would be a long time before she fully recovered and was her vibrant self again. They had been warned about how a mother suffers emotionally after losing a baby. They could see the pain and deep sadness in her eyes. She was noticeably weak and frail. They all agreed to be extra good and were more than willing to pitch in and help out around the house.

With his personal appreciation for the amazing gift of having his mother survive the frightening ordeal, Foss Man made the requisite quick trip down to the old apple orchard and climbed up to his favorite safe haven in the tall oak tree. He said one more heartfelt thank-you to God and then pulled that dependable old Indian Head penny out of his billfold and gave it a kiss. Mr. Slim was right—the special penny was proving to be truly magical! It had never failed him!

The second week in December signaled the time for the popular Christmas concert. Foss Man was sitting in the audience with his parents, cherishing every minute he could spend with his mother more than ever, and they were beaming with pride when Catherine received another standing ovation as she once again stole the show with her annual rendition of "Oh Holy Night." Catherine also teamed up with Big Jake for a duet featuring the stirring harmony of everyone's favorite, "Silent Night." Foss Man was proud of his tall friend, and how about that—it appeared Big Jake was going to remain upright and on his feet for the entire program this year. He once again marveled how composed Catherine handled herself under the glare of the bright lights.

Thanks to his growing friendship with Horse, hunting became another favorite activity during Christmas vacation. Horse and Foss Man had become regular hunting partners and had gone pheasant hunting a number of times that fall. Horse had been hunting since he was eight years old and was an excellent marksman. Working together as a team, they always managed to bag a number of pheasants. Splitting the bounty for the day equally, Foss Man brought the birds home on a regular basis, providing welcome relief to the always-tight food budget.

The proud owner of several shotguns and a new high-powered rifle, Horse no longer had use for his old .22-caliber single-shot rifle. Knowing how badly Foss Man wanted his own gun, and after pleading and finally getting his parent's reluctant approval, Horse generously sold it to Foss Man for the bargain price of $10. With the presence of a dangerous gun in a house full of little ones, Foss Man's parents immediately put strict rules in place. The gun didn't create any problems until two days after Christmas that winter.

With the Troy River frozen over, a bunch of the guys worked diligently removing a foot of snow from a rectangular area, creating the perfect spot for what became all-day hockey games. The self-made hockey rink became a popular hangout over Christmas vacation. With the expected severely cold weather, they'd build big bonfires on the east shoreline and would keep them burning before, during, and after the lengthy hockey games.

Horse, Skunk, and Foss Man had been hunting squirrels and rabbits for a couple hours in the dense woods running along the west shore of the river. Not having much luck that afternoon, they wandered over by the usually crowded ice-skating rink. It was getting close to supper hour, and most of the skaters had thinned out and gone home. Before the three worn-out hunters called it a day, and having few opportunities to shoot their guns at live prospects, they decided to create their own self-made targets to polish their skills.

Standing on the frozen river between the hockey rink and the nearby gravel road, they each took their turn throwing chunks of ice in the air and the other two guys would fire away. Horse and Skunk, who were more experienced hunters and good shots with their big shotguns, were having success and were blasting the ice chunks in small pieces with almost every shot. Doing the best he could with his new high-powered single-shot rifle, Foss Man was having a heck of a time hitting anything. Frustrated and determined, he kept reloading and firing away.

After a half hour of target practice and about ready to head home, they took a short break and were sitting around the still smoldering fire pit warming up their hands. Officer Al, the Jefferson town cop, pulled up in his marked car and parked a short distance behind them on the gravel road that ran parallel to the river. Al was a sixty-year-old gentleman and had the distinction of serving as the lone town cop for over twenty years. Dressed in full uniform, Officer Al was aggressively walking toward them with a serious look on his face.

Validating the private citizen's alarming inquiry, the cop had also personally heard the multiple gun shots a little earlier. Skipping any warm greeting, Al got right down to business. "Okay, boys, I've got an important question: What kind of guns do you have there?"

Not really concerned at that point, they showed him their guns. Seemingly satisfied, Officer Al said, "Okay, that's what I was afraid of. You guys are going to have to come with me!" Confused and nervous by now, Skunk and Foss Man were ordered to get in the police car, and with permission from the officer, Horse followed closely behind in his car that he had parked on the roadside earlier. They proceeded to make the short trip back to Jefferson.

They pulled up and parked in front of a house owned by a guy named Bart Gunderson. Bart was a giant of a man and, perhaps with the exception of Herb, the crabby owner of the popular goat herd, he was clearly the orneriest and meanest bastard in town. Fittingly, Bart was the renowned town butcher and longtime owner of the local meat locker. After determined inquires and steady prodding on the way to town, the cop refused to give Skunk or Foss Man so much as a small clue in suggesting what this was all about. All he said before going up to the door was, "Bart called me, was very angry, and when you see him, I'm sure you'll understand why!"

More than a little shook up by now, the three hunting buddies walked nervously up to the house and the vigilant cop knocked on the door. Bart immediately jerked the door open, and after one brief look at the huge man, Foss Man's nuts shot straight north. That's just what they did. The other two guys looked like they were now officially shitting their pants. Not yet knowing exactly what happened, they could see this very angry man, actually more like a wounded grizzly bear, was standing there with a still festering deep red mark burned across his forehead.

Bart owned a pig lot and shed down by the river, just a short distance from where they had been target practicing. He was innocently feeding his pigs when a bullet whistled by his head. Severely shaken and very pissed off, he immediately tracked down Officer Al, who was parked in his regular spot in front of the fire station on Main Street, and registered his concern.

It was easy to conclude that the person who pulled the trigger of the .22-caliber rifle was the one who shot the potentially deadly bullet. The shotgun shell pellets could not have traveled far enough to have done the obvious damage to the butcher's forehead. The bullet had come so close it burned an ugly three-inch wound across Bart's forehead. Skunk and Horse, who were personally relieved, while trying to console Foss Man but in typical high school fashion, were indignantly shaking their heads sending the subtle message, "Boy, Foss Man, how could you be so damn stupid?" Foss Man thought to himself, *Yeah right. Thanks a heck of a lot, you assholes!*

Frightened and feeling terrible about what was now clearly his personal responsibility, Foss Man could do nothing but stand there staring at the floor. With his mind whirling, knowing very well how ornery and mean this guy was, he couldn't help but visualize Bart the Butcher taking a meat cleaver in the powerful hand on the end of his muscular right arm and chopping off his much improved and highly valued organ with one mighty whack!

But it was no time to be funny! Foss Man knew what happened was deadly serious. He fully understood. *Good grief, I came close to actually killing a human being!* He knew it was an accident, but it was now perfectly clear. *I've simply got to get my act together!*

Bart, while perhaps still in his own state of shock, was nicer about the whole episode than anyone could have expected. While clearly not a happy man, perhaps recognizing how bad Foss Man felt about his mistake, generously indicated he had no intentions of bringing any charges against him or of pushing the issue any further.

As it turned out, along with an emphatic sincere, heartfelt apology from Foss Man, Officer Al confiscated his new rifle and told him he'd give it back to him sometime next spring. This was more than fair as far as Foss Man was concerned, and frankly, he wasn't sure if or when he'd ever feel like shooting that stupid gun again anyway!

Foss Man's parents knew how upset he was and that he was fully aware of the fact his behavior could easily have produced a tragic outcome. They also knew he would accept full responsibility for it and do a good job of beating himself up. They decided to accept the consequences of taking away his gun privileges for the foreseeable future, and the subject was abruptly dropped.

But he still had to face Catherine. When his sister heard about it, showing mild support, she told Foss Man, "You've got to be more careful with that stupid gun. I suppose shooting at chunks of ice is better than killing innocent squirrels and rabbits. I've told you and Horse before, I think hunting is totally barbaric!" And Allen gave him what was by now a familiar look. "It's time to get your head out of your ass, little brother!" Foss Man figured these sentiments from his siblings were probably fair, but he couldn't help but think, *Boy, it would sure help my cause if one of you would screw up once in a while somewhere along the way!*

Their mother continued her brave struggle to regain her strength, and demonstrating her determined will to get things back to normal around the home front, she had every intention of returning to work after the first of the year. With her joyous return home and fast recovery, except for the shooting accident, it was the happiest holiday season of all time in the Foster home.

CHAPTER THIRTY-NINE

Foss Man and Big Jake were still the only two guys on the basketball team who didn't enjoy the benefit of driving or owning a car. It was only a few more months before Big Jake turned sixteen, but it was almost another full year for Foss Man. With the sub-zero temperatures and heavy snow, his dependable bike was stored in the shed for the winter. Sometimes he'd get a ride home after basketball practice with one of his buddies, but Allen drove his big Buick to school every day, and it only made sense to jump in with him for the much-appreciated ride home. A little incident in the locker room quickly changed that luxury.

Now a junior, Allen was a valuable starting forward on the basketball team. After practice one night in the middle of January, he got fed up with Foss Man persistently screwing around in the locker room. Proving he was getting his old fun-loving free spirit back, Foss Man was snapping wet towels and cracking guys on the ass and then throwing soap in the face of the next guy entering the shower room. Allen expressed his disgust. "Knock that crap off, you big idiot!" To the surprise of no one, the two brothers started scuffling and pushing each other around. In the process, Foss Man managed to stub his toe in the shower drain. It puffed up and looked so ugly he was afraid it may actually be broken. It was extremely painful, and as should be expected under the circumstances, he responded by calling his brother a few carefully chosen names.

After showering and getting dressed, Foss Man had trouble getting his shoe on his badly damaged foot. Angry about the shower room scuffle and the fact Foss Man called him those colorful names, Allen deliberately took off for home without him. With his buddies all assuming he'd gotten a ride with his brother, Foss Man had to walk home that night in below-zero weather on what he found out the next day was indeed a broken toe. It hurt like crazy, but Dr. Ellington told him he could go ahead and play basketball as long as he could handle the pain. Their family doctor assured him playing wouldn't do further damage to his foot. Tough as nails and loving basketball, Foss Man played in the game that Friday night.

The brothers were loyal teammates in the heat of battle, but let there be no doubt, they would continue their unique style of brotherly love throughout the basketball season and beyond. As far as his personal performance was concerned, in spite of making the infamous basket for Riceville earlier in the year, Foss Man had a rather impressive sophomore season.

While Foss Man was quietly hoping his brother Allen would screw up somewhere along the way, the very opposite happened. Allen proceeded to singlehandedly create some extraordinary excitement in Jefferson that winter. Much unlike his fun-loving brother, Allen was always dead serious about building a resume and preparing for his future.

H. R. Gross was the popular congressional representative for the fifth district of Northern Iowa and, in turn, a longtime resident of Washington, DC. Over the years, he had become friends with fellow Iowan Allen and Foss Man's Aunt Sylvia. Representative Gross and Aunt Sylvia, who by now held an important position in the Department of Agriculture in the nation's capital, had worked together on a number of congressional bills that directly benefited the farmers throughout the state of Iowa. Always creative and ambitious, Allen, without great expectations, wrote a letter to Mr. Gross and invited him to speak to his government class that winter. Perhaps influenced by his friendship with Aunt Sylvia and in conjunction with an already scheduled campaign trip to Iowa, Mr. Gross surprised Allen when he wrote back and accepted the invitation. The end result—Allen became an instant hero around the school.

When the day of his big visit rolled around that winter, as a result of the congressman's public relation's staff, several of the area newspapers showed up with reporters and a camera man and took a bunch of pictures. A large picture featuring just the two of them, a proud and smiling Allen and Congressman H. R. Gross, was plastered across the front pages of all the newspapers.

Along with Mr. Gross's speech to Allen's government class, Mr. Gladding, the high school principal, scheduled a general assembly for the entire student body. Shortly after receiving a warm applause following his inspirational speech to the faculty and students, the two of them, Allen and the popular congressman, sat down privately and got into what turned out to be a life-changing conversation. During the exchange, Allen informed the congressman about his lifetime dream of enlisting in the US Air Force when he graduated from high school. Very serious, Mr. Gross asked him if he ever considered attending the Air Force Academy.

Allen's heart about exploded in his chest! He was never more excited about anything in his life! Mr. Gross was obviously impressed with Allen and thought he was a perfect candidate for an appointment to the academy. After discussing the subject in greater depth, he told Allen they'd keep in touch and convinced him he had serious intentions of making the appointment at the right time, which was in the middle of his senior year.

Dreaming of the now very real possibility of moving to Colorado Springs, Colorado, and attending the US Air Force Academy, Allen couldn't sleep for a week. When the word got out, Allen had finally earned a cherished nickname. Skunk, the nickname man, quickly decided Allen would be called simply Air Force. Allen would be called Air Force the rest of his days attending Jefferson High, and too proud to admit it, he absolutely loved it!

All their battles withstanding, including the recent one that triggered the long frigid walk home on his broken toe, Foss Man was genuinely proud and happy for a brother he always secretly had the greatest respect and admiration for. Deep down, Foss Man knew his brother was the kind of airman anyone would want by his side in the heat of battle.

With sister Catherine already formally accepted in the prestigious Iowa State University school for veterinarians that fall, and now with Allen anticipating the revered appointment to the Air Force

Academy, Foss Man was feeling a little self-conscious about his rather modest plan of taking over or partnering with Nute in the local bait shop. He said to himself, *It's probably time to give some thought to moving my career goals up a notch or two.*

Chapter Forty

A shocking incident took place that winter that shook the community to its very core! Eclipse immediately became the prime suspect for what would be his most pathetic deed of an already long history of egregious behavior. The next-door neighbors on both sides of the Ferguson family house had fenced-in backyards primarily designed to corral their small pet dogs. They built dog houses and confidently left the dogs outside and let them run freely throughout the day and night. One morning, both neighbors were stunned when they discovered their beloved dogs were missing.

Endless speculation swirled around town about what happened to the poor dogs. As outrageous as the predominant theory was, notorious by now for his documented history of cruelty to animals and the conspicuous fact he lived right next door, everything dramatically pointed toward Eclipse. But once again, nothing could be proven, and the eerie and disturbing mystery remained unsolved.

After what had unfortunately been done so many times in the past, if Catherine had anything to do about it, this tragic incident would not be swept under the rug. Her passion for animals in general was well documented, but what put fuel on the fire this time was, Catherine had great personal fondness for the two missing dogs. Both dogs had been in the veterinarian's office on more than one occasion, and like all the pets she had the privilege of caring for, Catherine loved Lizzie the cocker spaniel and Willie the small terrier.

For years, Catherine had been repulsed by Eclipse's unspeakable behavior, but this despicable act struck her so deeply she was thrown into an unprecedented level of fury. This was simply outrageous, and she knew something simply had to be done about it. When was someone in this stupid community going to have the gumption to do something about this sick guy who was now obviously completely out of control?

A stroke of luck—a spontaneous confrontation with County Attorney Townsend took place during the halftime of the basketball game between Jefferson and Boulder the week after the dogs had gone missing. Dressed in her cheerleading uniform, Catherine saw the county attorney walking toward the refreshment stand, and she boldly walked up to him and politely asked him, "Mr. Townsend, when are you going to do something about those missing dogs? You have to know who is responsible!"

Caught a little off guard but knowing exactly what she was talking about, he casually brushed her off and said, "I appreciate your concern, young lady, but I highly recommend you mind your own business. Trust me, the case is being thoroughly investigated, and we're trying everything we can to find out what happened to the two dogs!"

She didn't like being brushed off, and now even more determined, she pushed the subject a little further. "What's it going to take before somebody does something about that Ferguson jerk?"

Having enough by now and starting to lose his temper, Townsend barked back at her, "Why don't you get your pretty little butt back to the business of cheerleading and let me take care of providing justice in Wright County!"

More angry about his indignant response, totally out of character, Catherine snapped back, "Don't *pretty little butt* me, you hopeless wonder," and with that she stormed away and got back to the rather frivolous duty of cheering for the mighty Panthers.

It wasn't until much later that spring and not until the heavy snowfall melted when proof of what happened to the dogs was accidentally discovered. Ironically, Foss Man and Air Force were in close proximity when the gruesome evidence surfaced. Nute and his two reliable helpers had made their first trip to Beaver Creek to seine minnows. Nute was walking along the heavily wooded shoreline of the fast running stream and was busy guiding Foss Man and Air Force in their search for minnows when he stumbled onto the ugly scene. He was startled when he almost stepped on a dead animal lying in the young grass and, within a few feet, discovered another badly deteriorated small animal. With normal curiosity, Nute soon realized they were small dogs. Familiar with the missing dog story that winter, the disturbing discovery registered with him immediately. After further examination, he could see their throats had been viciously cut from ear to ear, nearly decapitating the poor innocent dogs.

Fortunately, Foss Man and Air Force were preoccupied and focused on their seining duty. Quick thinking on his part, Nute thoughtfully decided to spare the boys from learning about his morbid discovery. And knowing better than to disrupt what he knew was now a crime scene, he proceeded with his business and left the bodies of the two small dogs exactly as he found them.

After returning to the bait shop and joining the boys for the requisite glazed donuts and glass of lemonade, Nute cut their normal bull session a little short. As soon as Foss Man and Air Force were on their way home, he immediately tracked down Officer Al and gave him the startling report. The town cop had the responsibility of informing the unfortunate dog owners of the sad news! The discovery didn't prove who was responsible for killing the dogs, but when the ugly details of the story spread, the entire community was outraged!

Again, with the well documented history of Eclipse's hatred for animals, the dead cats, pigeons, chickens, and more recently the squirrel in the biology lab and the glaring circumstance that he lived in the house directly between the two dog owners, there was no doubt in the minds of anyone in the community about who was responsible for the unthinkable deed. No one expected the crime to be solved by Al the town cop, but they did expect a thorough investigation by county sheriff Fred Ramsey and proper follow-up by county attorney Roger Townsend.

Following what could be considered an adequate investigation and reasonable effort by the sheriff and county attorney, with the snow having melted in the area where the dogs were found, any potential clues, particularly any critical footprints, were no longer present. The fact there were no eyewitnesses to the abduction of the dogs and there was no physical evidence that established a direct link to Eclipse, no arrest was made.

Townsend, the young ambitious county attorney, had a reputation for not wanting to indict a suspect or prosecute a case unless it was absolutely airtight. Putting a heavy premium on keeping his perfect prosecutorial record intact, overwhelming circumstantial evidence was not good enough for him. The defense lawyers in the area had long referred to the county attorney as "Slam Dunk" Townsend. As it turned out, while Eclipse was clearly presumed guilty of the horrible crime, for whatever reason, there was no request for search warrants, no personal interrogation, and subsequently no charges were filed against him. Eclipse had once again proven how cunning and very good he was at what he did!

Catherine was smart enough to understand that law enforcement officials were limited in what they could do from a legal stand point. But at the same time, she felt strongly there had to be something they could do from a practical common sense point of view. She was totally disgusted when she heard there were no search warrants for the knife in the Ferguson house or, at the very minimum, an intense interrogation of the obvious prime suspect.

After meeting personally with a number of respected and equally concerned community leaders and exhausting every conceivable option, Catherine had to accept the fact nothing was formally going to be done. Their feeble attempts of simply enrolling Eclipse in Boy Scouts and the crazy football team experiment proved they were at least trying, but in reality, she thought their efforts were a joke and they had to know that.

Recognizing this harsh reality and knowing it was unlikely she would make any progress with the powers-that-be, Catherine felt she had no choice but to make her own personal effort to try to influence the ruthless character's behavior. She was utterly disgusted and was going to make her case directly with Eclipse. Her final conclusion: *What do I have to lose?*

The next time she saw Eclipse in school, she walked right up and aggressively cornered him. Without the slightest apprehension, she started out with, "You know, Ferguson, when you made fun of my brother after he had polio and came home in the wheelchair, I thought you hit rock bottom. We all know you're famous for taking the elementary school kids' lunch money and for killing the squirrel in the biology lab. You know I could go on and on, but now you've reached a new low. You've been getting away with all this ugly crap your whole life."

A little surprised, Eclipse just stood there, but on a roll now and still fuming, she continued, "But cutting the throats of innocent little dogs is absolutely unforgivable. I'm giving you fair warning, Ferguson, I won't rest until you're put away once and for all. You belong down in the state penitentiary with your stupid brother!"

By his reaction, it was obvious that last comment struck a nerve with him, but still not responding, Catherine went right on, "I will become personally active in seeing to it that community leaders, school administration, and all the law enforcement officers in the county find a way of ending your ruthless reign of terror. Trust me, Ron Ferguson, I won't stop until you're put behind bars!"

Not slightly concerned and waiting patiently for her to stop ranting, all Eclipse did was laugh and warned her, "Well, you little wise ass, if you're smart, you'll shut your big mouth and mind your own goddamn business. You don't know what the hell you're talking about, and if you don't butt out, I promise you, you're going to be very, very sorry!"

Not even remotely intimidated by his threat, without hesitation, she boldly fired right back, "Your threats don't scare me one bit, you big jerk. It's about time someone in this community stands up to you, and if it has to be me, that's just the way it's going to be!"

Still not showing the slightest concern, but with a frightening cold look in his eyes, Eclipse said very calmly, "Trust me, you're going to be very sorry, you fucking little bitch!"

Still fuming and unfazed by his threats, she turned her back, walked away, and calmly proceeded to go to her next class. As it turned out, this proved to be just the first of a number of heated confrontations between the two of them that spring. Catherine was proving to be a very determined and strong-willed young lady.

Chapter Forty-One

That was the final straw for Eclipse. He had no choice. He was going to have to shut this little bitch up once and for all. He started putting his plan together that day! "When those smart asses meet in the shed like they always do on Saturday at the end of the school year, I'm going to have a little surprise for the assholes! That dick head Foss Man's sister Catherine will be there to greet them, but she'll be deader than a fucking doornail!"

The thought of killing Catherine brought great excitement to him. It would be his biggest challenge yet. He couldn't explain why he got so much satisfaction from hurting people and killing animals. All he knew for sure was that it always made him feel better. When he was younger, he used to feel a little bit bad about some of the stuff he did, but lately, it didn't bother him one bit. Picking on kids, hurting animals, vandalizing property, or breaking the law always gave him a special thrill and amazing gratification.

Furious about Catherine so boldly confronting him and determined to shut her up for good, knowing this was going to be his biggest accomplishment ever, many thoughts ran through his mind. *I wonder if any of those smart asses that keep having those cute little private meetings in the shed have ever been locked in the basement in the dark for hours at a time. When I was little, every time I cried, my parents sent me to the basement and locked the door. They wouldn't let me out until I promised not to cry again.*

One time, when I was in first grade and Frank was a freshman in high school, two ladies came to the house and wanted to talk to me. I guess they were from social services or something like that from over there in Boulder. I guess they were there because Frank's high school physical education teacher saw some strange welts on his back one day when he was coming out of the shower room. Before they got to the house, my parents threatened to put me in the basement every night after school for a month if I told them anything about them hurting Frank or me. I hated spending time in the dark basement, and afraid of getting beaten again, I told the ladies my parents never did anything bad to Frank or me. I don't know if they believed me or not, but they never came back again.

Nothing makes me cry anymore. I haven't cried for over twelve years now!

I wonder if those jerks that meet in the shed all the time could catch a baseball very well if they never got to play catch with their dad. I saw all the other guys in the neighborhood playing catch with their dad. I never played catch with my dad. I don't even have a glove. They all played little league games. My parents never even signed me up. Their parents would jump up and down and cheer when they got base hits and then go to Sallie's Drive-In for malted milks.

When I was younger and I'd see my brother Frank doing mean things and always getting in trouble, I couldn't understand why he did it all the time. All he ever said was it made him feel better. Now I understand. I'm doing all the same stuff he did now, and he's right—it's the only thing that makes me feel better.

Do those smart asses in the shed ever feel like a caged animal? If you said or did anything your parents didn't like, you'd get stuck in the basement in the pitch dark for hours. I must have spent half my life in the basement. How would they like having an older brother down in the basement with them, warning you that we had to keep our mouths shut about everything that was going on or we'd get the living shit beaten out of us? Our father was a giant, and he was so mean we thought he might kill us if we told anybody about what was going on. We didn't dare say a word about how we were being treated or everything would just get worse. Frank and I both felt like caged animals. Whenever I see an animal in a small pen or fenced-in area, I want to put them out of their misery. It makes me feel good when I take them out of their misery. The perfect truth is, I have thought many times about taking myself out of my own misery.

When I go with my parents down to the penitentiary to see Frank, they never let us be alone. They didn't want us to talk to each other in private. One time, when they left and we managed to be alone, Frank asked me if they were still hurting me. I told him the truth, and he went ballistic. He was furious. He said he had to do something about what was happening to me, but he was afraid to tell the authorities because he feared for my life. Frank was afraid our dad might kill me if he told the truth about our parents. Frank told me that he was working on a plan. He told me to hang in there, that when the time was right, he was going to bring this ugly crap to a halt! He told me going to jail was the best thing that ever happened to him but he always felt guilty about abandoning me. I'm not sure I want to go to jail, but the truth is, it doesn't sound like the worst thing in the world either.

Killing that smart little bitch Catherine Foster is going to be an amazing feeling. I killed those dogs, and those stupid idiots never found a clue. I've only got a few weeks to put together another perfect plan! I can't wait to kill that fucking bitch! This is going to be the best thing ever!

Chapter Forty-Two

Baseball brought the gang back together again that spring. They were all in the starting lineup for the first varsity game of the season. Skeeter was at third, Air Force, one of the only three juniors in the lineup, was playing short. Skunk won the second base job. Big Jake at 6'5" was the perfect target and played first. Rocket was the starting pitcher and Foss Man was catching. Horse played center field, and the other two juniors were in right and left.

Recognizing the great potential of this young enthusiastic group, Coach Sanders didn't hesitate to put the younger underclassmen in the starting lineup and told them if they proved to be a winning combination, he would keep them together with the realistic goal of winning the state championship within the next two years. Air Force was the no-nonsense leader of the team, and Coach selected him to serve as the captain! He knew he had his hands full with the six free-spirited sophomores in the lineup, particularly his fun-loving brother. They all played hard and were fierce competitors, but there would clearly be an abundance of laughing and having a good time along the way; that was just the way it was going to be with this unique group.

They proceeded to get the season off to a good start putting a nice winning streak together. Skunk and Skeeter may have been only pint-sized but were quick as cats on defense, gobbling everything up that came near them, and batting in the top two spots in the lineup; they were both hitting over .300. They were pests on the base paths, flying around stealing bases. Foss Man, after having a great year last summer on the Town Team, was having a tough time at the plate and was contributing very little, at least offensively. His shotgun arm was still impressive, throwing out virtually every foolish base runner that attempted to steal on him, but the fact was, he was not hitting the ball like everyone had grown to expect.

About midway through the season, the game between the Panthers and their big “rival” Riceville provoked an unexpected confrontation. In the bottom of the first inning, batting third in the lineup, Foss Man came up to the plate. The burly catcher for Riceville, he was about the size of a small brown bear, greeted him with, “Hey, bowed legs, I’ve been meaning to thank you for so generously contributing that basket in our two-point victory over you guys last winter!”

Fuming but caught a little by surprise and resisting the temptation to say anything to the big jerk, Foss Man settled into the batter’s box. Looking out at the pitcher, he dug his cleats in and thought to himself, *Please put the first pitch over the plate, you bastard!*

His wish was granted. The first pitch came right down the middle, and Foss Man hit it on the screws easily clearing the center field fence, probably the longest ball he’d ever hit in his life!

When he was circling the bases, he was absolutely ecstatic but at the same time was trying to decide what he was going to say to the giant catcher with the obvious runaway pituitary gland when he crossed home plate. Not able to come up with anything too profound, as he proudly jogged by him, he came out with an uncharacteristic but very simple “This run counts for the Panthers, you big asshole!” Not able to make out exactly what Foss Man said as he strutted by, the catcher could do nothing but stand there with a dumb look on his face. With Rocket on the mound, the one run stood up and they went on to shut out the Wildcats, 1–0.

As expected, the Panthers won another conference championship, but the last game of the season was not a particularly good one for Foss Man. After a couple of wins in the playoffs, they were playing the regional championship game with the winner advancing to the sectionals. The game started and ended in a rather dubious fashion.

When Foss Man was making the routine throw down to second base to get the game underway, for some unknown reason, Rocket failed to step off the mound like he had always done in the past, and the ball hit him squarely on the back of the head. With the powerful velocity of Foss Man's shotgun arm, Rocket fell to the ground like a dead pheasant's reaction to a blast from Horse's big 12-gauge shotgun.

Coach Sanders, a badly shaken Foss Man, and all the infielders rushed over and huddled around Rocket, who was lying flat on his back. It looked like their star pitcher was, at the very minimum, unconscious if not dead. But fortunately, Rocket was as tough as they come and came around in only a matter of a few minutes. Greatly relieved, Foss Man still felt like crap and all he could say was, "Sorry about that, Rocket!" In spite of the screaming headache, sounding sincere, Rocket generously responded, "Don't worry about it, Foss Man. It was my own fault. I'm okay," and proceeded to pitch one of his best games of the season.

The Panthers trailed 2–1. There were two outs, the bases were loaded in the bottom of the last inning, and Foss Man was at the plate. A base hit—the Panthers would score two runs, win the game and advance to the sectionals. As badly as he wanted to be the hero, Foss Man knew a walk would tie things up and they could safely move on and very likely win in extra innings. He was patient and worked the count full, 3 and 2. Disciplined, knowing without a doubt it was several inches outside, he took the next pitch. After the game, he had to admit that under the circumstances, the pitch was probably too close to take. But of course, the blind umpire had rung him up. He struck out, and the baseball season was over. The dream of going to state was suddenly over for the promising Panthers.

It was another long ride home on the bus, and just what he didn't need, like the ride home from Riceville last winter, he could detect through that always-present cloud of smoke, his no-nonsense Aunt Francis was once again shaking her head and rolling her eyes as he was climbing up the steps and entering the open door of the big yellow school bus.

By now Foss Man had learned to get over stuff like this pretty fast, but Coach Sanders could see how extremely upset he was when they arrived back at the school. Coach was trying to come up with the right words to pick his spirits up a little bit but wasn't making much progress. An idea suddenly struck him. He looked at his watch and knew this was the perfect time to show Foss Man something. He suggested, "Hey, Foss Man, instead of riding home with your brother tonight, I want you to come with me for a few minutes. I want you to see something. I'll give you a ride home." Foss Man was a little curious and knew Coach Sanders must have something special up is his sleeve. All he really wanted to do is go home and feel sorry for himself for a while, but he reluctantly agreed to go along with his trusted coach.

It remained unusually quiet in the car, and when they arrived at Coach Sanders's house, the coach said, "Come on. Let's go inside for a minute, Foss Man."

When they got inside, they walked back to a big picture window where you could easily see the neighbors' fenced-in backyard. Fourteen-year-old Sammy Randle was sitting over there in his wheelchair. When he was about eight years old, Sammy had been hit by a car when he was chasing a ball that had rolled into traffic in front of his house. A spinal injury left him paralyzed below the waist. Sammy became a weightlifting fanatic and had an amazing athletic, muscular upper body. He was flipping a plastic ball in the air and hitting it as hard as he could with a short wooden bat. Their big lab hunting dog would immediately chase it down and bring it back to him. With a big smile on his face, Sammy would take the ball out of the dog's mouth and pat him on the head. Foss Man and Coach Sanders stood there without saying a word and watched Sammy go through the little ritual a number of times. Each effort concluded with that same huge smile on his face and with Sammy hugging his loyal beloved dog.

When Coach Sanders stopped in front of the Foster house to drop him off, Foss Man said rather sheepishly, "Thanks, Coach, I guess I deserved that!" The coach, recognizing his intentions perhaps hit home a little harder than he wanted and trying to soften the impact a little bit, responded, "I know I'm a little rough on you sometimes, Foss Man, but you know it's because I love you, buddy!"

That little experience would prove to have a powerful impact on Foss Man! Knowing the Sammy Randle story would probably be good for all his buddies, he was looking forward to the regular end-of-the-year bull session in the shed.

Chapter Forty-Three

Thursday was the last day of school. With no classes on Friday, the gang agreed to meet in the shed around four o'clock that afternoon instead of Saturday.

Along with the excitement of wrapping up another wild and crazy school year, Skunk and Foss Man were helping Big Jake celebrate receiving the keys to the new car his dad had rewarded him with for receiving the coveted Eagle Scout award that spring. They were sitting with Big Jake in his shiny new wheels parked right next to Rocket's big convertible at Sally's Drive-In. With the top down, Horse and Skeeter were proudly sitting there with Rocket. The six of them were bantering back and forth, laughing, and having a big time. They had already placed their orders with Mary Jane, one of the newly graduated Becker twins. Going off to college that fall, the guys had to take full advantage of having the two spectacular beauties around for the few remaining summer months.

After their fill of chocolate malts and hot fudge sundaes, they took off for Foss Man's house and stormed into the shed. Foss Man opened the window above the old couch, and they got down to business.

Foss Man couldn't wait to ask, "Hey, Rocket, who were those older guys that were talking to you after the game last week? I heard they might have been big league scouts or something?"

Trying to play it down, Rocket had to admit, "Yeah, after you guys took off, it was kind of crazy. There were two guys that cornered me. I guess the one who was a professional scout working for the Chicago Cubs was impressed with my fast ball. He figured it was at least around eighty-eight miles an hour and claimed that's pretty good for a sophomore. The other guy was a coach from the University of Iowa and he promised to keep in touch. He said he was seriously thinking about offering me a scholarship. It's good news, I suppose, but my dad told me to not get too carried away with it all and to just enjoy playing ball. The truth is, I'm just as excited about playing football this fall as I am about my baseball future!"

Foss Man was impressed but had to add, "I suppose they were probably impressed with my velocity too when I smoked you on the back of the head!"

Everybody but Rocket laughed, and he complained lightheartedly, "Yeah, thanks a lot, asshole, I've still got a big lump back there!"

Moving on, Rocket modestly changed the subject. "I've been meaning to ask you, Foss Man, what do you hear about the Texas migrant workers coming back to Iowa this summer? And you know exactly why I'm asking. Is that beauty—what's her name, Rosita or something like that?—is she going to make it back to town?"

Foss Man had spent hours wondering the same thing, and all he could say was, "I don't know about Rosita, but Walter told me how glad he was to report that the same much-appreciated gang is on the way back to Jefferson and should be reporting in a few days. I start work Monday morning, and I'll know what the deal is then. I have my fingers crossed that Rosita will be with them—I can promise you that!"

They were all chiming in and replaying all the crazy stuff that happened during the school year. Getting serious for a minute, Skeeter pointed out how relieved they all were that Foss Man's mother recovered from that scary ordeal. He also reported his dad's new bowling alley was just about ready to open. The bowling alley was replacing the old Roxie Theater. Directly related to that development, he said his dad was making great progress on the new drive-in theater.

Horse asked, "Hey, Foss Man, did you ever get your gun back from Officer Al? There's a million squirrels running around in our woods that are just asking for it. You going to come out and help Skunk and I shoot a few this summer?"

Foss Man didn't hesitate. "Heck, no, my hunting days are officially over. I'll leave shooting any stupid squirrels up to you and Skunk!"

Big Jake had been sitting there, listening intently. Although most of them were good students and regulars on the honor roll, Big Jake had by now clearly established himself as the most serious and deep thinker of the group. He was reluctant to bring up what he knew was an extremely delicate and personal subject, but his instincts told him it was something he had to do.

He started out with, "Boys, talking about jock itch, those untimely erections, and the hazards created by those nasty zippers in our new jeans was vitally important at the time, and it certainly wasn't easy but we even got Foss Man through puberty. But I'm afraid times have changed, and like it or not, going into our junior year, it's inevitable we're going to be facing some 'big boy' decisions. With the risk of sounding like a preacher, there's a sensitive subject I've got to get off my chest. I think this is as good a time as any!"

Sensing how serious Big Jake was, Horse quickly comforted him, "That's okay, you big drink of water. What's going on in that giant brain of yours anyway?"

Appreciating the encouragement, he went on, "Skunk, I know this is still a tough time for you and Stub, and this is going to hit a little close to home, but I'm gambling you won't mind, and maybe you'll even feel better after we talk about it a little bit."

Skunk was quick to support him. "That's all right, Big Jake. I don't know what's on your mind, but I'm doing fine, go ahead, spit it out!"

"Thanks, Skunk, that makes me feel better about getting a little serious with you guys. It's been exactly one year since we were all out at the cemetery while they were lowering Skunk's sister Ellie into the ground. I don't have to remind any of you about what kind of a miserable day that was for all of us! The circumstances surrounding her death, the fact she was pregnant, is what I want to talk about for a minute. You know it was my cousin Randy who had been dating Ellie at the time and the one everyone assumes was responsible for her pregnancy. Let me tell you, boys, you can't imagine the pure hell that poor guy has been through this last year. You know he had already been accepted at the University of Iowa when the whole thing exploded, and as you may or may not know, he never did report for classes last fall. His parents have indicated he's been in a severe state of depression since the tragedy, and they're afraid he's never going to get over it. He hardly leaves the house anymore, and you remember what an outgoing, fun-loving guy Randy always was. I'm sorry for bringing this up, but I think there's a valuable lesson to be learned here!"

Everyone had quit screwing around and were sitting there clinging to his every word! It was obvious the message hit home! Recognizing this fact, Big Jake abruptly cut it off. "That's it. My sermon is over!"

Skeeter, who had been paying close attention, resorted to his timely sense of humor and added one additional thought: "I think what Big Jake is trying to say is this, boys. In all due respect to old One Eye, you can't let the big guy do your thinking for you. You have to put your brain in gear at some point!"

Appreciating Skeeter's more lighthearted interpretation, feeling better, Big Jake added, "Yeah, I guess that's another way of putting it!"

Horse, always the quiet and introspective one of the group, once again hadn't said much throughout the unusually intense discussion. He had been thinking it but finally openly confessed, "After mocking you guys a little bit about the silly and frivolous discussions here in the shed,"—showing emotion none of them had seen before— "I want to reinforce what Big Jake and Skeeter have expressed here. Most of us have sisters. I don't care how corny this sounds, boys, but I say we treat girls the way we want our sisters to be treated." It was never something formally agreed on, but that's when the sister rule was planted in all their minds.

As they were walking back to their cars, Skunk reminded them, "Don't forget about the town team tryouts tomorrow afternoon." They were all looking forward to regrouping at five o'clock sharp the next night for the one thing they all had in common: their love for baseball.

For shocking reasons, it would be their final gathering in the popular old shed. And little did Foss Man know at the time, the next day would be the very worst day of his life!

Chapter Forty-Four

Foss Man sprung out of bed early Saturday morning. This was the second day of what he knew would be the greatest summer vacation of all time. He jumped on his bike and checked in at the grocery store at 7:00 a.m. sharp for his last day on his part time job until next fall. After filling the milk coolers and sprucing up the vegetable displays, it was finally 9:00 a.m. and time to check out. His boss Vaughn made a special point of complimenting him. "Foss Man, I've got to be honest—you've been a darn good worker this year and I'm looking forward to putting you back to work this fall." That made him feel good. They shook hands, Foss Man thanked his boss, and he took off to get started on the three lawns he was scheduled to mow that day.

Catherine headed for her job at the veterinarian's office. She worked from nine o'clock in the morning until three o'clock in the afternoon every Saturday. Catherine was diligently saving her money for college that fall. Thursday night, sitting with his parents, Foss Man was proud when she was given the huge applause as she walked across the stage to get her diploma from the president of the Jefferson school board. Everyone in town clearly respected her for finishing third in the class when they considered the heavy load she had at home. It was sure going to be a lot different not having her around next year! As tough as she always was on him, Foss Man knew he was going to miss her dearly!

Air Force was currently putting in ten hours on Saturdays. With grease jobs, oil changes, and pumping gas, Saturdays were big days at Rosie's Gas Station. He was making good money and saving most of it for when he headed out to Colorado to attend the Air Force

Academy a year from that fall. Foss Man didn't always appreciate the fact Air Force appeared to have his act together, and he knew it would be no different this summer.

Foss Man's dad had been working a lot of overtime hours on Saturday mornings lately. He loved working on Saturdays with his generous boss Paul Peterson paying him time and a half. His mother was home on Saturdays now, and along with the endless demands of the five younger kids still at home, she was enthusiastically doing the laundry, house cleaning, and shopping. She was completely recovered from the tragic event last winter; Foss Man had never seen his mother any happier, and he loved listening to her once again singing out loud as she was working around the house. As far as Foss Man was concerned, things had never been better around the Foster house.

Determined to save up enough money for a car that fall, Foss Man was glad he had those three lawns to mow every Saturday. He finished off the two smaller $1 jobs in less than two hours and saved Grandpa Wentworth's big $3 lawn for last. Pedaling his bike down the gravel road on the way to his grandpa's place west of town, he rode past Walter's sprawling cabbage field. He could see the long winding rows of cabbage, but with all the rain this spring, he could see the weeds were taking over. It was a good thing his friends from Texas were scheduled to return to town next week. He couldn't wait to see his great friends and had been hoping and praying that Rosita would come along with them. He was anxious to get her brother Pedro back on the baseball field after hitting the crap out of the ball the way he had by the end of last summer. Pedro was a great kid and had a good chance of suiting up and contributing to the success of the town team this summer.

He got his grandpa's lawn done at about 3:30 p.m., and on the way home, he pedaled by Sally's Drive-In for a quick hot fudge sundae with crushed nuts. He was glad to see Rocket with the top down in the big convertible and Skeeter sitting there next to him. Foss Man jumped into the back seat. Rocket and Skeeter already had their baseball gear on and were just killing a little time before heading down to the baseball field for town team practice scheduled for later that afternoon. After shooting the breeze with his buddies for a while, with a final glance at Mary Jane Becker, Foss Man told the boys he'd see them at practice a little later. He jumped on his bike and headed home.

After parking his bike in the shed, his plan was to jump in the tub for a quick bath and head over to the field for baseball practice. His thoughts were bouncing back and forth between two happy subjects, the prospect of seeing Rosita in the very near future and how he was going to crush the ball during batting practice later that night. Everything was falling in place, and his outlook was at an all-time high.

Meanwhile, that same day, Eclipse was never more excited in his life. Today was the day he had been looking forward to and had been carefully planning for during the past several weeks. That smart mouth little bitch was going to be sorry for all the wise-ass crap she keeps spreading around town. The thought of choking her and watching her beg for her life sent chills up his spine. This would be his most gratifying accomplishment of his lifetime. He couldn't wait for the big moment that afternoon when she got off work!

His parents left at eight o'clock that morning for one of their phony trips to see Frank. Whether they even talked to him when they got down to the state penitentiary was doubtful, but they kept making their monthly trips to make it look good for the neighbors and the rest of the community. What a fucking joke! But the one good thing about the trip was it gave him some time to be alone without having to deal with the two despicable people he had grown to hate. They had developed a set routine for these visits by now, and he knew they wouldn't be home until after ten o'clock that night.

Their absence made it perfect for him to carry out his elaborate plan. He had figured out a way to break into the liquor cabinet without being detected. Both of his parents were heavy drinkers, and they always had a healthy number of partially filled bottles of liquor in the house. Vodka and gin were their favorites, and they managed to drink several quarts of it every week. He had it down to a science. He could help himself to a generous amount and refill the bottles with water and they would never know the difference. It was an easy task for a crafty and cunning person like him!

He had carefully deliberated about whether he was going to drink any booze this time. His special plans for the day were by far his biggest challenge, and he wanted to make darn sure he didn't screw it up. He vividly remembered the fact he had drunk a lot of vodka the day he had killed those two dogs, and he had to admit, it made the experience more thrilling than ever. And that challenging project worked out perfectly. After much careful thought, he decided he would start drinking some of his favorite—vodka mixed in orange juice—around noon, and he would drink it slowly and steadily throughout the afternoon. He was determined to manage his drinking very cautiously so he would be in perfect condition for the big moment that afternoon!

He had been secretly observing Catherine's every move for weeks now and knew she worked at the vet's office on Saturdays until 3:00 p.m. With diligent surveillance, he knew she always rode her bike home, and after following her home a number of times, he was familiar with her route and the fact she would be putting her bike in the shed at precisely 3:15 p.m. With his meticulous preparation, he knew there was never anyone hanging around the vicinity of the secluded shed. He would be well hidden behind the big oak tree positioned a few yards from the entrance to the shed. The second Catherine entered the shed, he would ambush her from behind. The timing should be perfect. He could easily complete the mission before those smart asses meet at four o'clock that afternoon. He knew the guys always met on Saturday at the end of the school year. He had a little surprise planned for those dick heads—Catherine's strangled body! The thought of them walking in on that unexpected scene was almost more than he could handle.

It was 2:30 p.m., and he had already consumed a healthy amount of vodka. He was in the perfect frame of mind to carry out what would be his greatest feat of all time. The thought of actually choking that little bitch was going to be amazing. But one other thing kept creeping in his mind: the effect of the alcohol had aroused him and made him now reconsider the possibility of fucking her before he strangled her. His original plan was to take the shortest amount of time possible, simply strangle her and get the hell out of there. He had always been disciplined and cautious about not leaving any evidence behind. Many times in the past, everything pointed to him as the prime suspect, and the dip shits in this stupid town could never prove anything. That was the part that made it so satisfying. Everyone knew he was guilty, but the dumb asses couldn't do one thing about it. Thinking about the thrill of looking into Catherine's horrified eyes while he was raping her, and well aware of the fact she was an attractive little bitch, in his now drunken condition, he had hastily decided, *Why not, hell yes, I'm going to fuck her before I strangle her!*

Right on time, Catherine left her job at exactly 3:00 p.m., jumped on her bike, and headed for home. She couldn't wait to get home and get ready to go out that night. She had a big date with a good-looking guy she had dated a few times who just returned home the week before from his freshman year in college. They were going to the grand opening movie at Skeeter's dad's new drive-in theater. She opened the door to the shed, wheeled her bike over to its designated spot and, with her right foot, flicked the kick stand in place.

Foss Man arrived about five minutes later and pulled up to the shed with intentions of merely putting his bike away!

Two minutes later, Ron Ferguson would be dead!

Chapter Forty-Five

As Catherine limped and wobbled her way out of the shed, Foss Man, trying desperately to comprehend what had just taken place, stumbled over and collapsed on the overstuffed chair positioned right next to the long couch. Within arm's length, Eclipse was lying face down with blood pulsating from his freshly crushed skull. In a state of shock, Foss Man sat there, still holding the bloody baseball bat in his hands and staring at the badly warped wooden floor.

Unaware of how much time had passed, Foss Man's stunned father was shaking him and attempting to get him to come around. Knowing what he had just been through and recognizing the cold, distant look in his eyes, he was worried his son had fallen into that same mysterious deep spell he had struggled so mightily with in the aftermath of his baby sister Carol's drowning many years ago. As he was slowly coming to, Foss Man could hear the screaming sirens, and seconds later, Wright County Sheriff Ramsey came charging through the door.

Except for the fact a rape had occurred a short time earlier, with the unconscious body and the bloody bat now lying on the floor in front of where Foss Man was sitting, it was easy for Ramsey to conclude what had taken place. After parking the ambulance alongside the sheriff's car in Foster's driveway, a medic in a white uniform rushed into the shed a few steps behind the sheriff and immediately started giving aid to the unconscious boy lying motionless on the couch.

Recognizing the frightened and badly shaken condition Foss Man was in, the sheriff was calmly asking him to explain what had taken place. With his dad's assistance, the two of them attempted to explain to the sheriff about the horrific scene Foss Man had inadvertently walking into. As the sheriff was wrapping up his brief interrogation, the county medical examiner joined them in the now crowded building and approached the giant motionless body sprawled across the couch. A few minutes later, dazed and totally confused, Foss Man couldn't prevent hearing the chilling words coming from the examiner declaring Ron Ferguson officially dead on the scene. That unfathomable revelation would now be permanently etched in his mind.

With everything spiraling out of control, the county sheriff was boldly explaining to Foss Man that he was officially under arrest for his responsibility in killing the teenage boy lying there. With mild objection from his rattled and confused father, clearly late in the process, the sheriff was formally reading him his rights and methodically putting the handcuffs on him. As the sheriff was escorting him from the building, virtually numb, rambling thoughts were running through his mind, *Good grief, what on earth just happened in our always favorite hangout that provided so many happy times listening to those Saturday afternoon "Hawkeye" football games on the radio with my dad and all those special clubhouse meetings with my buddies?*

A short time earlier, emotionally distraught over the unspeakable ordeal Catherine had just been through while trying desperately to maintain her composure and fighting to remain calm, Foss Man's mother carefully put her ravaged daughter in the front seat of the family car and rushed her to their longtime family doctor's office.

Demonstrating her typical strength, Catherine proceeded to calmly explain to Dr. Ellington, who couldn't help but recall the day he had brought this special young lady into the world eighteen short years ago, about the horrific ordeal she had just been through. The doctor, in his many years of practicing small-town family medicine, had the great fortune of never treating a patient in Catherine's heart-wrenching condition.

After thorough examination, Dr. Ellinton was convinced that Foss Man had arrived on the scene early in the process of the brutal attack. That being the case, the doctor was optimistic that the physical injuries would prove minimal, and furthermore, there was very little chance of her being pregnant. While that was good news, he privately explained to Catherine's mother that it would be a long time before the emotional and psychological damages could be fully determined.

Catherine politely protested when she saw the doctor return to the examination room holding a flashbulb camera. Compassionate about what his young patient had been through, the doctor explained the importance of providing physical evidence for exactly what took place earlier that day. It was fortunate their doctor had the wisdom to take the appropriate pictures documenting the bruises on her wrists, arms, legs, and neck. What proved to be critical down the road, they would have clear and conclusive evidence that Catherine had indeed been raped that afternoon!

Meanwhile, the designated law officers were carefully and thoroughly searching for all the pertinent clues and any collaborating evidence that remained in the suddenly infamous small building. Cameras were flashing as the investigators were busy taking even remotely related pictures. Stirred by the sirens and the presence of multiple police cars and ambulances with their glaring bright spinning lights, there was a curious and fast-growing crowd gathering in the immediate surrounding area.

As should be expected under the dramatic circumstances in a small community like Jefferson, the shocking story and wild speculation spread swiftly. In what had to be record-breaking time, the inevitable swarm of reporters and cameramen from the area radio, television, and print media were pressing for interviews with anyone in uniform who was willing to provide information that might shed light on what had happened that afternoon in the always peaceful town.

There was a sudden eerie silence when the stretcher carrying the body exited the shed and was loaded in the ambulance. The scene provided a riveting picture for the next morning's newspapers as the reporter's flashing cameras captured the telling image of the two medics struggling with the enormous weight of the deceased young man under the ominous white sheet. The area around the shed was roped off with traditional yellow tape and was formally declared a crime scene. Again, as incomprehensible as it was, a rape and a death, possibly even murder, had just taken place in the previously innocuous hideaway.

Ferguson's parents were visiting their older son Frank at the state penitentiary in southern Iowa that day and weren't informed of the tragedy until they returned home much later that night. Needless to stay, they were stunned by the outrageous news. After their presumed deliberate effort to steer their second-born son in a better direction, the glaring results were now in. They had obviously failed miserably!

Foss Man was now sitting in the back seat of the county sheriff's marked vehicle. Sheriff Ramsey informed his dad that the state of Iowa was required to offer an arraignment hearing within forty-eight hours of the arrest of a juvenile, and it was possible he could be released at that time. That would be a decision made by the county attorney conducting the hearing. His dad was confused and clearly upset by this drastic turn of events. Was this even possible? First, their innocent daughter had been violently raped, and now, their son was under arrest. Having no choice in the matter, they were forced into accepting what they were told was the normal procedure under these extreme circumstances. After all, setting the provocative circumstances aside, as unbelievable as it was, their sensitive fifteen-year-old son was directly responsible for taking the life of another human being.

Ramsey coldly suggested, "You folks are going to want to hire a good lawyer as soon as possible. County Attorney Townsend is out of town for the week end but will be returning and conducting the hearing on Monday." Foss Man was now formally in the custody of the county and would be driven over to Boulder to be locked up in the Wright County Juvenile Detention Center.

Foss Man's mind was whirling in every direction. He should have been taking his turn in the batting cage with his buddies at that very moment. Instead, the shocking reality was he was flying down the road in the overly excited young sheriff's marked vehicle who, strictly for his own personal need for drama, had the deafening siren screaming at full tilt. Foss Man would now be spending the night in a lonely jail cell, far removed from his friends and confused and badly shaken family.

After selecting the ugly orange uniform about three sizes too big and stuffing his clothes in his assigned locker, Sheriff Ramsey lead Foss Man back to the holding cell anonymously tucked in the back end of the detention center. It felt good to finally have full circulation back in his hands when the handcuffs were removed from his wrists. He was already dreading the thought of trying to make it through the inevitable long night ahead of him.

The frightening echo of the steel barred door slamming shut suddenly made it all very real. Time seemed to stand still. As the hours managed to drag on, he was now sitting in the pitch black with his eyes closed desperately trying to make any sense out of what happened that day. This had to be some kind of cruel joke!

He got sick to his stomach as he kept hearing Catherine's desperate screams and couldn't erase the image of her pinned under the ruthless poor excuse for a human being. Not having a chance to talk to her, he was worried sick about how his big sister was doing. He hated to even think about it but he couldn't imagine what might have happened to her if he hadn't come home when he did. *If only I hadn't kept sitting there admiring the Becker twins this afternoon, I might have gotten home in time to prevent all this from happening.*

With the vivid picture of the ugly scene lingering in his head, Foss Man tossed and turned on the thin mattress covering the hard steel-woven bed. Sleep would prove impossible. As the misery stretched late into the night, like he had been forced into doing so many times in his turbulent past, he turned to his desperate but well-practiced routine of creating "hedges" against the night.

Chapter Forty-Six

Foss Man's buddies were putting on their cleats, and Sparky the team manager was busy strapping down the bases for infield practice when they first heard the screaming siren of the county sheriff's car and, minutes later, the blaring ambulance. An extremely rare event in Jefferson, they were all wondering what the heck was going on. They knew something unusual was taking place but were totally shocked when one of their older teammates showed up a little late for practice and, with panic in his voice, delivered the stunning report about what had allegedly just taken place in the shed behind Foster's house.

As much as they didn't want to believe it, it made some sense to Rocket, Horse, Skeeter, Big Jake, and Skunk, who had been curious where the heck Foss Man was. There was no way he'd be late for baseball practice. Skunk and Skeeter were scared out of their minds and immediately jumped in Skeeter's car and rushed over to Foss Man's house. Their minds preoccupied, the other guys made a feeble attempt to get on with practice, but when Skunk and Skeeter came back a few minutes later and verified the ambulance and several police cars were indeed parked in the Foster's driveway and that a huge crowd had already gathered in the surrounding area, Sparky hastily canceled practice.

Now worried to death, Big Jake suggested they all head up to his house to try to learn more about the unthinkable story they could only pray wasn't true. Big Jake's dad got home about the same time and indicated he had just talked briefly to Officer Al, who had filled him in on what had officially taken place in the Fosters' shed. He had the difficult task of informing Foss Man's five best buddies that the story was true.

Not able to sugarcoat it, Big Jake's dad shared the cold truth with them: "I'm afraid your buddy Foss Man walked in on the Ferguson boy while he was in the process of raping his sister Catherine. Good or bad, the evidence strongly suggests he hit Ferguson over the head with a baseball bat. Officer Al claimed Ferguson had been formally pronounced dead at the scene!"

The five teenage boys sat there in total stunned silence, trying to comprehend what all this meant. Big Jake's dad did his best to comfort them, but recognizing the severe emotional state they were all struggling with, thinking they could probably deal with it better on their own, he suggested they go home and perhaps spend some time with their families. Fighting back tears, Horse, Rocket, Skunk, and Skeeter all hung their heads as they found their way to their cars and headed straight to the much-needed comfort of their homes.

It was an unbearable night for Foss Man. He suddenly woke up. He figured he had slept at the very most one or two hours. He spent most of the miserable long hours flopping around on the hard bed. He was wide awake now, the cell had turned cold and damp, and he felt like he was in a basement. He had a horrible throbbing headache. How many nights was he going to be stuck in this repulsive place where he had been so rudely locked inside the night before? Thank God there was finally some daylight seeping through the steel bars of the one small window. He couldn't wait for the sun to come up. His reliable buddy Mr. Slim had always told him that when things looked the very worst, "Don't worry, Foss Man, you can count on it—the sun will always come up in the morning!" This was the first time he ever questioned his good friend's profound wisdom.

Sunday was always his favorite day! That obviously wasn't going to be the case today. He wondered what was going on back home after that unbelievable, crazy day yesterday. Still nauseating for him to even think about, his first thought was how Catherine was doing. He'd never felt so lonely and was hoping and praying for some company.

An old guy in a scruffy, beat-up uniform finally showed up with a tray of what would be his breakfast. There was a small box of cornflakes and a small carton of milk. The weird-looking guy unlocked the cell door and set the tray on top of the metal toilet with the lid down. The man didn't say a word.

Foss Man weakly asked him, "What's going on anyway? When do I get to talk to somebody?" Appearing annoyed by the question, the old man responded, "I don't know, boy. I just work here." He abruptly turned around, walked out, and slammed the steel door shut, just about killing Foss Man's already pounding headache.

He wasn't hungry and let the cereal sit there. He sat on the edge of the hard bed. With his elbows resting on his knees, he looked down at the floor, holding his head in his hands. *How in the holy hell did I get myself into this ugly mess anyway?*

The stunning news had spread like wildfire throughout the community. All the area radio and television stations were enthusiastically covering the outrageous story. The fact the three key players in the incident were minors, at least during the early stages, no names were included in the reports. By Monday morning, speculation of the unique circumstances surrounding the dramatic news had reached the associated press, and all three major national television networks, CBS, ABC, and NBC, would be sending reporters and cameramen to cover the story. There was a sudden wild ambush on the small formerly quiet and peaceful community. With the crazy media circus in town, there was unprecedented electricity in the air. The harsh reality was, life in Jefferson would never quite be the same again!

When Catherine had returned home from Dr. Ellington's office Saturday afternoon, with the help of the powerful sedative the doctor had given her, she was fortunately now sleeping soundly. Her badly shaken parents were sitting around the dining room table with Foss Man's brother Allen, Aunt Francis, Uncle Stan, and Grandpa Wentworth. The five younger kids were totally confused and couldn't begin to understand what had taken place. They could sense it must have been something pretty bad and were frightened and concerned when their dad ordered them to remain in the living room and were told to "be good kids now and keep yourselves busy watching television, okay?"

Relieved that Catherine was finally peacefully asleep, Foss Man's horrified loved ones were trying to focus on the first order of business: the strange, new experience of hiring a lawyer. They were nervously sharing their thoughts when the phone rang. It was Aunt Sylvia returning a call they had placed to her an hour earlier. Sylvia had been living and working in Washington, DC, for over twelve years by now, and with her lofty position with the federal government, they knew with her more worldly experiences she could probably provide valuable advice and expertise in dealing with the serious legal problem the family was suddenly facing.

After Aunt Francis quickly brought her older sister up-to-date, Sylvia's first reaction was, "My lord, what on earth was wrong with that young man anyway?" She was referring to Ron Ferguson of course. Although extremely upset with the stunning news, calmly and without hesitation, as they expected, she offered an immediate strong opinion about how they should proceed.

Her first recommendation was, "Forget the concept of using an assigned public defender. I insist we hire the absolute best defense lawyer in the area! And don't worry about the cost. When you find the right one, let me know, and I'll take care of the retainer fees and intend to pay for all the related legal expenses." What would prove to be the pattern throughout her life, having no kids of her own, Aunt Sylvia would always be there at crunch time for her sixteen beloved nieces and nephews, particularly for Luke, it seemed.

While Grandpa Wentworth had expressed the same sentiments and had already made a similar offer, he told Foss Man's parents he would go to work on hiring a lawyer first thing in the morning. His first call would be to one of his regular Wednesday afternoon golf partners, Harold McKinley, who along with his son Kenneth were notorious after becoming two of the most formidable defense lawyers in northern Iowa. Even though it was Sunday, Grandpa Wentworth confidently pledged he'd have a prominent qualified lawyer hired and on board by the end of the day. It was comforting to Foss Man's parents to know the kind of unwavering support they could count on from their loving family.

Chapter Forty-Seven

Early Sunday morning, after a long sleepless night, as Foss Man's parents were getting ready to make the twelve-mile trip over to Boulder to see their son, there was a knock on the door. As comforting as attending church services would have been at this difficult time, with everything going on and knowing very well their presence would create a minor spectacle, they opted to skip church that morning. This was just one small example of how the Foster family would be forced to make adjustments in the aftermath of the startling news that was now rocking the entire community.

Opening the door, they were surprised to see Foss Man's good buddy Big Jake, who of course was a towering 6'5" tall, and his older brother Will, slightly shorter at 6'4", standing together on the porch. Big Jake, always appearing the intellectual with his wire-rimmed glasses, was a good enough looking guy, but his brother Will, with his curly blond hair and square jaw, was nothing less than movie star handsome. The two giant young men created quite an impressive picture!

Will was eight years older than Big Jake and had just returned home for the summer. He graduated with honors from the University of Iowa two years ago, had immediately enrolled in Harvard Law School, had just graduated and received his coveted law degree, again with honors, and was going to spend the summer in his quiet and peaceful home town studying for the upcoming bar exams. He had already accepted a high-powered job with a large reputable law firm in New York and was scheduled to launch his legal career that fall. His carefully-thought-out plan was to get away from all the big city commotion so he could effectively focus and concentrate while preparing for the challenging exams.

Will, who was a terrific baseball player in high school, although he had not received a scholarship offer, was a "preferred walk-on" at the University of Iowa and got extensive playing time as a catcher with the Hawkeyes his senior year. To break up the monotony of studying, his plan was to spend time with his family and play some baseball with the Jefferson town team that summer—as a matter of fact, under the impressive lights his dad had played such an instrumental role in getting erected. While working in his dad's refreshment stand, Foss Man had witnessed a number of Will's towering home runs when he was in grade school and had darted under the counter and collected more than a few nickels for foul balls hit off his bat. Foss Man had idolized Big Jake's older brother Will for years, and the perfect truth was, he was the one who inspired him to become a catcher in the first place!

Foss Man's parents hadn't seen Will in a long time but certainly remembered him and were fully aware of what an exceptional young man he was. After warm greetings, Will quickly acknowledged, "We heard about the horrible incident that took place yesterday and that's why we're here." Speaking for both of them, he said, "Big Jake and I are truly sorry about what happened and know this is a difficult time for you and your family, but we have a very serious proposal related to what happened yesterday. We hope you'll forgive us for barging in like this!"

There was no hesitation. Foss Man's parents cordially invited the striking pair of young men in. These guys just happened to be two of the brightest students to ever grace the halls of Jefferson high school.

Settling down in the living room, Will proceeded to explain, "I'm not licensed to practice law in Iowa at this point in time, but I want to talk to you about the possibility of serving as Foss Man's counsel for the legal issues he will very likely be facing after what happened yesterday. My current licensing scenario may at a glance appear a little unusual, but let me assure you, it's totally legal and a viable consideration. My first order of business is to get your approval, and then of course we'll meet with Foss Man, get him on board, and get right to work putting an effective defense plan together." He emphasized, "While everyone will naturally be anxious to get this unfortunate episode behind them, it's important that we move the legal proceedings along as efficiently as possible in order to complete the process before I'm scheduled to report for work this fall. With that being said, it's very possible I could delay my employment starting date if it becomes absolutely necessary, but I'm confident the legal proceedings including a trial, if indeed there is one, should be over in plenty of time."

The single word *trial* sent shivers up their spine. Luke's parents could see how serious and enthusiastic Will was about the whole idea and were certainly more than willing to hear him out.

Will went on to explain the important role he thought his younger brother Big Jake could play in his already well-thought-out plan. "Big Jake told me he knows Foss Man like a book and exactly what makes him tick. This may not sound like a big deal to you folks right now, but trust me, knowing and understanding Foss Man's personal makeup will prove to be extremely valuable down the road. And I know Big Jake and Foss Man genuinely care deeply about each other and have mutual respect and trust for one another. Perhaps just as important, Big Jake can provide the moral support for Foss Man as we go through the difficult legal battle it's all but inevitable we'll be facing."

Will casually added, "Not being licensed at this time prohibits me from charging fees, and furthermore, I would have no intentions to do so anyway. My future law firm specializes in criminal defense, and I know the experience will prove to be invaluable for me personally. While I'm totally committed to seeing it through to the end, if at any time you folks or Foss Man feel uncomfortable or perhaps think things are not going satisfactorily, I won't hesitate to step down. I promise you, the number one priority and only consideration will always be making sure Foss Man is given the very best defense possible."

This development was nothing short of amazing! Knowing immediately this was how they wanted to proceed and confident that Foss Man would enthusiastically support the idea, they had to make sure to call Grandpa Wentworth right away before he made a substantial retainer fee and formally hired a lawyer. As it turned out, Grandpa's plan to track down his lawyer friend Harold McKinley was put on hold when he learned he was on a fishing trip over the week end and couldn't be reached until Monday morning.

Confident they would have the support of all the concerned relatives, this brilliant aspiring young lawyer and his younger brother were now officially welcomed on board and would officially be leading the way forward. Pleased about the sudden totally unexpected agreement, they shook hands, hugged, and invited Big Jake and Will to join them as they planned to head over to Boulder in a little while to see who by now was most certainly a very lonely and worried Foss Man. Impossible for them to comprehend the wild ride they were so bravely and boldly taking on, the brilliant Simmons brothers agreed to return in an hour.

They gave Grandpa Wentworth a quick call. He was a little apprehensive about the idea at first but reluctantly went along with the plan. They also placed a long-distance call to Aunt Sylvia and informed her of their decision. Her quick and supportive response was, "Oh yes, the brilliant Simmons brothers. I've heard about them, and as a matter of fact, small world, but I actually dated their father a few times back in high school. He was a very bright and a good-looking tall drink of water." With her continuing single marital status, she said, "When I think about it, I can't believe I let that charming guy slip through my fingers."

Aunt Francis, the chain-smoking, no-nonsense school bus driver, volunteered to spend the day with the kids, first making sure that Catherine was okay, and then working together with her deeply concerned brother Allen, tried her best to comfort the rest of the confused kids throughout the first day of what would be a long, frightening ordeal for all of them.

Chapter Forty-Eight

As tired as they were from the long restless night, Foss man's parents felt a new surge of energy as the four of them, including the two amazing young men, walked into the imposing Wright County Juvenile Detention Center.

There was a large formal glassed-in room with a conference table surrounded by leather chairs available to them but they chose to gather in the unoccupied public lounge area with the more comfortable overstuffed chairs and couches. The fact it was Sunday, there were few people on duty, and it was unusually quiet throughout the building. It was obvious Foss Man had also been through a rough night, but the presence of his great friend Big Jake and his big brother Will, and of course his beleaguered parents gave him a much-needed lift. The unexpected subtle smile on his face was comforting to his parents and got the rather strange reunion off to an encouraging start.

Following hugs and handshakes, Foss Man didn't know exactly what was going on, but after the miserable, lonely night, he was just happy to be together with this special group of people. Filled with emotion, Foss Man's first heartfelt words were, "Mom and Dad, how the heck is Catherine doing anyway?"

His mother attempted to tell him the best way she could. "She appears to be her same old amazing, strong self, Luke, but only time will tell. It will probably be a long time before we know what impact the horrible experience will ultimately have on her."

His dad added, "The last thing she said before we left the house this morning was, 'I can't wait to check into the dorm at Iowa State this fall. I need a break from this miserable, stupid town!' We all agreed that her already planning to get on with the next stage of her life was probably an encouraging sign."

His mother chimed in, "She struggled to put it in words, but she told us to make sure and give you a big hug and that she was looking forward to thanking you in person for the brave thing you did in the shed yesterday. She's extremely thankful and proud of her little brother Luke!"

He wasn't so sure about the brave thing, but he was deeply touched by these comments, and after his parents expressed their concern with how his night had gone, they got right down to business. Will explained what he thought he and Big Jake's role could be in dealing with this sudden turn of events. Spending virtually the whole night thinking about it, Foss Man was smart enough to know he was probably facing a serious legal battle. He was relieved to know a brilliant guy like Will, and his loyal and trusted friend Big Jake had volunteered to be in his corner. Without a second's hesitation, they shook hands, and as expected, Foss Man was totally and enthusiastically on board! He had to ask himself, *Is all this real? Do I actually need a lawyer for God's sake?*

The most immediate concern for him and his parents was how long he would have to remain in custody. Will had already thought it through and predicted, "The required arraignment hearing will be sometime tomorrow, Monday. Of course I'll be with you for that. Based on the violent and extreme nature of the incident, I'm assuming you'll be scheduled for a preliminary hearing most likely on Friday. Rather than putting Catherine through any interrogation at this difficult time, we'll get a written statement from Dr. Ellington first thing in the morning validating what was going on when you walked into the shed that provoked you to react like you did." He went on to make it clear. "Assuming it'll come to that, I'll be pushing to get the preliminary hearing scheduled as soon as possible. Depending on how the hearing turns out on Friday and to finally answer your question, that will likely be the earliest Foss Man could be released and turned over to you folks." He emphasized, "Very likely with limited freedom."

While this forecast was disappointing, the miserable thought of being locked up at least until Friday, the unfortunate truth was they had better get used to the idea; it was just the first of many undesirable circumstances Foss Man and the family would be facing for the foreseeable future.

Recognizing everyone's emotional state of mind as compassionately as possible, Will felt obliged to be perfectly honest and candid about the ugly battle they were very likely up against. With that genuine concern in mind, he went on, "Let me assure you, this whole thing is going to be difficult for everyone. We're simply going to have to be strong and learn to deal with the cold, hard facts surrounding the unfortunate hand you've been so rudely dealt."

"Let me summarize what we should focus on today. First, I want to give you the likely timetable for the various events that are going to take place not only this week but also further down the road. Second, I want to be upfront and honest about the chances for an indictment against you, Foss Man—in other words, the legal charges you'll very likely be facing. I don't want you to be alarmed about the blunt language you're probably going to hear from the county attorney for the first time tomorrow. Then finally, before we get into any specific defense strategies, we'll have plenty of time for that later this week, I want to explain exactly what to expect and how to handle the interrogation in the morning."

They were all listening attentively and clinging to his every word. Will went on, "Okay, first the events this week. Big Jake and I'll be with you during the arraignment hearing tomorrow. If things move along like expected, the medical examiner's general report and the autopsy should be completed in a few days. The county attorney will be motivated to schedule the all-important preliminary hearing as soon as possible, as I said before, probably this Friday. The preliminary hearing will be held in front of a judge, and at that time, it will be determined whether or not there will be a formal indictment and what specific charges will be filed against you. We'll learn more about the official schedule tomorrow, and we'll prepare accordingly. If all this indeed leads to a trial, it won't be scheduled for at least a month."

"Of course you, Foss Man, your parents, Big Jake, and I'll be at the hearing on Friday. We'll have time this week to decide if we want Catherine to testify that day. At that time, we'll petition for your immediate release. If we're successful, and with the fact you're not a flight risk and you obviously pose no immediate danger to the public, I'm confident your release will be granted. Also, under the existing circumstances, posting any kind of bond will very likely not be required. At that time, you'll be turned over to your folks and, like I said, probably with carefully outlined restrictions. And remember, we'll be getting together a number of times and will have plenty of time during the week to prepare for the hearing on Friday."

"Now I have to ask you one simple question, Foss Man—and this is the only question I'll be asking you at this point in time about what happened yesterday. While I can anticipate what most of the probable questions will be tomorrow, we'll deliberately let the county attorney introduce the questions to you at that time. I don't want to overcoach you or put words in your mouth. We don't want your answers to sound rehearsed. Your answers should be straightforward and, of course, the simple truth.

"Now my one critical question: How many times did you hit Ferguson with the bat?"

The recollection was sickening, but without the slightest hesitation, Foss Man responded, "Twice, the second one just a few seconds after the first one!"

With Foss Man's apparent eagerness to explain further, Will quickly put his hand up and politely insisted, "No, that's enough. For good reason, I don't want you to elaborate any further right now."

With that simple but important answer, Will went on, "Okay, with that, let me give you a little foundation for what the county attorney is likely to contend. He's not likely to get into this much tomorrow, but just in case, I don't want you to be surprised and overreact to what he's saying. Now, about the first blow to Ferguson's head. He'll strongly suggest there were better options for you than what he'll likely refer to as your reckless decision to use the baseball bat. Now in other circumstances, that might make sense, and without giving consideration to the fact it was your sister who was being raped in front of you and it was her you were desperately trying to rescue, with the dramatic discrepancy between your size and the size of Ferguson—while we can expect that the county attorney will totally disagree, and it won't be easy—but I'm confident the first blow can ultimately be deemed 'justifiable' behavior."

Letting that sink in for a minute, he continued, "Much more challenging for us will be the fact he's going to maintain that the second blow was totally unnecessary, that Ferguson was incapacitated and that by then, your sister was no longer in danger. Now, with the horrific nature of what was suddenly thrown at you, your state of mind and the amount of time that elapsed between the two blows will likely be the key element to their whole case. I can't brush it away lightly—it's clearly the second blow that will ultimately present our biggest challenge!"

Knowing he was being very candid and honest about the situation, it wasn't without careful thought. He didn't want to scare them unnecessarily, but Will felt strongly it was important for everyone to get the true picture and to start preparing immediately for the serious battle the Foster family was facing. With that in mind, he added, "We must remember, while the deceased young man in this case may very well have been a notorious, despicable monster, the county attorney has a responsibility to provide what he considers proper justice for his family, combined with the fact he is also representing the general public in Wright County. The simple obvious 'good versus evil' concept, which at a glance appears so very logical in this case, does not resonate very loudly in the pursuit of justice in the eyes of the law.

"Now I don't want to overwhelm or drown you with all the technical legal issues that may or may not present themselves down the road, but I can't overemphasize, tomorrow's interrogation is important. I really don't know much about the county attorney, this Townsend guy. What little I've heard is that he's a pretty decent guy, quite brilliant, and very ambitious, meaning it's very likely he sees this as his big chance to make a name for himself. Unfortunately—and again I don't mean to alarm you, but based on the immediate reaction by the local media last night, and with the widespread national interest already being shown—I'm afraid the highly motivated Townsend is well aware of the kind of fame and notoriety that would accompany this kind of victory."

With everyone still listening nervously to Will's every word, he went on, "Now, let's zero in specifically on tomorrow's interrogation. If Townsend is as overzealous as I expect him to be, he will deliberately but subtly attempt to get you to make statements that he can throw back in your face down the road during the trial, hoping to get you to contradict yourself. With the fact the contents of the session will be recorded and therefore be part of the official record, as part of traditional prosecutorial legal strategy, at some point in the future he'll try to discredit you. For that reason—and trust me, it won't be that difficult—it's important we talk about your basic approach and establish some simple guidelines before we sit down with him tomorrow.

"Now let me comfort you a little bit. My basic recommendation will be extremely easy for you to carry out. It's really very simple: you have to tell the perfect truth! It's important for you to understand you don't have to manufacture anything or make any excuses for what happened yesterday. While it was a violent scene, the fact is, in the end, there was no crime committed by anyone but the Ferguson boy! We have the truth on our side, and that in the end makes things easier for us! The truth won't change over time, and you will never have to struggle to remember what you said, perhaps several weeks earlier."

While dreading the thought of being stuck in this dreadful place at least until Friday, and as frightening as all this was, Foss Man appreciated Will's honesty about what he was now facing. After spending the long miserable night locked up, he obviously had a lot going through his mind. He totally understood where Will was coming from. He had complete confidence in him, and now, more than ever, he knew he was in good hands and looked forward to working with his longtime baseball idol.

Wrapping things up, Will continued, "So, finally, I want you to tell the county attorney the simple truth tomorrow. For example, if he asks you how you felt about the Ferguson boy prior to this incident, tell him the truth. If you hated his guts before and even more so now, feel free to tell him exactly that. Those feelings will be totally understandable to the judge and ultimately the jury. Understand—and this is important and we all know it to be true—how you felt about Ferguson prior to this incident is not why you took such decisive action yesterday!"

After sitting patiently and diligently listening to every single word, it was time for Foss Man to make a few comments. "I'm really glad to have you in my corner, Will. And I really appreciate you explaining how serious this whole thing is, and believe me, if I didn't understand it before, I certainly do now. I can't explain exactly why, but for some reason, I have no fear about answering the district attorney's questions tomorrow. I will tell him exactly how things happened, and I have no second thoughts about my actions. The facts will never change. I had to help Catherine. That monster was hurting her, and she was crying out desperately for help! If I'm guilty of doing something wrong, that's okay. I'll willingly accept that and any of the consequences I may deserve. And Big Jake, my good friend, I don't have to tell you how comforting it will be to have you by my side!"

With that, they stood up, hugged once again, and shook hands. Before departing, Foss Man had two requests for his parents. "Mom, be sure to call Walter Olson and tell him I won't make it to work tomorrow. Tell him I hope to be back by next Monday! And, Dad, will you tell Sparky"—who was the town team manager—"I won't make it to the game tonight? They'll have to find another catcher for the game."

Will had mixed feelings about mentioning the fact he was planning to play ball that night and, as it turned out, would prove to be more than an adequate replacement, ironically, at the catcher's position. After Will decided to be upfront about it, Foss Man was okay with it and lightheartedly warned him, "Make sure Rocket steps off the mound before you fire it down to second. His ears are probably still ringing from when I drilled him two weeks ago!"

With that, they all laughed, and the security guard guided Foss Man back to his cell for what undoubtedly would be another long miserable night!

When they arrived back at the house, her parents invited Will and Big Jake in with hopes they could talk to Catherine for a few minutes. Catherine appeared to be doing remarkably well under the circumstances, but the brothers were heartbroken when they thought about what this sweet, innocent girl had been through only the day before. They were already highly motivated, but after their short meeting, they were determined more than ever to get justice for this amazing girl, her brother, and the entire Foster family. Catherine thoroughly enjoyed the meeting and was impressed with the Simmons brother's professional attitude and had to admit this Will character sure was easy on the eyes.

Chapter Forty-Nine

To accommodate the swarm of reporters, the assistant county attorney, a guy introducing himself as Tom Dempsey, held a brief press conference on the court house steps in Boulder at nine o'clock sharp on Monday morning. He announced to the still-growing number of news media, "Following the arraignment hearing scheduled for this morning and assuming that goes as expected, we'll be holding another press conference at four-thirty this afternoon, at which time we should have a few more answers for you. County Attorney Townsend and County Sheriff Ramsey plan to attend and questions will be entertained at that time." With that brief statement and with a chorus of at least a dozen reporters shouting out questions simultaneously, he turned and walked back into the courthouse.

The reporters and their assigned cameramen would spend the rest of their day taking pictures of everything and anything even remotely connected to the crime. They were flying around the small town taking pictures of, first and foremost, the yellow roped-off crime scene around the shed, the homes of the purported players involved in the crime, the high school, and a variety of angles of the downtown business district. These valued shots would be broadcast on television sets virtually across the country later Monday night. While theoretically restricted because the key players were minors, in spite of that, while technically honoring the legal limitations, the news media managed to work their way around that, and by noon, all the relevant names were widely understood. The reporters were clamoring for interviews with local politicians, school teachers, administrators, and any acquaintance or neighbor who was willing to respond to their probing, highly trained questions. Understandably, the townspeople were intrigued by the amazing fallout from the crazy, unimaginable event.

Throughout the course of the day, every conceivable theory about what had taken place in the small shed had spread throughout the community. In order to establish credibility in the beginning, the major national networks wisely held off on any of the wild speculation until after the afternoon press conference in hopes of learning something more concrete to report on the evening news later that night. Prior to that, they focused on what a peaceful, pristine, and almost perfect little community Jefferson, Iowa, appeared to be. All that had changed dramatically in those few fateful seconds, approximately three-thirty on the previous Saturday afternoon.

As difficult as it was, Foss Man's parents reported to work on Monday morning. Demonstrating their typical strength, they had made up their mind it was the logical thing to do in spite of the inevitable spectacle they'd be dealing with from this day forward. In respect to Catherine's fragile condition, Air Force volunteered to miss work at the gas station that morning to watch the kids. But by noon, in her typical fashion, Catherine insisted she was fine and told her brother to report back to work, that she could certainly handle the afternoon shift.

It was a few minutes after 10:00 a.m., and Will, Big Jake, and Foss Man were sitting together, patiently waiting for the county attorneys to make their scheduled appearance. Although spending another miserable restless night, Foss Man appeared surprisingly fresh and was eager to get the questioning underway. Having these bright and caring friends at his side was comforting and gave him total confidence entering the nerve-wracking proceedings.

Before things got underway, Will handed Foss Man a big poster board the baseball team had prepared after the game the night before. Everyone on the team had signed it and briefly jotted down their best wishes. With Rocket on the mound and Will's competence behind the plate and even managing to belt one over the fence, they won the season opener 5–0.

Big Jake informed Foss Man, "Right after the game, Skunk, Horse, Rocket, and Skeeter came over to my house and were dying to know more about what the heck was going on. There first question was when was it okay for them to come over to see you. I told them the only visitors permitted were your parents and Will and me. Skunk kept telling us how worried he was about the thought of you being trapped alone in that miserable cell. When I filled them in on everything to the extent I felt comfortable with, of course they were all furious with Eclipse. They emphatically agreed how proud they were of you and couldn't believe you were actually arrested and taken into custody for merely doing what you obviously had to do. They wanted me to be sure and tell you that. You know how much they all think of your sister, and you know Skeeter and how crude he can be and how he absolutely adores Catherine. He thought Eclipse deserved to have his balls cut off and stuffed down his throat."

Their support and the signed poster board was a big boost for Foss Man, and it did wonders in lifting his spirits! After thanking Big Jake, they immediately got back down to the important business at hand. The only advice Will gave Foss Man was, "Just relax and be yourself. Be perfectly honest, speak from your heart, and keep your answers brief and to the point. Trust me, Townsend will try to find something you said to twist and distort sometime down the road. You'll have plenty of opportunity in the future to express your personal feelings, preferably when I'm asking you the questions on the witness stand, if indeed it ever comes to that."

The interrogation was held in the formal conference room there in the Juvenile Detention Center. Will handed Townsend Dr. Ellington's written report validating the fact Foss Man's sister Catherine was indeed in the process of being raped when his client walked in on the scene. Townsend glanced at it and quickly shoved it in his briefcase. Less than fifteen minutes later, the relatively short but intense session was completed, and Townsend called for a short recess. As Will expected, it was obvious the county attorney had already made up his mind to schedule a preliminary hearing and had every intention to press charges against Foss Man.

Will was extremely pleased in the manner in which his young client handled the questions. He was confident and strong, never wavering for a second, while effectively fielding every question the county attorney and his assistant threw at him. Following Will's distinct recommendations, Foss Man had deliberately saved any emotional fireworks for the inevitable more critical stages of the legal process.

When County Attorney Townsend and his assistant Tom Dempsey returned to their office, Townsend couldn't wait to point out, "This is going better than I could have ever dreamed, Tom, exactly the way I had hoped!" Without going into detail, he confidently boasted to his assistant, "I hope Simmons is stupid enough to put this kid on the witness stand. We'll have a field day with the poor guy, and I intend to take full advantage of his most glaring weakness."

Curious, Dempsey asked him, "What's that?"

"His flat-out honesty!"

"I don't get it, what do you mean by that?"

"Didn't you recognize it when I asked him what kind of feelings he had toward Ferguson prior to Saturday? He didn't hesitate for one second. He said he's hated his guts since the first day he met him way back in first grade. Talk about a fixed mind-set filled with a powerful prejudicial motive and even malice. Trust me, this is going to be like shooting fish in a barrel! Simmons may be a bright enough guy, but he's already proven he's totally incompetent and inexperienced. I almost feel sorry for the Fosters. It's a little sad they didn't accept one of our public defenders or were able to afford to hire a real lawyer!"

As this conversation was going on, and although they had never officially addressed the subject, after listening to Big Jake describe Foss Man's unique makeup, Will's instincts told him that Foss Man actually preferred or perhaps even needed to go to trial to find out for his own long-range peace of mind if he was truly guilty of committing a crime. Careful not to influence Foss Man's position on the delicate subject, the truth is, if his hunch was accurate, Will was quietly pleased about that! As much as Foss Man despised Eclipse, with his compassionate, sensitive manner, not a small issue and totally understandable, Will could sense Foss Man was devastated and absolutely sick about being responsible for taking the bully's life.

Following the brief recess, theoretically designed so Townsend could make his final decision, which Will knew all along was merely a formality, the county attorney informed Will, "Dr. Ellington's letter and Luke's testimony will not change anything. It's our full intention to formally indict Luke Foster for his responsibility in taking the life of Ron Ferguson. We're holding a press conference this afternoon at four-thirty on the courthouse steps. For your information, we're confident we'll have the full medical examiner's report and the autopsy in a few days. That being the case, it is our intention to schedule the preliminary hearing for nine o'clock on Friday morning. We'll keep you posted."

Foss Man was escorted back to his new home. Not surprised about the fact everything was now officially moving forward, Will and Big Jake planned to go home and get to work preparing for the hearing Friday. Deep in thought and with very little conversation between the two of them, Will and Big Jake headed back to Jefferson.

There were at least two dozen reporters and cameramen waiting on the courthouse steps for the promised press conference. At exactly 4:30 p.m., the two county attorneys and the county sheriff approached the podium and multiple set of microphones.

The sheriff started out by first introducing himself. "Good afternoon, ladies and gentlemen. My name is Fred Ramsey. I'm the sheriff here in Wright County." He spelled out his name. "In a minute, I'll be turning the mic over to Wright County Attorney Roger Townsend and his assistant Tom Dempsey." Again he took the time to spell out their names. "They'll be making a few comments, and following that, we'll all be available for a few questions."

The sheriff continued, "As you know, there is an ongoing investigation into the crime that took place at approximately four o'clock on Saturday afternoon over in Jefferson. It's too early in the investigative process to give you extensive details, but the attorneys will bring you up-to-date on what they have the liberty to report to you at this time. Let me emphasize, what we have right now is very limited, but I want to assure you and the general public that a complete and thorough investigation is underway and will be completed as soon as possible. When it's appropriate, more details will be forthcoming. With that, I'll turn things over to County Attorney Townsend."

Townsend started out, "Good afternoon, ladies and gentlemen. Thank you for being here and for your patience. As Sheriff Ramsey reiterated, we have very little information to give you at this early stage in the process. What I can tell you is that Ronald Ferguson,"—and he spelled out his name—"a seventeen-year-old minor from Jefferson was pronounced dead at the scene of the crime at approximately five o'clock last Saturday afternoon, June 7. We don't have the final medical examiner's report at this time, but what I can say is his death was caused by apparent blunt force trauma to the head. With his legal representation's permission, I can report that Luke Foster, a fifteen-year-old citizen of Jefferson, has taken full responsibility for administering a blow or blows to the head of the victim with a baseball bat. Mr. Foster is in custody at this time. There is an unsubstantiated report that a sexual assault was taking place at the time the blow or blows were administered. Validation of the sexual assault is pending. It would not be appropriate to identify the victim in the alleged assault at this time. It is our hope to have the alleged sexual assault victim's full doctor's statement, the final medical examiner's report, and the autopsy in our hands in a few days. If that happens, we have tentatively scheduled a preliminary hearing for this Friday morning when it will be determined if and what charges will indeed be made. We'll keep you posted as things progress throughout the week. Thank you again. Now we'll be happy to take a few questions. Again, please keep in mind, at this early stage in the investigation, the information we can provide you is very limited."

They were showered with a chorus of questions, all at the same time. The county attorney pointed to one of the many inquiring reporters.

"Is it true that the admitted killer is the brother of the alleged sexual assault victim?"

The county attorney answered, "At this point I don't want to refer to him as a killer—that sounds a little bold and premature. And furthermore, like I said a minute ago, we are currently protecting the name of the alleged assault victim until we have concrete validation that a sexual assault did indeed take place. When we have that information, we'll make a statement accordingly."

"How many times was the deceased boy hit in the head with the baseball bat?"

The sheriff answered, "We should know the official answer to that question after we receive the full medical examiner's report and autopsy in a few days."

"How long will the Foster boy be kept in custody?"

The county attorney took this one. "That will be addressed with the judge in normal fashion at the preliminary hearing on Friday, if indeed the hearing is held Friday."

"Will the case be tried in juvenile or adult court?"

"If there is an indictment and charges are indeed filed, and of course subject to how the defendant pleads on the ultimate charge, that is yet to be determined."

"Was there a history of bad blood between the victim and Luke Foster?"

Restraining himself, he said, "That has not been verified at this point."

"Is the Ferguson boy the same person who killed the two dogs last winter?"

The sheriff stepped to the mic. "We have no proof or reason to believe that at this point. If there is some correlation between this crime and the dead dogs and it is verified and becomes relevant, we'll address that when we have the facts."

"If charges are filed and hold up, how soon will the trial likely be scheduled?"

The county attorney answered, "That depends on a number of things, but I see no reason to delay it. So if a trial is indeed necessary, as far as I'm concerned, the sooner the better."

"Is this the worst crime you've had to deal with during your term?"

The county attorney said, "Thankfully, yes, I think so. They don't get much worse than this. Of course, I've only been serving in this position for two years!"

"What kind of charges are you likely to bring against Luke?"

The county attorney said, "That has yet to be determined. If we hold the preliminary hearing on Friday, and depending on what the investigation's final results are, that decision will be made at that time. That determination will likely come as early as Friday."

With that, the sheriff came to the microphone and announced, "That will be all the questions for now. When we have more meaningful information, we'll schedule another press conference accordingly. And for the benefit of you out-of-town reporters, that could very well be several days, most likely after the hearing on Friday. Thank you again for your patience."

Although the details were limited, the story made headlines and pictures were plastered on the front page of all the area newspapers. It was also the lead story for the local radio and television evening news programs. With the intriguing circumstances surrounding the dramatic story, the three national networks squeezed in a brief and cautious introduction to the story during the nightly news at five-thirty that night. After identifying the location and showing a few pictures of the crime scene and the community, they predicted more significant information would likely be forthcoming later in the week.

When the initial excitement settled down, the national reporters and cameramen thinned out significantly during the week and waited patiently for the outcome of Friday's preliminary hearing and the promised follow-up press conference. The impact the incident had on the local citizens would vary as time passed, but as the case progressed through the court system, the interest level would magnify accordingly. It was inevitable, the shocking incident was going to severely disrupt the previously innocuous small community throughout the always peaceful summer months.

Chapter Fifty

Along with Foss Man's Grandpa Wentworth, Will and Big Jake's dad, Daniel Simmons, was a regular Wednesday afternoon golfing partner of Harold McKinley, the renowned defense lawyer and proud owner of the big office located conveniently on Main Street in Boulder. The giant, elaborate "H. R. McKinley and Son" sign hanging in front of the well-known law office could be seen as soon as you entered town from the east or west. After a short debate on the subject, Daniel had convinced Harold to permit his sons to take full advantage of the firm's expansive law library.

Harold heard about the explosive story the minute he and his son Kenneth returned home from their weekend fishing trip on Monday. Although he knew the deck was stacked against the defense and it would very likely be an uphill struggle, Harold was disappointed not to land what would undoubtedly become one of the most controversial and historical legal battles in Wright County history. Furthermore, his notorious winning streak had been rudely broken when Roger Townsend, the smart-ass young county attorney, was elected two years ago. Harold, who was responsible for hanging the label "Slam Dunk Roger" on the county attorney, the by-product of his extreme caution only indicting "sure thing" suspects, was licking his wounds when he saw the intense national attention the case was stirring up. He would have loved to be the one to deal the punk kid his first major defeat. Upset even more when he learned his golf buddies' unlicensed son got the job, while it was certainly permissible and there was nothing illegal about the concept, he genuinely thought it was a risky move on the Foster family's part. In the beginning, he was selfishly reluctant to offer the boys the use of his library but soon felt it was probably the least he could do. Ultimately, he was okay with the whole idea and encouraged Will and Big Jake to come and go as they pleased and to, by all means, take full advantage of all the latest editions of the best law books money could buy. The two eager "quasi" lawyers spent over six hours during the day Tuesday digging around and focusing on the current 1957 Iowa Law Book.

As soon as Foss Man's parents got home from work Tuesday evening, they joined Will and Big Jake for the meeting Foss Man had been desperately looking forward to since the very moment they left the day before. The endless hours in the small cold cell were proving to be unbearable. The five of them gathered in the formal conference room in the juvenile detention center. Three days had passed since the horrific incident, and everyone had a chance to let the initial shock wear off, let what happened sink in a little bit, and think about and accept the enormous legal challenges they were now facing. They were all thankful to see Catherine had so quickly returned to her old self. Her amazing strength and resiliency inspired all of them, and they all agreed spending one minute feeling sorry for themselves would be a complete waste of time and energy.

Reflecting his high-powered Harvard training, Will quickly proved to be meticulously organized. Before starting the discussion carefully planned for the night, Will outlined the schedule he put together for the week. Wanting to make sure Foss Man got at least a short reprieve from that miserable cell every day and not wanting to overwhelm them with the complex legal issues they'd be dealing with at the hearing Friday, he suggested they meet for exactly one hour tonight and schedule the same length meetings again on Wednesday and Thursday night. Everyone understood his motive and fully endorsed the plan.

Wanting to bolster their trust and to comfort Foss Man's parents with his serious and dedicated approach to defending their son, Will pointed out that he and Big Jake had spent most of the day in the McKinley law library. He pointed out that criminal law varied not only from state to state but actually from county to county as well. He wanted to prove he had familiarized himself with the range of potential charges that could be filed against Foss Man on Friday.

To further dramatize his point, Will asked Big Jake to share what he thought was his most fascinating discovery that afternoon. Big Jake, who Will had to literally drag out of the impressive library, had to chuckle a little bit when he responded, "Sure, listen to this one. I was reading through some of the old 'blue laws' that still exist in Iowa, and would you believe the current recommended sentence for stealing horses or rustling cattle is nothing less than the death penalty? But the good news is most of the current penalties are more sensible and suitable to the times."

Will and Big Jake didn't pick up on Foss Man's dad's subtle reaction to this lighthearted revelation. But William had made a mental note to be sure and corner Rick, his former drinking partner and current working partner, the first thing in the morning and reinforce the importance of keeping a strict lid on their little escapade in Tank William's pig lot a few years ago. He quietly prayed the statute of limitations had expired by now.

Quickly shifting to more serious business, Will and Big Jake had agreed it was important to continue to be upfront, candid, and honest about the serious charges Foss Man would very likely be facing. At the same time, they wanted all of them to know, after their lengthy research that day, Foss Man's actions, as drastic as they were, and as horrific as the results were, would ultimately be deemed fully justified in the eyes of the law. They were careful not to make any promises or guarantees about the outcome, but they wanted the Fosters to know they both truly believed in Foss Man's innocence and felt genuinely confident he would ultimately be found not guilty of any and all charges.

Knowing the trust and respect Foss Man had for Big Jake, Will assigned him with the task of explaining their mutual conclusions about what took place in the shed Saturday. With their combined thorough research and after lengthy and intense discussion between the two of them, before getting into any of their specific legal strategies, they agreed it was important to share the basis for their confidence and fundamental approach in putting their defense plan together.

With that objective in mind, Big Jake proceeded, "None of us want to even think about the grave consequences we'd all be dealing with today if you hadn't arrived at the scene precisely when you did Foss Man. There's no question in our minds, you clearly saved your sister's life by miraculously showing up when you did Saturday. Excuse me for being candid, but after raping your sister, knowing she could and would identify him, there's no way Eclipse was going to simply let her walk away. It's difficult for any of us to comprehend, but the very truth is, Ferguson had every intention of killing Catherine. As we work our way through these unpredictable series of challenges over the coming weeks, no matter how tough things may look at times, please don't ever forget this fact!"

Foss Man's parents were visibly shaken by the frightening reference but listened intently as Big Jake continued, "While Will and I agree this is clearly the case, we all know this truth in itself won't magically remove your personal responsibility for your actions, Foss Man. Your decisive, bold actions are going to be thoroughly examined, questioned, and challenged. And knowing you like I do, I know you're willing to accept the ultimate outcome if that's the price you have to pay for saving your sister's life. You know how your family feels about it, but I can speak for all your caring and loyal friends—we are all thankful and extremely proud of what you did Saturday. I've talked to them, and in our eyes, you're truly a hero, Foss Man!"

Foss Man sat there quietly, not saying a word. He was willing to listen, but he knew he was no stupid-ass hero. In his mind, if he could have rescued Catherine with both of them walking away safely without killing Eclipse, then perhaps. But as far as he was concerned, the way he had handled it was more "chicken shit" than heroic. Anybody can hit somebody over the head with a stupid baseball bat.

Will nodded his head, indicating he agreed with everything Big Jake had so eloquently stated. He only added, "I'll take what Big Jake said one step further. Foss Man, once you became a witness to the rape, Ferguson would not have allowed you to simply walk away either. Nothing against your physical prowess, but had you not responded as decisively as you did, Ferguson would have been like dealing with a wounded grizzly bear. There's no doubt it would have turned into a blood bath, more than likely resulting in both you and your sister's death. While it may be difficult to prove, our research today clearly spells out that the great potential of Ferguson's violent retaliation provides valid grounds for an element of self-defense. When the time is right, we fully intend to demonstrate this very legitimate argument!"

Prior to these riveting declarations, Foss Man's parents had never given this horrifying outcome a remote thought—the very likely deaths of both their daughter and son. These stunning revelations made his always strong-willed mother break down. She was sobbing quietly and resting her head on her visibly shaken husband's shoulder. It wasn't his intention, but with this understandable emotional reaction, Will suggested they take a short break.

Other than Big Jake's hero reference, Foss Man was in full agreement with Will and Big Jake. He too had fully recognized the frightening reality of how ugly things would have gotten Saturday afternoon. While tossing and turning all night, although the entire episode only took a few seconds, he had gone over it in his mind again and again, dissecting every gut-wrenching detail of what happened. He was deeply sickened about being responsible for ending someone's life, even a despicable human being like Eclipse, and as much as he wished there was a better way, he knew he did what was necessary to guarantee saving his sister's life. With that honest and comforting conclusion, he agreed with Big Jake, he was more than willing to accept the consequences, however unbearable they may be!

With that being the case, emboldened by the emotional tolerance he had built up over the years and the help of God, Foss Man had formed strong feelings about what his position would be throughout what had clearly become the worst nightmare of his life. But for now, he was going to keep listening to his parents and trusted legal team and remain open-minded. When the time was right, he would not hesitate to contribute his firm opinion on what he considered to be the only acceptable approach to this unimaginable mess.

After a short break, they got back to work. Will started out with, "There are three major subjects that will be addressed Friday at the hearing. First and most importantly, based on the strength of the case presented by Townsend, will be the judge's final decision on what specific charge will be filed against Foss Man. I don't want to alarm you with the rather intimidating terminology, but the final charge is likely to range anywhere from second-degree murder, voluntary manslaughter, to involuntary manslaughter. Tomorrow night—and I intend to thoroughly research how Iowa law deals with each of these charges—I want to discuss with you how and to what extent we may challenge the various charges."

Will couldn't help but notice the startled and concerned look on Foss Man's parents' faces, but he felt the bold terminology had to be introduced—the sooner the better.

"Second, with your status as a minor, the next significant question will be, should the trial be held in juvenile or adult court? My guess is with the violent nature of the incident resulting in the death of a human being, the county attorney will be pushing for adult court, and frankly, that's not all bad. We'll have some input and influence on this decision, and I want to discuss this much further with all of you Thursday night, once again after I do more research on the subject. I want to do a full study of the recent history of the juvenile cases heard here in Wright County as well as throughout the state of Iowa.

"And third, with the high profile and notorious reputation of the Ferguson boy, Townsend will probably insist on a change of venue. Our position on this issue is clear-cut. We will argue this aggressively and simply won't let that happen! We clearly want the prospective jury pool to be composed of our local citizens. I have every reason to believe we'll win this battle!"

Foss Man knew deep down these were all-important considerations, but once again, after three long nights of contemplation, while he couldn't bear to think about how he would cope with any lengthy jail time, the perfect truth was, his ultimate peace of mind was his only real concern. He knew any lingering mental torment had to be minimized at all cost. He'd been through this kind of thing once before a long time ago. Above anything else, he not only had to find out if what he did was a crime in the eyes of the law, but he also had to find out if it was morally wrong. At this point in the process, the truth was, he really didn't care much about any of these technical legal matters; he only needed and looked forward to having his day in court.

While all this was true, he would save his personal thoughts until the end of the meeting Thursday night. He wanted to hear everything Will, Big Jake, and his parents had to say on what he knew were important and necessary legal decisions.

Chapter Fifty-One

Eclipse's funeral was scheduled for Wednesday morning, and it was a pathetically sad scene on many levels. Ronald's convict brother Frank was permitted to attend the funeral. With special permission, he had been transported, handcuffed, and was now being closely monitored by two personal police escorts. It was awkward for everyone involved, but the emotional and angry brother of the deceased boy refused to interact with or sit anywhere near his parents. The fact was, when the time was just right, he had an explosive surprise for the two people he despised more than anyone in the world. It was long overdue!

For months before the unfortunate tragedy in the shed, Frank had been trying desperately to put a plan together to expose the pathetic truth about what had been going on in their home throughout his miserable life. The only thing that kept him from blowing the whole sad story sky-high long before this was his honest fear for his brother Ronald's safety, even his life. He knew from his own personal experience that his ruthless father was capable of virtually anything.

All that had changed now. Frank was absolutely furious about what happened to his brother. He no longer feared the violent threats his parents had so effectively held over he and Ronald's head throughout their entire painful lives. He now, more than ever, welcomed any form of retaliation from his parents. Their reign of terror would soon be over!

The small attendance at the funeral was glaring. With understandable human emotions, Reverend Thompson struggled mightily to find the appropriate words to comfort the remaining Ferguson family members. It was difficult moments like this that made the preacher second-guess tearing up that retirement letter last winter.

Even for the severely troubled and renowned Eclipse, this was a sad ending. But it was only the beginning of a downward spiral for the Ferguson family!

At eight o'clock sharp Wednesday morning, the eager and motivated Simmons brothers were waiting in front of the McKinley law office over in Boulder. It was the second-generation law partner, Kenneth McKinley, who reported to open up for business that day. After making brief and polite small talk, Will and Big Jake made themselves comfortable in two of the large leather chairs and immediately buried themselves amongst the endless stacks of books in the firm's impressive library. Big Jake cherished every minute he was spending with his much-admired big brother and couldn't wait to dig into the research assigned to him for the day. It couldn't get better than this as far as he was concerned.

That night, they all gathered once again in the conference room. Foss Man had somehow managed to get through another long night and day in his undesirable personal dwelling. He felt like some kind of caged animal. He was praying he could make it to Friday morning and dreaded the thought if he for some reason wasn't released after the hearing. He cherished the short time he could spend with these two amazing guys and, of course, his parents.

Will immediately took charge. "Judge Cooper will give Townsend an opportunity to present his rational for requesting a preliminary hearing. Townsend will give his personal interpretation of what took place in the shed and introduce the fact he wants to formally bring charges against Foss Man. Then we'll be given a chance to dispute or challenge his case. If our objective is to have the indictment rejected or thrown out, we could go to great length to demonstrate that any charge against Foss Man is unjustified. For example, we could have Catherine attend and have her and Foss Man give testimony to what happened that day with the hope of having the case dismissed by the judge. By the end of our meeting tomorrow night, we'll have decided on our basic approach and to what extent we may or may not want to fight any specific charge.

"The sound of these charges will be frightening, but we're going to have to start getting used to the terminology that will be casually thrown around Friday morning. Townsend will probably start out aggressively attempting to convince Judge Cooper that Foss Man's actions justify second-degree murder charges. There's a very subjective gray area and fine line separating second-degree murder and voluntary manslaughter. *Involuntary manslaughter* is more clearly defined. Let me explain the basic criteria for each of the three charges, give a few examples, and then try to explain how they're similar, how they differ, and how they may directly relate to our case.

"The most serious charge, of course, is second-degree murder. This is 'killing another human being with malice. Doing a harmful act without just cause or legal excuse but without the element of premeditation or deliberation.'

"A man has a suspicion his neighbor might be having an affair with his wife. He comes home early from work one day and finds the familiar neighbor in bed with his wife. In an impulsive state of rage, he shoots and kills the neighbor. Was his reaction solely dictated by what was going on directly before him, or was it provoked by the preexisting suspicion? There was no premeditation, but there was the presence of malice. The current penalty for second-degree murder ranges from five to twenty years.

"Voluntary manslaughter occurs when one person kills another human being after adequate provocation and there has been action that was sufficient to incite an ordinary person to sudden and intense passion such that he loses control. The death occurred when the person was killed without malice, which means they did not intend to cause death.

"A man comes home from work early and finds a total stranger in bed with his wife. In an impulsive state of rage, he shoots and kills the stranger. His reaction was dictated solely by what was going on directly before him. There was no evidence of malice. The penalty for voluntary manslaughter ranges from three to eleven years.

"I don't want to confuse you but this next point hits close to home. A killing that would have been murder may be reduced to manslaughter if the defendant committed the killing because he mistakenly believed he needed to use deadly force to defend himself or another person. The fine line between these two charges revolves around the all-important state of mind.

"Following an intense argument with his boss, a man stops in the neighborhood bar and aggressively drinks alcoholic beverages until his alcohol blood level is well over the legal limit to drive. In a continuing state of anger, he jumps in the car and drives well over the speed limit, causing a violent crash that results in the death of a total stranger. There was no malice toward the victim, but there was a flagrant degree of recklessness. This would be another example of voluntary manslaughter in Iowa. In many states, it's labeled reckless homicide.

"Involuntary manslaughter is defined as the unlawful killing of a human being without malice aforethought, and the killing must have been unintentional.

"A person stops after work for a few innocent drinks with his co-workers. His alcohol blood level slips over the legal limit to drive. He loses control of his car on the way home when he hits a sheet of ice, slides through a Stop sign, and hits a car broad side, resulting in the death of a total stranger. The driver is responsible for his actions, but once again, there is no deliberate intent toward the victim. The penalty for involuntary manslaughter is one to three years.

"You can see the distinction between the two manslaughter charges is more clear-cut.

"During the discussion between Judge Cooper and Townsend Friday morning, you'll hear terms like *heat of passion*, *recovery time from provocation*, *malice aforethought and afterthought*, and *the state of mind*. Applying these concepts directly to our case, Townsend will very likely contend Foss Man's reaction was influenced not only by what was taking place at the time but by his past experiences or feelings toward Ferguson. Of course we know that's not the case. When it's all said and done, like I mentioned to you Sunday, the case will ultimately revolve around the amount of time that elapsed between the first blow and the second blow and Foss Man's state of mind during that brief time."

As Will expected, introducing these examples made everyone nervous and provoked many questions resulting in a healthy and lively conversation. Will felt good about the discussion and could see the Fosters were deeply worried but were starting to grasp what they were up against, and that was his only intention. When precisely one hour had expired, as planned, and as much as Foss Man would have preferred extending the meeting, he was rudely escorted back to his cell, and his concerned parents and legal team returned home.

Chapter Fifty-Two

As Will and Big Jake were settling in for another lengthy session in the McKinley law library Thursday morning, Will got a call from Townsend, who informed him he could pick up his copy of the medical examiner's report and the autopsy, which had just been completed.

From the lengthy five-page report, Will extracted what he considered were the three most significant discoveries. First, Ferguson's blood alcohol level was at .25, three times the limit to drive legally. This was a favorable finding for the defense. Secondly, while it was not 100 percent conclusive, it was determined that it was reasonable to conclude that the second blow to the head was the principal cause of death. Will had feared this outcome, and it was clearly the most powerful revelation and would prove to be their greatest challenge. And finally, important but fully expected, the doctor's report officially verified that a rape was indeed taking place at the time the deadly blows were administered. That meant the name of the rape victim would now be formally entered on the record.

On Thursday night, Foss Man eagerly joined his loyal supporters for their final meeting before the big hearing now officially scheduled for the following morning. After the normal small talk, in his typical highly organized fashion, Will got right down to business.

He started out, "As I promised, we're going to discuss the pros and cons of having the case heard in the juvenile or adult court system tonight." The fact was, instructed to think about it and now deeply worried about it, Foss Man's parents had discussed this question with some of their fellow workers that day. Before Will continued, Foss Man's mother asked him very politely, "Will, wouldn't a jury in the juvenile court system be just as capable of fully exonerating Luke as the adult court. I admit I don't know much about it, and I'm anxious to hear what you have to say, but it seems to me that would certainly be a more appealing option in terms of any potential sentence Luke might be facing. Remember, Luke is only fifteen years old."

Will was impressed with this very legitimate and astute point. After struggling all day with his own thoughts on the matter, he had deliberately put off expressing his own position on the critical decision until he could do extensive research on the subject. He had spent most of the day doing that very thing.

"That's a valid question, Mrs. Foster, and frankly, I had a heck of a time arriving at what my personal recommendation will be on the subject. But before we finalize anything, I want to share what I learned today and thought we'd hash it over tonight and hopefully arrive at a consensus we all feel comfortable with. Your feelings are important to me, and I promise will be given careful consideration.

"Here's what we've discovered. When there is a human death at the center of the case, like I suggested the other day, it is unusual in Iowa to have the case heard in the juvenile court system. But that doesn't mean we can't present an argument for it, it does happen, particularly for a fifteen-year-old. The records in Iowa suggest juries are inclined to believe the defendant is already getting a break by having the case heard in the lower court system, thus creating a mindset for the presumption of guilt. That being the case, the juvenile court system historically tends to come in with a higher percentage of guilty verdicts, oftentimes disregarding the strength of the defense arguments. This tendency, combined with the built-in expectation for softer penalties, the bar is set lower and juries subsequently feel more comfortable coming in with a guilty verdict."

Will paused for a minute for those considerations to sink in and continued, "Now let me remind everyone. While going through the adult courts clearly poses the potential for more severe penalties, with the higher bar and the more rigid 'beyond a reasonable doubt' burden of proof, it also improves the chance for total and complete exoneration."

As Will expected, these delicate and complex considerations once again resulted in a healthy debate amongst Foss Man's parents, Will, and Big Jake. Will could see that the number one concern and the driving force behind Mr. and Mrs. Foster's position on everything was minimizing the length of any potential jail time Foss Man might be facing. He totally understood and respected these sentiments, but he knew there were other important factors to consider and he couldn't overlook his personal legal obligations. Will was genuine about asking for their input, and while he was developing strong feelings about where he stood, he wanted to be careful not to pressure them or influence their honest opinions. He knew it wouldn't be easy, but when it came down to it, at the end, it was up to him to make a bold recommendation and take a final stance on how they would proceed.

Fortunately, like a gift from above, what was about to take place took Will off the proverbial hook. He wanted to give Foss Man a big hug for expressing so bravely and candidly how he had personally hoped they would all agree to move forward.

Foss Man had been sitting quietly and listening intently to his loyal supporters debate for over a half hour. Like his dad, who had learned to be a good listener with eight bubbly and outgoing kids, Foss Man proved to be a talented listener. Knowing already how strongly he felt about these issues, he felt he owed it to them to finally speak up. With that in mind, he boldly interrupted, "Let me make this easier for you guys. I know all of you are looking out for my best interests, and in the end, I hope you will agree with me, but I know how we have to go about this whole thing. We really have no choice!"

The intense discussion stopped immediately. Having a pretty good hunch about what he hoped was coming, Will seized the opportunity and eagerly encouraged him, "Go ahead, Foss Man. After all, it is your future we're talking about here. What are you thinking?"

Foss Man proceeded to express his well-thought-out position. "Last night, we debated over what our response should be to the range of charges Townsend will likely file against me. Then tonight, the healthy discussion about our preference between the juvenile and the adult court system. We all know Will has to take a final position on both of these issues tomorrow morning."

"The second I walked into the shed last Saturday, and believe me, I thank the good Lord every day for putting me there, but a built-in part of the deal, I was given what really amounts to a lifetime sentence. After five days of replaying what happened over and over in my mind, as much as I wish I had better options, we all agree I did what had to be done to stop what was going on and to actually save Catherine's life. Now I'm no stupid hero, but like Big Jake rightfully suggested the other day, I'm totally willing to pay whatever the price may be for that fortunate outcome. But along with that, the harsh truth is this: I am now personally responsible for taking another human being's life, and nothing can change that. Amongst us—and I know how much you all care—only I know exactly how my mind works and what is necessary for me to have a legitimate chance of suspending this lifelong sentence I am already serving or to ever have a minute of true happiness again in my lifetime."

He had everyone's attention. "So here's what we have to do with the issues we've been wrestling with this week. We simply put our full trust in the legal system. We don't fight it—we accept whatever charge Townsend decides is appropriate for my actions. He knows what happened in the shed Saturday. And I don't want any breaks. If it's normal for a case dealing with the death of a human to be tried in the adult court system, that's exactly where I want, and more important than that, we need to have the case heard. And finally, I agree with you, Will—the jury should be made up of local citizens. Who better to evaluate what happened and make an honest judgment of my actions? And in the end, we have to put our full trust in the jury.

"If I'm found guilty, it won't be easy—I'll just have to learn to live with that. If I'm found not guilty of any wrongdoing—and we all firmly believe that should and will be the case—I then have a legitimate chance of getting on with my life with my head held high!"

No more had to be said. Will was ecstatic, and the fact was, he totally agreed with everything Foss Man proposed. Now better understanding what Big Jake had been saying all along about his great friend, Will's fondness and respect for his young client skyrocketed. He could now let Townsend set the bar for the burden of proof. And this would allow him to save Catherine's critical testimony to maximize the impact and would prevent Townsend from any opportunity to attack and tear it apart. The same thing would be true for Foss Man's full testimony. While this had turned into a bold "all or nothing" approach and would put enormous pressure on him, he knew in his heart it was the right thing to do.

Foss Man was guided back to his cell for what they all hoped and prayed would be the last time prior to the trial, and the others departed with a full understanding of how Will would proceed in the morning.

Chapter Fifty-Three

The preliminary hearing got underway at nine o'clock sharp on Friday morning in front of the duly appointed fifth district circuit court judge, the long-standing Honorable George Cooper. Cooper was a serious, no-nonsense judge with unquestionable integrity, was held in high esteem, and was famous for his unwavering dedication to upholding the law.

Based on the agreement the night before, Catherine remained home and Foss Man, his parents, along with Big Jake and Will, were now seated together in the large rather intimidating Wright County court room. Foss Man had been escorted the short walk from the juvenile detention center and was still dressed in the unbecoming orange coveralls.

Following introductions and the normal formalities, Judge Cooper went through a brief list of the expected requisite instructions. Wasting no time, County Attorney Townsend proceeded to present his recommendation for the formal indictment in the case pitting the State of Iowa versus Luke Foster. Before any discussion on the nature of the specific charge to be brought against the defendant, the judge asked Will, "Would the defense like to make a statement on behalf of Mr. Foster?" Will leaned forward without standing up and politely responded, "Thank you, Your Honor, not at this point." A little surprised there was no debate or objection to making the initial indictment, Judge Cooper ordered the county attorney to introduce what specific charge he proposed to file against the defendant.

Townsend proceeded to explain his rational for the range of charges he felt were appropriate. The fact the case was not a "whodunit" crime, the primary focus was on technical dialogue, reviewing and debating the difference between second-degree murder and manslaughter. The key element that stood out in the discussion between Townsend and the judge was the fact the decision would depend less on abstract legal rules than on a subjective judgment about the defendant's state of mind at the time of the alleged crime.

Foss Man listened diligently to what sounded like legal mumbo jumbo to him, but as Will predicted, terminology like "malice aforethought," "heat of passion," "recovery time from provocation," and "state of mind" were being thrown around. He'd let the lawyers sort all that legal stuff out, but only he really knew what was going on in his head that day. He simply had to make sure he saved his sister this time!

Townsend had an aggressive and confident matter-of-fact style about him, and after intense and thorough debate with Judge Cooper between either second-degree murder or voluntary manslaughter, it was finally determined that Luke Foster would be formally charged with the lesser charge, voluntary manslaughter.

With that, Judge Cooper addressed Will, "Thank you for your patience, Mr. Simmons. You've heard the prosecution's rational and the court's decision for formally bringing the charge of voluntary manslaughter against your client. This is the time for you to present any arguments you may have in protest to the charge."

Will stood up and approached the bench. He planned to be brief and to the point. "It's been obvious to us from the very beginning that County Attorney Townsend has ignored the glaring circumstances that, beyond the obvious, were dramatically present in the shed on Saturday, June 7. The defense fully understands that the violent rape of Luke's sister, on its own merit alone, may put his bold reaction in question. But it's our emphatic belief that a more responsible, complete, and thorough analysis of the threatening and explosive dynamics that loomed so very large that day, again beyond the surface, would fully justify Luke Foster's actions that sad day. The defendant genuinely regrets the horrific outcome, but if Mr. Townsend read and understood Catherine Foster's personal statement, it was made perfectly clear Ron Ferguson had every intention of killing her that day. It is our firm belief Luke Foster's actions were not only justified but necessary in saving his sister's life. The only crime that took place in the shed on that tragic day was the violent rape of Catherine Foster. That being the case, the defense firmly believes that any criminal charge filed against Luke Foster should be dismissed immediately. That's all the defense has to say at this time, Your Honor!"

While Will's statement was filled with logic and was convincing, Big Jake, Luke, and his parents sat there, knowing all along it was merely a formality and designed exclusively to present at least a minimal protest to satisfy what position the judge would expect a responsible defense lawyer to take.

Clearly taken back by Will's provocative statement, with no debate or response from Townsend or Judge Cooper, the defense's premise was promptly rejected. With that, Judge Cooper was obliged to go through the formality of asking the defendant what his official position was on the charge. A guilty plea would end the proceedings, and a hearing would be scheduled for the penalty phase.

Standing beside his young client, on behalf of Foss Man, in a firm voice, Will bellowed, "Luke Foster pleads 'Not Guilty,' Your Honor!

The second major consideration dealt with the expected "juvenile vs. adult court" decision. Judge Cooper pointed out that with rare exceptions, it was a normal practice with the death of a human being involved, the case would be heard in the adult court system. With that in mind, and with no objection from the defense, the judge readily agreed with the county attorney's recommendation, and it was quickly determined the case would indeed be tried in adult court.

Once again, Judge Cooper was surprised no protest was made by the defense. While he thought the young unlicensed Simmons was bright and articulate, he had to wonder if the Foster kid was being properly represented.

Then the important "change of venue" issue was addressed. Emphasizing the notoriety of Ferguson's behavior history, Townsend made the anticipated argument for a change of venue. Although there was firm rebuttal coming from Townsend, very little debate was entertained by the judge, and as Will expected and hoped for, Judge Cooper emphatically rejected the proposal. Loud and clear, the judge demanded, "This case will be heard right here in the local Wright County Court House!"

After reviewing everyone's personal calendars and general agreement was made by all parties involved, the trial was scheduled for the tenth of July, approximately one month from that day.

It was agreed that Luke Foster would be released to the custody of his parents with no bond required. His release was referred to as "house arrest" with exclusive freedom for work privileges. He would be restricted to remain at home under his parents' supervision but was permitted to report to work for Walter Olson between the hours of 6:00 a.m. and 6:00 p.m., Monday through Saturday. He would be free to attend church and Sunday school from 9:00 a.m. until 12:00 noon on Sundays. It was emphasized that he would not be allowed to play baseball or any other recreational activities outside of the home. Any violation of these restrictions would result in the revocation of these liberties and his immediate return to the juvenile detention center, and he would remain in custody until the completion of the trial!

With that, Judge Cooper proclaimed, "Thank you for your cooperation, and if there are no more questions or concerns, this hearing is now adjourned!" With that, he slammed his gavel.

Relieved it was over, Big Jake, Will, Foss Man, and his shaken parents returned to Jefferson. After six long days and nights in that cold miserable cell and dressed in the same uncomfortable orange one-piece set of overalls, a dramatic understatement, Foss Man was happy to be going home. He couldn't wait to sit down and spend some time with his family, particularly with his big sister Catherine. Forgetting the fact he had no real choice in the matter anyway, his plan was to spend the rest of Friday quietly at home.

With his client's full support, Will was satisfied with how everything turned out. He now had a full month to prepare the best defense possible for his new young friend, Luke Foster. He knew he had a huge challenge ahead of him but totally believed in Luke's innocence and was more than eager and willing to do whatever it took to get the sensitive and bighearted kid through this ugly mess. And he looked forward to having his brilliant younger brother—Big Jake, his buddies called him—at his side. He had to be honest with himself, there were moments along the way when he questioned if he was adequately prepared for such a monumental case. But he realized now more than ever, *This is indeed going to be an interesting summer!*

Other than the "change of venue" decision, thirty-five-year-old Wright County Attorney Townsend was thrilled about how everything was going. With his ambitious long-range political aspirations, already having his eye on the fifth district congressional seat in Washington, DC, incumbent H. R. Gross had to retire someday. He knew this case provided a golden opportunity to elevate his profile and stature in the entire state of Iowa!

While he had no personal vendetta against the young defendant—he seemed like a decent-enough kid—he was certainly going to do his job in not only representing the Ferguson family but the Wright County general public as well. Furthermore, he genuinely felt the defendant was guilty of taking the law into his own hands and certainly had better options at that critical moment he instead chose to bludgeon the obviously troubled Ferguson boy. For all those reasons, he was determined to win the case and keep his unblemished prosecutorial record intact.

With that in mind, he and his assistant Tom Dempsey had to get to work and prepare his opening statement for the press conference scheduled for later that afternoon. With no time to waste, he made arrangements to have sandwiches delivered to his office. Both thoroughly enjoying the excitement of the moment, they closed the door, sat down, rolled up their sleeves, and enthusiastically dug in. The press conference was scheduled for less than two hours later, and peeking through the side window in his office, there was already a swarm of reporters gathering on the courthouse steps. He could see this was creating a level of interest never before seen in Wright County, and he had every intention of taking full advantage of it!

As they promised, on Monday, Sheriff Ramsey and county attorneys Townsend and Dempsey walked up to the bank of microphones at exactly 3:00 p.m. sharp. The unruly media crowd was twice as large as the one they addressed on Monday. With his adrenaline already at a fever pitch, he couldn't help but notice the identification on the side of the television cameras from the three national networks. *Holy shit, it looks like a live broadcast. This is incredible!*

Sheriff Ramsey graciously greeted everyone and introduced himself, once again spelling out his and the two county attorneys' names, made a few brief comments, and turned the mic over to Townsend.

With the unique circumstances surrounding the dramatic rape and murder scene last Saturday, and the charge now formally filed against the teenage defendant, there were all the provocative components needed and desired for a lead story for the evening television news shows, as well as front page "above-the-fold" headlines for the print media. The intrigue and interest was so powerful the three major national networks felt justified in interrupting the regular scheduled programming for the live broadcast of the highly anticipated press conference.

Will and Big Jake were huddled in front of the television set at home, and watching his brilliant performance, they couldn't deny it, Townsend was really quite impressive. Will had already recognized the fact this guy was pretty sharp that morning at the hearing, but the way he was handling himself this afternoon, he now fully realized the young but extremely polished county attorney was going to be a formidable opponent. He wasn't necessarily intimidated or worried about it, but he had to admit, in that expensive tailored suit, flawless dark complexion, combined with being 6'2" tall and blessed with an undeniably handsome face, Will could see the case serving as a major launching pad for a seat in the House of Representatives in Washington some day or perhaps even a bed in the governor's mansion. It was pretty obvious Townsend had his sights set on something far beyond the Wright County Attorney's office.

Townsend explained, "I'll be making a rather lengthy statement, so please bear with me. We'll be happy to take some questions in a few minutes." The first subject he addressed provided the perfect opportunity to demonstrate what a compassionate, thoughtful, and gracious human being he was. He opened up with, "Ladies and gentlemen, with permission from her family, I can now report that our investigation has officially concluded that Catherine Foster, the older sister of the defendant in this sad case, was indeed in the process of being raped at the time Luke Foster entered the shed last Saturday afternoon. I ask—no, I insist—that you show the ultimate respect for Catherine's privacy at all times. Now I want this made perfectly clear. This young lady deserves to live a normal life throughout this entire process, and anyone who approaches her or shows the smallest hint of anything that even resembles harassment will be arrested on the spot. The same thing goes for the defendant, Luke Foster, who incidentally, was released and turned over to his parents this morning. Catherine and Luke should feel comfortable to go about their lives without interruption from the media. Keep in mind, these young people have both been through an unimaginable traumatic experience, and they deserve their privacy and your utmost consideration. It's really very simple—I politely order you to stay away from them!"

Sitting next to Will on the couch in their family room at home, before Townsend went any further, Big Jake couldn't resist, "Good grief, how did the ruthless executioner from this morning so quickly turn into this eloquent Billy Graham in such a short period of time?" Will, who was shaking his head and chuckling, added, "And it's pretty obvious, he's cleverly designing everything he says to charm and influence the potential jury pool out there. Oh yes, this guy's a smart fellow all right and is going to be a tough opponent, believe me, little brother!"

Townsend went on. "Now I want to talk about the specific facts of this case, the decisions that were established at the preliminary hearing this morning. After lengthy and careful evaluation of the facts, formal charges of voluntary manslaughter have been filed against Mr. Luke Foster in the death of Mr. Ronald Ferguson. The defendant has formally pleaded 'not guilty.' Two other major determinations—the case will be held in adult court, and there'll be no change in venue. The case will be heard right here in the Wright County Court House. The trial is scheduled to begin approximately one month from now, on July 10."

With that, as promised, he opened it up for a few questions. There was an immediate resounding chorus of questions shouted out simultaneously. It proceeded to be a lively exchange, and every conceivable question was thrown at them.

"Why weren't second-degree murder charges filed against the defendant?"

"What kind of a sentence is the defendant facing if he's found guilty of manslaughter?"

"Doesn't a boy have the right to rescue his sister if she's being raped?"

"Is it normal to have a murderer released back into the community?"

"Was the deceased boy guilty of killing those dogs last winter?"

"Is it true that the young man raping the girl was drunk at the time?"

"How long will the trial take?"

The conference went on for over a half hour, and as the questions were often repeated and soon became redundant, Sheriff Ramsey stepped up to the mic. "Thank you for your interest and your patience." And with that, the press conference abruptly ended.

There was widespread media interest over the weekend. With the trial scheduled a month later, things gradually settled down, and at least on the surface, within days, things returned to normalcy around Jefferson once again. Throughout the ten days since the crime was committed, endless pictures of the shed, the Ferguson and the Foster homes, high school, downtown business district, and more recently, a picture of the defendant riding his bike to work, one of the entire Foster family exiting the First Lutheran Church that Sunday morning, and every remotely related scene was splashed in the local newspapers and on the evening television news shows.

Meanwhile, Frank Ferguson, older brother of the deceased boy in the case, while his counselors were fooled into thinking he had made great strides during his intense rehabilitation program and the general recovery process, the underlying truth was, triggered by his younger brother's brutal death, he was growing angrier and more bitter by the day. He made one unwavering promise to himself: *The court system better put the punk that killed my brother away for a long time, or I'll take care of him myself! Rape, my ass! Ron didn't rape that girl any more than I was guilty of the sexual assault I was convicted of over eight years ago. Those little bitches strut around town just asking for it, and when you do something about it, they go running to the police. Ron did not deserve to be killed any more than I deserved to be locked up down here. That county attorney better take care of that fucking punk kid, or believe me, when I get out of this place, I will!*

With that alarming declaration, unknowingly, the stakes in the criminal case of the *State of Iowa v. Luke Foster* were elevated dramatically!

The Jefferson community's wholesome reputation may have been tarnished by the recent event, but with the overwhelming presence of all branches of the media, the restaurants, taverns, and motels within a fifty-mile radius of town had enjoyed an unprecedented booming business. A quiet underlying bonus—the local economy got a huge shot in the arm. And it would be the same if not greater when the tenth of July rolled around.

Chapter Fifty-Four

With Foss Man's return home Friday afternoon, the family spent the rest of the day struggling to get their minds around the incredible developments that had so rudely turned their lives upside down in that one short week. When Luke walked in the door, Catherine ran directly toward him, hugged him, and totally uncharacteristic of her always disciplined demeanor, holding him in a firm bear hug, began sobbing uncontrollably. Foss Man couldn't help it; he too broke down. For his parents, it was a powerful, moving picture.

Everyone regained their composure, and during the next few minutes, Foss Man would have two of the most meaningful conversations of his lifetime. It was rare for Catherine and Foss Man to have direct heart-to-heart talks, but for obvious reasons, Catherine was in a serious and emotional mood and said with genuine sincerity, "Luke, I want to tell you something that is really important. I know how much you tormented and beat yourself up over what happened years ago when Carol fell out of the boat that night of the bad flood. We all know it wasn't your fault, but I know, deep down, you've always blamed yourself. And now it's a simple fact, Luke—you saved my life. Do you hear what I'm saying? There is no doubt in my mind you saved my life!"

Foss Man couldn't say anything. More than anyone would ever know, it was an extraordinary moment for him. No words had to be spoken. They just stood there and, spontaneously, once again hugged each other.

Then another first. Air Force came over to Foss Man, shook his hand, and said with newfound admiration, "Good work, little brother, I'm really proud of you!" Totally out of character, he continued, "No matter how this thing comes out, Luke, what you did last Saturday was absolutely the right thing to do!" Then a sight their parents could hardly believe—they proceeded to hug each other! Once again, it was a rare and touching sight!

This was a pivotal moment in Foss Man's young life. The unwavering support of these two respected siblings would be instrumental in coping with the monumental challenges he was now facing. Their mother encouraged the three of them to sit down and ordered the rest of the family to either go outside or up to their rooms and find something to keep themselves busy. Looking back quizzically, the five younger ones politely scampered out of the room. Foss Man, Air Force, Catherine, and their loving parents sat down and had a serious family discussion.

After their desperate attempt to make some kind of sense out of all this, it was established that together, as a family, they would get through this frightening nightmare. They were committed to be stronger than they had ever been in their lives and agreed to not waste one minute feeling sorry for themselves. They knew it was a blessing that Foss Man walked into the shed when he did, had done nothing wrong, and with their strong belief in God, everything would work out for the best. They all genuinely agreed and believed, "Everything happens for a reason, and the outcome is now in God's hands!"

There was a knock on the door. Mr. Slim and Nute were standing there, and as always with smiles on their faces and a box filled with Foss Man's favorite glazed donuts. The two old gentlemen were warmly invited in to join them. Noticing his glaring weight loss, a concerned Mr. Slim suggested, "Good grief, it looks like you're nothing but skin and bones, Foss Man. You better eat the whole box of donuts yourself." During what turned out to be a brief conversation, Mr. Slim made an interesting suggestion. "You know what, young buddy, this would probably be a good time to keep that special old Indianhead penny in your mitts. It's always been a little magical for you, hasn't it?"

Foss Man quickly agreed, "You know what, that's a good idea, Mr. Slim. You're right, it hasn't failed me yet!" Recognizing it was a private time for the Fosters, the two old codgers quickly excused themselves. Foss Man could always count on these two special friends to give him a timely lift!

As soon as they left, Foss Man made a call to Walter Olsen informing him that he would be reporting for work in the morning. Walter responded, "That's good news. It's high time we put you back to work."

Foss Man was thrilled about the opportunity to sleep in his own bed that night with Gerald, his confused eleven-year-old brother. Gerald looked at him with curious eyes and asked him, "You going to be okay, Luke?" Not really knowing the answer to the valid question, he bravely attempted to convince him, "Yes, little brother, don't you worry about it. Everything is going to be just fine!"

Gerald actually jumped out of bed before Foss Man the next morning to deliver newspapers. It had been another long restless night, but about a half hour after Gerald disappeared, Foss Man bounced out of bed and enthusiastically reported to work promptly at 7:00 a.m. After being cooped up all week, he couldn't wait to work off all that pent-up nervous energy and was anxious to make up for all the hours and income he had missed out on the previous week.

Walter expressed how sorry he was about what he was going through but quickly switched gears and gave him the good news. "You're going to be happy to hear this, Foss Man—I'm expecting the migrant workers sometime before noon tomorrow morning. With all the rain this spring and the way those weeds are growing, it's a darn good thing!" And with that, he immediately put him to work with the glamorous task of scooping manure out of the two big chicken coops.

That was exciting news, not scooping manure but the part about his great friends coming to town. Foss Man was never more enthused about going to work. Even shoveling chicken shit was okay, knowing it would help keep his mind off the upcoming trial. He couldn't wait to see his old friends from Texas, and more important than anything, he was excited about the possibility of seeing Rosita. After playing such an instrumental role in getting him through last summer's heartache, dealing with Ellie's death, would Rosita be here to keep his spirits up through this summer's drama? He was praying she'd be there in the morning with her amazing family.

Perhaps preoccupied, Foss Man got his summer job off to a rather shaky start when he backed the tractor with the manure spreader hooked on behind into the side of the chicken coop that morning. Not exactly happy about the accident, but seeing the damages were fairly minor and knowing Foss Man had a lot on his mind, Walter kept his sense of humor and told him lightheartedly, "Damn, Foss Man, if I wanted you to enlarge the chicken coop door, I would have told you!" Feeling rotten about it, Foss Man apologized and worked his butt off the rest of the day. He worked until a few minutes before 6:00 p.m., jumped on his bike, and made sure he was home before the miserable curfew kicked in.

Big Jake had carefully organized a little surprise for his troubled and dispirited friend. Skunk, Skeeter, Rocket, and Horse hid their cars down the street and all ambushed him when he walked in the front door. With the shed now officially off limits for obvious reasons, they settled there in the Foster's living room for a rather awkward but much-needed and appreciated reunion.

Trying desperately to avoid the subject that weighed heavily on all their minds, they attempted to pretend nothing had changed. Rocket started off with, "Damn, Foss Man, you look like you've lost a lot of weight. You going to be able to even hit the ball when we get you back in the lineup?"

In typical Skeeter fashion, he chimed in, "With Big Will hitting in your spot, I don't know if that's really a big deal." He quickly added, "Just kidding, old buddy."

Foss Man slugged Skeeter on the shoulder and changed the subject. "Hey, how are the Becker beauties looking lately? You been keeping an eye on them for me? Now that I think about it, I'll be lucky if I get to see them again this summer before they head off to college."

Rocket said, "Now that you mentioned it, they both told me to say hello and that they were sorry about what you're going through. You know they're both good friends of Catherine. They said they were really proud of you!"

As hard as they tried to carry on in their normal fashion, it just wasn't working, and the conversation drifted back to the disturbing event that had taken place exactly one week earlier. In a rare display of genuine affection, his buddies convinced him they were truly proud of him. Like his big brother said the night before, "You stepped up and did what you had to do, Foss Man. It's a sickening thought, but we know you saved your sister's life!" The support from the old gang gave him confidence he could handle the scariest thing he'd ever faced in his life!

The next morning, the family attended church together, and as always, filled one pew while spilling into a second one. The congregation was aware of the Foster's conspicuous presence but, out of respect, attempted to keep things as normal as possible. Reverend Thompson discreetly singled them out, giving them a warm thoughtful welcome. Going to church was an important first step in the family's bold attempt to get on with their lives! But a quick reminder that it wasn't going to be business as usual—they were showered with camera flashes from the remaining reporters standing across the street as they were exiting the church.

Taking full advantage of the three hours of freedom he was allowed on Sunday mornings, with the First Lutheran Church conveniently located only two blocks from Walter's farm, filled with anticipation, Foss Man ran over to see if his migrant friends had made it back to town. As he approached Walter's farm, he looked across the sprawling cabbage field with his eyes glued on the five shacks looking for any clues. He took off running and came charging into the campsite when he saw the long caravan of cars with the overloaded wagons hooked on behind.

Everyone was busy unpacking their belongings when one of the younger kids saw him and started screaming, "It's Boss Man! Hey, you guys, it's Boss Man!" And everyone stopped what they were doing and swarmed around him. It was obvious they all loved Foss Man when everyone started hugging and jumping up and down and patting him on the back. It was an amazing greeting, and it made Foss Man feel special. When things settled down, he was desperately looking around, hoping to see Rosita. Trying not to panic, he nervously asked Rosita's mother, "Where's Rosita, Mrs. Rodriguez?" With a sad look on her face, she quickly responded, "Sorry, Foss Man, Rosita not come this year, stay back in Texas with grandmother!"

Foss Man's heart sank! Rosita wasn't there, and it suddenly dawned on him he'd probably never see his special friend again. The news felt like another punch in the stomach.

It was a struggle, but he tried his best to remain as upbeat as he could about seeing everyone else. Heartbroken and in great need for something to cheer him up, he made a special effort to spend some time with Rosita's brother Pedro. He had grown at least three inches taller and put on over twenty pounds. Pedro was anxious to tell Foss Man, "I work hard on baseball all winter and hit baseball very far now, Foss Man!" Feeling a little better, Foss Man said, "That's good news, Pedro. You're going to be a big help to the town team this summer, and I don't mean serving as the bat boy!" Foss Man really liked Pedro and was going to have to get used to the idea of not having his amazing sister around this summer!

A few minutes later, still in the dumps and after the adults returned to the task of unpacking, as he was sitting on one of the picnic tables and chatting with some of the kids, somebody came up behind him and put their hands over his eyes and said, "Guess who, Foss Man?" Confused but a little excited, thinking he recognized that voice, he quickly turned around and was afraid he was seeing things. He couldn't believe his eyes. Rosita was standing there with a big smile on her face, and in her usual sexy manner, she said, "Hi, Foss Man." He wanted to jump up and down and scream out loud! What a sight! Rosita looked much taller than last summer, and with a short skirt and the typical low-cut blouse, she created an absolutely stunning picture!

They all stopped what they were doing and came over to the picnic tables, cheering and clapping their hands. Everyone had been in on it! They had carefully put the plan together, unaware of what Foss Man was going through and had no idea how much he needed the lift. It was a happy time for everyone.

Anxious to be alone, a few minutes later, Foss Man and Rosita managed to tactfully break away and took a walk through the woods along the familiar shores of Beaver Creek. With frequent stops and passionate embraces, there was no secret about how happy they both were to be back together again. As much as he hated it, having no choice, he caught her off guard: "I've only got a few more minutes. I've got to be home by noon."

She was obviously disappointed and asked him, "Why Foss Man in big hurry?" He told her it was pretty complicated but made an honest attempt to at least briefly explain what was going on. She was obviously confused about the frightening story, and all she could say was, "I know Foss Man not hurt somebody! I help Foss Man get through sad time again."

With that encouraging news, cutting it close, Foss Man raced home, arriving about one minute before the 12:00 noon deadline.

He was stuck at home now. It was a long afternoon, and making things worse, he was well aware of the fact the town team had a big game that night. Everyone felt bad for him, but having no choice but to get on with their lives, fulfilling a job always reserved for Foss Man, dressed in full uniform, Air Force willingly pitched in and helped his dad fill the pop cooler. With the refreshment stand set up and now open and ready for business, Air Force joined the team for batting practice. Minutes later, Air Force took his position at short, and Will squatted behind the plate.

The ball park was just a few blocks from their house. Foss Man could hear the crowd cheering when they were in the process of taking the lead in what he knew was the bottom of the first inning. He was still sitting there when the impressive bright lights were turned on as the game progressed into the later innings. When his folks got home, they gave him the good news: with Rocket on the mound, the Panthers had won another game, 5–2. He had to get used to the idea they were winning games without him, and as a matter of fact, Will, his more-than-able replacement, had crushed a two run homer in the bottom of the fourth inning.

That afternoon before the game, in full uniform, knowing how much Foss Man was struggling with not being able to play ball that night and knowing he was stranded at home, Big Jake thoughtfully stopped over to keep him company. Both in a solemn and reflective mood, the two great friends got into an unusually serious and intense conversation.

Filled with emotion, Foss Man said, "You know, Big Jake, now that the dust has settled a little bit, I've got to tell you something. I'm really scared about this whole thing. I know I talk a big game, but I honestly don't know if I could handle spending a long time in jail!"

Recognizing how deadly serious his buddy was, Big Jake just sat there for a couple of minutes in deep thought and finally responded, "You know, Foss Man, I've always been honest with you, right?"

Foss Man vigorously acknowledged that was precisely the case.

"Well, the perfect truth is, I'm scared too! We all know what you did that day was the right thing to do. You had no other choice. But the fact is—and believe me, Will and I have talked about this in great length—when the outcome is determined by a wide-ranging jury comprised of twelve human beings, it's impossible to predict the outcome. But don't forget, Will is a really smart guy, and after all his research, he honestly thinks he can justify your bold actions. But of course that doesn't mean it's going to happen. Yes, Foss Man—and I don't want to alarm you, but I can't lie to you—I'm scared too!"

They sat there quietly, not saying anything for a few minutes. Foss Man really appreciated Big Jake's always being honest with him. Having no idea how this jumped into his mind, out of nowhere, he asked, "Big Jake, I'm going to ask you something on a totally different subject. Do you remember when you lost your paper route money bag that Saturday way back when we were playing basketball over on Robbie Duncan's court?"

Caught completely off guard with the strange question, Big Jake honestly had to stop and think about it. Finally, he said, "Yes, I guess I can remember that, but why the heck are you asking me about that now?"

Foss Man came back with, "Remember, as always, we're being totally honest now. Big Jake, tell me the truth, do you think I put your money bag in my paper bag?"

"Good grief, Foss Man. Hell damn no, I never thought that for one second. Matter of fact, if I remember right, Robbie told me before they moved out of town that he did it as a joke. I told him it was a pretty stupid thing to do, but trust me, at no time did I ever think you were trying to steal it. If I thought for one minute it was bothering you, I would have said something to you. In thinking about it, I guess since it never came up, I just decided the less said about it, the better. Foss Man, you may be a little goofy sometimes, but I know one thing for a fact: you're as honest as they come!"

"Thanks, Big Jake. Shit! I wish I would have asked you about this a long time ago! I spent a lot of time tormenting over that stupid thing. And hating Robbie for all this time. Mr. Slim always told me hating somebody was a waste of energy! Okay, good, at least I can check that off my worry list now!"

They continued their unique, heartfelt conversation for a little while longer, and Big Jake took off for the game.

Foss Man was up at six o'clock the next morning and reported directly for work in the cabbage fields. After scooping manure all day Saturday, he was looking forward to getting back to his regular assignment for the summer—overseeing, working alongside, and bringing fresh drinking water to his good friends, the migrant workers. One major difference this summer, Foss Man had to be home by six o'clock every night until the trial started, which was a full month down the road. He would miss out on those bonfires every night and, afterward, the cherished private walks with Rosita.

Chapter Fifty-Five

As the days unfolded, living under the strict guidelines of having to be home by six o'clock every night and by noon on Sundays, Foss Man and Rosita had trouble finding time to be alone. Rosita's mother, who was only thirty-eight years old and a knockout in her own right, wanting to subtly put her trust in him, cautiously warned Foss Man, "Rosita be only sixteen, act like she be twenty-five sometimes. That main reason she be here this summer and not stay back in Texas with grandmother!"

Foss Man noticed a more aggressive and sassy attitude in Rosita as they were getting back to the daily routine throughout the long workdays. She still had that irresistible charm and likeable personality but was persistently flirting with him and daring and tantalizing him with a steady supply of suggestive comments. Of course he loved every minute of it, but at the same time, it was driving him a little crazy. It was probably a good thing he wasn't around at night or things would undoubtedly be getting a lot more intense. She had clearly matured physically over the winter, and her provocative mind seemed to be constantly working overtime.

They managed to sneak off a few times during the noon hour and squeezed in some rather intimate embraces, but again, the built-in nonprivate circumstances kept things under control. Like last summer, Foss Man got invited to join the group for the hardy noon feasts on a regular basis, and he frequently took them up on their generous offers. However, for the first time in his life, he continued having trouble eating much food, undoubtedly related to the persistent worry and fear related to the upcoming trial. But now more than ever, he thoroughly appreciated being around these wholesome, happy, and fun-loving people. Their basic approach to life was pretty simple. Work hard and squeeze the utmost enjoyment out of every single day. He looked forward to the day he could once again join them for the sing-alongs around the roaring bonfires at night. That of course would depend on whether or not he was a free person after the trial!

With his poor appetite creating time to spare during lunch hour, once in a while, he'd jog over to the nearby old apple orchard and climb up to his favorite spot in the tall oak tree standing conspicuously amongst the much shorter apple trees. He'd sit up there and replay what happened in the shed and fret about how it was impacting his life. There was something about that special place—with the seemingly ever-present cool breeze and captivating view, it helped him sort things out and he always felt better when he went back to work. He never left before he prayed for God's guidance and thanked him for saving his mother's life last winter.

One day, not knowing she was behind him, Rosita quietly followed him over to the apple orchard. He just reached his spot high in the tree, got settled in, and he heard her voice: "Hey, Foss Man, what you be doing up there?" Before he could answer, she was scampering her way up the tree. Surprisingly agile and athletic, she had no problem with the tricky steep climb and, within minutes, was safely perched on the convenient branches right next to him.

Proud of herself, with a big grin on her flawless face, she said, "Hi, Foss Man!" He marveled at her sassy attitude and couldn't help but laugh out loud. She had become a truly amazing, crazy, and lovable character. He couldn't help it—he was more intrigued by her every day and whether it would ultimately prove to be a good or bad thing, he absolutely loved being with her. Her mere presence was an absolute godsend for his troubled world.

Not wasting a second, she leaned over and planted a big kiss square on his lips. She leaned back and boldly asked him, "Foss Man, like see Rosita's breasts?"

Startled, confused, but excited at the same time, Foss Man managed to respond, "Oh yes, I think that would be okay." He thought to himself, *What a stupid-ass answer!*

With that, Rosita immediately pulled her top up over her head. Foss Man had never seen anything quite like it. He came frighteningly close to losing his bearings and falling straight to the ground. Catching his breath, he couldn't remember the climb down the tree, but before things got totally out of control, they had somehow managed to return safely to land and back to work in the steaming-hot cabbage field. Lost in dreamland and with newfound energy and enthusiasm, Foss Man breezed through the afternoon, effortlessly pumping endless pails of the much-needed cold drinking water.

About a week later, just before the noon-hour break, Rosita came over by Foss Man and, in her breathy voice, said quietly in his ear, "Climb tree today?"

There was little doubt, with Rosita only a few steps behind, he had to set some kind of land speed record, and in the process of flying up the tree, he managed to tear his work shirt in three places. With things quickly heating up and aggressively advancing forward but in a much smoother and less awkward manner this time, it turned into another amazing noon hour.

The next two weeks seemed to fly by. The limited freedom was tough to deal with, but working every day, making the best money in his life, and with the regular trips to the treetop bringing a new dimension to his life, Foss Man was actually getting along pretty well. The endless worry about how the trial was going to turn out and, of course, not playing baseball were the worst parts. Reports from his buddies indicated Pedro was now the regular center fielder, successfully chasing down every fly ball in sight, and was hitting the crap out of the ball. Rosita's brother turned out to be a terrific player, had a modest and humble attitude, and everybody loved having him around. In Foss Man's absence, Skeeter and Skunk effortlessly made sure Pedro felt comfortable with all his new teammates.

Will wanted to give Catherine time to recover from the traumatic experience but was anxious to sit down with her to get her detailed version of exactly what took place that horrific day. He knew her testimony could make or break the case. He had virtually memorized the written statements, but after listening to her put it in her own words, he knew immediately it was going to be a game changer.

The jury would simply fall in love with her. He couldn't wait to get her on the witness stand. The deck was stacked against him, and defending Foss Man would be tough, but their meeting gave him a much-needed surge of hope and renewed confidence.

Will had deliberately not interacted with Foss Man or the family for over two weeks but thought it was probably the right time for them to get together and talk. More than anything, he wanted to see how everyone was doing and let them know he was doing his homework and would be fully prepared for the trial.

Will called Foss Man's parents, and with a big game scheduled for later that night, they agreed to meet Sunday afternoon when he knew Foss Man was probably going a little crazy being stuck in the house on such a beautiful summer day. His dad didn't have to report for refreshment stand duty until later, and his mom was going to be home and was available for the meeting. Catherine joined the group for the first time. Of course, Big Jake was included in the discussion, and Foss Man always loved having him around.

Will brought everybody up-to-date on his research, and they talked informally about some of the key issues Foss Man was up against. His relaxed and confident style was comforting to all of them. At a glance, his basic and simple approach to putting the defense plan together may have sounded a little bold, and he wanted to make sure they all felt comfortable with it.

Before he got started, he noticed Foss Man really didn't look that good. He came right out and asked him, "Good grief, Foss Man, you look like you've lost a lot of weight!"

Foss Man admitted, "For the first time in my life, I haven't been able to eat a whole lot of food."

His mother agreed, "He's been eating like a bird since this whole thing happened."

Will scolded him, "You've got to eat, Foss Man. Darn it, this thing is going to work out!"

Putting that aside and getting down to business, Will started out, "Let me explain how I think we should look at this whole thing. I'm not going into great detail right now, and this won't take long, but when I get done here, I want to know everyone's honest reaction to my basic plan. Remember, we're going to work together as a team now."

Trying to ignore his undeniable masculine appeal, Catherine, excited about being included on the team for the first time, quickly agreed and playfully addressed him as Big Will. "Go ahead, I'm anxious to hear what your big plan is!"

Impressed with her mature, relaxed, yet dignified manner, Will explained to her and the others, "I don't see any need for planning cute courtroom antics or drama-filled strategies. The prosecution will present their case. We'll merely listen to their witnesses' testimonies and react accordingly. Like my lifelong idol, the great General and President Dwight Eisenhower, preached about the concept of preparation, it really doesn't mean much once the battle is underway. We'll do our homework, try to anticipate every needed contingency plan, and as the trial unfolds, we'll pay close attention and adjust as we see fit.

"Through it all, we'll keep everything basic and simple and focus on one thing and one thing only. Our sole objective will be to point out to the jury the perfect truth! Let me remind everyone, the trial will probably take many twists and turns, but one thing will remain constant: we have the truth on our side! Like you correctly said yourself, Foss Man, we must have complete trust in our system of justice and belief in the jury system, and the fact is, I do!"

"We'll probably meet again before the trial and will go over the final list of witnesses, and, Foss Man, we'll have many chances during the trial to talk about your testimony."

Foss Man's dad thanked Will, patted him on the back, and they shook hands. He had to get down to the ball park and get the refreshment stand ready for business. Gerald and Glenda jumped in the car with their dad and they were eager and ready to go to work. Gerald was looking forward to chasing down those foul balls. Will and Big Jake hustled home and got their game uniforms on. Foss Man wished them good luck. This was the most difficult part of all this: he loved playing baseball. His mom decided to stay home with him and the little ones.

Later that night, he sat outside in a lawn chair and could see the bright lights surrounding the field and could frequently hear the crowd cheering. It was, more than likely, Will hitting another homerun as he was filling in as the more-than-able catcher.

Chapter Fifty-Six

Two long weeks remained before the trial. While dealing with the frightening cloud hanging over their heads, the Foster family did the best they could to bury themselves in work and made every effort to get back to living as normal as possible under the difficult circumstances.

Catherine was reluctantly attending one hour counseling sessions at seven o'clock on Wednesday nights. She thought they were rather silly but went primarily to make everyone else feel better about her recovery. Her mother felt guilty going to work every day, but Catherine insisted she go to work and not worry about the home front, that she could handle it.

The fact was, Catherine had the five younger siblings whipped into shape in no time. Specific chores were systematically assigned to each sibling, and when the work was done, then and only then they could go out and play! She prepared the noon meals and went beyond normal expectations, voluntarily completing the daily house cleaning and the weekly laundry needs, all before her mother got home from work.

On Saturdays, Catherine reported to work for Dr. Dockstader, spending from six to eight happy hours taking care of the sick pets in town. She was making good money, which would come in mighty handy, considering the fact it was only a few more weeks until she reported to Iowa State University and launched her lifetime dream of becoming a veterinarian! She couldn't wait to go off to college! Her parents continued to marvel at her incredible strength and perseverance!

Skunk and Foss Man's friendship went back to day one in the school bus. And Skeeter had virtually lived with the Foster family for years and was more like a brother. The two loyal friends were sick worrying about Foss Man and the very real threat of him spending years behind bars. They were consistently stopping in to see him and reported to him religiously after every baseball game. They knew how much he enjoyed hearing the details about the games and that he would also be interested to know that his friend Rosita was attending most of the games to watch her brother Pedro play ball.

Unknowingly and with no effort on her part, Rosita had been stealing the show on game days. There wasn't a player in the league who wasn't aware of Rosita Rodriguez's striking presence, and they went out of their way to insist Pedro and his sister stick around for the postgame celebrations. Knowing it would make Foss Man feel good, Skunk was happy to report, "Rosita was smart enough to see what was going on and politely informed them, 'Rosita Foss Man girlfriend!'" Rosita and Pedro always hurried back to the campsite to join the clan for the last hour of the traditional Sunday night sing-alongs around the big bon fire. Skunk and Skeeter were simply the best friends a guy could even dream of having!

Along with preparing for the trial, Big Jake was spending several hours a day drilling his big brother in preparation for the upcoming bar exams. With serious intentions of joining Will in the legal profession someday, Big Jake was highly motivated, and it wouldn't have surprised anyone if he too was ready to pass the difficult exams by the end of the summer. The trial date was closing in on them, and they were getting anxious to get things underway. They had boldly and generously taken on this huge challenge and were fully aware of how much was at stake! As each day passed, they could feel the pressure mounting, and Will was increasingly pleased about recruiting his little brother for the legal team!

Foss Man was doing his best to keep busy at work but was getting a little nervous about the frequent wild and crazy trips up the tall oak tree with Rosita. Her presence helped keep his mind off the pending trial, but he wondered if she was trying a little too hard to get him through this ordeal like she had promised that first day when she returned to town. In addition to the treetop escapades, they made a few midday trips to the remote swimming hole a safe distance from the campsite. On some of the unbearably hot and humid days, Rosita's dad would excuse her from hoeing weeds, and she'd sneak over to the swimming hole to get out of the hot sun and get refreshed by taking a dip in the perfectly clear and cold water.

As she planned to head over to the swimming hole, usually over the lunch hour, she encouraged Foss Man to bring his lunch bucket and join her. On Saturday, his last work day prior to the trial, Foss Man was sitting on the shoreline in full work clothes thoroughly enjoying the view with Rosita frolicking and splashing in their private swimming hole, as always, in her skimpy bikini. He was shocked when she slowly and provocatively strolled out of the water directly toward him with both the top and bottom pieces of her swimsuit in her hand. He almost choked on his baloney sandwich. It was the most amazing sight he had seen in his entire life. He thought to himself, *Good Lord, you can take me now—I've finally seen it all.* As she approached him and was gesturing for him to hand her the towel, she teased, "Foss Man like Rosita body?" He was speechless, probably for the first time since he was three years old.

She quickly filled the awkward silence with, "Foss Man be gone tomorrow. Rosita make Foss Man very happy, that be okay?" He was rattled and fighting to regain his composure. She was making the same offer she made at the end of last summer the night before she went back to Texas for the winter. She was well aware of the very real possibility of never being alone with Foss Man again if the outcome of the trial went the wrong direction. They had talked about that harsh reality on a number of occasions.

While trying desperately to decide exactly how to handle this not-totally-unexpected development, he was amazed with her bold, relaxed, and totally comfortable attitude about her sexuality. Of course he was thoroughly enjoying what had been going on between them this summer; it was the way he always pictured heaven. But like last summer, he knew she was simply trying to comfort him and help him through another difficult time in his life! He was facing another giant moral predicament! Rosita was obviously quite the character, but she was also a very sweet girl! He did not want to hurt her. But at the same time, he was only human!

Foss Man had managed to at least indirectly make a reference to his progressive relationship with Rosita to Mr. Slim and Nute that summer, and they always took the same position on the subject. "Cool your jets, Foss Man, there's plenty of time for that stuff when you get older!"

Foss Man knew he couldn't afford to make another giant mistake before he got through the frightening ordeal he was already dealing with. Rosita's parents had full trust in him. Without giving consideration to the sacred "sister rule," he knew it wasn't going to happen!

Once his tactful rejection to her proposal was fully understood, while it was awkward for a few minutes, with her typical graceful attitude, the bold idea passed smoothly, and it was only minutes later and they were back to work under the scorching-hot son. Rosita was hoeing weeds with her family, and Foss Man was busy pumping and delivering the badly needed buckets of cold water to his friends, perhaps for the last time.

The migrant clan had given Foss Man a special invitation to be sure to join them for the regular 5:00 p.m. supper break. They knew he had to be home for his 6:00 p.m. curfew. As planned, at about 5:30 p.m., they all suddenly gathered around the picnic table where Foss Man was sitting and attempting to eat. Rosita and Pedro's little eight-year-old brother Fernando had been selected to present him with their special gift. All thirty-two members of the five families crowded around, and Fernando came up to Foss Man holding something secretly tucked behind his back.

Fernando had always affectionately called him Boss Man. With a huge smile on his face and in his innocent, childlike voice, Fernando proudly said, "This is for Boss Man," and he handed him the carefully wrapped box he was struggling to hold on to without dropping.

Foss Man was deeply touched by all this attention and, filled with emotion, proceeded to unwrap the big box. When he saw what was inside, he couldn't help it; he broke down and cried. It was the most beautiful catcher's mitt he had ever seen. He couldn't talk. In a strange trance, he made his way around and hugged every single one of these amazing people. A few minutes later, as he jumped on his bike and was pedaling down the road, they were all cheering and clapping.

Earlier that afternoon, Foss Man had reminded Walter that he wouldn't be reporting for work Monday morning! Walter was well aware of this fact and, showing genuine concern, wished him well. When he handed him what might very well be his final paycheck, with a sincere and emotional voice he told him, "Don't forget, Foss Man, like I've told you before, if there's anything I can do for you or your family, just let me know. Promise me you'll do that, okay, young friend?"

Foss Man was ordered to report to the Juvenile Detention Center by noon on Sunday. Seeing no logical reason for him spending the long Sunday afternoon in the miserable place, Will had formally requested a 6:00 p.m. arrival time, but it was quickly rejected by the inflexible, no-nonsense Judge Cooper.

The entire Foster family attended church services together at ten o'clock on Sunday morning. Knowing by now their presence would create a small spectacle, they made an honest effort to quietly blend in and keep a low profile. However, beyond their control, the next hour turned into an amazing display of love and affection. Following Reverend Thompson's typical short but meaningful sermon and tactfully reciting a short prayer asking for God's blessing on behalf of the Foster family, as the chorus was preparing to sing their final scheduled hymn, completely unplanned, the preacher asked Catherine and her mother if they would consider joining the choir in singing what he knew was Foss Man's favorite hymn, "Just a Closer Walk with Thee"!

When the congregation responded with spontaneous polite applause, feeling they had no real choice, within seconds, Catherine and her mother found themselves standing front and center with the popular church choir. Like they had done on many previous occasions, the talented, well-practiced duet was singing with a powerful raw emotion that grew with each verse. Their inspirational performance electrified the entire congregation, who of course were fully aware of what the Foster family was facing that week. Everyone was now standing and enthusiastically applauding. There wasn't a dry eye in the place.

There was about a half dozen members of the early arriving news media carefully positioned across the street who were treated to the moving scene of the emotionally charged Foster family huddled together as they excited the church. The picture was plastered on the front page of the local papers, formally introducing to the public what was very likely the biggest trial in Wright County history scheduled to begin the following day, Monday morning.

On the way home, at Foss Man's request, his dad dropped him off at the bait shop, and as he had hoped and expected, Mr. Slim and Nute were in the middle of a heated cribbage game. He spent a few final minutes with his favorite old codgers, and after hugs and best wishes, Mr. Slim, always brief and to the point, said one more time, "Always remember, God's in your corner! Be strong, my young friend!"

From there he hurried home, tried to force down some food, got more heartfelt hugs from his badly shaken family, and cutting it close, his dad delivered him promptly to the Juvenile Detention Center at precisely twelve o'clock noon.

Will and Big Jake were granted special permission to spend a couple hours with Foss Man that afternoon. It helped break up an endless day and gave them a chance to go over their final game plan. The focus of the discussion revolved around the list of potential witnesses the prosecution had submitted during the required pretrial discovery exchange Friday morning. You could eliminate witnesses as the trial unfolds, but it took special permission to add witnesses once the trial was underway. It was pretty obvious from the list, as expected, the prosecution was going to attempt to demonstrate a pattern of reckless behavior in Foss Man's past. The name of some of the potential witnesses triggered a few scary memories, and the one that really stood out was Bart the butcher. The last time Foss Man ran into Bart, he could still see the fading red mark across his forehead. It made Foss Man sick to his stomach thinking about it.

As hard as Will tried to keep things lighthearted, for obvious reasons, there was an undeniable tension in the air. It was all suddenly very real. As they were shaking hands one final time, Big Jake said it again, "Foss Man, like I've told you a dozen times, you did the right thing that day. We all know you saved your sister's life! Don't ever forget that. Now please sleep well, my friend!" Choosing his words carefully, feeling well prepared for the very first client in a career he had spent a lifetime dreaming of and planning for, he said once again, "This is going to work out, Foss Man!"

Foss Man was repulsed by the familiar echo of the steel doors of the miserable cold cell slamming shut, knowing it would once again be home for an unknown number of nights. Sitting on the edge of the hard cot, he pulled his new catcher's mitt out of his overstuffed duffel bag and began pounding his fist into it over and over. Admiring the incredible gift that he knew had cost his hardworking migrant friends at least a half day's wages, he sat there replaying the special events that had taken place during the last twenty-four hours.

Clutching the catcher's mitt, Foss Man settled in for what he knew would be another long night!

Chapter Fifty-Seven

During what was probably the most important step in the entire legal process, Monday was spent on the critical selection of the jury. Most of the time involved the intense interviewing of the individual prospective jurors. Including the two alternates, the final fourteen were now officially chosen. Will thought it went well and felt good about the final jury composition. The jury included eight females and six males with ages ranging from twenty-two to seventy-four. There was a balance of professionals and common laborers. Admittedly inexperienced with the process, Will felt the makeup of the jury turned out to be a good mix.

After careful consideration given to the option of sequestering the jurors, reviewing the hefty related expense and the severe inconvenience to the people involved, the concept was declared unnecessary. In view of that and knowing it was a particularly high-profile case, Judge Cooper went to great lengths to restrict the jurors from reading the newspapers and watching the television coverage throughout the course of the trial. They were ordered that any discussion of the trial amongst the jurors prior to the final deliberations was strictly prohibited. Any valid indication reflecting violations of these rules would lead to immediate expulsion from the jury, and a firm warning was emphasized that such behavior could easily result in a mistrial. Knowing they still had a number of contentious issues to discuss before the trial commenced and not wanting the jury to have to sit around for hours, the judge ordered the jury to report at one o'clock the following afternoon.

Along the same line of thinking and in respect to the exhaustive efforts put forth in the jury selection process and the fact it was almost 4:00 p.m., Judge Cooper decided to adjourn for the day. The judge wanted the lawyers to be rested and fresh when they addressed the always difficult decisions related to the liberties and limitations of the evidence to be presented throughout the trial. His vast experience told him the nature of this particular trial would likely require a few tough decisions. Townsend and Will both readily agreed, and the meeting was set for nine o'clock on Tuesday morning.

Will and Big Jake stopped over to the detention center to give Foss Man a much-needed break after having been cooped up for what they knew had to be another long, miserable day. Knowing the actual trial wouldn't get underway until sometime Tuesday, Foss Man's mom and dad squeezed one day of work in, knowing they'd be in court for the rest of the week. Both of their bosses, proving their respect and unwavering support, informed them they would be paid for the full week. With that wonderful news, they rushed over to Boulder right after work to see Foss Man and were glad to see him sitting there in the public lounge area with Will and Big Jake. Will suggested they move into the enclosed conference room, assuring a more private atmosphere. Will brought them up-to-date on how the jury selection had gone, and they sat around and chatted informally for a while. Will cut the meeting short, wanting to get home for one final tune-up of his opening statement scheduled for the next day. Foss Man braced himself for what would be another long and lonely night of flopping around on the steel bed.

Townsend, his assistant Dempsey, Will, and Big Jake met in Judge Cooper's chamber at precisely nine o'clock as planned on Tuesday morning. The lawyers were keenly reminded of the widespread interest in the trial when they observed the already crazy scene in front of the courthouse a full hour before the trial was originally scheduled to get underway. Townsend's adrenaline was skyrocketing when he saw the three national television network trucks all strategically positioned across the street. This was only the beginning of the kind of exposure he had been dreaming of throughout the two years he had served as the Wright County Attorney.

Judge Cooper outlined his plan for the day, explaining he had reserved the morning wanting to have plenty of time to address any and all questions and concerns from both sides. Furthermore, in the spirit of fairness, he wanted to assure both opening statements would be consecutive, back to back, not separated by the lunch break. After polite small talk, they got down to business.

The first major question dealt with how much of Ron Ferguson and the defendant's personal behavior record would be permitted. After brief discussion and fully expected by both sides, the judge made a quick ruling: "In view of the fact this is not a 'whodunit' case but, as we discussed during the preliminary hearing, a subjective debate revolving around the state of mind of the defendant, as it lends itself to the basic element of motive, behavior history of and between both parties would appear to be instrumental." Impossible to comprehend which side this abrupt ruling may ultimately benefit the most, and having no real choice in the matter, no one objected.

Both sides were given an opportunity to look over and react to the list of witnesses submitted by the opposition the previous Friday. There was minimal debate until Will expressed concern with the currently imprisoned Frank Ferguson's potential testimony. Will had given it serious thought since he received the witness list and speculated his testimony would more than likely focus on the by-now highly suspected undesirable living conditions around the Ferguson home throughout the years. He could anticipate the subject would enable Townsend to play the potent sympathy card significantly benefiting the prosecution. The debate went back and forth with Will insisting that the original source of Ferguson's egregious behavior prior to the incident had absolutely nothing to do with the defendant's degree of innocence or guilt. This provoked a lengthy and heated exchange. Judge Cooper ultimately ruled in favor of the prosecution. Frank Ferguson would be allowed to testify if the prosecution chose to do so.

On the surface, this decision may have been interpreted as a serious setback for the defense. Will fully expected the judge to rule in favor of the prosecution on the issue, but in accordance with his deliberate carefully calculated strategy, he wanted to go on the record of disagreeing and chalking up an official defeat, hoping a subsequent disputed call might be ruled in his favor. Furthermore, after much thought on the subject, readily acknowledging the potential sympathy value of Frank Ferguson's testimony, he honestly felt it could prove to be more beneficial to the defense. Falling back on his basic premise, he had no fear of anything that contributed to finding the truth behind anything that may have contributed to what happened in the shed that afternoon!

County Sherriff Fred Ramsey knocked on Judge Cooper's door and inquired about the likeliness of the trial starting before noon as originally planned. He informed the judge that the crowd outside of the courthouse was growing by the minute and was becoming almost unmanageable in their eagerness to get in front of the line to assure a seat in the courtroom. Apologizing for the misunderstanding and knowing it would not make them very happy out there, the judge told the Sherriff to announce to the crowd that the trial would not commence until one-thirty that afternoon.

All this time, Foss Man was going a little crazy sitting in his cell wondering what the heck was going on. Finally completing the scrutiny of the witness lists, Judge Cooper pressed both parties one final time for any new relevant discoveries, and if there were such, they must be disclosed to the other side at this time, emphasizing, "I don't want any surprises, cute antics, or grandstand plays once we get underway. Have I made myself clear?"

It struck Will, while there were no significant surprises, the extreme liberal nature of the potentially explosive rulings made by Judge Cooper that morning would all but guarantee more than a few dramatic dynamics and fireworks rarely seen in a courtroom. It was gradually sinking in—there was now no doubt about it—his first courtroom experience was going to be most memorable. The scores of news media from across the country would not be disappointed!

Judge Cooper's final admonition was, "Again with no 'whodunit' element, and with the relatively modest list of witnesses submitted, I would hope and expect to turn the case over to the jury before the end of the week." He demonstrated his famous no-nonsense approach. "I see no reason for this thing to drag on!" Repeating his seemingly favorite theme, he said, "Beyond that, I feel obliged to say it one more time. Because this is a minor being tried in adult court, I expect both parties to show the ultimate respect and consideration for the age of all the parties involved and the sensitive nature of the central issues in the case!" With that, the meeting was adjourned.

Will couldn't help but notice Townsend's natural swagger, an irritating arrogance combined with an undeniable level of confidence that suggested he anticipated an easy victory, if not the proverbial slam dunk. Will was determined to do everything humanly possible to prevent that from happening!

With advanced knowledge that the trial was scheduled to get underway that week, the media circus started flooding the Jefferson area on Sunday, and the pace had picked up Monday. Like a month ago during the pretrial hearing, business in the local bars, restaurants, and hotels was booming. By Tuesday the visitors were in full force. The battle was on for a presence in the courtroom. There were no television cameras allowed in the courtroom—no cameras of any kind, for that matter. The doors were finally opened, and considering the sudden wild ambush, the court room was filled in surprisingly orderly fashion. With the modest-sized room jammed and filled to full capacity, many of the unsuccessful reporters were forced to wait on the courthouse steps along with their cameramen as they patiently waited for any pertinent unfolding news that may seep from inside the courtroom. It was now perfectly clear—the level of interest in the case was unprecedented in Wright County history.

Will had petitioned for a number of reserved seats in the courtroom. After thorough study of his submitted list of candidates, the judge granted the defense twenty-five permanent passes. Catherine, Air Force, and their mom and dad were nervously sitting in the front row behind the railing just a few feet behind Big Jake, Will, and Foss Man, who were now sitting huddled behind the old, beaten-up wooden rectangular table. Anxious to get things underway, Foss Man was happy to be back in the comfortable presence of his faithful legal team. The four grandparents, Mr. Slim, Nute, Walter Olson, Reverend Thompson, Dr. Ellington, and Coach Sanders were sitting in the row behind the Foster family. Skunk, Skeeter, Horse, Rocket, and Stub were squeezed together in the next row alongside Rosita,

Pedro, and their parents. The twenty-five loyal family members and friends would be present for every minute of the proceedings. No pass would go unused.

County Attorney Townsend and his assistant Tom Dempsey were seated at a matching corresponding table approximately six feet to the right of the defense team. Behind them in the first row behind the railing, making a rare public appearance, sat the over three-hundred-pound father of Ron Ferguson, dwarfing his timid and miniature wife sitting next to him.

Normal for the state of Iowa in the middle of July, absent the luxury of air-conditioning and magnified with the overflowing, bustling crowd of excited and sweating human beings, with only the modest aid of four large carefully positioned fans, it was unbearably stuffy and hot in the overcrowded courtroom. The uncomfortable conditions would do nothing to minimize the level of anticipation, excitement, or the growing tension so very prevalent in the air.

Chapter Fifty-Eight

At precisely one-thirty Tuesday afternoon, the Honorable Judge Cooper hammered his gavel and announced, "The case of the *State of Iowa versus Luke Foster* will now come to order!

"Before I bring in the jury, I want to give everyone in the courtroom a few behavioral guidelines that will be enforced with utmost consistency throughout the trial. With the central players in the case being minors, I have instructed the prosecuting attorneys and the defendant's representatives to be cognizant of this at all times. Furthermore, the fact the heart of the case revolves around an extremely sensitive subject, the rape of a minor—while graphic dialogue may be necessary and will be permitted at times, it will be done cautiously, sparingly, and as discreetly as possible. In turn, everyone in the gallery will be expected to conduct themselves accordingly. With that understanding, assuming there are no further questions or comments from counsel, I will have the bailiff escort the jury in and we'll get started."

Judge Cooper warmly greeted the jury members, and following a few brief final instructions, with his commanding voice, he ordered, "Attorney Townsend, will you present your opening statement?"

Trying desperately to control his nerves, as they entered the courtroom a few minutes earlier, Foss Man asked Big Jake, "I forgot to ask you last night, how'd the game come out Sunday night?"

Big Jake shook his head, "Oh man, it wasn't pretty. Rocket walked in two runs in the first inning and, for the first time this year, got knocked out of the game in the second inning. Air Force came in to pitch and didn't do much better. Skunk and Skeeter couldn't catch a grounder, and when they did, they threw it over my head at first base. Nobody could hit the ball. I think Will struck out three times. And you know, Sparky, he kept telling us to get our heads out of our ass. We were behind 8–0 when Sparky got so desperate he put me in to pitch. That was a bad idea. They were drilling line drives all over the place. All I was doing was running around backing up wild throws to third and home base. I couldn't get anybody out, and mercifully, the game ended when Riceville invoked the ten-run rule in the fifth inning. We got beat, 10–0, for our first loss of the year."

Foss Man came back with a simple "Ouch" and squeezed in one more question: "Was Rosita at the game?"

Big Jake said, "No, matter of fact, for the first time all summer, Pedro didn't show up either. It was obvious no one's head was in the game. We should have cancelled the stupid game!"

As Foss Man was settling in at the defense table, he casually turned and glanced up and saw Rosita, Pedro, and their mom and dad sitting together in about the fourth row. Rosita gave him a worried smile and a nervous wave. As they would be doing all week, the four loyal friends had already put in several hours of hoeing weeds earlier that morning and would squeeze in four or five more hours and fighting the pesky mosquitoes every night. Like every place she went, Rosita had created quite a stir when she entered the courtroom.

Following a confident and firm "Thank you, Your Honor," Townsend got the formal proceedings underway with a well-rehearsed pause while prancing slowly back and forth in front of the jury box, effectively assuring he had every eye in the courtroom glued on him. Completing the requisite courtesies, making an obvious special effort to appease the judge, with a relaxed and steady voice, he said, "Before I present the prosecution's case, in respect to Judge Cooper's warning regarding the sensitive events involving the young teenagers, please understand—and I apologize in advance—there will be the need for occasional candid and explicit vocabulary, not only today but throughout the trial. I beg for your continued indulgence in this regard."

Townsend was impeccably groomed, dressed in an expensive tailored navy-blue suit, crisp white shirt, bright red-and-white striped tie, glittering silver-cuff links, and with his flawless, well-tanned complexion and thick brown hair, he had the striking appearance of a polished future big-league politician. Will asked himself, *Good grief, it's got be close to one hundred degrees in here. Isn't this guy going to sweat at least a little bit?*

Townsend began, "On Saturday, June 7, a little over one month ago, the fifteen-year-old defendant, Luke Foster,"—taking a second to politely acknowledge his presence by nodding toward the defense table—"upon innocently returning home after mowing several lawns that day, entered the small building located behind the Foster family garage with intentions of merely putting his bike away like he had done many times before. Totally unexpected and to no fault of his own, the teenager walked into a horrific scene that no human being should ever have to encounter."

Will and Big Jake glanced at each other, raising their eyebrows and rolling their eyes. Although they'd seen this act before, they had the same thing going through their minds: *Just this morning in the judge's chamber, this same character was arrogant, aggressive, and brazen and is now suddenly transformed into this compassionate and gentle soul. Oh yes, this guy is good!*

Townsend continued, "Ronald Ferguson, a seventeen-year-old young man, it has now been officially confirmed, was in the process of raping the defendant's eighteen-year-old sister. Luke Foster, a 6'1", 160-pound terrific athlete, understandably upset, deliberately chose to take the time to locate a baseball bat!" Wanting time to elapse for the desired effect, Townsend slowly walked over and picked up the bat from the designated evidence table.

"Members of the jury, this is the thirty-four-inch weapon the defendant was now holding in his hands!" Firmly gripping the bat, he said, "Luke Foster then made the cold, calculated decision to crush the back of Ron Ferguson's head." Townsend proceeded to demonstrate a dramatic full over-his-head swing. "I don't have to tell you the young man on the receiving end of that violent blow fell forward and, without doubt, was totally unconscious."

Townsend, once again letting a little time elapse, went on, "Now you'd have to assume a reasonable person could easily see his sister was no longer in danger, wouldn't you? There are two important factors that have to be considered when attempting to answer that critical question. First, Luke Foster, who readily admits the fact, had a long history of bad experiences with the Ferguson boy and had developed an extreme hatred for him. And secondly, the defendant just happens to have a well-documented record of reckless and irresponsible behavior.

"While all this is true, in the spirit of drawing an accurate and fair picture, the prosecution acknowledges that the defendant was understandably badly shaken and upset at the time. However, ladies and gentlemen of the jury, I respectfully ask you, does that justify the deliberate calculated decision to—once again, for a second time—violently crush the head of the already unconscious teenage boy? Now what makes this so troubling is the fact the medical examiner's formal report concluded it was the second blow that was the principal cause of death."

That simply wasn't true. Will was fuming over the fact the medical examiner's report on which blow caused the death was clearly not conclusive. He knew it was inappropriate to make an objection during an opening statement. He made a mental note to be sure and correct this inaccurate comment during his opening remarks. Undermining his credibility this early in the proceedings could serve him well down the road. For the time being, he could only bite his lip!

Townsend continued, "Again, the prosecution readily agrees what the defendant encountered that day was a shocking and horrible scene. However, what we will prove, beyond a reasonable doubt, is the defendant's actions were not only designed to effectively disrupt what was going on before him but rather, unleashing anger built up over the years, he seized the perfect opportunity to get even with his longtime nemesis.

"Sadly, there's only one conclusion that can be drawn. Luke Foster simply took the law in his own hands and chose to brutally murder Ron Ferguson. And therefore, ultimately, ladies and gentlemen, the defendant's violent deliberate actions were clearly not what the law would consider an appropriate response by a reasonable human being under similar circumstances.

"In closing, while the defendant's bold actions could conceivably qualify for second-degree murder charges, they easily fall within the established parameters of the lesser charge of voluntary manslaughter! That being the case, and we will prove beyond a reasonable doubt, you will have no choice but to find Luke Foster guilty for the unfortunate death of the young teenager, Mr. Ron Ferguson!

"Thank you again for fulfilling your civic duty, and I appreciate your undivided attention! That's all I have, Your Honor!"

Chapter Fifty-Nine

With obvious heightened tension throughout the overheated courtroom, Judge Cooper abruptly moved things forward. "Thank you, Attorney Townsend. Mr. Simmons, will you please present the opening statement on behalf of the defense!"

Before Will stood up and attempted to proceed, he calmly leaned over and had a quiet discussion with his trusted confidant, Big Jake. There was no denying it—they were both in a minor state of shock and deeply concerned with the unquestionably effective opening statement presented by Townsend. Will braced himself for what had quickly become a cruel baptism to the big leagues!

While they were familiar with the recommended rule of not "trying" the case in your opening statement, they agreed he had to do something beyond what he had originally planned to neutralize the huge momentum the prosecution had clearly established. There was no doubt the pendulum had dramatically swung in favor of the prosecution. Foss Man was sitting there nervously, listening to their conversation. It was pretty obvious things had not gotten off to the greatest of starts.

Attempting to remain calm and trying not to push the panic button, following a quick exchange of ideas, Big Jake agreed that Will had no choice but to expand his opening statement. Knowing it would be at least two days before the defense's key witnesses were put on the stand, it would be risky to let the powerful arguments offered by the prosecution settle in the juries' minds for that lengthy period. Supporting his idol Ike's theory on flexible preparation, fully aware it would become necessary at some point in the trial, Will had to make some major adjustments and do some urgently needed fancy thinking on his feet. Big Jake's final reminder was "Do what you have to, Will, but try to stay under the ten-minute rule if you can."

Seated by Big Jake and his nervous client, still sorting out his hastily modified game plan, Will reminded himself, *This is the minute you've been dreaming of and preparing for since you were in eighth grade. Now settle down, you big idiot—you can handle this!*

Suddenly, out of nowhere, a quiet calm seemed to magically come over him and, with it, a surge of confidence undoubtedly generated by his unwavering belief in Luke Foster's innocence. Foss Man was a nervous wreck and where he got the gumption to say anything he really didn't know, but quoting Will's final words of encouragement the night before, he leaned over to him and said, "Don't worry, Will, this is going to work out!" The timely comment from the most unlikely source made Will chuckle a little bit. He was primed, and it was time to go to work!

He stood up, walked over, and for the very first time in his legal career, positioned himself squarely in front of the jury box. Following all the appropriate courtesies to the judge and jury, Will began with, "It's nothing less than a travesty that this amazing family, the Fosters, following the violent rape of their daughter and sister, have been put in this unfathomable position to, of all things, actually defend themselves. While it's only fifteen-year-old Luke Foster who is personally facing these highly disputable charges, let there be no doubt, with the relentless loyalty, support, and determined spirit of this large closely knit family, a family that has gone through many hard times and against great odds, with their powerful faith in God and in the justice system, will not only survive the unimaginable hand they were dealt but will become stronger and even closer because of it!"

That seemed to go okay. Will felt comfortable and was gaining confidence. "I want to take a minute to introduce the central figure in this sad story, Luke's eighteen-year-old sister Catherine, who after experiencing the unthinkable just a few short weeks ago, is bravely sitting here and showing her loving support for the person that very likely not only disrupted her from being violently raped—and we will convince you—actually saved her life!"

Will paused and made sure the jury could pick Catherine out in the front row. "Sitting with her is her brother Allen, who took a giant step toward fulfilling his lifetime dream of becoming a pilot in the Air Force when he was recently offered the coveted appointment to the Air Force Academy from our fifth district congressman, H. R. Gross. Like the defendant, both Catherine and Allen are honor roll students. Sitting next to them are their humble and proud parents, William and Elizabeth Foster. Their five younger siblings are sitting nervously at home in a total state of confusion and fear about what is going on today with their much loved and admired older brother."

Turning back to the jury, Will continued, "There has been one and only one mistake made by the Foster family. The parents innocently raised their daughter, Catherine, in a manner that produced a lifelong passion for loving and caring for animals. And sadly, that passion is directly responsible for what happened in the shed that day and the very reason we're here today.

"To demonstrate the extent of her love for animals, Dr. Dockstader, the longtime veterinarian in Jefferson, after employing Catherine part-time on Saturdays during the past two years and personally observing her tender and genuine love and care for animals, has offered to put her through college providing she, upon graduation, promises to return to Jefferson and go to work for him. The truly innocent victim in this sad case, it will be Catherine's unquestionable fortitude that will lead her family through this incredibly sad ordeal!"

"Let me draw the picture. Ronald Ferguson, the deceased young man in this case, had a mysterious lifelong hatred for animals. As we proceed the next few days, we will provide unquestionable evidence supporting this harsh reality. Mr. Ferguson had a long and bloody history of treating animals in cruel and unspeakable ways. Catherine, like many others in the community, was well aware of this persistent atrocious behavior. This dynamic provoked a continuous sequence of confrontations between the two of them—Catherine the lover of all animals, and Ronald Ferguson, the ruthless abuser and killer of animals.

"Catherine had become so disgusted with the lack of accountability for his actions she took it upon herself to do something about it. She became actively involved with bringing attention to these repulsive cruel acts and debated extensively with county law enforcement officers, school administration, and even the limited department of social services to first understand and then do something about his behavior. Unfortunately, no one seemed to take her seriously, and she made very little progress. Ron Ferguson was too cunning and crafty and therefore was rarely, if ever, held responsible for his endless indiscretions."

Townsend was boiling! "That bastard had better not suggest it was my fault that Ferguson was never arrested. It suddenly dawned on him. When Catherine Foster had been pointed out a little earlier, he thought she looked familiar, and now he remembered. She was that damn cheerleader he had the heated conversation with about the two dead dogs during halftime of the Jefferson/Boulder basketball game last winter. Shit! He knew what was coming!"

The more time Will spent in Jefferson that summer and learned about the endless evil deeds of the Ferguson brothers over the years, he knew something just wasn't right. He was always proud of his hometown and knew it was filled with loving and caring citizens, but someone had obviously fallen asleep at the wheel. He didn't want to recklessly pin it on any one person, but this horrible incident should never have happened. It wasn't his objective this summer to correct whatever ills may exist in his beloved hometown, but he was not intimidated. He figured, *If the shoe fits, so be it!*

He got back on track. "These confrontations boiled over this winter when it was discovered Ferguson's two neighbor's dogs had been brutally killed by having their throats slit from ear to ear. All suspicions pointed directly toward Ronald Ferguson. But once again, nothing could be proven. Well, finally, Attorney Townsend—and I know you'll be happy to hear this—there's been a major breakthrough. We now have proof that Ronald Ferguson was indeed responsible for killing the dogs."

Townsend about exploded!

"Now here's the point of all this. In recent weeks, since the killing of the dogs, the heated confrontations between the two growing adversaries increased in their intensity. Catherine promised him she would have him arrested if it was the last thing she did on this earth. Ferguson responded by merely laughing at her and telling her, and I quote, 'You don't know what the hell you're talking about, you little bitch.' As the anger grew between them, Ferguson made his most chilling and frightening threat. He promised, and again I quote, 'I'll shut you up for good if you don't back off and shut your big mouth!' You see, members of the jury, it wasn't the intentions of Mr. Ferguson to merely rape Catherine that day in the shed. He had a carefully calculated, premeditated plan to kill her!"

Will paused and walked slowly over by the table where his little brother, all 6'5" Big Jake, gave him a look saying, *You're doing fine, big brother, keep going now!* With his elbows leaning on the table, Foss Man was looking down, resting his now-throbbing head in his cupped hands. If he didn't know it before, he clearly knew it now: this was serious business and he was obviously in the middle of the battle of his life. But the good news was, after listening to Will for just those few brief minutes, he knew he was in good hands. He sat up and deliberately switched the Indianhead penny from his right hand to his left hand!

Will knew he was getting a little windy and didn't want to break the cardinal rule of not "trying" the case in his opening statement, but he also knew too big a lead was hard to overcome, and Townsend had clearly made a powerful impression on the jury. Cases are often won or lost during the opening statements, and with that in mind, he decided to add a little more substance to his original game plan.

Will regrouped and started out freshly. "Now I want to tell you a little about the defendant, Luke Foster. With credible testimony from highly respected sources, we will demonstrate to you that the defendant, while clearly a highly spirited and fun-loving kid, contrary to the image the prosecution is so determined to draw, is a sensitive and gentle soul and, trust me, does not have a mean bone in his body!

"While this is true, and it's something we were planning to address in due time, since Townsend has made such a grand effort to point it out here in the beginning, it was never our intention to deny the fact there was a history of bad blood between Luke and Ron Ferguson. Let's make something perfectly clear: Luke Foster was a lifelong victim of Ron Ferguson's ruthless bullying. Luke has despised Ronald Ferguson for many long, miserable years. Let me say it again, Luke despised Ron Ferguson!

"But don't misunderstand, contrary to what the prosecution is so hellbent to maintain, not for one minute should Luke's prior ill feelings toward Ferguson be distorted or construed as a motive for his actions at that critical split second in the shed that day. The prosecution is trying desperately to make Luke Foster out to be some kind of reckless and vindictive monster, and trust me, nothing could be further from the truth!"

He switched gears. "And before I forget, I do have to correct something Mr. Townsend so emphatically claimed during his opening statement—his deliberate blatant, misleading statement about the medical report suggesting 'conclusively' that the second blow was the principal cause of death. What it actually said—and you'll be provided the opportunity to read the complete official report yourselves—it was inconclusive and only probable that the second blow was the cause of death."

Designed to first undermine Townsend's credibility, he also wanted to plant the seed that the impact of the second blow was conceivably irrelevant. Confident the jury would be more willing to accept the obvious provocation for the first blow, Will asked, "When you carefully consider the likely physical damage that was inflicted with the first undeniable powerful blow, like the one Mr. Townsend so dramatically demonstrated, wouldn't it be reasonable to believe the first blow was the actual cause of death? Unfortunately, the answer to that pivotal question will never be proven conclusively during the course of the trial!

"Ladies and gentlemen, Luke Foster was doing one thing and one thing only that afternoon, trying desperately to rescue his sister from being violently raped! It's only logical to conclude there was no time to think or calculate his actions. To even remotely suggest there was time for some kind of deliberate calculated act so Luke could even the score with Ferguson is absolutely absurd. Admittedly, filled with a mixture of immediate rage, fury, and fear, Luke responded with one flurry of anger to bring a stop to the outrageous scene thrown at him that horrific day!"

Summarizing his final position, he said, "While the burden of proof is on the prosecution, it is our contention that Luke Foster's actions were not only justified but, rather, also directly responsible for saving not only his sister's life but very likely his own as well!

"Members of the jury, I sincerely thank you for your attention." And with that, Will turned to the judge. "That's all I have, Your Honor. Thank you."

Confident he had done a decent job for a rookie, Will humbly returned and sat down at the defense table. Big Jake leaned over and playfully pointed out, "If old Slam Dunk's body language or sick look on his face means anything, I think you did the job, big brother." Looking at his watch, he added, "Although it was closer to fifteen minutes, I think it was time well spent!" But Foss Man's was still scared to death!

It was the farthest thing from Will's mind, but at 6'4" and 190 pounds, with his muscular, athletic build and thick curly blond hair and striking good looks, combined with his high-powered Harvard education, the truth was, he hardly had to take a back seat to Attorney Townsend, his more than competent counterpart. If it wasn't evident before, there was now little doubt it was going to be an interesting battle between these two brilliant and determined young professionals.

Chapter Sixty

Judge Cooper thanked Will, and in respect to the late start for the proceedings and determined to keep things moving, he glanced at his watch and promptly ordered, "Mr. Townsend, we'll get started with the prosecution formally presenting its case. Please introduce your first witness."

Skipping the strutting, show boating, and with no fanfare, Townsend promptly responded, "The prosecution calls our first witness. Would Mr. Gary Sanders please come forward?"

After being sworn in, he said, "Mr. Sanders, would you tell the jury what your job is for the Jefferson school district?"

"Yes. I teach high school math and coach the varsity football, basketball, and baseball teams."

"Have you taught or coached the defendant, Luke Foster?"

"Yes, I certainly have. I had Luke in algebra class this last year and had the pleasure of coaching Luke for many years in little league baseball and, for the past two years, in varsity football, basketball, and baseball."

"I want to ask you about his football experience. Is he known for his aggressive style and toughness in football? And specifically, I understand he was named to the all-conference team as a middle linebacker?"

"Yes, he is one of the toughest kids I've ever coached. The guys being tackled by him have often said it was like getting hit by a runaway truck! And yes, he was second team all-conference last fall as a sophomore, which is quite rare."

"Now, Coach, I know you're fond of Luke, and I remind you there's a lot at stake here, but tell me, do you think he would be capable of confronting and physically disrupting the rape of his sister, even someone the size of Ronald Ferguson, whom I understand you're also familiar with?"

"Yes, I think he would be capable of disrupting the rape, but that doesn't mean—" Before he could go any further, Townsend deliberately interrupted him, "No, please don't editorialize any further, Mr. Sanders. I need a precise answer—yes or no, in your best judgment, could Luke have physically interrupted the rape of his sister?"

"Yes, I suppose he could have!"

Turning toward the jury, Townsend offered and emphasized the theory. "Members of the jury, get the current picture now. The defendant has effectively tackled Ron Ferguson, the rape is over, and Catherine Foster would now be free to remove herself from the building!"

"Thank you, Coach. That's all I have for Mr. Sanders, Your Honor!"

"Your witness, Mr. Simmons."

When they saw Coach Sanders's name on the witness list, Will and Big Jake were surprised at first but then assumed that would be their only logical objective, to validate Luke's physical prowess. Beyond that, the prosecution had to know the coach had a great relationship with Luke.

As highly unusual as it may have appeared at a glance, depending on how the prosecution's interrogation of Mr. Sanders had gone, they had decided Big Jake was the perfect one to handle the cross examination. Will knew how comfortable and confident Big Jake would be in handling it, and with his special relationship with Coach Sanders, he could get the best answers from him. It was a bold and unique move for the defense, but Will thought it would set a good tone for winning over the hearts of the jury. As it turned out, he couldn't have been more right.

Big Jake may have been a little nervous on the inside, but you sure wouldn't have known it by looking at him. The sixteen-year-old tall and gangly Gary Simmons, wire-rimmed glasses and all, like his older brother dressed smartly in a dark suit and tie, like a seasoned pro, stood up and confidently walked over in front of his coach.

With impressive composure, he started out casually, "Who could have ever pictured this scene, huh, Coach? Pretty amazing when you think about it, isn't it, you and me here in the Wright County Court House!" The coach smiled and nodded his head in agreement. "But let's get down to business. Coach, you said that Luke was a tough kid, but would you say he was a mean kid?"

"No, not at all. He has one of the biggest hearts I've ever seen. When he tackles a guy, he usually helps him up, and sometimes when he thought he hit the ball carrier a little too hard, he asks them if they're okay. No, you know how it is, Big Jake, Luke doesn't have a mean bone in his body!"

"Another question, Coach. I know Ron Ferguson played football for you. Could you tell the jury how that worked out?"

"Everyone thought football would be good for Ron. Unfortunately, it turned out to be pretty much a disaster. I took a chance and put Ron in on defense during the first varsity game last fall. He only lasted two plays. He punched players on the other team on both plays. They threw a flag for unnecessary roughness, and we were penalized fifteen yards for each violation. I was in the process of taking him out of the game, but the referee beat me to it—he threw him out. That was the end of Ron's football career."

"Would you say Ron Ferguson was a mean kid?"

"Ron had a lot of problems—we all know that now—but yes, he was an extremely mean kid!"

"Coach, of course you're familiar with what happened a few weeks ago, but could you give any examples that might help us better understand Luke's personal makeup that might reflect his likely state of mind when he walked into the shed that day?"

Townsend jumped up. "Objection, Your Honor, Coach Sanders wasn't put on the witness stand as a character witness for the defendant. This is clearly not appropriate or relevant to the case."

"Overruled! When you presented the witness counselor, you know how it works—he's going to be eligible for cross examination. At the same time, Mr. Simmons, Attorney Townsend does have a point. I'll permit this question, and we'll move on. You may answer the question, Mr. Sanders."

The coach thought for minute how to answer the question, and he finally came up with, "This might be a good example. Luke was the only kid in the starting lineup who always made a point to help the managers put the blocking dummies in the storage shed after football practice every night. He wasn't expected to do it, but for whatever reason, he just wanted to help out. It was actually a little comical. He even had names for the three big old blocking bags—Carl, Fred, and Ted. By the first game, all his teammates knew the names. It was great for team morale during those grueling, hot August two-a-day practice sessions. Again, you know how it is around school, Big Jake, all the teachers get a big kick out of Luke!"

"Thank you, Coach. No more questions, Your Honor."

Will beamed with pride; he couldn't have been prouder. Big Jake had knocked it out of the park. Amazingly, while Townsend had made an effective point with Foss Man's physical prowess, Big Jake had at the very minimum neutralized the testimony and, even more than likely, turned the first witness for the prosecution into a victory for the defense. He looked over and saw the frustration on Townsend's face. It may not have been a game changer, but Will thought round one had backfired on the prosecution! Will knew his little brother's first shot at playing lawyer was clearly one he would always remember!

Checking the time again, the judge ordered, "Your next witness, Mr. Townsend."

Attorney Townsend promptly announced, "The prosecution calls the Wright County chief medical examiner, Dr. Howard Baker. Dr. Baker, would you please come forward?" Baker was sworn in.

Hoping to get things moving in a better direction, Townsend proceeded, "Dr. Baker, would you explain to the court what your extensive tests indicated were the principal cause of death for the central figure in this case, Mr. Ronald Ferguson?"

Without hesitation, the doctor responded very concisely, "Blunt force trauma to the head!"

"And could you determine exactly how many blows there were to Mr. Ferguson's head?"

"Yes, there were two distinct blows."

"Would you please tell us, in your medical opinion, which of the two blows was responsible for the death of Mr. Ferguson?"

"It's not one hundred percent conclusive, but medical logic would conclude that the second blow was most likely the ultimate cause of death."

"Okay. Now, not for one minute do we accept the reckless and irresponsible decision the defendant made to deliver even the first blow, but for obvious reasons, if the defendant had not delivered the second blow, in your professional judgment, is it possible the deceased young man may have survived?"

"It's impossible to determine conclusively how much damage was caused by the first blow, but yes, it's possible."

"So do I understand you right? If the defendant would have stopped his violent reaction to the scene before him after the first blow, the victim may very well still be alive today."

"It's questionable what his condition might be, but yes, that's possible, he may still be alive."

"Thank you, Dr. Baker. Your witness."

Will deliberately left this significant piece of evidence out of his opening statement, but with the doctor's testimony now tying the second blow directly to the cause of death, he felt the urgency to introduce the fact Ferguson was severely intoxicated at the time of his death. He felt obliged to point out how the high alcohol concentration in his bloodstream would have significantly contributed to his increased vulnerability for death in the immediate aftermath of the first blow to the head. But more important than all that, Ferguson's drunken condition would have made him react like some kind of wild and completely unmanageable animal. Will would have preferred introducing this critical evidence closer to the final jury deliberations when it was fresh in their minds. But that simply wasn't going to be the case now. It was already proving to be a game of continuous adjustments.

With that in mind, Will walked directly to the witness stand. "Dr. Baker, did you perform any tests that might indicate if there was alcohol in Mr. Ferguson's system at the time of the incident?"

Dr. Baker answered, "Yes, his blood alcohol level was .25."

Will stated, "You and I both know this high level would substantiate the fact Ronald was extremely intoxicated at the time of his death, but, Dr. Baker, would you explain to the jury how this alcohol level might have directly or indirectly contributed to his death."

"In the State of Iowa, a driver of an automobile is considered legally drunk when his blood alcohol level reaches .08. Ronald's blood alcohol level was over three times that. Yes, this would clearly support the concept that Ronald was severely under the influence of alcohol at the time of his death. As far as how it contributed to his death, that would be impossible to determine. There are too many medical variables, depending on the magnitude of the blunt force trauma he experienced. In my professional judgment, it was the blows to the head more so than the amount of alcohol in his bloodstream that ultimately took his life."

Will came back with, "Before we talk more about the potential of the alcohol's medical contribution to Mr. Ferguson's death, if the defendant tried to take a less aggressive approach to disrupting the rape of his sister, like physically confronting him and trying to reason with him as the prosecution suggests, would the alcohol have made Ronald, who keep in mind, had just been caught in the act of rape, increasingly more likely for the 230-pound powerful young man to respond in an aggressive, angry, and violent manner? In other words, Dr. Baker, would the alcohol have affected his frame of mind, judgment, and subsequent behavior at that critical moment?"

"It's safe to say, in general, yes, alcohol could have profoundly affected his judgment and behavior."

Will continued, "Okay, let's get back to the cause of death issue. Dr. Baker, the extremely high concentration of alcohol in Ron Ferguson's system would have made him more susceptible to death wouldn't it? And if so, in that condition, wouldn't that suggest the first blow may have actually caused his death?"

"That possibility was carefully considered in making our final judgment, but yes, it's possible."

"Not that I believe it's necessarily germane to the case, but isn't it safe to say it's not conclusive that the second blow was the cause of death? It may very well have been the first blow that was responsible." It was all about creating doubt whenever possible!

"Yes, I suppose that's possible."

"Thank you, Dr. Baker. I have no more questions, Your Honor."

Judge Cooper responded, "Thank you, Dr. Baker, you may be excused. Should it become necessary to revisit any of the information you have provided for us this afternoon, the court asks you to please make yourself available throughout the week."

Satisfied with the progress made to this point, Judge Cooper decided to shut down for the afternoon and announced decisively, "We're going to adjourn in a few minutes, but before doing so, I want to thank the people in the gallery for your admirable demeanor today and will expect that to continue throughout the rest of the trial." He turned to the jury. "I also want to thank you for your attention, and again, I want to apologize for the late start today but remind you that court will resume at nine o'clock sharp tomorrow morning, and I want you to report no later than eighty-thirty. You may be excused." And hammering his gavel, the judge proclaimed, "Court is adjourned!"

Chapter Sixty-One

Foss Man's sixth-grade brother Gerald had been delivering the Des Moines Register for over a year by now. This was the third morning in a row he had sprung out of bed without the comfort of having his big brother sleeping next to him. It was just like a month ago when Foss Man had been gone for a week and Gerald hated it then too. He missed when every night Foss Man would tickle, jostle, and wrestle with him before they eventually called it a night. He knew something bad was going on, but his parents never explained exactly what it was. He and his sister Glenda heard something about this rape thing and knew it somehow involved Catherine. The truth was, his parents were struggling mightily to effectively explain what happened to the younger kids. How do you explain rape to a twelve- and fourteen-year-old? They were doing their best to insulate the little ones from the sensitive facts surrounding the incident. They were no magic answers.

That morning, when Gerald was stuffing the 50 Des Moines Register newspapers in his paper bag, he couldn't help but notice the huge picture on the front page. His eyes got huge when he realized it was a picture of his mom, dad, Catherine, and Allen squeezing their way through a huge crowd of people as they were coming down the steps of the courthouse. He stood there for a minute with his eyes glued to the large black-and-white picture. Gerald said to himself, "What the heck is this all about anyway?"

Like all the Foster kids, Gerald was a good student and an excellent reader. He sat down on the steps of the post office where the papers were dumped by the big delivery truck every morning. He proceeded to read the story. His dad had promptly shut the television set off the night before when NBC, ABC, and CBS were all covering the story on the 5:30 p.m. news.

The bold headline above the big picture read as follows:

TEENAGE MURDER/RAPE CASE
CAPTURES NATIONAL ATTENTION

> Jefferson, Iowa, the small historically peaceful farming community located about one hundred miles north of Des Moines, has been swamped this week with the national television network news trucks along with scores of newspaper reporters. The widespread interest was created by the intriguing trial for the teenage boy, Luke Foster, who, while innocently putting his bike in the small storage shed, walked in on the renowned teenage town bully, Ron Ferguson, who was in the process of raping Catherine Foster, his eighteen-year-old sister. The young Foster boy has been charged with voluntary manslaughter in the death of Ferguson after repeatedly crushing the back of his head with a baseball bat.
>
> The trial will determine if Foster, who has accepted full responsibility for Ferguson's death, was indeed reckless, irresponsible, and overzealous in his reaction to the rape of his sister, behavior the prosecution contends was fueled by a well-documented history of bad blood between the two high school classmates. The defense has taken the initial position that the defendant's actions were not only justified, but when considering the size and strength of the rapist and the fact he was severely intoxicated at the time, it was a necessary act of self-defense in view of the subsequent battle he would inevitably have been facing in the aftermath of walking in on the unimaginable scene. The accused fifteen-year-old

> boy curiously volunteered to have the case tried in the adult Wright County Court system.
>
> The controversial trial appears to have split the closely knit community into two distinct camps. Combining that with the fact the inflammatory case pits two brilliant young legal minds, Wright County Attorney Roger Townsend and Harvard graduate Will Simmons, both from the immediate area, has elevated the local and national interest to a fever pitch. Notorious no-nonsense Judge Cooper is hoping to have the case in the hands of the jury by no later than Friday. Until then, the national media frenzy combined with the intense local interest will not only guarantee a circuslike atmosphere throughout this week but will also undoubtedly leave an indelible mark on Jefferson, the wholesome and previously pristine small farm town.

The story continued on a back page, but Gerald had read enough, and after delivering the fifty papers in record-breaking time, worried and filled with reinforced curiosity, he handed their copy of the paper to his mother. Busy getting ready and about to head to the courthouse for the day, Gerald's parents were forced to take a few minutes and conduct another rather awkward meeting with Gerald and his older sister Glenda. They struggled but cautiously did their best to explain and comfort the two confused siblings. Substituting the term *hurting* for *raping*, they emphasized their brother Luke had bravely come to the aid of their older sister. Knowing their answers were inadequate, leaving the two kids with quizzical looks on their faces, they were reminded once again, this wasn't going to be an easy week for anyone.

Reading the report in its entirety, it was notable that the magnitude of the widespread national interest and subsequent extensive coverage was nearly as big a story as the dramatic trial itself.

With an even larger throng of national and local media along with the growing interest from the general citizenship in the surrounding area, the scene on Wednesday morning was wilder and crazier than ever. In anticipation of this development, County Sherriff Ramsey had solicited the assistance of the Iowa State Highway Patrol in keeping the crowd safe and orderly. When the front doors of the court house were finally opened and the courtroom immediately filled to capacity, the overflow of bodies were jammed in the adjacent hallway, courthouse steps, and spread out on the street. Waiting for the chance of any spontaneous piece of news, the herd of curious people would linger in the general vicinity of the courthouse throughout the day.

With the four fans whirling in their futile attempt to counter the ninety-five-degree temperature and intense humidity in the once-again overpacked courtroom, following a brief side bar meeting with the lawyers, and with the jury now freshly positioned and wide eyed in the jury box, Judge Cooper slammed his gavel twice and boldly demanded, "Order in the court, order in the court!"

As he was escorted into the courtroom, Foss Man quickly scanned the gallery. He tried to avoid making eye contact as he walked in front of Ferguson's parents, who were sitting in the front row along the railing and directly behind the defense table. They had no idea what was coming that morning. He easily singled out the striking face of Rosita and, in the row behind her, Mr. Slim, who was demonstrating his typical positive attitude, giving Foss Man the thumbs-up signal.

The judge ordered, "Mr. Townsend, please call your next witness to the stand."

Decked out in another impressive fresh, new outfit, Townsend skipped the prancing and show boating and got right to it. "The prosecution calls for Mr. Alford Hughes to the stand."

"Mr. Hughes, would you state your official position in Jefferson, please?"

Everyone in the courtroom had to be impressed. Alcohol Al, as he was affectionately referred to and, of course, reflecting his inclination to consume alcohol on the job, looked as sharp as they had ever seen him. Officer Al was completely sober, and in his freshly pressed uniform and shined shoes, he had never looked better. It was a stressful experience for the cop, and he wasn't looking forward to it, but having no alternative, he was willing to fulfill his obligation.

In a nervous voice, the officer responded, "Yes, I'm the town cop over in Jefferson."

Townsend asked him, "Do you recall an incident this past winter involving a Mr. Bart Gunderson and his concern with a stray bullet?"

"Yes, I certainly do."

"Would you tell the jury exactly what took place that day, Mr. Hughes?"

Appearing more comfortable and relaxed, the cop went through the whole story. "Bart called me and was extremely upset about the fact a bullet had grazed his head just a few minutes earlier. He told me the incident took place down by his pig shed, which is located a short distance from the popular skating rink out on Troy River. I went down to the river and discovered Luke Foster and two of his buddies, who all had guns on their laps. They admitted they had been target practicing on the frozen river. I picked the three boys up and took them over to Mr. Gunderson's house. Bart had been feeding his pigs when a bullet whistled by his head. Recognizing the fact the other two boys had shotguns, it was easy to conclude it was Luke's rifle that shot the stray bullet. Bart had a long festering red mark across his forehead."

After a series of probing questions and subsequent answers dramatizing the story in complete detail, Townsend asked the cop, "Were any legal charges filed against the defendant at that time?"

"No, Luke apologized and expressed his sincere regret for what happened. Bart was particularly reasonable, considering the potentially deadly circumstances, and said he didn't want to press the issue any further. I took Luke's rifle and told him I would return it sometime in the future—as a matter of fact, I still have possession of his gun."

Will was familiar with the incident and had previously talked it over with Foss Man in great length. The testimony was fully expected and obviously not a favorable revelation. The incident clearly suggests a degree of reckless behavior on Foss Man's part. Knowing it would be a futile effort if not even counterproductive, Will had made a calculated decision not to challenge the anticipated testimony of the town cop. After all, it happened and was a legitimate story. There are times when you simply have to bite the bullet, so to speak.

Townsend knew this was a pivotal moment in the trial and he was going to take full advantage of it and keep hammering on the story. "So do I have this right? You're saying that Luke Foster's reckless behavior with the high-powered .22-caliber rifle nearly resulted in the death of another human being. Is that correct, Mr. Hughes?"

Frustrated with the way the story was growing in importance, Will jumped up. "Objection, Your Honor. This isn't the time to be making summations. At this early stage of the proceedings, let the jury evaluate the testimony on their own!"

The judge said firmly, "The objection is overruled. You may proceed, Mr. Townsend."

Townsend responded rather indignantly, "Thank you, Your Honor. You may now answer the question, Mr. Hughes."

"Yes, the bullet could just as easily have gone through Mr. Gunderson's head, and I suppose it's safe to conclude it could have killed him."

"I have no more questions for Mr. Hughes, Your Honor." And looking arrogantly and victoriously at Will, knowing he had just hit a home run, he said, "Your witness."

Will was carefully thinking how he might counter this powerful revelation. He quickly decided, *Less is probably more right now.* However, he knew he had to respond in some manner to blunt the obvious momentum that Townsend had established with this dramatic testimony. Again he hated to admit it, but it was becoming abundantly clear—this Townsend character was a real piece of work and damn good!

Desperate, he finally came up with, "Mr. Hughes, when it was decided not to press charges in this incident, was it based primarily on the fact it was an accident?"

The reasonable town cop came back with, "Yes, there was never any doubt about that. Luke obviously had no intentions of doing any harm to Mr. Gunderson. I knew that, and Bart knew that. Mr.

Gunderson was extremely shaken up about what happened, but he knew it was just a rare, freakish accident. Bart and I both knew Luke was a good kid, and we just wanted to make sure he understood and appreciated the fact he had to be more careful with that powerful rifle!"

Wow, that turned out better than Will could have ever dreamed. It didn't erase the negative impact of the incident, but he couldn't have written a better answer himself!

Feeling a little better and wanting to drive the point home, Will wrapped it up with, "Mr. Hughes, in your respected professional opinion, as serious as this incident was and as bad as I know Luke feels about it, would you say this incident could be chalked up as a youthful mistake, a teenager's error in judgment, an accident with a great lesson to be learned attached to it?"

Not thinking of what Luke was currently facing or fully recognizing the irony of what he was saying, the cop said sincerely, "Yes, I don't think Luke will make another mistake like that!'

Not wanting to let the jury digest the inadvertent prophetic nature of that last statement, he quickly wrapped it up. "Thank you, Mr. Hughes. I have no more questions, Your Honor."

Chapter Sixty-Two

Townsend knew the bold decision to put Frank Ferguson on the stand was a questionable proposition. Knowing it was a risky maneuver, Townsend had called and talked in great length to the psychologist in charge of Frank's more recent rehabilitation program in the penitentiary. Citing strict confidentiality laws, the psychologist was careful to point out at the very beginning that she was limited in what she had the liberty to share with him.

However, she did proceed to volunteer, "I'm familiar with Frank's personal history here at the penitentiary. Let me explain a little bit. I've only been on the staff here for three years. I was hired during the second year of the Eisenhower administration when they attempted to appease the loud voices of national civil rights leaders, protesting how prisoners were being treated in the federal and state prisons across the country. Congress cleverly tied federal funding to the individual states with strict mandates requiring local funding to provide improved counseling, particularly for the inmates in high-security prisons.

"When I came on board, I dug into Frank's personal records. He was clearly quite a stinker throughout his first five years down here. He got in so many fights they didn't dare let him join the general population without direct supervision. He was such a bitter and angry young man. Unfortunately, like many others, he was kept in solitary confinement most of the time. It's a pretty sad commentary, and it's only slightly improved, but prisoners were caged like animals back then.

"During our early sessions, Frank refused to tell me much. Then after about a year of our persistent meetings, something changed. Now don't misunderstand, he was far from a model citizen, but it wasn't very long before he no longer had to be confined and was enjoying more freedom and a few privileges as a result of his improved behavior. As he grew to trust me, always expressing deep concern with his younger brother's safety, he made me promise not to tell anyone about what I could sense he wanted so desperately to share with me. Of course I can't discuss what was at the core of his deep fear, but I will say this, when his brother was killed a few weeks ago, he went ballistic. Since then, apparently no longer fearing for his brother's safety, he has really opened up to me!"

Liking what he was hearing, Townsend asked her, "I understand you're limited on what you can tell me, but do you think Frank would be a good witness on behalf of his brother?"

The psychologist knew all about the pending trial. She responded, "What I will risk telling you—and it's up to him—is he certainly has quite a dramatic story to tell. And he definitely has great compassion and a powerful love for his younger brother. Thinking he was responsible for what happened, he was absolutely devastated with the news of Ronald's death, particularly the way it happened. I probably should warn you, he gets pretty worked up talking about it, but yes, I think he would be a good witness. I better not say any more!"

Sensing where she was coming from and recognizing the golden opportunity to slam the door on this whole thing, he intended to take full advantage of the potent highly valued sympathy card. Townsend was familiar with the cardinal rule "Don't ask a witness a question to which you don't have a pretty good idea how it will be answered," but he knew there was virtually no response Frank could give that would harm the prosecution. The opportunity for a lengthy practice run was prohibitive under the unusual circumstances, and furthermore, in his experience, while risky, unrehearsed spontaneous testimony can also be extremely effective. During his brief conversation with Frank, Townsend was encouraged and could sense he was eager and more than willing to testify! The complex logistics of transporting him to Boulder should be well worth it.

There was a sudden electricity in the courtroom when Frank Ferguson made what was a rather spectacular grand entrance. The prosecution had lost the argument permitting Frank to change from the traditional bright-orange prison uniform into street clothes. Handcuffed and carefully secured between two tough-looking uniformed law enforcement officers, he was dramatically escorted into the room. Every eye in the place was now glued on the convict. His dad was stunned when he saw him walk in. He had no idea his older son was scheduled to testify. Conveniently positioned in the front row directly behind the railing, Frank easily singled him out and glared at him with frightening cold, penetrating eyes.

Knowing there was nothing he could do to halt the proceedings, totally desperate, his father could do nothing but glare back with the same fierce, intimidating look that had been so effective throughout every day of Frank's miserable life. But it wasn't working this time. With his equally alarmed petite wife right next to him, the two had no choice but remain sitting there with the remote hope their presence would influence Frank's pending testimony.

When everything settled down, the timing was almost perfect. Judge Cooper ordered, "Attorney Townsend, your next witness please."

With his adrenaline reaching a new all-time high, Attorney Townsend boldly announced, "Would Mr. Frank Ferguson please come forward and take the witness stand."

A decision the judge would soon live to regret, offering a small dignity, there was a slight delay while the police removed the handcuffs. Foss Man knew he was on the witness list, but the very sight of Frank Ferguson was deeply disturbing for him. First, the eerie fact that at 6'4" and over 240 pounds, he looked almost identical to his younger brother. Foss Man's first thought was, *Good grief, what a giant!* He thought he could remember seeing Frank years ago, but he would have only been six or seven years old at the time. Frank had a defiant and arrogant look about him as he strutted forward and raised his hand to be sworn in. Again, you could cut the tension with the proverbial knife!

In a calm voice, Townsend started out, "I know this is a difficult time for you, Frank, but on behalf of your deceased brother, it may prove helpful for the jury to learn more about you and your brother's childhood with the chance it may have contributed to Ron's extreme behavior that day. Are you willing to do that for us?

Fearing where this was heading, his angry dad looked like he was about ready to come charging out of his seat.

With a strong, aggressive tone, Frank fired back, "No, Attorney Townsend, you're wrong about one thing! This is not difficult for me! I've been waiting years for this opportunity!" He glared directly at his dad. "You damn right, I'll tell you about our miserable childhood. Maybe that piece of shit sitting over there would rather explain it to you!"

With that, his dad stood up and bellowed, "Shut your mouth, you worthless bastard. If you know what's good for you, you'll shut your goddamned mouth right now!"

Judge Cooper was hammering his gavel and shouting, "Order in the court, order in the court!" Prepared for this kind of rare event, the judge ordered the excessive number of law officers present to immediately remove Mr. Ferguson from the courtroom. Fortunately, avoiding what could have been an ugly scene, humiliated and instinctively not wanting to hear anymore, on their own volition, Frank's parents rushed out the nearest exit in the back of the courtroom. Everyone in the gallery, the fourteen members of the jury and the three concerned guys sitting at the defense table, were gasping for air and shocked by the crazy unexpected event.

Perhaps a little startled but liking the direction this was going, when things eventually settled down, Townsend restarted, "Okay, Frank, let's try to relax a little bit and get back on track here. Please explain to the jury what it was like living in your home."

He knew it was a futile effort, but wanting to at least plant the legitimate contention in the minds of the jury, Will asserted himself, "Objection, Your Honor, exactly what does this have to do with the guilt or innocence of the defendant?"

Recognizing exactly what the defense was trying to do and with the fact this issue had been argued and well established earlier, Judge

Cooper was not happy with Will and barked, “Overruled. You may proceed, counsel!”

Calming down and in a more civilized and controlled tone, Frank proceeded to tell the story. “It was like a torture chamber around our house, going back as long as I can remember. I think it started when I was about six or seven years old. It’s sickening, but I’ve learned how to talk about it. My sorry excuse for a dad started taking me in his bedroom and molesting me. I couldn’t do anything to stop him. When I cried, he would beat me and put me down in the dark basement. What he was doing to me was unbearable, but I learned not to cry. My sick mother, the match made in hell, sat outside the bedroom door most of the time and did nothing. Sometimes when my dad insisted on it, she would come in and watch what my dad was doing to me. She would just sit there. My dad made ugly sounds like an animal. He made me do every disgusting thing you can imagine to him. During the early years, I’d get real mad and threatened to report what he was doing. He told me he would kill me if I told anybody. I believed him! He was the meanest and most evil person I’ve ever known and I knew he would kill me!”

Townsend could see Frank was getting emotional and considered asking Judge Cooper for a short break. He knew the jury didn’t need to hear any more to get the picture, but he wanted to tie all this more directly to the younger brother. He suggested Frank catch his breath for a minute or two and, buying a little time, walked over to the prosecution table and talked briefly with his assistant, Attorney Dempsey. The guys at the defense table could only sit there and take it all in.

The judge intervened and ordered Townsend, “Get on with this or we’ll break for lunch.”

With that, Townsend responded, “Sorry, Your Honor, we’ll get going here.”

He walked over to Frank, “I want to switch gears for a minute. What about your brother Ron, was it the same for him?”

Hearing his brother’s name struck a raw nerve, and Frank became visibly shaken. Animated and with more volume in his voice, he barked, “That’s what really makes me sick. For all these years being locked up, I knew Ron was being abused the same way I was. It was bad enough when he was little—he sat outside the bedroom door with my mother and had to listen to what was happening to me all those days and nights. When I got in high school, for some reason my dad left me alone, but I knew and Ron knew, someday the same sick crap would be happening to him. Unfortunately, we were right. My dad threatened to kill Ron if I told anyone. I didn't dare do anything about it, and it's been even worse sitting in jail because I felt like I abandoned my helpless little brother. I had nightmares knowing exactly what was going on at home, but I knew my dad would kill him if I reported it to anyone. Ron told me it stopped three years ago when he got in high school. That's when I gambled and started talking about it with the psychologist."

The judge could see the witness's emotions and anger were building. He decided with the sensitive nature of the testimony, everyone had heard enough, and with it approaching lunch hour, he decided to call for a much-needed break. "Court will now adjourn for lunch. Mr. Townsend, you may recall the witness this afternoon if you want, and of course the defense will be given a chance for cross-examination."

Addressing the jury, Judge Cooper reinforced his strict instructions about not discussing the morning testimony amongst themselves over lunch. With that, he adjourned and announced that court would resume at 1:30 p.m. sharp and slammed the gavel. With the promise of more explosive fireworks in the afternoon session, many people in the gallery chose to remain seated rather than risk not getting back in after the lunch break. Recognizing what was going on, Judge Cooper ordered everyone to leave. Having reserved seats, the twenty-five friends and family of the defendant had the luxury of going out for lunch and not having to worry about getting a valued seat.

Chapter Sixty-Three

Will, Big Jake, and Foss Man had a lot to talk over during the lunch break. Putting it mildly, it had been a rough morning. First the gun incident and then the well-played sympathy card. It wasn't unusual for the prosecution to have things move in their favor in the early stages of a trial, but Will was not happy about the abundance of fresh information the jury would be digesting over the lengthy lunch break. Contrary to the strict rules put in place and their best intentions, he knew the jury couldn't resist quietly interacting about the explosive dynamics that morning.

Sensing the tension in the air, as they were attempting to eat the sandwiches Will had delivered to the conference room, he quickly reminded Big Jake and Foss Man, "All right, you guys, let's not get all bent out of shape here. We knew there would be a few bumps in the road. We have to keep calm, pay attention, and trust me, we'll get this thing turned around. I don't see any logic in trying to undermine Frank's testimony with any clever cross-examination. But you know something, my gut tells me this cute little move bringing Frank Ferguson back here to testify could blow up in Townsend's face! And don't forget, we'll be getting our witnesses on the stand tomorrow!"

Judge Cooper slammed the gavel, and the afternoon session for the *State of Iowa v. Luke Foster* trial was underway. The jury was back in place, and Attorney Townsend could smell blood and was eager to put Frank Ferguson back on the witness stand.

Townsend informed Frank he only had a couple more questions. With no real purpose other than stirring the sympathy pot a little more, Townsend asked him, "With everything going on—and I fully understand why you personally couldn't do anything about it—did anyone in a position of authority ever get suspicious and try to intervene with your family dynamics?"

Frank thought about it for a minute and finally answered, "One time, when I was in eighth grade, my gym teacher asked me about some ugly welts on my back. I made up something, but a few days later, a lady did come to our house. I think she was from social services or something like that. She talked to my parents for a little while, and I really don't know what happened after that. Now that I think about it, that's when it stopped, for me at least. Of course it wasn't too long after that before the ugly stuff started with Ron."

Then the unexpected stick of dynamite. Townsend said, "That's interesting," and with innocent intentions, he said, "Okay, we're about done here, Frank. I don't expect you to know, but do you think the way Ron was treated at home all those years contributed to his behavior in the shed that day?"

The question obviously struck a raw nerve, and with sudden anger, Frank snapped back, "That's what all the experts claim down in the penitentiary, but the truth is, no one knows for a fact that Ron was raping anyone." He had already picked Catherine out sitting in the front row, and the fact she reminded him a lot of the girl who pressed sexual assault charges against him eight years ago made him proceed to go berserk.

Like a wild man, he stood up, waving his arms, and shouting at the top of his lungs, he blurted out, "My brother may have been fucking that smart-ass little bitch sitting over there but he sure as hell wasn't raping her when that punk brother of hers started hitting him over the head with that fucking baseball bat!"

Before they could stop him, his final rant—"You better put that little fucker away for a long time, or I promise you, I'll take care of the asshole for good! Trust me, I'll kill the little bastard with a goddamned baseball bat just like the punk used to kill my brother!"

The whole room erupted! The judge hammered his gavel and commanded, "Order in the court! Order in the court!"

With Frank still ranting and raving, the judge ordered the four uniformed police officers to have him immediately removed from the courtroom. The attorneys on both sides could do nothing but watch.

The same thing was true for the startled jury and all the stunned people in the gallery.

It took the four male police officers at least five minutes to get the crazed giant under control. They were all rolling around on the floor while Ferguson was throwing wild haymakers and, oftentimes, connecting. After a long, fierce battle, with ugly red welts on their faces and disheveled with their shirts pulled out of their freshly pressed trousers, the four burly officers finally managed to get handcuffs on the powerful, insane giant of a man!

Foss Man's five buddies were standing and all but cheering out loud. They'd never seen anything quite like it! No one in the gallery had for that matter!

It was an incredible scene, and with the now-handcuffed severely disturbed convict being literally dragged from the courtroom and with Judge Cooper in the process of declaring an emergency recess, there was suddenly another big commotion in the gallery just four rows behind the defense table. Like everyone else, Foss Man turned to see what was going on and was devastated when he saw his great friend Mr. Slim lying on the floor in the aisle at the end of the bench where he had been sitting. The always-present medic dressed in a white uniform had already taken charge and was vigorously applying CPR on the old gentleman. Will and Big Jake had to hold Foss Man back as he attempted to get to the side of his stricken friend.

Even a grisly seasoned veteran like Judge Cooper had never experienced anything quite like this during his long-storied career. First the wild wrestling match with the crazed witness and now what appeared to be a heart attack victim in the gallery. With the circus atmosphere and now worried about the poor gentleman in the gallery, knowing the jury could never regain their composure and focus on the subject at hand, as much as he was hoping to wrap up the prosecution's case that afternoon, the judge hastily decided to adjourn court for the day. More demonstrative than he had been all week, Judge Cooper stood up and demanded the trial will resume at nine o'clock sharp in the morning while simultaneously hammering his gavel and bellowing, "Court is adjourned, court is now adjourned!"

Chapter Sixty-Four

Everyone in the courtroom was in shock. Frank Ferguson had put on a show for the ages. Townsend had felt comfortable that everything had been going as planned, but unfortunately, his big gamble at the end had clearly blown up in his face!

Foss Man's parents were deeply concerned about their great friend being wheeled out on a gurney but were preoccupied with comforting Catherine, who was visibly upset with Frank's direct reference made to her and even more so for the frightening threat leveled at her brother. Foss Man's five buddies loved the chaos, and other than what happened to Mr. Slim, they were totally impressed with all the craziness. They were genuinely worried about how things appeared to be going against their friend that day, but there was no denying how excited they were as they piled in Rocket's car and headed back to Jefferson. In typical teenage fashion, they couldn't wait to return the next day, hoping for more of the wild fireworks in the courtroom.

With a wide range of emotions, Will, Big Jake, and their badly shaken client headed back to the conference room. Foss Man was fighting back tears and no longer thinking about what he was facing; he was worried sick about how his old friend was doing. He insisted Will talk to Judge Cooper about letting him go over to the hospital, where he was afraid Mr. Slim might be literally fighting for his life. Attempting to settle him down, Will promised he'd talk to the judge.

The meeting with Judge Cooper did not go well. After intense debate, Will returned and was as angry as Foss Man had ever seen him. He told him the judge had rejected his request. Without going into detail, still furious, Will simply said, "The judge doesn't understand the nature of your special friendship with Mr. Slim and didn't think it was necessary or appropriate to release you even for just an hour or two. You know I'm not happy about it, Foss Man, but we have too much at stake for me to push it any further and risk alienating our relationship with the judge. I'm sorry, Foss Man. When we get done with our final preparations for tomorrow, I promise you Big Jake and I will stop over and give Mr. Slim your best wishes!"

Foss Man was deeply upset about this whole thing. It was impossible for him to concentrate as they were going over the questions Will planned on asking him during his testimony which would most likely be the following day. As they were struggling and failing to make much progress, Foss Man assured them, "Don't worry, you guys, I've had plenty of time to think about this stuff. I know exactly what I want to tell the jury. Like you've both been telling me all along, just speak from the heart and tell the truth. That won't be hard. To be perfectly honest, I can't wait!"

As they were wrapping things up, Foss Man added, "When you guys go over to the hospital, tell Mr. Slim I'm going to write him a letter tonight, and remind him, like he's reminded me over and over, when it looks like everything is going against you, don't worry, the sun will always come up in the morning!

"And one more thing, I want you to give this to him." He handed Will that almost-perfect old Indianhead penny he, unknown to them, had been squeezing in his right hand all that week. "Mr. Slim knows all about the magic penny and recommended I only bring it out for special occasions. It's never failed me, and now he needs it more than I do!"

When they got to the hospital, they were informed that Mr. Slim was in intensive care and wasn't allowed to have visitors. The doctor in charge told them he had experienced a serious heart attack so severe, he already had to be resuscitated twice after going into repeated cardiac arrest. Having no immediate family, Mr. Slim's best buddy, Nute, was there and would remain at his side until things hopefully stabilized.

Sitting in the public lounge, Nute shared a rather amazing story with them. "You guys won't believe this. Mr. Slim was so upset listening to Townsend's attempt to make Foss Man look like such a reckless and bad kid he told me just this noon, "If I have to listen to much more of this crap about this young kid with such a big and caring heart, I think I'm going to have a damn heart attack!" Will and Big Jake picked up on the irony behind the unique story, but more than that, they were impressed with the mutual affection between this old codger and their young client.

It was a sad reality—the much loved eighty-six-year-old gentleman was in critical condition—but the doctor assured Will and Big Jake, "That doesn't mean he won't pull through, it happens all the time!" The doctor convinced them there really wasn't anything more that can be done for him right now. Nute promised to give Mr. Slim the special penny, they shook hands, and the brothers made their way back to bring Foss Man up-to-date.

Will and Big Jake were granted permission to visit Foss Man in his cell in the back end of juvenile center. When they walked by the smaller and much less intimidating juvenile courtroom, Will had to ask himself, *Were we too quick in making our decision to voluntarily forfeit the option to have the case heard in the juvenile court system?* He vividly remembered Foss Man's parents sincerely questioning the decision. Although he still felt strongly they had made the right decision, there was no denying it, the pressure was building.

They didn't want to worry Foss Man more than they had to, but at the same time not wanting to give him false hope, they did their best to describe the scenario. "Your friend is resting peacefully, and the doctors won't really know what the outlook is until tomorrow when they hope to have him stabilized. Mr. Slim had a serious heart attack, but the doctor said many people pull through this kind of thing."

Foss Man was badly shaken with the frightening news. Will and Big Jake were anxious to get back home to get to work. It wasn't a pretty picture walking away from Foss Man once again trapped in that miserable, cold cell. On the way back to Jefferson, it was quiet in the car until Big Jake broke the silence. "Do you think it can get any shittier for that friend of ours, Will?"

When Will and Big Jake got home, setting all the emotions aside, they had to settle down, get their minds back on track, and carefully evaluate everything that had taken place that day. Will had to admit he had never anticipated anything quite as crazy as all this when he signed on for the job, but he was still thankful he made the bold decision to help the Foster family. Big Jake agreed and made a special point to tell Will it was a darn good thing he took this thing on because he knew there was no one better suited to get the best possible outcome. Will said, "I appreciate that, Big Jake. Now let's get to work!"

As they replayed the highlights of the day, first the good news. There was no question about it—the dramatic Frank Ferguson display that day was an absolute bonanza for illustrating and proving the potential self-defense concept, which of course was one of the key elements in building their defense. There was no testimony or words in the dictionary that could have more effectively described the fight Foss Man would have been facing that day in the shed if he hadn't responded as decisively as he did. It took four burly highly trained law enforcement officers to get the crazed wild man under control. Frank was virtually the same size as his brother Ron. And Ron had been drunk and caught in the act of rape. Not in their wildest imagination could they have visualized that kind of battle! And the jury had witnessed it all firsthand! The defense couldn't have orchestrated it any better!

All that well and good, with the prosecution getting close to resting its case, they had to bear down. After two hours of replaying and reviewing the prosecutions key plays, except for taking full advantage of the gift-wrapped development that day, Will and Big Jake saw no need for making major adjustments to their original plans. Satisfied with their preparation and totally exhausted, they both agreed, "We better get some sleep, we've got a big day ahead of us!"

Foss Man decided to wait until early the next morning to write his letter to Mr. Slim. He spent most of the night tossing and turning like always, and although he knew he'd very likely be taking the witness stand the next day, he wasn't worried about that. Instead, he spent most of the night worrying about Mr. Slim. He fell asleep thinking about what to say in the letter.

Dear Mr. Slim,

Sure enough, with everything going on, just like you promised, the sun came up again today.

What's up with you and me anyway? Me sitting here in this stupid jail cell and you lying over there in that hospital bed. I bet you're giving the nurses a hard time. You're probably making them laugh. You told me laughing is good for you. We haven't been laughing enough lately.

I could sure use one of our little talks. I can just hear you, "Don't worry buddy, everything's going to work out!" I know you're right. This stupid trial is going to be over in a couple of days, and if they haven't sent you home by then, I'll be right over to see you. Before you know it, we'll both be back in that new hot spot we found a while back and pulling in some more of those huge catfish.

I want you to know a couple of things, Mr. Slim. We've been good buddies for twelve years now. You and Nute are just about the best friends a guy could ever have. You guys always help me deal with my problems, and boy, it sure seems like I have my share. I don't know about this one but most of them are my own fault. I don't want you worrying about me. You're right, it's all going to work out!

Now keep that special penny squeezed in your right hand and you and Nute and I will be back together fishing and laughing again. I can't wait!

Your best buddy,
Foss Man

Chapter Sixty-Five

Pictures of a handcuffed and angry Frank Ferguson being escorted from the court house and stuffed in the back seat of a marked police vehicle were plastered across the front pages of the local and national newspapers that night. The national television networks had kept their viewing audience up-to-date on the evening news programs, reinforcing their lead story by showing the same dramatic pictures. The spectacular nature of the story was generating a larger contingency of interested parties, and the growing intrigue was picking up steam as the trial progressed through the week.

The news outlets reported that the questions debated in the bars, cafes, and at the breakfast, lunch, and supper tables across the country all revolved around one central theme: Was the fifteen-year-old teenager justified in the drastic manner in which he rescued his sister who was being violently raped by the oversized seventeen-year-old mutual acquaintance of theirs? The young defendant was being charged with voluntary manslaughter for crushing the teenage boy's head with a baseball bat. Focusing on the reckless behavior in the defendant's recent past and suggesting there was premeditation on his part, the testimony had clearly favored the prosecution, and the general consensus was that the outcome did not look good for the young defendant. With the prosecution about ready to rest their case, the defense was expected to start presenting their side on Thursday. The judge in the small northern Iowa community was still hopeful of getting the case in the hands of the jury by Friday.

Foss Man handed Mr. Slim's letter to Big Jake first thing Thursday morning. When Big Jake saw Nute walk in the courtroom, he rushed up and gave him the envelope. Nute looked like he had been up all night, and it was very close to being the case. Nute informed him Mr. Slim had stabilized late last night and had gotten a pretty good night's sleep. He said he was resting peacefully when he left him this morning. Nute promised Big Jake he'd get the letter to him over the lunch break. Big Jake gave Foss Man the message, and it made him feel a little bit better.

The courtroom was jammed as always, and Judge Cooper intended to get things underway promptly at 9:00 a.m. Having let the emotions simmer down overnight, the judge had met with Townsend earlier that morning. He made it clear he wasn't very happy about the fiasco yesterday. A somewhat dispirited Townsend humbly apologized. The judge knew it certainly hadn't been choreographed and said, "I understand. Let's put all that behind us and get on with today's proceedings."

The night before, huddled in Townsend's office, as they were attempting to recuperate from the crazy episodes that day, Townsend and his assistant Tom Dempsey were discussing the repulsive revelations revealed during Frank's explosive testimony that afternoon. It quickly dawned on them that with no statute of limitations on child abuse in the state of Iowa, there was another high-profile case staring them in the face and looming large well within the boundaries of their jurisdiction. Licking his chops, Townsend temporarily removed the unbecoming events of the day from his mind.

The citizens of Wright County were sickened by the pathetic story and along with their utter disgust, there was strong speculation across the supper tables that night that they could soon expect to see a "For sale" sign on the front lawn of the Ferguson family house in the very near future.

Unrelated to the events the previous day, Townsend told the judge he was cutting back on his witness list. He had hastily cancelled two names whom he originally hoped would reinforce the defendant's careless and reckless tendencies. The harsh truth was, with the defendant's popularity and the witnesses' vulnerable cross-examination potential, learning his lesson from putting the football coach on the stand the day before, he decided it could easily prove counterproductive. It simply wasn't worth putting them on the stand.

He also wanted to be careful not to overplay the sympathy angle, but Dr. Freemont, the psychologist from the state penitentiary, had driven all the way to Boulder, spent the night, and with her extraordinary cooperation, they felt obligated to have her testify, if only briefly. He gave Judge Cooper the heads up he'd be officially resting the prosecution's case after the psychologist's short testimony.

The judge decided the less said in the courtroom about what happened the previous day, the better. Knowing they were probably a little rattled over the extraordinary events, he had met with the jury before he excused them for the evening. A resilient group, they appeared ready to move on. With no further discussion needed and the jury now in place, Judge Cooper slammed his gavel, and the Thursday morning session was underway.

A proven courtroom veteran, unfazed, and reinvigorated with a fresh attitude and unshakeable confidence, Townsend got right back to work. "The prosecution calls Dr. Angela Freemont. Would Dr. Freemont please come forward and take the witness stand."

After validating her rather impressive set of credentials and the fact she was a highly experienced and currently practicing psychologist, Townsend explained, "I know you've worked extensively with Frank Ferguson in recent years and, by design, were present for his rather alarming testimony yesterday. Without going into great detail, I have a few brief questions that I hope will remove any doubt in the jury's minds about the effect the most unfortunate living conditions in the Ferguson home would have on the boy's general state of mind and subsequent behavior."

Fully understanding his request, Dr. Freemont collected her thoughts and proceeded. "Well, the horrible things the boys had to deal with on a regular basis throughout their childhood would clearly have a profound impact on their basic level of happiness, their disposition, their attitude, and how they went about their life in general. It's hard to put in a few short sentences, but suffice it to say, the unspeakable events that persistently took place in their home environment would undermine their level of confidence and ability to interact with children their own age and even more so with adults."

Townsend tried to steer her in the direction that fit his objectives. "I know it's hard to summarize in the limited time we have here, but specifically, in your own words, how would those childhood experiences affect their behavior?"

"Well, all kids react differently, but it's very common for young people to be extremely bitter and angry, and they frequently have a tendency to lash out and express themselves in an antisocial manner, totally against what would be considered normal behavior. Aggressive behavior is a common expectation for youngsters that live in the conditions the Ferguson brothers were forced to live in. The more aggressive and the meaner they are to those around them, the better they feel about themselves."

She was getting close to expressing what Townsend wanted, and keeping it simple and with his desire to wrap it up, he asked her, "Not to excuse any of it but to accurately identify the source of the well-documented long history of bad behavior of the Ferguson brothers, would it be safe to conclude it was directly related to the extremely abnormal manner in which they were brought up?"

"Yes, Mr. Townsend, without a doubt!"

Townsend knew her testimony wasn't anything earthshaking and Dr. Fremont had only stated the obvious, but he wanted to nail down the precise source of Ferguson's general behavior. In view of what took place the day before and a subtle effort in damage control, pushing the sympathy card one more time only made sense.

"Thank you, Dr. Fremont. No more questions, Your Honor."

"Your witness, Mr. Simmons."

Will thought the psychologist's testimony was redundant and, for all practical purposes, totally irrelevant. In thinking about it, her comments actually reinforced some of the theories he would be introducing to the jury later that day. Will promptly responded, "No questions, Your Honor."

On that relatively quiet note, the prosecution formally rested their case.

Chapter Sixty-Six

Judge Cooper thanked County Attorney Townsend and, without wasting so much as one second, turned to the defense table and politely asked, "Mr. Simmons, will you please introduce your first witness?"

Will's basic approach was to save the more critical testimony for the end. For obvious reasons, he wanted his key witnesses' testimony to be fresh and as close to jury deliberations as possible. With that in mind, he would be putting Catherine and then, very likely, Foss Man on the witness stand last. If things went as planned, he hoped to get to them later that afternoon.

It was game time! Will stood and with a relaxed and confident voice, he said, "The defense calls Larry Willingham to the stand.

"Larry, it's my understanding that you were a frequent hunting partner of Mr. Ronald Ferguson. Is that right?"

"Yes, Ron and I did a lot of hunting together."

"During these excursions, it's been brought to my attention that you personally witnessed some rather unusual behavior from your hunting partner. If this is true, would you tell the jury about some of these incidents?"

"Ron enjoyed shooting just about anything that moved. When we wrapped up our regular efforts to shoot squirrels, rabbits, or pheasants, he was always looking for other animals to kill. I'm really not proud to admit it, but I witnessed it on a number of occasions. His favorite targets were pet cats. As the cats were innocently scampering around farm buildings, he'd walk over, aim his big shotgun at them, and blast them to pieces with the fur flying in all directions.

Probably the ugliest thing I ever saw him do was the day he shot a big German Shepherd.

"On top of shooting animals, he used to pour gasoline on chickens, throw a lit match on them, and watch them squawk and run frantically until they fell over dead. He'd capture pigeons out of the hay lofts in barns and tie a firecracker to one of their legs, light it, and let them fly away. Within a few seconds, the pigeon would explode. He always got a big kick out of this kind of stuff and would usually burst out laughing. I have to admit, it was kind of spooky."

Not wanting to go overboard with the sickening stories, Will politely interrupted, "Thank you, Larry, that's enough. I think the jury gets the picture. And, members of the jury, I do want to apologize for the graphic nature of Mr. Willingham's testimony. I have no more questions, Your Honor. Your witness."

Townsend had just one question. "Larry, I'm just curious, did you ever at any time try to interrupt these unbecoming proceedings?"

A little embarrassed by the suggestion, Larry admitted, "I told him more than once how stupid I thought it was. He was a big guy, but if I had it to do over, I wish I would have done more. He was kind of a difficult guy to tell what to do. When he kept doing that kind of stuff, I quit going hunting with him. That's about all I could do."

"Thank you, Larry. That's all I have, Your Honor."

Will asked for Mr. Tom Randolph to please come forward.

After Tom was sworn in, Will asked him, "Would you please tell the jury what position you currently hold with the Jefferson School District?"

"Yes, I'm the guidance counselor for grades one through twelve."

Will proceeded, "During your many years serving in this position, did you ever have experience dealing directly with Ronald Ferguson?"

"Oh yes, I've got one file cabinet just about filled with Ron's referrals. I'm afraid I could write a book about him and his endless behavior problems."

"Would you give us a few examples of your knowledge on the subject, and when it's appropriate, if it specifically involves Luke Foster, the defendant, please point that out?"

"In one word, Ron was a bully, probably the worst bully we've had in the school system since his older brother Frank attended school years ago. He picked on everyone, but he loved to make fun of how other kids were dressed. He was famous for threatening to beat up kids after the year-end school picnic celebrations. I know about one of the worst examples involving the defendant. When Luke returned to school after his battle with polio and was stuck in a wheelchair for almost a year, Ron was constantly taunting him and making fun of him."

The counselor paused for a minute. "Before I go any further, I want to answer the question that I know is probably on everybody's mind. Why didn't we, the school personnel, who were well aware of this behavior, do more to stop it? The truth is, we spent hours discussing things we might do to change his behavior. We tried everything. We must have met with his parents a dozen times over the years and tried almost everything."

Obviously troubled by their lack of success dealing with Ferguson, the counselor paused for a minute. After a brief pause and catching his breath, he said, "With what I witnessed here yesterday and the beyond-tragic event a month ago, everyone at school is sick about our failure to discover what was going on in the Ferguson home all these years. For years we recognized the fact the Ferguson boy's parents were confused and appeared lost and helpless, but we honestly had no idea anything like that was going on. Triggered by this incident and always suspicious there was at least some form of abuse in the Ferguson home, we've had a number of emergency meetings to develop strategies in detecting this kind of thing in the future."

Like everyone else present, Will couldn't help but be a little disgusted with the nature of the sad revelations, but recognizing this was most difficult for the proud professional, Will attempted to soften his approach a little bit. "Over the years, Mr. Randolph, did you see any improvement, or did this behavior continue when he reached the upper grades?"

"Sadly, it never let up. Let me give you a more recent example. Just last year, the pet squirrel in the biology lab was found dead with a sharpened pencil driven through its neck. We were sure who did it, but fearing retribution, the other students were always afraid to come forward to pin anything on him. Ron was intimidating and very cunning about his deeds. Again, I wish we could have done more. This is such a sad and terrible way for all this to end!"

Hearing more than enough, Will held his hand up. "That's good enough, Mr. Randolph. I think the jury gets the picture. Thank you for your honest and candid report. I know it was difficult for you. Your witness."

Townsend gave a resigned response. "No questions, Your Honor."

Wanting to immediately start demonstrating the sharp contrast between Foss Man and Ferguson's persona, well known for his incomparable work habits, Will wanted to get Foss Man's current boss on the stand. He asked the distinguished and highly respected businessman, Mr. Walter Olson, to please come forward.

Will began, "Mr. Olson, I know the defendant has worked for you for a number of years. Would you tell the jury how you feel about him as an employee?"

Walter didn't hold back. "It's really pretty simple. Luke's the best young worker I've ever had, and I've been in business for a long time. He's always on time, he'll take on any job, never complains, willingly puts in long hours, and he simply works his butt off."

Will asked him, "I've heard he's kind of a—let's see, what would you call it—kind of a free spirit. What would you say about that?"

"Oh, Foss Man likes to have his share of fun all right. I've caught him throwing rotten tomatoes, rotten potatoes, and of course his favorite is dumping a bucket of cold water over the heads of his fellow workers. But he knows where to draw the line and never carries it too far. Work in the vegetable fields is difficult, tedious work and the truth is, his antics tend to lift the spirits and morale of the rest of the crew. And you know, it's kind of amazing, but at the end of the day, we seem to get more work done when he's there. Everybody loves having Luke around. He's currently my right-hand man. He loves the title I gave him last summer, junior foreman. Luke has a special way of getting along with everybody. Yes, he may be a little reckless at times, and I would agree with that 'free spirit' label, but honestly, I wouldn't want it any other way!"

Will was hoping that brief reference to being reckless would be overlooked, but he was generally more than pleased with Mr. Olson's testimony. Will thanked him and indicated he had no more questions.

No such luck! Not wasting a second, Townsend pounced on it. His first question during the cross examination was, "Mr. Olson, you made reference to the fact the defendant was inclined to be reckless. Could you give us a few examples of his reckless behavior?"

Wanting to keep his credibility, Walter responded very candidly, "Well, there really haven't been that many incidents that I would call reckless, but Foss Man was always in a hurry to get the jobs he's not too crazy about done as fast as he can. One example, about a month ago, he was cleaning out the chicken coops. I know he hates shoveling manure, and in his haste to get it done, when he was backing up the tractor with the manure spreader hooked on behind, he hit the side of the chicken coop and did a little damage. He felt bad about it, and it really wasn't a big deal."

Seizing the opportunity, Townsend jumped on it. "About how much damage would you say was done to the chicken coop, Mr. Olson?"

"It didn't amount to much—a couple hundred dollars I suppose."

Townsend came back quickly. "So, Mr. Olson, now please give me a very simple yes or no answer. Your statement today is that the defendant is inclined to be reckless."

"I think you're taking this whole thing way out of context!"

"For the record, Mr. Olson, is your answer yes or no?"

With obvious frustration, Walter responded, "Yes."

"No more questions, Your Honor."

Will knew the jury could see it was merely an accident. He didn't have to point it out.

Will called on two of Foss Man's favorite teachers as character witnesses. They gave glowing reports and made it clear he was well liked around the school. Will planned to call Coach Sanders to the stand, but after Big Jake did such an effective job with him during cross-examination yesterday, he crossed him off the list. He planned to put Mr. Slim and Nute on the witness stand, but of course after what happened yesterday, he had to cancel that idea.

His two best buddies, Skunk and Skeeter, were nervous wrecks as they walked up to the witness stand, but Will kept their testimony brief and it was more of the same, glowing remarks reinforcing what a loyal and dependable friend Foss Man was.

From the prosecution's standpoint, Townsend had an isolated question here and there during the cross examinations, but for all practical purposes, he could only sit there and fume. He couldn't fight it—the defendant was obviously a popular kid. But from strictly a legal standpoint, that carried very little weight. He had a job to do, and he genuinely felt the defendant had stepped over the line and flagrantly took the law into his own hands. And furthermore, he knew he had a very winnable case and was going to take full advantage of this rare high-profile opportunity to make a name for himself. There was no doubt in his mind he'd be adding to his perfect prosecutorial record. There were no second thoughts—being a good kid doesn't put you above the law!

It was close to noon, and Judge Cooper decided it was a logical time to break for lunch. Sizing the schedule up, it looked like the time table would work out nicely. The defense would hopefully wrap things up this afternoon, and there would be plenty of time Friday morning for the summations. He could turn the case over to the jury before noon. With that in mind, the judge hammered the gavel, and with his commanding voice, he announced, "Court will resume at one-thirty sharp this afternoon."

CHAPTER SIXTY-SEVEN

During the noon break, with Foss Man's letter in his hand, Nute went straight over to the hospital to see how his stricken buddy was doing. Nute was deeply worried about Mr. Slim. His heart had been badly damaged, and as much as he wanted to deny it, the outlook was not good.

When he walked into the private room in the intensive care unit, Mr. Slim, hooked up to multiple tubes and wires, opened his eyes and, with his right hand, gave Nute a little wave. Nute was encouraged and relieved to see he was conscious. That alone had to be a favorable sign. Through his bushy beard, he could detect an effort to smile.

Explaining what it was, he handed Mr. Slim the envelope. Unable to do much with his arms and hands, he asked Nute if he'd open it up and read the letter to him.

Nute read it out loud. You could tell Mr. Slim was deeply touched and thoroughly enjoyed hearing from Foss Man. In a weak voice, he asked, "How's it looking for our young buddy?"

Nute brought him up-to-date on the nature of the morning testimonies. He added, "I think things are looking a little better than they did yesterday, but you never know. Townsend is determined to put the kid away!"

Struggling to talk, Mr. Slim said, "This is all so damn ridiculous. That young man should not be in this mess. All he was doing was rescuing his sister. Tell him to hang in there, will you, Nute?"

Nute handed him the special Indianhead penny. He could see the powerful impact this had on him. Gaining his composure, Mr. Slim managed, "That's just like the young man. If you get the chance, give him hug and thank him, will you, Nute? He should have kept it tucked in his own hand. It's never failed him. Now I know everything's going to work out for him!"

There was a knock on the door. In walked Foss Man's mom and dad along with Catherine and Air Force. They had eaten their carefully prepared sandwiches on the ride over, and with reserved seats in the courtroom, they had plenty of time to stop in and see their special friend before the afternoon session resumed. Catherine knew she was the first one to take the witness stand that afternoon, but more than ready, she wasn't worried about that.

Mr. Slim lit up and was thrilled with his new visitors. With a renewed spirit, he said, "Well, for heaven's sake, would you look who's here? My two most favorite girls in the whole world. Now how lucky am I, the two prettiest girls in town here just to see an old broken-down, ugly cuss like me." He looked over at Air Force and his dad and added, "Oh, and it's good to see you two ugly guys too."

They all laughed, and deliberately avoiding any discussion about the trial, they proceeded to enjoy some of their favorite memories and replayed the exciting day twelve years ago when Foss Man snapped out of his trance down by the Troy River.

Before the Fosters left a few minutes later, Mr. Slim asked the girls if they would do him a big favor. "I don't expect there'll be a very big crowd, but would you two beautiful ladies be willing to sing that favorite song of mine, 'How Great Thou Art,' at my funeral?" Mr. Slim had been a bachelor his whole life and had no immediate family.

Foss Man's mom quickly answered, "Well sure, Mr. Slim, we'd be honored to, but we all know that's not going to be any time soon!"

The doctor had warned them that Mr. Slim was pretty weak and they shouldn't stay very long. It was time to head back to the courtroom anyway. The Fosters all made a point to give their wonderful friend's arm a warm and affectionate squeeze before they left.

The relentless media and the general public were well aware that the defense's key witnesses, Catherine and Luke, were both taking the witness stand that afternoon. Today would be no different; there was a wild ambush when the courthouse doors were finally pushed open. The temperature in the overcrowded courtroom had to be approaching one hundred degrees but no one seemed to care. This was the moment everyone had been looking forward to!

Will, Big Jake, and Foss Man were huddled in the conference room. There was a strange calmness in the room, and rather than any last-minute cramming, they talked about baseball and debated who was going to be behind the plate next week. They knew very well the outcome of what had clearly become a fiercely contested legal battle would probably be decided in the next few hours.

Will abruptly called his key witness, the defendant's sister Catherine, to the witness stand.

There was complete silence as the striking beauty made her way through the crowd. She was dressed immaculately and walked with an easily detectable air of confidence. Her profile and demeanor sent a clear and precise message: "Yes, I'm the girl who was raped, but I'm getting on with my life, so please, just get over it, everyone!"

It was evident Catherine was more than ready to give her testimony that, while being totally honest about every detail, would serve her much loved younger brother well. After all, he was not only the most undeserving victim in this whole mess but a hero in the truest sense of the word. Feeling fully responsible for his predicament, all the damaging testimony yesterday had her worried to death. The thought of her innocent brother being locked up in jail for his brave actions made her sick. That would be an absolute travesty! She was composed and more than ready to tell the jury the full story!

With every eye in the place glued on her, Catherine was sworn in.

Will, with genuine compassion and sincerity, started out with, "Now, Catherine, I know how difficult it is for you to go back to that ugly day in your life. But the fact you are the only one who was present in the shed that day, along with your brother of course, you know how important your testimony is to this case. You are in the unique position to tell the jury exactly what took place that horrible day. I know you are eager and willing to provide the true story. I apologize in advance for putting you through this miserable ordeal again."

Before Will could go any further, in her typical confident and strong manner, Catherine politely interrupted, "You don't have to apologize, Mr. Simmons, and you're right, I am ready and pleased to finally explain what led up to and exactly what took place that day. And don't worry about the sensitive nature of what happened to me that day, and don't hesitate to ask me anything that might help draw a true and accurate picture for the jury. Trust me, Mr. Simmons, I'm fully aware of how important this is!"

Expressing his appreciation, Will said, "Thank you for that, Catherine. Quite amazingly, you, of all people, have helped put all of us at ease. Now take your time, and in your own words, will you explain to the court exactly what provoked this horrible ordeal?"

Responding directly, she said, "Ronald Ferguson and I had a long-running battle. It goes way back to when he used to bully both of my brothers in grade school. It started with little things like making fun of their clothes. It got progressively worse until it led to things like making fun of Luke sitting in his wheelchair or the day he deliberately shot Allen in the leg with his BB gun. I thought he had hit rock bottom, but then, hard to believe, I learned about him torturing and killing animals. You know, I love animals. That's all I could take! I had no choice but to confront him. I told him if no one else was going to do anything about it, I was going to do everything I could to stop him from killing animals. But unfortunately, it continued, and we had many confrontations over the years. Finally, following an utterly despicable revelation this winter, our arguments intensified and got uglier and uglier."

Looking forward to what he knew was coming next, Will politely interrupted her. He positioned the slide projector and the pictures he had carefully prepared to dramatize and reinforce the next portion of Catherine's testimony. Fully aware of how inflammable and potentially prejudicial the slides were, following a lengthy debate with the prosecution team Tuesday morning, the judge had reluctantly approved having the pictures shown to the jury. Knowing very well how damaging these vivid illustrations would be for the prosecution's case, Townsend was absolutely furious about the ruling. That being said, with Ronald's candid confession of killing the dogs to Catherine just minutes before the rape took place, these pictures, as graphic as they may be, were critical proof that Ronald was indeed capable of virtually anything, including murder!

Going back a few months, Townsend distinctly remembered getting the phone call from Nute, the bait shop owner over in Jefferson, who had discovered the two dead dogs on the shoreline of Beaver Creek earlier that spring when he and ironically, the Foster brothers, were seining minnows. It appeared the dogs had been thrown there sometime during the winter months and had been deliberately buried in the snow. When the snow melted, any footprints or any other meaningful clues disappeared. As a result, Townsend could find no concrete evidence, and the case of the two dead dogs remained unsolved. The fact was, Townsend had been to the shoreline and diligently taken pictures of the gruesome scene. He wasn't aware that someone else had done the same.

With his adrenaline building, Will asked the next question. "Catherine, would you explain to the jury exactly what it was that escalated the tension between you and Ronald?"

Still cool and calm, she enthusiastically responded, "Last winter, when the two dogs were reported missing, naturally the owners were upset and had no idea what happened to their pets. With Ronald's well-known reputation for being cruel to animals and the documented history of actually killing animals, he soon became the prime suspect. After the investigation by the county sheriff and county attorney,"—one glance at Townsend, and you could see he was fully aware and prepared for this unbecoming story—"mysteriously, once again, nothing could be proven!"

Holding his hand up and making a special effort to bring attention to what he was about to say, Will interrupted with a polite gesture. "Catherine, before you get into the specific circumstances that led to Ronald's confession of killing the dogs, I want to show the jury a few pictures."

The lights in the courtroom were dimmed. He had taken the time to visit the owners of the dogs that had disappeared last winter. The dog owners were more than willing to share an impressive variety of pictures with them holding and cuddling their beloved pets.

Of course the carefully selected pictures were outrageously sweet and loving.

Will proceeded to slowly go through the individual pictures on the big screen strategically positioned and designed for easy observation by the jury. Will didn't say a word, he deliberately went from one perfectly clear and vivid picture to the next. The slides included a variety of settings, some illustrating the owners holding the dogs in their laps, others displaying playful scenes, but all dramatizing how cute, cuddly, and innocent the small lovable dogs were. Generating the deliberate and desired effect, as Will proceeded, there was a persistent loud sympathetic display of murmurs and groans from the people in the courtroom. They were emphatically displaying their disbelief that someone could actually slit the throats of these poor sweet, innocent dogs. Then finally, even more startling, one dramatic picture showed both of the dogs lying together on the ground and they were obviously dead. Then the ultimate picture, a close-up showing indisputable evidence that the dog's throats had been cut from ear to ear. There was a sudden spontaneous outburst of uncontrollable anger and disgust from the vast majority of the gallery. Several emotional members of the crowd actually screamed out a few obscene names aimed at the perpetrator.

Judge Cooper, upset with the reaction, hammered his gavel three times and shouted, "Order in the court, order in the court! One more display like that and I'll clear out the courtroom. Now control yourselves or you'll all be gone!"

This, of course, was why the judge was reluctant to permit the pictures to be shown in the first place. He knew how potentially inflammatory they could be, but rather than take the time to preview them, he had gambled with the chance they wouldn't unduly influence the jury. While he fully appreciated the importance of illustrating the magnitude of the Ferguson boy's violent capabilities, having now seen the pictures and the reaction to them, he was seriously questioning the wisdom of his rather bold decision.

Everyone in the courtroom was well aware of the fact it had been Ronald Ferguson that had slit the throats of these lovable creatures. It was obvious the before-and-after pictures of the dogs had a powerful, chilling effect on the fourteen members of the jury. Which, needless to say, was Will's whole objective.

Will requested the lights be turned back on. It was suddenly eerily quiet in the courtroom, and he turned to Catherine and cautiously asked her, "Now would you tell the jury what the circumstances were that led to Ronald's confession of killing the two dogs?"

Knowing the next few minutes could make or break the case, Catherine regrouped and calmly began, "Our last confrontation involved my direct accusation of him being the one responsible for killing the two dogs. He got real angry and told me, please excuse the language, if I didn't shut my fucking mouth, he was going to shut me up for good. I was a little scared when he said that, but being used to his threats by then, I was never really worried that he would actually physically hurt me. I told him I wouldn't back off until he was held responsible for killing the dogs.

"All Ferguson said was, 'If you know what's good for you, you'll shut your big mouth.'" With her chin quivering and her voice weakening for the first time, she said, "Obviously I regret it now, but I didn't back off. I continued my one-person campaign, and he warned me on more than one occasion, 'You better back off, bitch, I told you I'd shut you up for good!'"

Recognizing her growing emotional state, Will interjected, "You're doing fine, Catherine. Now just relax, take your time, and tell the jury what happened next."

It only took a few seconds before she regrouped and was back on track. "About a week later, I was coming home from work and was putting my bike away in the shed like I always did. As soon as I entered the shed, someone came up behind me. Of course I wasn't expecting anyone, and with the giant suddenly towering over me, I was scared to death. The first thing I noticed—and it was very obvious—was that Ferguson was extremely drunk. He had this frightening, evil look in his eyes. When I tried to run by him, he grabbed me and threw me on the couch. He was so strong he pinned me down and I couldn't move.

"Standing over me, slurring his words, he started screaming, 'You fucking little bitch, I'm sick and tired of your big mouth. I warned you that you would be sorry if you kept spreading that bullshit. Now it's over, I'm shutting you up for good!'

"Totally petrified, I tried desperately to be calm and reason with him. I said something like 'You have to be crazy, you know you'll never get away with something like this.' I pleaded with him, 'Please stop and just leave. I promise I won't tell anybody about this!'

"In his drunken stupor, he hollered back at me, 'You mean like those stupid dogs? The dip shits in this stupid-ass town couldn't even figure that out. I cut their fucking throats in broad daylight and they never found a goddamn clue. I'm going to strangle your skinny ass, and there won't be a shred of evidence. They won't be able to prove a goddamn thing. Now quit whining and shut your big mouth!'"

Catherine went on, "Then he started babbling something like 'You know, you are kind of a pretty little bitch. It would be kind of stupid if I didn't fuck you before I strangle your dumb ass!'"

Sensing her still rising emotions, Will interrupted her, "Are you doing okay, Catherine? We can take a short break!"

"No, I'm fine, I want to get this over with."

"Okay, but please try to just relax and take your time."

She bravely continued, "Then he started tearing at my clothes. I fought him as hard as I could, but he was so strong, it was hopeless. I was screaming as loud as I could. He pulled his pants down and started raping me. All of a sudden—it was like a miracle—Luke walked through the door. With this monster grunting like some kind of animal and my loud screaming, he couldn't hear Luke come in."

Then the most critical part of her testimony. Totally distraught but eager to get through it, she said, "The next thing I heard was a loud cracking sound and the monster went limp and fell off to my right side. I was struggling to get out from underneath him but was stuck when I heard another loud crack. It took me a few seconds to get him off me, and I grabbed my underpants and ran into the house. I didn't say anything to Luke at the time. If he hadn't come in there when he did, I would have suffered a lot more, and I know I would have been dead in the next few minutes!"

Townsend jumped up and shouted, "Objection, that's pure speculation on the part of the witness!"

Judge Cooper responded quickly, "Sustained. Strike that last sentence from the record!"

Fighting back tears but in rebellious protest, she said, "I've held this inside long enough. I'll say it again—my brother saved my life that day!"

The judge angrily came back again, "Strike that last statement! Counsel, please control your witness or I'll hold you in contempt!"

Will politely responded, "I'm sorry, Your Honor, the emotions are running pretty high right now, that should be understandable!" Quietly he thought to himself, *Incredible job, Catherine, simply incredible!*

Will let the suffocating silence in the courtroom take its effect. Catherine's testimony was absolutely riveting. She was so convincing; her credibility was indisputable. The true picture was now out there for the jury to digest. Looking over at the prosecution table, Townsend looked like he was going to explode. The case was by no means settled, but Will knew they had at the very minimum neutralized the prosecution's well-established momentum.

After another brief calculated delay, Will said quietly, "Thank you, Catherine. I know that was hard for you. You are indeed a strong-willed young lady! I have no more questions, Your Honor."

Townsend sat there for a minute, desperately trying to come up with some kind of rebuttal. Catherine's impressive testimony, reinforced by the dramatic picture display of the dogs, had been nothing less than a grand slam for the defense and he knew it. But he did detect one critical issue that was left out of her story.

He walked slowly over in front of the witness box and gently stated, "I know replaying and zeroing in on this specific period in the horrible incident is difficult for you, Catherine, but it's important for the jury to clearly understand the precise answer to this critical question. You described the two separate cracking sounds you heard when the baseball bat crushed the back of Ron Ferguson's head. Do you recall hearing any sound coming from the Ferguson boy between these two blows and approximately how much time elapsed between the two?"

Catherine was fully cognizant of the importance of her answer to this question and how pivotal it could be in the ultimate outcome of the trial. She had told the perfect truth up to this point and wasn't about to jeopardize her credibility. She would answer the question exactly how she remembered it. "Ferguson let out a sickening groan after the first cracking sound, and I think he was still groaning when I heard the second one."

Townsend loved her answer, and he pounced on it. "And how much time elapsed between the two cracking sounds while he continued this groaning?"

Catherine told it exactly like she remembered it, "I don't know for sure, it couldn't have been more than a few seconds."

"Thank you, Catherine. That's all I have, Your Honor."

On that note, Catherine was excused from the witness stand. Once again, all eyes were on her as she made her way back to her seat next to her emotionally-wracked parents and brother. It was pretty obvious, the sentiment of everyone in the audience had switched from sympathy to one of great respect and admiration for this impressive young woman.

CHAPTER SIXTY-EIGHT

It was a clever response by Townsend but Will wasn't overly concerned. Catherine's answer to the critical question was already baked into the general picture and merely shed light on the obvious. Catherine's presentation was so powerful Will gave serious consideration to not putting Foss Man on the witness stand. The long-standing rule relating to the risk of calling on the defendant and subjecting him to cross-examination was not lost on Will. Up to this point, he not only had intentions of having Foss Man testify but had assumed he'd be their most important witness.

He and Big Jake huddled for a few minutes and ultimately agreed it was still a good idea to have Foss Man testify but to modify the questions to keep things very simple and non-controversial. After many hours of careful preparation for this critical moment, Will had to be on top of his game to eliminate questions without undermining his primary objectives. This would be his second major test of thinking on his feet in the heat of battle.

His adrenaline was pumping and his mind whirling with all the quick alterations to the plan. Will called for Foss Man to please come forward. Once again, every eye was glued on the defendant as he walked nervously toward the witness stand. Everyone was on full alert, knowing this was another significant juncture in the tense week-long proceedings.

After the formalities, Will began. "Luke, your long history of being on the receiving end of Ronald's bullying tactics has been well-documented throughout the trial. For that reason, I'm not going to spend our time listing and describing the many unfortunate experiences you've had to deal with over the years. But let me ask you one question: Is it safe to say you developed a great dislike for Ronald Ferguson long before this terrible incident?"

After witnessing firsthand the straightforward honesty that Catherine had just displayed, he was relaxed, felt totally comfortable, and eager to do the same. It was really pretty simple. He would speak openly and freely and not fret about how the jury might interpret or react to what he was saying. It was like Will said during their preparation meetings: Speak from the heart and tell the perfect truth! If you do that, everything will come out the way it's supposed to! That's all he ever wanted!

Another kind of weird thing happened. He suddenly recalled the advice Reverend Thompson had given him following the scary gun accident. "Take full responsibility for your actions, show your genuine remorse, and everything will work out for the best." That simple message was ringing loud and clear in his mind and gave him a renewed surge of confidence and strength.

Appearing totally relaxed and composed, Foss Man firmly answered, "I like just about everybody in the world, but I've hated Ron Ferguson for as long as I can remember. It actually started on the first day of school way back in first grade!"

It hadn't been rehearsed, but Will knew that answer was coming. "You've had plenty of time to think about this by now. Luke, do you think your hatred for Ron Ferguson had anything to do with the way you handled things when you walked in the shed that day?"

"Boy you're right about having plenty of time to think about it. Over the last month, I've asked myself that question a million times. There's no question about it—I recognized Ron Ferguson right away when I walked in there. But I don't remember thinking or deciding anything. I just know I was scared out of my mind and that I had to do something right away to help Catherine. She was crying, and I knew Ferguson was hurting her. Hurting her really bad. I don't remember grabbing the bat—it was just suddenly in my hands. I remember hitting him as hard as I could with the bat two times. I can still hear the ugly sound of the bat hitting his head. It happened so fast, but I remember being relieved when I saw him fall over and

Catherine was able to get out from under him and could run out of the shed."

Great answer—again the simple, perfect truth. "Luke, let me ask you the question in another way. Did you see this as your chance to finally get even with Ronald for all the mean things he had done to you over the years?"

"No. I didn't have time to think about that. Ferguson was hurting Catherine real bad, and I had to stop him. But I knew how strong he was and how mean he could be."

This was going perfectly. Will could see he could keep the questions directly on the key issues and saw no need to ask many more questions. He was sorting and shuffling everything through his head.

This next question was dangerous. He didn't want to bring unnecessary attention to it, but he knew the prosecution was going to focus on it in their summation, so here it went. "Luke, do you remember how much time transpired between the first blow and the second blow? Did you think about it or make a calculated decision about whether or not the second blow was really necessary to save your sister?"

"I don't remember thinking about anything. I just knew I had to make sure this giant mean guy stopped hurting Catherine. I remember being really scared and I was furious about what he was doing to her. It happened so fast—it's still like one big blur. It didn't seem like two separate parts, but I know I hit him twice because I can still hear the two loud sounds. There may have been a little time between the first and second swing. Maybe it took a little time to wind up for the second swing—I don't really know for sure."

Will asked another extremely delicate question. "Luke, how do you feel about the fact your actions ended up killing another human being? Some people have called you a hero. How do you feel about that description?"

"I've hated Ron almost my whole life. I can't deny the fact I'm glad I don't have to worry about him anymore. But I'd give anything if I could have figured out a better way of handling things that day. I'm glad Catherine's going to be okay, and now I know she will be. If what I did was necessary to save her life, if that's really true, I can't be sorry for what I did. I just wish there could have been a better way. I don't think Ron deserved to die for his terrible behavior, especially now after hearing about the horrible way he lived at home. I hate to even think about what that must have been like. Somebody should have been able to do something to help those guys. I wish he was still alive. Now it's a big mess for all of us, and I have to live with the fact I killed him for the rest of my life. If people think I did something wrong, I'm sorry! I'm really, really sorry! But *hero*—no, no way, that's ridiculous. I'm responsible for a high school boy being dead now. How could I be a stupid hero? Catherine's the hero, she didn't deserve any of this! She was the only person in town that had the guts to stand up to Ferguson."

More than satisfied with the convincing, genuine, and credible tone of Foss Man's testimony, Will made the quick decision there was no productive reason for asking any more questions. Less was clearly more right now, and he crossed off about a half dozen of what he previously thought were relevant questions.

Will abruptly ended things right there. "Thank you, Luke. No more questions, Your Honor."

Townsend had to come up with a legitimate "cross." The emotional testimony from Catherine and now the defendant was going to be a challenge for the prosecution to overcome, but the cold, hard facts were still the cold, hard facts. There had been a brutal and violent death of a human being in his jurisdiction. Taking Ron Ferguson's life was unnecessary, could not be justified, and someone had to be held accountable. Nothing had changed; he was determined to do his job!

Townsend began, "Luke, looking back at it, don't you think you could have disrupted what was going on that day by confronting the now deceased young man and perhaps even physically intervening if necessary? Do you really believe hitting him twice over the head with a huge baseball bat was a reasonable or sensible way of handling it?"

Luke wasn't worried about answering any of Townsend's questions, no matter how difficult or how damaging the answers may or may not be. All he ever wanted was for the members of the jury to decide whether or not what he did was wrong. If it was wrong, he would simply have to live with the consequences. It was the only way he could go on with his life and have any peace of mind. He had waited over a month to get this matter cleared up once and for all.

With that in mind, Foss Man eagerly responded, "If I knew for sure Catherine and I would have survived the battle we would have on our hands facing the huge, drunk, and angry Ferguson boy, yes, I agree with you, I wish I would have maybe tried a different approach. But after watching the four big policemen wrestling with Frank Ferguson yesterday, boy, I really don't know!"

Townsend's silent reaction—*Holy shit, there is no doubt that question certainly blew up in my face. At this point, I have to come back with what is clearly my most indefensible argument.* He had to throw his best punch.

"Not that I think the first hit was necessary, but let me ask you, Luke, how big of a battle do you think you would have gotten from the deceased young man after you bludgeoned him the first time with the huge bat, obviously leaving him totally unconscious? Do you really think the second violent blow, perhaps even more vicious then the first one—and don't forget, the doctors labeled it the likely cause of death—was really necessary to assure you and your sister's safety?"

Will had made it clear to Foss Man that he was going to be asked this question, and as defenseless as it sounded on the surface, all he could do is tell the truth. He knew this question could ultimately determine the outcome of this whole thing. But once again, Foss Man appeared relaxed and eager to deal with it.

Without hesitation and straight from the heart, he said, "Mr. Townsend, that question has been haunting me around the clock for the last month. Will told me this would be the hardest thing for anybody to understand or for me to explain. Why didn't I stop after the first time I hit him? I really can't give you a very good answer. All I know is I just reacted to what was going on, and I knew he was a big, mean guy, and I wanted to make sure I stopped him from hurting my sister. There was never a first and then a second decision. I guess I just went a little crazy when I saw what Ferguson was doing."

Will did a mental handspring. This was clearly the most explosive and potentially dangerous issue. Once again, Foss Man had absolutely hit it out of the park. And it all seemed so simple for him. He was totally relaxed while obviously speaking from the heart and merely letting his true feelings flow. Like with Catherine, it was really an amazing thing to see. The truth can be a remarkable weapon. Now what he had to do in his summary tomorrow was reinforce the now-obvious fact Foss Man would have been facing an insurmountable battle and his actions were ultimately a necessary act of self-defense.

However, it was far from a done deal. He knew all juries were unique and made up of a dynamic combination of emotional, determined, and well-intentioned citizens that as a group could easily go either direction. It only takes one or two vocal and influential jury members to swing things to their way of thinking. He believed in the jury system wholeheartedly but at the same time knew they were totally unpredictable! It was far too early to organize a victory parade.

Losing ground and now more desperate than ever, Townsend continued, "Luke, I have one final question for you. This isn't a typical trial about who did it—you are clearly the one individual totally responsible for taking a severely disturbed young man's life. Do you really believe it would be right for you to walk out the door a totally free person?"

Will's first thought was, *What a dumb-ass question.* He couldn't wait for Foss Man's answer. Once again, he couldn't have drawn it up any better. He knew exactly how he was going to answer it. *Hang on to your sorry ass, Townsend.*

Again, without the slightest hesitation, Foss Man continued, "Before the trial started, I kind of thought I should be able to because I really didn't think I did anything wrong. But when you think about me almost killing Mr. Gunderson, I know it was an accident, but it was pretty dumb and I was pretty reckless."

"But I don't know about this thing though. I don't think I did anything wrong. My buddy over there, Big Jake, he keeps telling me every day, 'Foss Man, you did the right thing, quit beating yourself up and feeling so bad. You had no choice. You did what you had to do.' Big Jake knows how big and mean Ron Ferguson could get when he's mad. So I hope Big Jake's right about me doing the right thing. He's pretty smart, and you know something, he isn't wrong very often."

Will loved that answer and struggled to keep from chuckling a little bit. But he was worried about this next part; Will knew what was coming, and he knew exactly what Foss Man was going to say and it made him nervous. He knew he could object on the grounds of the rules specifically designed to prevent self-incrimination, particularly for a minor in adult court, but he also knew if Foss Man handled it right, it could be a game changer. Big Jake leaned over and said, "Let him continue, Will. I know Foss Man. He'll do just fine. Trust me, just let him talk."

Will reminded himself, "This is exactly why I wanted to have Big Jake by my side, for critical times like this. He knows Foss Man like a book!"

Totally sincere, Foss Man went on, "I sure don't want to go to jail, but I suppose I probably should serve some time when you consider I almost killed Mr. Gunderson and now this. I'm sleeping in jail every night right now, and it's the second time this month, and it's really miserable. The worst part is I feel really bad about killing Ferguson and can't sleep at night. But I don't want sympathy or mercy from the jury. I know they have to do their job just like you do. I'm not mad at you for doing your job and I won't be mad at the jury for doing their job. I just hope what I did wasn't wrong because I hate jail so much! You may think I'm stupid for saying this, but I really don't disagree with anything you're doing here. I totally understand, Mr. Townsend, you're just doing your job!"

Will thought to himself, Good grief, I hope Townsend keeps asking questions. *His cross is proving to be more beneficial to the defense than anything I could have orchestrated in a million years.* He knew Foss Man was speaking from the heart and meant everything he said. *Granted, it's a little dangerous, but that's simply how the kid feels.* And the bottom line, as his legal representatives, the reality was, he ultimately had no real choice in the matter anyway.

Meanwhile Townsend was thinking, *Who the hell is this kid anyway? Is he for real for Christ's sake? Is he really that genuine, or is he simply a clever little bastard? I know the jury bought into everything the damn kid said, from the beginning to the very end. One thing is definite—he sure doesn't sound like a killer, and I'm sure as hell not going to ask him any more of my stupid-ass questions!*

Dejected, Townsend surrendered, "No more questions, Your Honor."

Feeling relieved this whole thing would soon be over one way or the other, Foss Man returned to the defense table and sat down by Big Jake, and he couldn't help but notice the big contented smile on his buddy's face. Big Jake always had a way of making him feel better!

Judge Cooper looked at Will and quickly ordered, "Your next witness please."

Will stood up and happily announced, "We have no more witnesses, Your Honor. The defense rests!"

After giving the jury brief instructions, Judge Cooper informed everyone, "The court will adjourn until nine o'clock tomorrow morning. At that time, we'll promptly ask the prosecution to summarize its case to the jury, and immediately following that, the defense should be prepared to summarize its final position as well. I see no reason why we shouldn't be able to get this case in the hands of the jury before noon tomorrow."

With that, he slammed his gavel. "Court is adjourned."

Chapter Sixty-Nine

Following the intense afternoon session, Townsend and Dempsey were having a serious conversation. They were more than a little concerned with how things had gone the last two days. They were already worried after the crazy fiasco with Frank's wild behavior in the courtroom the day before. There was no doubt, his almost inhuman physical display in overpowering the four full-sized veteran police officers helped the defense immensely with their potential self-defense argument. They were well aware of the fact Ronald was just as big as his brother Frank. Add Catherine's riveting testimony and defendant's impressive oratory this afternoon, and they had to face it—their case could be in serious jeopardy.

As much as they hated the idea, they both finally agreed it was time to approach the defense to offer some kind of "plea" deal. With that difficult decision finally agreed upon, they rushed into Judge Cooper's chamber and were glad to see he hadn't gone home for the night.

They explained their reasoning. The judge thought about it and agreed it probably made sense but made it clear it was strictly their decision. He told them he had some work to do and would be sticking around for a while anyway. Rather than calling both parties together to hold a formal plea hearing, he suggested they sit down with the defense and work on it privately and on their own. He knew there were distinct advantages of keeping the discussions off the record. The judge told Townsend to keep him posted on the progress.

With no explanation, Judge Cooper sent a bailiff with the message to Will in the nearby conference room to be sure to stick around for a while, that Townsend and Dempsey wanted to talk to him. Will, Big Jake, and Foss Man were huddled and working on their summation. Curious about this surprising development and deserving an explanation, Will went straight to the judge's chamber. Cooper quickly brought him up-to-date, and Will hurried back to the conference room with the stunning news!

Without getting too carried away with this remarkable development, they put the all-important summation aside and put their heads together and tried to anticipate what Townsend may actually have in mind. They couldn't do much to prepare for the pending meeting but agreed it was up to Townsend to show his hand. There was little doubt it was going to be an interesting night.

They didn't have to wait very long. With County Attorney Roger Townsend and his dedicated assistant Tom Dempsey marching close behind, observing the defense team through the glass walls in the conference room, they knocked on the door. Will waved for them to come in. Townsend started the conversation, "I know the judge got word to you that we were coming over. We'd like to talk to you guys privately for a few minutes. We'd like to politely ask the defendant to be excused while we talk this thing over a little bit."

Will said, "Sure, we'll have him go down to the lounge for a little while." Knowing Foss Man sure as heck didn't want to go back to that miserable cell across the street in the Juvenile Detention Center before he had to, Will called the bailiff back and he accompanied Foss Man to the nearby public lounge.

Townsend began with his explanation, "After listening to the testimony this afternoon, as much as we still feel there was a serious crime committed in the shed that day, Tom and I both feel the Foster family has been through enough. Listening to the defendant's testimony this afternoon, it is pretty clear he has accepted full responsibility for Ferguson's death and has demonstrated his genuine remorse. We see no value in having him serve a lengthy sentence at this time. We would like to work out some kind of agreement so that can be prevented. I'm sure you're willing to work something out so we can put a logical conclusion to this unfortunate incident."

Will was very gracious and thanked Townsend for his thoughtful comments. But knowing he was now in the driver's seat, as he and

Big Jake had anticipated and previously agreed, he proceeded very cautiously. After everything the county attorney had put Foss Man and his family through, they were not going to be easy to deal with!

Will came back firmly, "If you're willing to drop the charges against my client, I guess we'd have no real choice but to entertain that possibility. But anything less than that, I honestly don't think my client would be interested."

Not happy with this unreasonable counter offer, Townsend snapped back, "Well, you know that's not going to happen. Now I recognize you're taking a strong opening position here, but let's get serious—with a little compromising on both sides, we should be able to work something out that both sides can live with. Don't forget what's at the center of this whole thing, Will—a young man was killed! And we all know it didn't have to happen. We can't just pretend it didn't happen and simply sweep it under the rug!"

Will decided to take the time to remind the two suddenly humble county attorneys how all this materialized in the first place. He said, "Let me explain why it's highly unlikely we'll do much compromising at this time. Let's go back to the first day we met. You had your mind made up and decided to move forward without even interrogating the rape victim, the only one who really knew the whole story. You accepted her written statement, and I have reason to believe you didn't even read it. Everything said in the courtroom this afternoon, virtually word for word, was in that statement. Now it was always clear to me that no crime had been committed in the shed that day, except for the rape of course. You chose to ignore the honest and candid testimony and were hell-bent to move forward and recklessly proceeded to indict Luke Foster!"

Will could tell he had Townsend's full attention. He went on, "Do you recall the fact I never debated you for one minute about your decision to indict Luke? You see Mr. Townsend, my client wouldn't let me. As hard as it may be for you to believe, he said at the time he only cared about one thing—he had to officially find out if he was guilty of any wrongdoing. And do you recall the fact I never debated you about what specific charge you were going to file against Luke? Again, he wouldn't let me. He didn't care. He wanted to know conclusively if he was guilty of wrongdoing. The particular charge you brought against him really didn't make any difference to him. And finally, do you happen to recall the fact that when you decided to have the case heard in adult court, I never challenged the decision? Once again, my client didn't care—he didn't want any special consideration given to the fact he was a minor."

Will continued, "It's high time you understand something, Mr. Townsend. We have an honest young man here who has the strength of character to accept whatever the consequences may be for his actions that day. That's the one and only way he can have the peace of mind to get on with his life. To this day, he honestly and sincerely wonders if there wasn't a better way of handling the situation that was so rudely thrown on his lap that horrible day. He knows he's made mistakes in his life and now wants the legal system to make a formal determination if what he did that day was wrong in the eyes of the law. After endless thought and careful evaluation of exactly what happened in the shed, he honestly believes he did what he had to do but wants a jury to make the decision. You see, Mr. Townsend, it's my client who's steering the basic direction we've taken to this point, not me. And that's not about to change!"

More than a little perturbed, Townsend abruptly came back with, "Okay, that's all very impressive. Now do I understand you right? It's your position that either we drop all charges or we simply move forward with the case?"

Will knew the judge would be upset if he wasn't willing to work with Townsend, at least be willing to listen to his final proposal. He was familiar with the very real possibility of when a defendant refuses a plea bargain and it turns out he is ultimately found guilty, with the judge's responsibility and discretion in handing out a sentence, right or wrong, it oftentimes is more severe under those circumstances.

With that in mind, Will opened the door for more discussion. "Well, there's probably nothing wrong with listening to what you have in mind, Mr. Townsend." Pausing for a minute, he came up with, "Let's do this. You and Mr. Dempsey go back and put together your best offer. There's really no reason for us to go on and on, back and forth. Bring us your best offer and we'll either accept it or reject it. Take your time—we'll be here for a while. But let me say it one more time, dropping all charges is very likely the only thing that's going to expedite the case at this point!"

With that, Townsend and Dempsey stormed out of the conference room.

After they left, Big Jake said, "Boy, I hope I don't ever have to negotiate with you, big brother. That was impressive! I do have to say, though, I totally agree with everything you said."

Will shook it off and humbly said, "Hey, I'm following Foss Man's lead. I just told them the truth!" They agreed that there was no sensible reason to drag Foss Man through these negotiations. When they had the final offer on the table, of course they would let him in on the final decision. The very truth was, based on the way things were going, it would very likely end up being strictly and exclusively their determined client's decision.

It was about an hour later that Townsend and Dempsey returned. Same routine, Foss Man was escorted back to the lounge. With obvious tension in his voice, Townsend got right down to business. "In view of everything that has transpired, we're willing to lower the charges to involuntary manslaughter with a recommendation for a one-year suspended sentence. No additional time served, include a lengthy probationary period, and with significant community service left at the discretion of Judge Cooper." He went on to explain, "Like I said earlier, the Fosters have suffered enough. I don't think the defendant is a bad kid, but he has to be held responsible for that wild and totally unnecessary second blow. Jail time would serve no real purpose!"

Will wanted to jump up and down. His first reaction was powerful relief. This was a reasonable offer. But he refused to show an ounce of emotion. Keeping his best poker face and generously overlooking the fact Townsend had boldly rejected not dropping the charges as he specifically demanded, he was stubbornly nonresponsive. Demonstrating no optimism with his offer, he said, "Okay, I'll have to talk to my client and get back to you."

Again, the two prosecuting attorneys nervously exited the glass-walled conference room.

Will calmly explained the plea deal to Foss Man. For the first time in over a month, Foss Man realized if he accepted the offer, he would no longer be facing another minute of time in jail. Holy shit, that in itself was huge. This at a glance was wonderful news, but he wanted to know more about this new "involuntary manslaughter" charge and what it really meant.

Will knew he had to be extremely careful how he characterized this whole thing. He knew Foss Man wasn't about to make a reckless decision. He knew what his ultimate goal was and that he wasn't likely to compromise in reaching it. Will cautiously explained everything as honest as he could while still not truly even knowing for sure himself where he stood on the matter.

He proceeded to made it clear. "If we accept Townsend's offer, you will be found guilty of involuntary manslaughter. You will serve no more jail time. Involuntary manslaughter is a felony. It will be on your criminal record. They'll try to make a big deal out of the fact it will be on your juvenile record, trying to convince us it's not as serious as having it on your adult record. However, a record's a record. It's there permanently—it can't be erased. You will be a convicted felon for the rest of your life.

Foss Man asked, "Okay, I got that, but more important to me, does this mean the jury won't be making the final judgment if what I did was wrong that day?"

Will said, "That's exactly right. The case would be over right now! You would be free to go home!"

Foss Man was shaking his head. "Will and Big Jake, I'm sorry, I don't like it. I don't want to be stubborn here, and trust me, I want both of your opinions before we arrive at a final decision. First, you'll never know how relieved I am about not having to serve more time in that miserable cell. Believe me, it's really tempting. I'm responsible for killing Ron Ferguson—that will never change and I will have to live with that reality for the rest of my life. But after carefully evaluating all the circumstances surrounding what happened that day, if twelve adults decide that what I did was understandable or—like you always say—justified, it will at least give me a chance to recover some day from the guilt and endless torment when I'm trying to sleep at night. Guys, I'm sorry, I don't want to be stupid about this, but I need the jury to make the decision!"

Will knew right then and there what he had to do. He had to reject Townsend's offer. At the same time, knowing how unpredictable juries can be, he knew the gravity of the risk they'd be taking. This had become a monumental, ball-busting decision. He had to make absolutely sure Foss Man totally understood what the risks were of rejecting Townsend's offer.

Will went through everything one more time. Big Jake finally spoke up. "Will, I know Foss Man. The thought of him sitting locked up for any length of time is sickening. But what this all boils down to is this: Foss Man had to do whatever it took to assure he saved his sister's life. Goddamn it, what he did was reasonable under the circumstances! I'm with Foss Man. I say we trust the jury!"

Will had a lot of respect for his younger brother, all gangly 6'5" inches of him. With no further discussion, he said with total conviction, "Foss Man, I recommend we reject Townsend's offer!"

It was a huge moment in all their young lives. It was a life-changing decision, not only for Foss Man but for all of them. Unwavering, they reached a mutual agreement. With that, more united and determined than ever, they hugged and shook hands.

Will reported to the judge's chamber. Townsend had just finished explaining his offer to the judge, and optimistically, the two had been waiting for Will's arrival. Will expressed his sincere appreciation to Townsend for what he thought was actually a reasonable offer. Then he boldly explained the defense's position. You could see Jude Cooper and Townsend were surprised with his bold rejection of the proposal. Townsend thought he had made a generous, honest, and sensible offer, and Judge Cooper had agreed.

When the dust settled from the rather stunning outcome, not showing the slightest preference or concern one way or the other, Judge Cooper was now glad he kept the negotiations informal and off the record. With that in mind, he interjected, "Let me point something out to you guys. The jury is not privy to the fact any plea bargain was discussed. If I learn either side is guilty of leaking it to the jury, I will consider it contempt of court and will be on you like the wrath of God!"

The judge had made another significant decision and promptly informed them, "Setting the consideration of a plea bargain aside, after listening to and carefully analyzing the testimony to this point and recognizing the subjectivity to the key element of the case, the defendant's state of mind at the critical moment, I'm going to exercise my legal authority."

He explained further, "After thoroughly educating the jury on the legal definition and idiosyncratic differences between voluntary and involuntary manslaughter, I'm going to give them the freedom to apply the charge they feel is most appropriate." Recognizing the defense's natural concern that in giving the jury two choices, it might imply the jury may feel obligated to choose one or the other, he reiterated, "Of course, 'no charge' is also an option! And trust me, Mr. Simmons, this last point will be made perfectly clear to the jury."

Although he had no choice in the matter, Will was not pleased about that last development. But well within his authority, the judge had made his final ruling. It was now perfectly clear the danger and risk of their bold decision was now greater than ever. Knowing very well how he would react, Will saw no reason for explaining the new dynamics of the now-optional charges to Foss Man. He had made his position perfectly clear. He insisted on being cleared of any and all charges by the jury; there were simply no other options.

Disappointed in having his offer flatly rejected, Townsend was pleased with the judge's recent ruling. This flexibility was clearly to the prosecution's advantage. Townsend had to refocus and get his thoughts back on track. Goddamn it, this young, cocky, unlicensed punk lawyer would regret his stubborn and ignorant decision to reject his generous offer. He was more determined than ever and would be working overtime on his summation late into the night. He had every intention of keeping his prosecution record perfect.

Will and Big Jake had a big night ahead of them. The pressure had always been there, but now it was off the charts. Foss Man spent the night fretting about how his buddy Mr. Slim was doing. The last report from Nute was that there was no great change—he was stable but remained in the intensive care unit. He was still in critical condition.

Chapter Seventy

Pictures of Foss Man decked out in his Jefferson High School baseball uniform and Catherine in her cheerleader outfit were plastered across the front pages of the newspapers and featured in the television evening news programs following their dramatic testimony that afternoon. The headlines and emphasis throughout the media coverage focused on the one big question, "Will the fifteen-year-old boy be facing serious jail time for his vicious attack on his longtime nemesis, whom he walked in on when he was in the process of violently raping his older sister?" The majority of the storylines suggested their heartfelt testimony may have helped the teenage boy's defense, but the harsh reality was, the prosecution had built a strong case, insisting he had better options than bludgeoning the other young man to death with a baseball bat. The general consensus was that the final verdict remained in doubt! Interest was heating up for the critical closing arguments scheduled for Friday morning. Judge Cooper was pleased and confident he'd be getting the case in the hands of the jury sometime before Friday noon.

While it could take days, there was growing expectation that the final ruling of the jury could be coming as soon as Friday afternoon. The number of national television and newspaper reporters and cameramen had reached a new high. Interest of the local media and general population in the immediate area had reached a fever pitch. All combined, it had become a persistent hectic scene around the Wright County Court House. The law enforcement personnel had never experienced anything quite like it but was doing an admirable job of keeping things safe and orderly.

With all that, Friday morning arrived, and as expected, when the doors were opened, there was another mad scramble to get one of the cherished seats inside the courtroom. It was another scorching hot and humid July day, and the four large fans were already whirling but hardly improving the sweltering conditions in the overly crowded room. Filled with anticipation for the climatic events scheduled for that morning, there was a heightened level of tension in the air. Additional reporters were admitted and were now jammed around the perimeter of the gallery, jostling for the most favorable position to observe firsthand the speeches that would very likely determine the outcome of what had become a contentious and highly controversial case.

Both legal teams worked late into the night, rehearsing and making adjustments to their final arguments. During their thorough and meticulous preparation, Will had developed a special calm and quiet confidence when it dawned on him all he really had to do was follow Catherine and Foss Man's lead—simply tell the truth.

Townsend and his assistant Tom Dempsey were carefully reviewing their final arguments, and after getting over their frustration of having their generous offer rejected, they were energized with a fresh and renewed confidence. They would be relentless in fulfilling their responsibility by holding Luke fully accountable for his taking the law into his own hands. Their apprehension yesterday, which hastily lead them to making the failed plea offer, had only reinforced their resolve and determination to provide justice for the Ferguson family and the citizens of Wright County.

He didn't need further motivation, but Townsend was fully aware that the national interest in the case had grown throughout the week. With the streets leading to the court house now lined with well-marked national network television trucks, Townsend knew the day's proceedings could generate a huge boost in reaching his ambitious political goals. Townsend was anxious and fully prepared to get things underway!

With the jury once again comfortably seated, at precisely nine o'clock on Friday morning, Judge Cooper slammed the gavel and ordered, "Attorney Townsend, will you present your final arguments for the prosecution at this time!"

Dressed immaculately in what Will concluded had to be another new tailormade suit, the always confident, poised, and composed county attorney approached the jury box.

What had become his practice, pausing briefly for effect and thanking the jury for their diligence and careful attention, Townsend settled in. "The fact is the case is not about who did it but rather the subjective state of mind of the defendant at that critical second. It presents an exceptionally complex challenge for each of you. I have total confidence you will see the perfect truth about what took place that fateful Saturday afternoon just five short weeks ago!

"To make your job a little easier, I want to briefly summarize the facts of the case, and it will become a glaring and obvious fact the defendant demonstrated total disregard for human life in the ruthless and reckless manner that he handled things that tragic day in the shed."

When Townsend paused even briefly, all that could be heard was the steady whirling of the four overworked fans.

"We readily acknowledge Mr. Ferguson's long behavior history was deplorable. Furthermore, let there be no misunderstanding, what he was doing on that sad day was egregious. The prosecution clearly acknowledges and agrees with both of these disturbing realities. The recent discovery of the torturous conditions that Ron Ferguson lived throughout his short life doesn't change any of that. Here's my point in all this: The tragic loss of his life cannot be diminished by his past behavior."

Townsend wanted to be careful to not overstate this accusation but felt it was fair. "It's a very sad commentary, but this has been, at the very minimum, the underlying subliminal message the defense would like to have you believe. I am obliged to remind you, Ron Ferguson was indeed a human being just like you and me and did not deserve to lose his life that day!"

Townsend spent the next fifteen minutes expanding on, first, the defendant's physical prowess and viable options he had at that critical second. Second, Luke's history of reckless behavior of course citing the serious gun accident. Then the idea he hammered home profusely, the theory that the defendant had seized the opportunity to get even with the Ferguson boy for all those years he was a victim of his bullying.

So far, Will and Big Jake hadn't heard anything earthshaking. It was about what they expected. However, they couldn't deny it—the jury appeared to be totally mesmerized by the convincing story Townsend was so cleverly and craftily replaying. He was obviously on the top of his game, and they knew exactly what was coming next.

"Now, members of the jury, everything I've said so far reinforces the following question, without a doubt the most critical question that needs to be answered. If you could somehow generously find justification for the first vicious blow to the side of Ron Ferguson's head—and don't misunderstand, the prosecution clearly does not support that drastic notion—a reasonable person would have to ask himself this question: When it is now a glaring fact the young man was totally incapacitated and at the very minimum unconscious, how on God's earth could anyone explain why a person would once again wind up and deliberately deliver another even more vicious blow on the back of the head of another human being? And please keep in mind, the medical examiner's report strongly suggests it was the second blow that was ultimately the cause of Ron Ferguson's death. That, ladies and gentlemen of the jury, in a nutshell, is what you have to evaluate."

It was questionable if Judge Cooper wanted Townsend to lay this out for the jury, but knowing it would play favorably for him, he boldly proceeded to point out, "Due to the ambiguous and subjective nature of the defendant's state of mind at the critical moment while committing this violent crime in the state of Iowa, it's admittedly difficult to distinguish between voluntary and involuntary manslaughter. For that reason, based on Judge Cooper's recent ruling, you have been given the freedom to select which of the two specific charges you feel best fits the ruthless and reckless actions of the defendant. Based on your careful judgment of the facts before you, it will be your responsibility to pick the criminal charge you feel is most appropriate."

Will was surprised Judge Cooper had chosen not to interrupt Townsend's opportunistic explanation of this questionable ruling. Will was not happy about this.

Townsend knew he had gotten away with it. He proceeded to wrap up what had to be considered a highly effective summation. "Now in closing, the critical question is this: Were the actions taken by the defendant that sad day representative of what a reasonable person would do under similar circumstances? I repeat, what a reasonable person would have done. With the clear facts presented to you this week, you have no choice but to find the defendant, Luke Foster, guilty on the basis of one of the two specific charges—voluntary or involuntary manslaughter!"

Townsend graciously thanked the jury, and knowing he had connected with the jury, he victoriously announced, "That's all I have, Your Honor."

It was obvious to Will that Townsend was making every effort to subtly influence the jury into thinking they had no choice but to pick one of the two options put before them and therefore ignoring the third legitimate "not guilty" option, which of course was contrary to the spirit of the ruling by the judge. This is precisely why Will disagreed with the judge's decision to give the jury two options in the first place. There was little doubt Townsend would abuse the liberal ruling and attempt to use it to his advantage.

CHAPTER SEVENTY-ONE

Will recognized the renewed determination and passion in the general demeanor of Townsend throughout his summation. In his way of thinking, Townsend genuinely felt he had offered a legitimate compromise with the plea bargain and they had indignantly thrown it back in his face. Will was not happy about Townsend's most recent cute little trick, but in thinking about it, the jury would more than likely see through it and it could easily backfire on him. Setting that aside, Will had to admit the impressive prosecuting attorney presented a viable and powerful argument. It was now abundantly clear to him he absolutely had to be on top of his game these next few minutes or the outcome could easily swing in favor of the prosecution.

Will was fully aware of the skyrocketing nationwide interest in the case. He too had observed the network television trucks lined up on the streets adjacent to the courthouse before he arrived early that morning. There was no question about it, the unlicensed lawyer had clearly put himself in the hot seat. And this young man's future was now resting squarely on his shoulders!

He couldn't help but ask himself, *What in holy hell was I thinking! Was this bold idea of volunteering my services to this wonderful family a responsible decision? Was I adequately prepared to take on a case of this magnitude? Was it exclusively with the Fosters' best interests in mind. or was I even partially motivated for my own selfish reasons?* Only one thing was certain: he would soon have the answers to all these questions!

Wanting to get the case in the hands of the jury as soon as possible, Judge Cooper promptly announced, "Thank you, Mr.

Townsend. Will the defense counsel please present your final arguments at this time?"

Will and Big Jake huddled for the last time. Big Jake reinforced one familiar word of encouragement for the big brother he had idolized his whole life: "Will, Foss Man did the right thing in the shed that day!"

Smiling and accepting his brother's well-chosen words, Will took an extra minute and got his thoughts together one final time. He stood up and found his way in front of the jury box. For no apparent reason, he slowly turned and calmly walked back to the defense table, and while doing so, with his eyes involuntarily scanning the gallery, he couldn't help but notice the frightened looks on the faces of Foss Man's family and their many special friends. With the emotional impact of seeing all the people who were so desperately depending on him to turn this thing back in favor of their son, brother, or friend, he felt a renewed surge of determination and, with it, a powerful resolution to succeed in the enormous challenge facing him. He was more motivated than he had been at any time in his life!

After fulfilling the proper formalities but before plunging into his carefully planned presentation, something was bugging him, and he decided to squeeze it in. "I don't want to dignify Mr. Townsend's absurd notion that the defense doesn't respect Ron Ferguson as a human being in the same manner we would anyone else in this courtroom, but the obscene accusation couldn't be further from the truth. And frankly, that isn't what this is all about. We're here for the sole purpose of determining the innocence or guilt of this wonderful young man, Luke Foster."

With that off his chest, he said, "Having said that, it would be misguided for you to get lulled into subconsciously underestimating the nature of Ron Ferguson's ugly behavior that sad day. The subject does force me into pointing out the deliberate—and what I would consider shallow—distortion on the part of the prosecution. Mr. Townsend has gone to great lengths to identify the underlying source of the Ferguson brother's anger and subsequent lifetime history of poor behavior. It goes without saying, we all have the greatest sympathy for the unthinkable way the Ferguson boys had to live. But

I ask you, does the source of Ron Ferguson's behavior have even the slightest thing to do with the innocence or guilt of Luke Foster? Mr. Townsend has been playing the sympathy card all week, but it's an insult to all our intelligence to think it even remotely has anything to do with the important decision now squarely in your hands.

"Before I get into what I consider the more critical parts of my summary, it's important for the jury to understand a behind-the-scene dynamic that contributed significantly to our initial approach in putting Luke Foster's defense together. Judge Cooper, Mr. Townsend, and Mr. Dempsey all witnessed firsthand during the course of the preliminary trial how serious the defendant felt about being held fully accountable for what took place in the shed that day. In the very beginning, the defendant made something perfectly clear to all of us. These were his exact words: 'I'll always be thankful for arriving on the scene when I did that day, but it's just a fact, the second I walked into the shed I was handed a lifetime sentence.' You see members of the jury, Luke was absolutely devastated with the harsh reality he was directly responsible for taking another human being's life. He knew beyond a doubt that the only way he could ever recover from the ordeal was by finding out if his actions were truly a crime in the eyes of the law. He demanded we simply trust the county attorney to make the decision what the appropriate charge should be, and furthermore, if the adult court system held the promise of stronger scrutiny, that was exactly what he needed. His only request was to have the trial held here in Wright County so the jury would be composed of local citizens. Beyond that, all he ever sincerely wanted was for the jury to make an honest judgment about what he did that day.

"That's just the way it was going to be, and I have to say, early on I struggled mightily with his position, but in the end, it made sense and has certainly made my job much easier. From that day forward, all we ever had to do was analyze to the best of our ability exactly what happened that day. We felt it was important to show you the dog pictures to demonstrate the extreme violence Ron Ferguson was capable of doing, but beyond that, we didn't have to spend time strategizing or fretting about any sophisticated plan of defense."

He paused for a minute or two to get his thoughts together. "Let me explain a little bit how I'm going to move forward with the summary. There's a few of what I would consider far-reaching, if not frivolous, contentions by the prosecution that should be quickly addressed and then totally dismissed in the spirit of focusing on the real issues surrounding the case. There are only two legitimate questions that need to be addressed: First, why the baseball bat, and second, why the second violent blow? I should readily acknowledge right here and now, all of us on Luke's side have spent endless hours contemplating those serious questions. I'll get back to those, what I consider vitally important issues, in a few minutes.

"The first theory that should be dismissed immediately revolves around the suggestion that the defendant is a careless or reckless young man. Now there's no denying Luke is a spirited and fun-loving teenager—that is well documented—but other than the isolated frightening accident with the gun last winter, there is absolutely no evidence of any pattern of reckless behavior. It's just simply not the case. You heard it over and over in the testimonies we presented, Luke is well-liked—a gentle soul and doesn't have a mean bone in his body.

"And second, the wild concept that the defendant was deliberately taking full advantage of this incident to get even with Ferguson for bullying him all those years is utterly preposterous. Please think about this for a minute. Does anybody honestly think the defendant said to himself, 'Wow, what a golden opportunity to show Ferguson how I feel about all those things he did to me all those years!' There couldn't have been anything further from his mind at that critical second."

Will could see he was getting through to the jury and felt comfortable in moving forward with what he felt were the real issues he was obliged to address.

"Members of the jury, before I give you my personal interpretation of what truly transpired that horrific day, I want you to calmly put yourself in the shoes of the defendant at that critical second. Just for one minute sit and think about what you would be facing. And please, take a second and recall the outrageous scene you witnessed two days ago when Frank Ferguson lost his temper on the witness stand. And think about the ruthless way he killed the two dogs. Ron was virtually the same size as his brother Frank. Add to that fact Ron Ferguson was intoxicated and had just been caught in the act of rape. And don't forget, it was your sister who is currently in the process of being violently raped.

"Before I go any further, in the spirit of drawing an accurate picture, the defendant didn't know Ferguson was drunk at the time and wasn't aware of the fact his intentions were to murder his sister. All he knew for a fact was that the guy was Ron Ferguson and that he was raping his sister. Now the prosecution has presented many wonderful solutions to the problem Luke was suddenly dealing with. Luke, his parents, Big Jake, and I have spent hours thinking about what his real options may have been at that critical second. But here's the reality—it's an exercise of futility for the prosecution or anyone else to speculate on the perfect solution. With the luxury of time to contemplate, the only thing that is really important is to try to understand why it unfolded the way it did."

Once again, Will paused to let that important concept sink in. He could see by their alert reaction that he was clearly resonating with the jury. He was totally composed, relaxed, thinking clearly, and eager to move on.

He proceeded, "I don't want to insult your intelligence by replaying all the testimony you so diligently listened to this week. With that in mind, let me get back on track. You've put yourselves in Luke's shoes, but let's break down and focus on what Luke actually did at that critical split second and take the liberty to speculate about what his likely state of mind was at that time.

"Totally stunned with the horrific scene in front of him, immediately recognizing it was Ron Ferguson raping his sister, without time to calculate, he instinctively grabbed the baseball bat that was conveniently leaning against the wall by the entrance, took two or three short steps forward, and without the slightest hesitation, immediately hit Ferguson over the head with the bat. Still in a state of shock, scared to death, and in a sudden state of fury, he impulsively hit him over the head a second time.

"Now let's, just for a minute, accept that as a reasonable explanation of what took place that day. The challenge you have now is to decide if Luke's actions are what a reasonable person would do under similar circumstances. Like I said a few minutes ago, there are two critical questions. First, why use the baseball bat, and more important, why hit the rapist a second time when, now looking back at it, it was obvious he was incapacitated and not capable of doing further harm?

"First, why the bat? Let me suggest, the bat was just there, perhaps too convenient, but like Luke said in his testimony, there was no decision. It was like a blur. He has no memory of grabbing the bat, it just ended up in his hands. Is it reasonable to consider that while instantly recognizing it was the historically powerful Ferguson kid, Luke instinctively reacted to the magnitude of the challenge he was facing? Now let me shift for a minute to the second even more important issue, why the second attack? This brings us to the almost impossible and much discussed psychological analysis, what was Luke Foster's state of mind during those few intense seconds between the first and second blows? With the luxury of time and hindsight, perhaps to your surprise, the defense readily accepts the contention that Luke's actions were not the perfect solution to the unthinkable scene he was suddenly facing.

"Now we can debate these two very legitimate questions until we're blue in the face, but let me ask you, when considering the explosive circumstances, the inevitable built-in enormous battle, the endless unknowns, wouldn't even the most reasonable person in the world be capable of a certain degree of irrational behavior? Members of the jury, I respectfully ask you, weren't Luke Foster's instinctive and impulsive actions at the very minimum, understandable, in a fair, unbiased, and objective point of view?

"I'm sure it comes as no surprise to you folks, but it's the defenses' position that after our intense scrutiny and much honest debate, we strongly believe, beyond a reasonable doubt, the actions of the defendant were indeed understandable and that no crime was committed by Luke Foster. And the only crime that day was the violent rape of Catherine Foster.

"But here's the bottom line: Luke will never accept what we think. He doesn't only want you to make the ultimate decision, he virtually needs you to make the decision. You heard his testimony yesterday. You have to decide how genuine and sincere he is about all this. You have to decide how much he regrets the fact Ron Ferguson lost his life that day. You have to decide how sick he was when he learned about how the Ferguson brothers lived their lives. You have to decide how much he wishes there was a better solution and he would have handled it in that manner.

"When you've made your final decision, if you find him guilty, he'll be disappointed in himself, not you. He's put full trust in you to tell him if what he did was truly a crime. He doesn't want your sympathy, and he doesn't want your mercy. He needs one thing: your honest evaluation of what he did.

"Now in closing, this is me speaking, not the Foster family or Luke. I can assure you, at the end of all this, whichever way it goes, Luke will survive. There's no ruling today that will permit him to ever walk freely again—he'll live with this burden the rest of his life. It's like he correctly recognized in the very beginning, the second he walked in the shed that day, he was rudely handed a lifetime sentence. But the good news is, Luke's an extremely strong-willed young man. He will learn to live with your ruling knowing in his heart he saved his sister's life. That will carry him through whatever the additional consequences may be. The same is true with his loving family. They know in their heart, Luke is a loving, caring, and gentle soul. With their unwavering support, like I pointed out in my opening statement, they've had to deal with many setbacks in their lives, and together, they not only survived but were closer and stronger in spite of them. The same is true with this frightening and sad time in their lives. Let me comfort you, no matter how this turns out, the Fosters will survive and become stronger than ever.

"Finally, let me repaint the picture Luke Foster was enjoying back on Saturday, June 7. This highly sensitive fifteen-year-old teenager, who was merely planning to put his bike in the shed like he had done so many times before and one who loves baseball and was excited about going to practice scheduled for that beautiful sunny afternoon, was instead, through no fault of his own, suddenly thrown into this unthinkable, horrific scene.

"Ladies and gentlemen of the jury, when you've made your final decision, regardless of the direction it goes, it will signal the beginning of the long healing process for Luke and his family. I sincerely thank you for your patience and dedication through all the unexpected events of what has clearly been a most difficult week. That's all I have, Your Honor."

There was a wide range of emotions running through everyone present in the courtroom. There were tears for many of those directly impacted by Will's dramatic presentation, but overshadowing that, there was a spontaneous distinctive vocal display of approval and support from the gallery in general. Not happy about the impulsive reaction, Judge Cooper immediately slammed his gavel and severely admonished the audience. The sudden respectful and instant silence provided the most poignant single moment of the nearly-week-long tension-packed proceedings!

Will returned to the defense table and took his seat by his obviously elated younger brother and his very first client, an emotional and severely shaken Foss Man. He knew he had just delivered the most important speech of his life. While feeling good about his performance in general, he knew very well, with the historically unpredictable nature of juries, the final outcome was still clearly in doubt! It was far too early for any celebrations!

The prosecution hastily turned down their option for rebuttal.

Following careful and lengthy instructions from the judge, the case was unceremoniously put in the hands of the jury. With no further need for the two unknown alternate jurors, the prosecution and defense each had the opportunity to eliminate one jury member of their choice. Will and Big Jake had serious concern with a couple of jurors prior to the final summations, but Will felt he had effectively connected with both jurors and was no longer concerned with either one. After the alternates were formally excused from duty, that left the required number of twelve to promptly return to the jury room, elect their foreman, and proceed with the deliberations.

All that was left now was the unbearable and agonizing period to simply wait for the life-changing verdict. It could be hours, and it could be days.

Chapter Seventy-Two

Judge Cooper informed everyone in the courtroom that it was always difficult to predict how long the jury deliberations might take and the final verdict reached. While the defendant would of course remain in custody, in response to his instinctive gut feeling, the judge encouraged the representatives for both the prosecution and defense teams, "In the remote chance of a quick verdict, please remain in close proximity of the courthouse until at least five o'clock, the normal time for wrapping up the afternoon session."

The gallery, including the vast majority of the news media, exited the courthouse in typical speedy fashion, assuming it would be at least several hours and more than likely over the weekend before the jury reached the required unanimous agreement. Like everyone else, Foss Man's immediate support group left the courtroom but decided to remain close by for that rare chance of a quick ruling. They found the much-needed comfort by remaining together, and something intuitively told them to stick around.

And it proved to be a wise decision!

It came as a surprise to everyone, but the bailiff assigned to monitor the jury room sent the magic word to Judge Cooper that the jury had indeed reached a verdict. A generous supply of sandwiches and refreshments had been promptly delivered to the jury room, and they wasted no time in getting down to work. It was now 3:00 p.m., exactly four hours from the time the judge had given his final instructions and ordered them to commence with the deliberation process.

With the unexpected news quickly spreading, the courtroom was once again jammed in a matter of only a few minutes. The many reporters who had made the hasty decision to leave the courthouse area to get the jump on preparing the evening storyline with the self-imposed limitation of focusing exclusively on the morning summations, would be disappointed about missing out on the firsthand reading of the verdict and the newsworthy reaction of the gallery.

Judge Cooper had to temporarily hold up the proceedings until he could track down Attorney Townsend and his assistant, who had gone out for lunch and then back to their private offices. Will and Big Jake had conveniently remained in the building and were just a short distance down the hall in the conference room at the time of the startling announcement.

Will, Big Jake, and Foss Man were trying to remain calm in the comforts of the big leather chairs in the conference room for what, one way or the other, would be their final time. They had been nervously discussing what the procedure would be if Foss Man was indeed found guilty. Will felt obliged to prepare him for the cold realities of what he could potentially be dealing with. Then they got the word. The verdict was in. Will knew a quick ruling was no reliable predictor of the outcome. He knew very well the final decision could go either way.

For Foss Man, Will, and Big Jake, the dramatic event about to take place had suddenly become very real. Up to this point, everything seemed more like some kind of surreal game for which they had been chosen to merely play their assigned roles. But not anymore—it was now far from a game. The soon-to-be-learned outcome would have an indelible impact on all their lives. Finding no words that fit the moment, Will and Big Jake gave Foss Man a private supportive hug, and the three of them began the tension-packed long walk back to the courtroom. It was an almost unbearable time for them and totally understandable the young "quasi" lawyer and two young teenagers were totally petrified!

It had taken about an hour to get all the key players informed, rounded up, and back into the courtroom, and it was approaching 4:00 p.m. With no further delay, Judge Cooper ordered the bailiff to guide the jury back to their seats in the jury box for one final time.

Like everyone present in the courtroom, Foss Man was trying desperately to get a read on the jury's facial expressions and body language. It was impossible to draw any conclusions, but the subdued and serious look on their faces scared Foss Man to death. He was suddenly more worried than he had been at any time since this whole thing began. He had disciplined himself to be prepared for the worst possible outcome and knew he had to be strong not only for himself but for his family and friends.

His last thoughts were, *Good grief, to think I could have avoided any form of jail time by simply accepting the offer made by Townsend yesterday.* He knew he did what he had to do, but right now he had to seriously question how smart that bold decision really was!

Judge Cooper started the formal proceedings by firmly inquiring, "Has the jury reached a verdict in the case of the *State of Iowa vs. Luke Foster*?"

The newly elected foreman stood up and weakly and almost apologetically announced, "We have, Your Honor!"

Foss Man did not like the tone in the foreman's voice!

The judge methodically asked the bailiff to bring the ballot form to the bench.

With a strong voice, Judge Cooper ordered, "Would the defendant please stand?" Will, Big Jake, and Foss Man followed his command. Big Jake wrapped his left arm around Foss Man's shoulders exactly like he had done with his buddy Skunk a year ago at his beloved sister's heart-wrenching graveside ceremony. Big Jake's embrace was comforting and gave him a quiet confidence that everything was going to be alright. After all, Big Jake was always right, wasn't he? And hadn't he told him over and over, "You did the right thing, Foss Man"? Deep down he thought he had too, but he was about to find out once and for all!

Sitting directly behind Foss Man was his frightened and worried family. Always the pillar of strength, Catherine was bowing her head and appeared to be sobbing and praying at the same time. From the very beginning, she had blamed herself, knowing if she hadn't been so bullheaded about confronting Ferguson, none of this would have happened. Air Force was bravely looking straight forward but with a glazed look in his eyes. He genuinely wished it would have been him that walked into the shed that day! His father was embracing his mother, who had buried her face in her husband's broad shoulder. The rest of his great friends, all sitting close together directly behind his family, were nervous and anxious.

With sudden finality, Judge Cooper announced, "In the case of the *State of Iowa v. Luke Foster*, the jury finds the defendant not guilty of all charges. Mr. Foster, you are free to go!"

Simultaneous to the loud echo of the gavel slamming on the bench for the final time and the judge dramatically and loudly declaring, "Court is now adjourned," the gallery erupted in loud and joyous celebration. It was perfectly clear virtually everyone in the courtroom, perhaps with the exception of the prosecuting attorneys—and even that was now in doubt—agreed with and had hoped for this wildly popular outcome. The place went wild!

While clearly ecstatic about the verdict, Foss Man, Will, and Big Jake calmly embraced each other while maintaining a graceful and dignified manner. In genuine respect to the prosecuting attorneys, who had merely done their job and had done it well, and in recognition and appreciation for the sad nature of the horrific events at the heart of the case, the three of them deliberately minimized any outward display of victorious emotion. It was a sensible and deserved response, particularly in view of the fact Townsend and Dempsey immediately approached them and, while disappointed, had graciously congratulated them on the outcome. Will humbly responded to the county attorney and his assistant, speaking from the heart, "There were no winners in this sad chapter in the history of our beloved community, but at least now the healing can begin." Foss Man sat down and was holding his head in his cupped hands and began the process of vociferously thanking God. Big Jake sat down beside him and draped his long arm around him.

Foss Man's family maintained a very similar demeanor. They too were naturally thrilled with the results but were so overwhelmed with emotion and great relief they could only quietly embrace each other with the expected flood of tears. Vigorous and lengthy hugs provided the comfort they so badly needed and richly deserved at this pivotal juncture in their lives.

Within minutes, the family and many friends were crowded around the defense table. While Foss Man's parents were hugging and emphatically expressing their immense appreciation for the remarkable job Will and Big Jake had so generously and effectively done for their son, Foss Man was in the process of hugging his thankful and greatly relieved big sister. No words had to be spoken between them. Catherine simply clung to her little brother with a renewed level of respect and appreciation. Air Force stood close by and affectionately patted his younger brother on the back.

Following the long, touching embrace with Catherine, Foss Man suddenly saw Rosita standing just a few steps in front of him. Her huge radiant smile and wholesome breathtaking beauty could once again be truly enjoyed and fully appreciated. After a mindless hug and intense display of mutual affection, Foss Man managed to break free and hugged Rosita's smiling parents and thanked them for their loyal, unwavering support throughout the long week. Pedro was smiling and patting Foss Man on the back. Standing nearby, Rosita quietly asked him, "Foss Man work tomorrow?" Foss Man answered, "Oh yes, I'll be back in the morning, bright and early!" Rosita pulled his head down and whispered in his ear, "Climb tree tomorrow, yes?" Foss Man didn't respond. He could only think to himself, *Oh yes. Thank you, God. Thank you, dear God!*

There was absolutely nothing reserved or remotely dignified about Skunk, Skeeter, Horse, Rocket, and Stub's reaction. They held nothing back! In classic teenage style, they were literally jumping up and down and cheering out loud, similar to the way they acted after a rare victory in football last fall! Their good friend Foss Man was finally going to be back with them, not only on the baseball field but also back to his important role in contributing to the kind of fun the summer months were supposed to offer. There was still a few weeks before the demanding football season began, and they were determined to make up for all that lost time yet this summer.

Nute, Coach Sanders, and Walter Olsen had huge smiles on their faces and were politely shaking hands and expressing their great pleasure and relief with the outcome. They all had a special and unique relationship with Foss Man and were genuinely happy for their young friend.

Walter Olsen, the Foster's longtime landlord and Foss Man's prosperous and thoughtful employer, hastily offered to throw a celebration at the nearby restaurant in Boulder that featured the popular Friday night "all you can eat" fish fry. Walter generously offered to pick up the tab for the Foster family as well as the rest of their close circle of friends.

While acknowledging Walter's generous offer and expressing his true appreciation, Foss Man encouraged his family to feel free to attend the celebration, but he only had one thing on his mind: he wanted to get over to the hospital and see his buddy Mr. Slim. In a similar manner, his family thanked Walter for his generous offer but told him they were going home and wanted to spend a quiet night together.

With no further explanation needed to explain the emotions they were experiencing, it soon became understandable to everyone present, while justice had now been served, it didn't suddenly or magically wipe away the memories of the mind-boggling events that had transpired over the recent weeks. While it was a time for great joy and happiness, it quickly became evident to everyone that this unthinkable tragedy was far from over for the Foster family.

For all those reasons, the joyous celebration came to a happy conclusion, and the members of Foss Man's loyal support group quietly dispersed in their own desired direction, which in most cases was to the privacy of their homes.

Except of course for Foss Man's five loyal comrades. After the short-lived reunion and all the happy back-slapping and juvenile frolicking with their good buddy, the gang would remain together and carry on like every healthy sixteen-year-old boy should do on a beautiful summer Friday night. They all piled in Rocket's convertible and, with the top down, drove up and down Main Street in Jefferson, triumphantly honking the horn and whooping it up like they had just brought home the state championship trophy. There had been very little to be happy about in Jefferson for a long time and the beaten-down community was in need of some good news.

With the wild frenzy in the aftermath of the sudden final verdict in the provocative teenage rape and murder case, it was once again the featured lead story on the evening news of the major television networks. Pictures of the Foster family forcing their way down the courthouse steps while surrounded by a crushing crowd of delirious and jubilant supporters flashed across the television screens around the country.

Bold headlines were plastered on the front page of the local and major newspapers: “Teenage Boy Found Not Guilty of All Charges.”

After fighting through the army of reporters and camera men, the jubilant, happy, and relieved Foster family headed back to Jefferson, and like never before, the true comforts of home. Foss Man quietly hustled out the back door of the courthouse and quickly jumped in Nute’s car and the two of them headed across town to the Boulder Memorial Hospital. Foss Man had anxiously looked forward to this opportunity for the last three days. He couldn’t wait to tell Mr. Slim the great news. He knew it would make him feel better and inspire him to want to get back home and they’d be fishing together sometime in the next few days!

With Foss Man two steps behind Nute, the two of them eagerly entered the private room in the intensive care unit. Mr. Slim’s eyes were closed, and he appeared to be in deep sleep. Nute gently shook his arm and triumphantly announced, “Hey, Mr. Slim, wake up, there’s somebody here to see you.” There was no response. A little concerned, Nute shook his arm again, “Hey, you big, ornery cuss, wake up! Our buddy Foss Man’s here to see you!” That appeared to do the trick! Mr. Slim opened his eyes, and through his scraggy and scruffy beard, you could detect an immediate broad smile on his face.

Foss Man moved in closer to the bed. Mr. Slim reached out with his right hand and squeezed Foss Man’s hand.

With the huge smile suggesting immediate relief and a welcome peace, the almost perfect Indian Head penny fell gently into Foss Man’s hand. Mr. Slim closed his eyes for the last time!

A note to readers: *Foss Man II* will soon be available.

The story picks up in the immediate aftermath of Foss Man's celebrated "not guilty" verdict. His personal struggles in recovering from the traumatic experience were magnified by the chilling threat Frank Ferguson made on the witness stand to "take care of him" the very minute he was released from prison.

Following his two-final tumultuous high school years and turning to a surprising secret life, and after accepting the highly coveted baseball scholarship and unwavering financial support from favorite aunt Sylvia, the stage was set for a simply outrageous and unbelievable college experience.

Soon inseparable from his three dynamic and influential freshmen roommates, while posing a serious threat to his promising baseball career as well as his academic standing, Foss Man got caught up in a crazy social life and in the middle of a highly sophisticated cheating scandal. Upset by the treatment of a valued friend, Foss Man personally challenged the misguided and deeply engrained "Greek Culture". His very future, powerful loyalty, and deep rooted principles were put to the test when he learned of the shocking criminal side to one of his long trusted roommates and was forced into making a potential life threatening decision.

Let us know what you think at:

www.keithfossey.com
fossmanseries@kiethfossey.com
www.facebook.com/keith.fossey.18

About the Author

Receiving his undergraduate degree in physical education and mathematics and his master's degree in secondary school administration, Keith thrived for thirty years as a classroom instructor, dean of students, and middle school principal and served as the varsity football coach in New Berlin, Wisconsin. After assisting many "under the radar" football prospects in successfully landing full-ride scholarships, including one from Mankato State University in Minnesota for his son Rick, and recognizing the glaring lack of direction for other parents navigating the oftentimes confusing recruiting process, Keith wrote and published the acclaimed *Football Scholarship Guide*.

Closing in on fifty years of marriage to his always supportive wife, Avis, and now fully enjoying the retirement scene, provoked by encouragement from many peers, Keith once again returned to writing and is currently in the middle of his fictionalized/autobiographical three-part Foss Man series. Along with writing, Keith spends summers with his four children and eight grandchildren in Minnesota, while enjoying winters golfing, biking, and socializing with his seven siblings and their spouses all residing in sunny Arizona. Reflecting his active lifestyle, Keith is currently training for his third Lifetime Fitness Triathlon.

CPSIA information can be obtained
at www.ICGtesting.com
Printed in the USA
LVOW03s1954310118
564761LV00002B/141/P